Bowling Avenue

By Kay Gardiner and Ann Shayne

Mason-Dixon Knitting: The Curious Knitter's Guide
Mason-Dixon Knitting Outside the Lines

Bowling Avenue

Ann Shayne

CHENILLE PRESS   NASHVILLE, TENNESSEE   2012

ISBN: 978-0-9852100-0-7 (pb)
ISBN: 978-0-9852100-1-4 (ebook)

Published by Chenille Press, Nashville, Tennessee

Cover design by Bryce McCloud, Isle of Printing

First Edition

Visit annshayne.com and masondixonknitting.com.

To Elizabeth Meador Driskill

All water has a perfect memory and is forever trying to get back to where it was.

Toni Morrison

I still operate from a base position that people are a lot of effort.

Henry Alford

Welcome Wagon

The burglar alarm is wailing like a wounded child, and I have no idea how to turn it off. There's a horn honking, a shrieking sound on top of that, and it's all bouncing off the neighboring houses back at me—echo upon echo. On top of that there's a recording of the Voice of God announcing that the police are on the way, looping over and over. Jebus, it's the apocalypse! The neighbors must hate this house. They're not exactly rushing over to help.

I shut the kitchen door that set off this mess, drop my bags, and come around to the front of the house to wait for the police. I sit down on the broad flagstone steps. The Voice of God is so convincing. I know! I freakin' know it! I'm glad they're coming!

The din from the alarm is amazing. I dial my phone, covering my head with my down coat to muffle the racket.

"Mother?"

"Delia!"

"I'm here."

"What? I can't hear you."

"I'm at Ginna's."

"What?"

"Do you know the code?"

"The what?"

"THE ALARM CODE. FOR GINNA'S HOUSE?"

"WHERE ARE YOU?"

I hang up, hopeless, and peek out from under my coat. Too hot for this thing down here. The view from Ginna's front steps is lush, with the spring-green trees glowing in the late afternoon sun. Her deep lawn is a velvety fairway, so smooth that it looks fake. How did she keep this place going? How do you find someone who can make grass do this? Her maples are an almost fluorescent green.

"The police are on the way."

"So where are they?" I yell back.

A chunky woman in a pale blue nylon tracksuit swishes past the driveway, staring openly at me. Skinny people run, fat people walk. That was the meanest thing Ginna ever said, but she knew I loved it when she was snarky, loved hearing Nashville gossip. Whenever I came to town, we would wander the neighborhood, this leafy suburb with no sidewalks, and I'd make up stories about the walkers we passed. "Desperate," I would whisper. "Blackballed by the Garden Club of Nashville." "Sleeping with the minister but is actually hot for the organist." "Has hemorrhoids the size of grapes." "Likes peeling dead skin off her heels." Making Ginna laugh was so easy.

I don't believe in ghosts, I really don't. So the prospect of staying at my dead sister's house is not daunting in terms of worrying that I'm going to run into a spectral Ginna wandering the hall in her Lanz of Salzburg nightgown. Actually, that would be terrifying. She wore those things all her life: eyelet trimmed, flannel, hot as fiberglass insulation. I always joked to her that a Lanz nightgown was the quickest path to divorce. When Bennett left her a year ago, after sixteen years of marriage and two kids, I had the hateful thought that a peignoir or two might have made a difference.

I need to get away from the racket to call Mother again. She must have the code. I'm about halfway down the curving, pea-gravel drive when a police car turns into the entrance. I stand, sort of at attention, trying to look responsible and not sketchy. Does this skirt look hippieish? I wave limply at the officer as he stops beside me and climbs out. He is paunchy, with a fat Village People moustache and a gun belt with a hell of a pistol in there. A twelve year old's face on a fifty year old's body. I'm suddenly nervous.

He comes unnervingly close to me, but I realize he's just trying to get near enough that I can actually hear him. "Are you the homeowner?" he says loudly.

"No. Her sister. The homeowner's sister. I am—I mean, Ginna Schwartz. Is my sister. Was. I'm Delia. Delia Ballenger." I hold up my phone. "Trying to get the code from my mother—how long do these alarms go off?" I shake my head, smiling, trying to get him to share in the absurdity of this situation.

"Seventeen minutes. Metro ordinance." Officer McDaniel—his badge is right at my eye level—looks at me with a flat, neutral expression. No solace coming from this guy.

A jitter starts in my hands. "May I call her?"

He nods. They must give these guys lessons in deadpan.

"Mom? It's me. I'm here. At Ginna's. Do you have the alarm code for her house? It wasn't supposed to be set."

"Oh, dear, goodness no. Can't imagine. Never did like those things—"

"MOTHER. The policeman's right here."

"No. I don't have it." Her voice is louder, as if she's holding the phone closer and paying better attention. "Wonder how that happened. Never even used to lock the house. When will you be—"

"Gotta go."

"Come see me."

"Right," I say as I end the call.

The age-old twang of annoyance rises in my chest. Always after me, Mother is. Officer McDaniel shifts on his feet. I aim for a grave expression. "Here's the thing. My sister died. Six months ago. I just got into town. We're selling the house. I'm selling the house. I'm supposed to sell the house. You know."

"Do you have any ID, ma'am?"

I nod, then remember it's all in the tote bags by the kitchen door. I'm suddenly exhausted by the noise, by the cop, by the reason that I am in this irritating situation.

I see a man coming up the driveway, waving. He looks like a neighbor in this neighborhood would look: khakis, a button-down shirt, dark sweater, mild face. There are a million men like this in west Nashville. Fifty or sixty? I can't tell how old people are anymore. Everybody looks tired, mostly. "Hello," he semi-yells. He's quite tall, gangly. "I have the code, if you need it."

I don't know who this man is, or how he would have the alarm code. He's looking closely at me. "Oh," he says, as if he's just spotted a strange bird. "What are *you* doing here?"

Officer McDaniel is watching Khaki Man. "Do you know each other?"

Khaki Man studies his shoes, uncomfortable. "*I* know *her*. Ginna's sister," he says in a sour tone. He looks up, brightening as if he has just figured out something. "She can't go in the house, officer."

I give him a hairy eyeball, mystified. Who is this guy? Officer McDaniel turns to me. "Are you authorized to be here, ma'am?"

Authorized? Now there's a good question, but unfortunately, I don't have a good answer.

"Like, a piece of paper? I don't have that, but I am supposed to be here. I have a key. I mean, the executor of the estate wants me to be the one selling this house."

"And who might that be, ma'am?"

Khaki Man is now chewing the inside of his cheek, agitated.

I don't want to complicate all this, but there's nothing to do but lay it out. "The executor is Bennett Schwartz. Ginna's husband. Her estranged husband, I mean. They were separated, when she died. He wanted a divorce."

Officer McDaniel is thinking very hard. "Okaaaaaaay, so let's get this Bennett Schwartz on the phone."

Ugh. I knew this was next. When Ginna died, six months ago, she and Bennett had been separated for six months. Ginna, eternal optimist Ginna, would not give Bennett the divorce he wanted, because she felt that he was suffering from Physician's Lust Syndrome and would snap out of it, given enough time. She saw no reason to let go, she was patient, and she loved him. Ginna's will, therefore, was the will of a woman happily married to an orthopedist. Except for one confounding little page that she cooked up a month before she died.

This isn't going well. Yelling over the alarm is so stressful. All I want is to take a nap, and I don't want to deal with Bennett. I text him, because he is impossible to reach by phone. "urgent!!! at ginnas. police wont let me in. call me asap"

I turn to Khaki Man and say hotly, "What're you talking about? Why can't I go in the house?"

There is something very strange about this guy, a sagging about him, a wholesale droop of someone who is having trouble getting a day going.

"Your sister," he says, in the rich Nashville accent common to those families with old insurance company fortunes. "Your sister wouldn't like it. That's all. I'm sorry—but she had such strong feelings. About you." He looks horrified to be saying something so direct. So southern, this guy.

Ah. Khaki Man knows about me. I shake my head, frustrated. "She was fine—"

The alarm stops, shockingly. It's as if a vacuum has sucked up all the sound in the world, and we are left with the scruffle of robins rooting through dry leaves. I turn to Officer McDaniel and suggest that we sit on the front steps to wait for Bennett to call back.

Strong feelings. That's one way of putting it. "I'll get my ID," I tell the officer. I'm hit with a wash of sadness about my sister. So stupid, all this. I wish

Bennett would call back so I can get inside and get some sleep. Officer Mc-
Daniel is right beside me as I head for the back door—what does he think is
going on here? I'm going to pull a pistol out of my L. L. Bean Tote Bag?

Next to my tote bags, beside the back door, is a bucket still filled with
Ginna's garden tools. Folded neatly on top are Ginna's leather rose gloves, with
long cuffs to protect against thorns. Ginna's rose garden is one of the many
things about this house that seems impossible. I reach down, slide my hand
into a glove, and feel the shape of her hand in the worn leather. "Gauntlet," I
say as I hold up my hand in a knightly salute.

Officer McDaniel is not playing. I point toward the rose garden, the broad
formal circle, now in heavy spring bud, on the verge of beginning its extraordinary display. "She was an amazing gardener." He nods, minutely. I sigh and
hand him my driver's license.

Exactly at the moment that I decide Bennett is never going to call back, I
see a gleaming, white Cadillac pull into the driveway.

Mother.

This poor cop has no idea what is coming his way. Mother drives around
the police car, onto the grass, across the yard, basically, so that she can park directly in front of us. It's her upbringing on a farm in Columbia coming
through. If you want to get somewhere, drive there. Road optional.

"Still waiting?" she says as she emerges, wearing a taupe evening gown with
a lace jacket and her strand of whopper pearls. Taupe is one of Mother's colors.
I always forget how striking she is: all angles in her face, strong in the chin and
a stern brow. If Abraham Lincoln were a beautiful woman, he would be my
mother. "How do you do, officer? I'm the mother of this one here. Grace Ballenger. Judge Ballenger. Sixth Circuit Court of Appeals. This is my daughter's
house—my other daughter, who died a few months ago. There's no problem
here. Delia here has just come into town. We have a house to sell, unfortunately. I know you understand."

This is all delivered in a matter-of-fact way, fast and with no room for discussion. Mother's way. Officer McDaniel is dazzled by this white-haired
woman, but also stumped. "Yes ma'am—your honor—I'm sure it's all fine, I
just need—"

"We're fine. You run on, officer." Mother's pale rose perfume has wafted
over us all. That scent is one of the most potent memories I have about this
woman. I'm pretty sure it's why I never wear perfume.

Khaki Man chimes in, "I do have the code, officer."

Mother looks at Khaki Man, confused.

"Well," Officer McDaniel says warily.

"Thank you for coming. You're a beacon of security in a world of trouble, sir," Mother says. She actually reaches out and pats him on the shoulder. It's as if she has broken the spell, and he realizes that he can go home now.

I should have known that calling Mother would activate her. There is no way she would have sat at home, knowing that I was a tantalizing four miles away. We watch the police car come around the curve of the driveway and exit through the other entrance.

Mother turns to Khaki Man, extending her hand. "How do you do? I'm Grace Ballenger. And how exactly do you have the code?"

A brilliant pink creeps into Khaki Man's translucent face. I'm embarrassed that he's embarrassed.

"Angus Donald," he says. "Neighbor. Ginna gave me the code a while back when she was . . . when she wanted to make sure somebody nearby could," he shrugs, "turn off the alarm. If it went off. She hated the thing. A bit much."

Mother gives him her best superfakey smile and says, "Well. That's just wonderful. Perhaps you could share this code with us?"

Angus looks troubled. "You don't have it? I shouldn't even have it. But when I heard the alarm going off for so long—I almost let it go, but then I figured—"

"Angus," my mother smiles in her most ferociously cordial way. "We're family. Honest."

"Yeah," I chime in, holding up my phone. "And I'm waiting to hear from her husband. Who has it. Obviously."

His eyes narrow, wary. "Well, OK then." He pats his pockets for a pen.

"Memory like an elephant," Mother says, impatient. "Lay it on me."

Angus is embarrassed all over again. "Right." He squints at Mother. "Six eight eight one. To turn it on. Six three three one two to shut it off."

Mother is studying Angus. "Your wife was Augusta Donald."

Here we go. Mother cannot resist the impulse to connect every single person she knows to every other person in the universe. Angus admits that yes, his wife was Augusta Donald, and for the next three minutes, Mother rhapsodizes about Augusta and their experience together on the Metro Arts Commission six years ago, and how desperately sad she was when Augusta died, and what a lovely thing it was for Angus to help with this silly alarm.

Angus tries to be game about it all, but he keeps crossing and uncrossing his arms as if they're tangled, absolutely avoiding eye contact.

"I'm exhausted," I announce. "Mother, I'll call you." Being definite with Mother is pretty much the only way to communicate with her. Every conversation with her is a sort of argument.

"Delia, you just got here."

"I'm tired."

"I need to talk to you."

"Later, Mother."

Angus watches this tennis match with quick eyes. Mother sighs in that theatrical way I really despise, and says as she roots around in her little taupe evening bag, "Well, I have a dinner." She looks like the mother of the bride in that get-up, rail thin and as comprehensively groomed as ever. She shakes her head in a tiny way, this quiver of disapproval. "I know. I know exactly how this goes. How about you call me when you feel like it, OK?" She pauses. "Delia." I know she is not happy about this, but I also know that she understands exactly how unproductive it would be to push it. She pulls out a handkerchief and wipes her nose. "Go on and get settled in your haunted house. Can't imagine why you're not staying with me." She evaporates in her white Cadillac as quickly as she came, her special-issue Tennessee license plate announcing, as ever, "Judiciary." As if she's ever going to need to peel off to court like a fireman. I wonder how many traffic tickets she's avoided with that thing.

Angus creeps down the driveway. "OK, then. I'll be going," he says and turns to go.

"It's my house," I say weakly, half hoping he won't hear me.

Angus turns back. "What?"

"The house. It's my house. Ginna left it to me. I'm 'allowed' to be here," I say, hooking my fingers into quotation marks.

Angus's pale face looks aggrieved. "That's not it," he says. "You *shouldn't* be here, that's all." He troops down the driveway, legs like stilts, suddenly animated by his disgust.

Auspicious. Welcome to 603 Bowling Avenue.

I finally make my way inside my sister's dim house, feeling guilty to be there after that welcome by my new neighbor Ichabod Crane. I find the alarm system control panel by the kitchen door, but I've already forgotten the code. Mother may have a mind like a steel trap, but numbers slip out of my head like noodles off a fork.

However annoying she is, Mother should have at least stayed with me long enough to turn on some lights. No, I don't believe in ghosts, but I do believe that an empty house can be full of creepy, especially one that has been vacant for six months. Let's just say that there are fourteen lamps downstairs at Ginna's house, and it takes about five minutes to turn them on. When a person is moving fast.

So dusty, so uninhabited. Ginna always kept things so fresh and polished, the constant touching of every surface in a house, over and over. Rub scrub polish paint. Back in Chicago, I do as little home maintenance as possible. A can of Comet will cover just about any emergency. Just shake some of that stuff on there.

This is a big house by Nashville standards, gigantic by mine, built in the twenties, a brick colonial revival, sturdy as a ship. It's in an old trolley car neighborhood right off West End Avenue, which is pretty much the Amazon River for the natives who call Nashville home. Never mind the fact that the metropolitan Nashville region covers ten counties—there are people in Nashville who live their entire lives within a mile of West End Avenue. You can grow up in Belle Meade, go to elementary school, high school, and college without leaving the long artery that is West End Avenue. Ginna was pretty much one of those people, and if I had been as careless as her, I could have had the same gruesome fate.

It's hard to know where to sit in Ginna's house. The living room. The library. The den, the study, the nook in the kitchen, the screened porch, the terrace, the nest at the top of the front stairs. Each room is a world, carefully and carelessly pulled together. Ginna's house feels exactly like Ginna: welcoming, soft, so filled with beautiful things that you can't reach out without touching something lovely. The curved leg of a side table. A bowl of marble eggs. None of the fabrics in the living room match, but they are all friends: blues, creams, greens. She told me that once this room was finished, her decorator took a look around and said, "Good. It doesn't look like a decorator has been in here."

My apartment in Chicago would fit inside Ginna's living room. Literally. I live in a room, though they call it a loft because that sounds better. I'm fifteen floors up, with a minuscule balcony that whistles with cold in the winter, suited only for jumping to your doom. I can go weeks without setting foot on grass. I don't crave a yard; I crave the absence of one. In the time I've lived in Chicago, that apartment has been all I need: a pied *de* terre, a foot off the ground.

I give up and sit in the breakfast room.

It's the ruins of Pompeii, this breakfast room. Nobody's lived here since Bennett took the girls the day of the accident. There's a *Tennessean* from last October on the sideboard, folded to the middle of the Living section, a Sudoku half worked. A pile of Amelia's geometry papers. Flip flops under the table. What are the girls up to? It must be miserable for them right about now. I don't really know them. Another thing to feel bad about.

My phone rings. Bennett.

"You got in?"

"Yeah. Thanks."

"Right. Got a hip to do."

"OK, bye then."

Typical. Bennett is a man of few—actually, he's a man of no words. He's a beady-eyed rodent, with two front teeth that he sinks into his lower lip all the time, gnawing at himself. He's dark haired and pale, a creature of the operating room and subterranean hospital passageways. Exhausting to talk with him—I can't imagine how he and Ginna managed to sustain a marriage on such a thin diet of conversation. Every word is an event with Bennett, a nugget, a hard-won prize. Who wants a chatty surgeon, right? With Bennett, chatty is not a problem.

I keep thinking about that Angus guy. "You shouldn't be here." He reminds me of a character in a fairy tale. The Doomsayer. Nose like the prow of a sailboat, permanently aloof.

Maybe he's right. What am I doing here, anyway?

I tick through the plan that I've figured out over the past few weeks. I'm in town to sell this house. It actually is mine. Ginna left it to me, in this stark little addendum to her will. Notarized, witnessed, everything, dated about four weeks before she died. Her attorney wouldn't or couldn't say a word about how it came to be. I don't know why she would do something like that. At one point I wondered if she did it as a cosmic joke: here, sister, here's some lifestyle for ya. Here's the life you left behind—it's time for you to come take care of Mother.

Ha! As if Mother needed one iota of help. She is the least helpless woman I know. I can't count the number of people who rhapsodize about my mother: so brilliant, so inspiring, such a trailblazer for women. A treasure, a beacon, name a bridge for her. What they never say is how great a mother she is, because I'm guessing that no one ever saw her do anything maternal. *Sweet* is not a word you hear about Mother. Her extravagantly lame rearing of us resulted in two very different daughters: warm and cool. Ginna had a giant, warm heart, and she was always the great uniter, operating with a strong sense that personal happiness would come from being a part of a family. I had a highly developed sense of Get Me Outta Here.

My only guess about why I've ended up with this house is that Ginna wanted to be sure her daughters wouldn't end up living in her beloved house with her husband and his slutty surgical nurse. I can't blame her a bit.

The phone call from Bennett when he told me about the will was a classic one-minute revelation. I had a million questions. Did she write it out on a napkin? She owned the house singly, not with him? What about the girls? Why would she do such a thing?

Bennett had no insight into what Ginna had done. He told me that she had paid most of the down payment, thanks to an infusion from the Grace Ballenger Buy Your Daughter's Love Fund, so he had wanted her to have the house in her name. He said he had no interest in the house anyway, and that Ginna's codicil had saved him the awkwardness of dealing with his daughters about it. The thing he couldn't figure out, though, was the timing of it all.

It's a horrible, depressing lottery prize, this house. Congratulations! You've just won your dream house! The only catch is that your sister has to die for this to happen. And you can't afford to have a house like that. And, by the way, it's in Nashville.

Oh, Nashville. I worked pretty hard to get out of this place. Have you ever been to a party that you hated, where you spent half the time working on the excuse for why you were going to have to leave early? That's what Nashville is like—that cloying thing, that thing where everybody is having a great time, and you think you ought to be right in the mix too, except you suddenly notice that they're all talking about football and church and their spring break trip to Rosemary Beach. That's Nashville. From the time I was in high school, I knew I had to get out of there. Nobody was thinking.

And Mother. I guess that was part of it, too. A large part.

So. My plan is pretty simple. Next week, the house officially becomes mine. I'm going to sell it as fast as I can, then give most of the proceeds to the girls—there's no way I would take something that obviously should have been theirs. I will, however, keep some of it. An embarrassing fact in all this: I kind of need the money. Money is one of those hot topics in our family. It's not that there isn't money floating around; it's just that it floats my way only when Mother is rowing the boat. It is available only with many, many strings attached, so I decided a long time ago that I'd just as soon make my own way. I guess I have only myself to blame, but I blame Mother anyway.

I figure if I divvy up the proceeds, then everybody will come out ahead. By selling the house myself, I'll save the six percent real estate agent's fee, which with a house like this would be in the neighborhood of $120,000. That's considerably more than I'm making at my own job. I'm thinking of this as moonlighting. I can keep doing my travel agent stuff, such as it is, while I deal with the house, so this is going to work out great. It's such a desirable neighborhood, and such a choice house, that it won't take long to git r done.

It's late. I've finally decided which bedroom of the five to use. I knew I couldn't deal with Ginna's bedroom, with its little patio outside the bedroom where you can sit and presumably have coffee brought to you by someone whose job it is to bring you coffee. That king-size bed screams "empty," and there's no way that I'm going to find comfort amid those shams and goose-down duvet. The juju coming out of that maritally challenged bed could be big trouble for me. It's already bad enough, the man situation.

Incredibly, on her dresser, there's an eight-by-ten photograph of Ginna and Bennett, bride and groom. How could she possibly stand to look at that thing? If my husband ditched me for a nurse, I'd make a bonfire in the back yard for stuff like that. Her wedding day? I wonder what she saw when she looked at that childlike pair.

I didn't want to stay in the girls' rooms, either, because they might come over at some point and find me camping out amid their drifts of crap. Cassie's looks like a pink bomb went off, and Amelia's is covered in Tibetan prayer flags and posters of poorly nourished singer-songwriters. I don't know why they didn't take more of their things to Bennett's. Sad. It looks like they were airlifted from this place, judging by the amount of stuff still here.

That left the guest rooms. One is the Official Guest Room, looking much fancier than the last time I was here, now covered in a crazy amount of $300-a-yard dun-colored linen that a decorator talked Ginna into last year. It feels like an expensive hotel, and I've never been one to care about thread count. The other is on the third floor, a secret hideout up a set of narrow back stairs, with tall attic windows stuck into the three dormers across the front, and a half-moon window down low to fit some outside symmetry. Maybe it's a little spare, and leftover, and not really a bedroom at all.

If the wi-fi makes it up the steps, that's where you'll find me.

I go downstairs, hungry, though it's going to be a stretch to find anything to eat. I take the back stairs, steep and tunnel-like. It's a breathtakingly crappy kitchen by west Nashville standards. The cabinets are plain sheet metal, pale green, at least forty years old, from the days when the cook did the cooking. They're so out of fashion that they're almost back in style: a brutally efficient space. The linoleum isn't ironic linoleum; it's lazy, tired linoleum. It's funny to me that Ginna resisted the pressure to have a dreamy kitchen like all her friends do. A few months after moving in, she decided that it was a perfectly OK kitchen, and she liked it.

I hear a rustle in the pantry, and I figure that mice must be having a fine time in this uninhabited house. A cat meows, and I just about jump out of my skin. Mr. Serious comes lumbering in from the sunroom. Such a huge animal, like a Thanksgiving turkey, too much body for not enough head. A threat to no mouse. Ginna loved that cat. I'd forgotten that Mr. Serious was still here. And I'd forgotten that Shelly was still coming to take care of the poor orphaned beast. Bennett claimed that he had developed an allergy to cats, that asshole, and the girls were adamant that Mr. Serious could not be given away. So Shelly—mother's steady, loyal housekeeper—took on the responsibility of feeding and scooping Mr. Serious as part of her caretaking duties at the house.

I wonder when Shelly will turn up. I think of her on occasion, so fondly, but we've lost touch since high school.

The pantry is crammed with kid food: Skittles, Cheetos, Cool Ranch Doritos, Dr. Peppers, Sprites. Did Ginna never hear of the food pyramid? I unearth a box of Brown Sugar Cinnamon Pop-Tarts that by my calculation can be no fresher than six months old, and I slide a couple into the toaster. Dinner.

Reconnaissance

I drove down yesterday from Chicago in my Toyota, with a trunkful of dread and my office in the back seat: my computer, a box of client files, and three bricklike backup hard drives. That's my office. It's doesn't look like much, but there is a ton of stuff in there—all my clients, destination research, my Golden Rolodex of tour guides, concierges, restaurant maître d's, airlines, lawyers, priests, oral surgeons, plastic surgeons. I pride myself on being able to find the name and number of the exact person to solve the particular problem of one of my travelers. I'm Special Ops, Travel: you ask me the name of a dentist in Vienna, I tell you that Mrs. Doktor Sara Schreiner kicks Doktor Christian Vetter's ass.

Susan Castrano, my business partner, lives in Portland, Oregon. "Business partner" sounds more official than it is. "Roommate from college" is probably a better description. We have a travel business, not a travel agency so much as a travel hand-holding service. Travel agents are a miserable lot these days, now that the Internet has devoured anybody's ability to make good money booking tickets and hotels. We still book trips, but mostly we're doing something much more time-consuming and less profitable: we help old rich people, mostly, who are on trips.

We're a kind voice; Susan's is kinder, actually. I'm efficient, and for certain people, men usually, efficiency is the greatest comfort when things are screwed up. We're good at what we do. We guarantee that we will be there, on the phone, whenever they need us. People don't expect miracles from us; they just want to have us inside their cell phones, waiting to help.

It's usually low-grade trouble—a lost hotel reservation, a tour guide who doesn't show up. Ideally, we never hear from our clients, because their trips run smoothly. However, due to the demographic we serve, clients have died on us while in faraway places, which is always traumatic. I've got a list of medevac companies, unfortunately.

It's a career that showed up the way a lost cat appears on your doorstep, and you give him a dish of milk. Accidental.

I can put my finger on the moment when it started. One chilly May night, nine years ago, Ginna and I were at Mother's, celebrating her sixtieth birthday by throwing her a Mexican patio party. Mother loves theme parties (her daughters do not), so we were all dressed in serapes and sombreros, and Mother had a giant fake red rose tucked behind her ear. Her girlfriends likewise dressed for a flamenco convention. The men wore khakis and button-down shirts, as ever. A less game group of men you'll never find. Their bland tolerance of all this was something they cultivated during a hundred sorority parties at Auburn, at Tuscaloosa, at Vanderbilt. They'll come, but do not ask them to dress up.

The margarita machine had just broken when the phone rang. I answered it, and Mother's best friend Tweenie Gilbert started talking. No introduction, but I knew it was Tweenie because Mother had been expecting Tweenie's birthday call, had been talking all night about how it just about killed her that Tweenie was going to miss this party, because she was in Spain and Portugal this very week and would have added so much to the party.

"He's gone! I am just absolutely beside myself! Nobody is helping me! It's all Portuguese!" Tweenie said in her high, flappy voice. "Gracie?"

"No, this is Delia."

"Delia, Delia! Grantham has vanished."

I sussed out that she was calling from Oporto, Portugal, and that her husband had gone out to get some souvenir bottles of port and had not come back for more than six hours.

It's funny. Something clicked in me. I was the one who should help Tweenie find her husband, never mind the fact that she was an ocean away and I didn't speak Portuguese. I told her I would get in touch with the hotel and go from there. And I told her, even though it was one in the morning in Oporto, that it was going to be OK. I could feel the relief radiating from her, the simple fact that she had found someone who was going to help.

Grantham, it turned out, was not OK. He had indeed gone to the wine shop down the street, but he had a heart attack in the back stairwell of the hotel, as he climbed the four flights of stairs back to their room. A hotel maid found him, laid out on a landing, with his two bottles of 1953 Cockburn standing neatly beside him.

At the visitation the following week, Tweenie took me out to her boatlike Cadillac and rooted around in the vast trunk. She fished out a Kroger grocery bag, handed it to me and said, "Delia, this is the wine that Grantham was out to buy. Our fiftieth anniversary is coming up, and he wanted us to celebrate it with this port. I want you to have this, because the sound of your calm voice was the only thing that got me through that night." She nodded toward the bag. "Maybe you can celebrate a grand occasion with it, some marvelous trip." She paused and looked me full in the face. "I must've told a hundred people about you. You ought to be a 911 operator!"

I took the wine, and I took her advice, and at the tender age of 22, with a degree in geographical studies from the University of Chicago, I found myself helping Mother's many, many friends take their trips all over the world.

As I said, this was all unexpected. I had thought I would get a job working in city planning. I wanted to fight the crapification of the world. But I'm no good at politics—my internships in Chicago showed me how much backslapping went on when it came to things like zoning and land use, how sickening it can be to see a good idea sink in the mud of mediocrity. I hate losing, and I hate it more when stupid people win. The travel business was so much easier: dropping travelers into the maps of the world. I could do it from the comfort of my living room. With only myself to boss around.

Susan came on after a year, such a great piece of luck. I learned pretty fast that being a travel concierge means never having to say goodnight—it's always ten a.m. somewhere in the world. Just as I was hitting a wall, Susan hit a wall of her own—she had been working at a PR firm whose best client was the world's largest manufacturer of disposable enemas. Susan is good with a euphemism, but she told me then that she would rather use her powers of persuasion in a less poopy way.

There was a time when our travel business was going well. It is not, however, going well at the present time. The current financial upheaval pretty much heaved my customers' interest in exotic travel out the window, leaving Susan and me with the occasional Alaska-bound widow who is worried about a global warming-affected iceberg falling off Hubbard Glacier onto her cruise ship. People traveling domestically just don't need a lot of assurance by telephone. It's a good time for me to have something else to do, though I can think of at least fourteen part-time jobs I'd rather have than selling my sister's house.

I have no idea how to go about selling a house. But I have made a career of figuring out things. I got a book, *Beverly d'Angeleno's How to Sell Your House in Two Weeks*, which has pretty much been my Bible so far. I picked it because it has a photograph of Beverly d'Angeleno on the front, and Beverly looks like a gal who knows how to move the real estate. She says I need to be "pro-active" in my efforts, that I need to "incentivize a buyer" to come see the house. It doesn't seem that hard, in the case of this particular house. Ginna was always telling me about how fast houses in her neighborhood sold, how every doctor in town wanted to be on Bowling Avenue because it was the street with the biggest houses closest to Vanderbilt and the hospitals. All I need is one of those Vanderbilt doctors to have a wife who's got that third baby on the way. The doctors' wives freak out when that third baby's coming. That's the sweet spot for a house like this.

Last night I went looking for an extra blanket for my bed, and when I opened the closet at the top of the back stairs, I found shelf upon shelf of yarn. Ginna was a knitter. It's scary, the amount of yarn that she had. I headed into Ginna's room to steal a blanket, and I found one of her bright afghans in a basket by her bed. I picked it up to take it upstairs but found needles and a ball of yarn still attached at one end, like Ginna was down there, holding on to the end of the blanket.

Shelly was the one who taught us to knit, back when I was little and Ginna was marooned at home, still too young to drive. One day, high summer, when we were bored out of our minds, she separated us from a tangle of pointless bickering with the words, "Come on. I'll show you something." She took us up to the attic, the lofty-ceilinged attic, hot as fire, and dug out a cardboard box. "Your grandmother loved to knit," she said, "and it's time for you girls to get the hang of it." Shelly knew our own mother would never teach us. Shelly was like that—filling in the gaps, all the time.

I know it's kind of a cliché to have a kindly black housekeeper supplying privileged Southern white girls with tender experiences like this, but that's how it was. Shelly taught us to knit and to make fried pies and how to press a shirt, but she was actually a dad to us in some ways, seeing as how our father had died when I was a baby. Mother was always off at court, and God knows Shelly was patient in a way that Mother never was. So it was Shelly who showed us how to handle a pocketknife, how to bait a hook. She was a feminist, 100 percent, and didn't have much use for men. In our house, wholly lacking in men, I took her point early. But when Frank Harrell ditched me at the senior prom, and I cried the next day, still humiliated, it was Shelly who said, beneath the tissue she was using to wipe her own eyes, "Delia, welcome to the world, honey. Welcome to the damn world." I could tell her exactly how it felt to walk out of that dance, past a wall of prom girls, with Mrs. McAllister, the geometry teacher chaperone who drove me home. Only Shelly could take the sting out of that.

Holding Ginna's unfinished blanket in my lap, I find that I can't wait to see Shelly again.

When I arrive downstairs, groggy and stiff from sleeping too long in that stout, narrow canoe of a daybed, Mr. Serious watches closely from the sunroom floor. Shelly is at the breakfast table, spreading pimento cheese onto toast. Shelly has been eating pimento cheese toast in Ballenger family breakfast rooms for as long as I can remember.

"Look what the cat dragged in," she says dryly.

"Oh, Shelly, thank God you're here." She must be almost seventy by now, diminishing. Her large, wide-set eyes are old around the edges, her hair a flat gray in its tight little ponytail, but she still looks exactly like a Persian cat. If you didn't know her, you might read grumpy in her face, but I never saw it as anything but Shelly Who Never Let Us Down. There were times when I thought it was the most beautiful face I'd ever seen. I bend down to give her a hug. She feels as small as a child, diminished, after all these years. She still carries that gentle scent of witch hazel, her all-purpose treatment for just about any ailment. When we were young, she'd get out the witch hazel for our blemishes, sunburns, poison ivy, bruises, dry skin—Ginna used to joke that Shelly mixed it in with her iced tea. To this day, I keep a bottle of witch hazel in my bathroom.

"Lonesome, isn't it?" she says with a sigh.

"Terrible."

"Six months of this. Can't hardly be over here these days. Wasn't for that pitiful cat . . ."

"Worst night's sleep. This place creaks, sounds like people walking all over the place."

Shelly smiles. "Haints."

"Stop it!"

There's a cane by her chair. It pains me to see this symbol of decrepitude. "What's that?"

"Knees."

"Sorry."

"They want to do something about 'em. Long as I can outrun the doctor, I'm good." Shelly takes a sip of coffee. "So, Delia, what's the plan?"

My plan had been, until I laid eyes on that cane thirty seconds ago, to have Shelly help me clean out the house in order to get it ready to put on the market. "Well," I say. "That organizer woman. Need to get her to come. The one Mother said."

Shelly grunts.

"That bad?" Shelly gives me a look of deep knowing, then slowly shakes her head. I don't want to do anything that Shelly doesn't like. "Well, maybe somebody else—"

"Don't get me wrong—Miss Priss'll get this house in shape. She's just ..."

"What?"

"You'll see." Shelly shrugs, then stands as if she's unfolding a rusty pocket knife. "When you want to start?"

I don't want to start, ever. I want to sell the house as is, with the stacks of sheet music on the piano, the Rice-a-Roni in the cabinet.

I cut my finger—any fool should know better than to try to saw a frozen bagel in two—so I head toward Ginna's bathroom for some first aid. On the way, I pass Bennett's former closet, a deep cavern of custom-built shelves, now absolutely stuffed with yarn. Circular knitting needles dangle from the tie rack. Too funny. Man treats you like crap? Stashing well is the best revenge.

I pick up the phone to dial up Miss Priss, and the stuttering dial tone tells me that there are messages on Ginna's voicemail. Who could that be? I don't know how to get at her voicemail. This house is an aircraft carrier with no captain.

"Hello? Is this Barbara Odom?"

"This is she. And with whom am I speaking?" Shelly wasn't kidding. She sounds like somebody who accessorizes.

I tell Barbara about my situation, and she sets a time to come over. Immediately. She appears to have nothing to do that is more important than discussing this house-cleanout project. Man, do I not like the sound of this. I like the padding of a day or two before any appointment, just to give me the mental space to dread it. But I can't come up with a reason to delay this.

———

The doorbell rings. To my colossal chagrin, I see the size 2 figure of Barbara Odom at the door, whitegold hair slicked back in a high ponytail. She has a handbag the size of a suitcase over her arm, and I worry that her pencil-thin wrist will snap off. I recognize this creature. Brandy Butler has upgraded to Barbara Odom, but she's still the high school classmate who always terrified me.

"SURPRISE!" she screeches. "I wanted to surprise you!" She is clapping her hands in a tiny way and shifting from one gargantuan wedge heel to the other. "Didja know? Couldja tell it was me?"

Brandy's dumb act served her well for many years. In high school, dumb was how she managed to date, with an efficiency that left the rest of us awestruck, the three most desirable guys in the school. Once she got to Auburn, dumb got her a degree in marketing, and once out of school, dumb got her a job working at CMT, the country music cable channel. Brandy was the one who was responsible for coming up with the career-making slogan, "CMT: MTV for Americans."

We weren't friends in school, but you wouldn't know that by the way she's acting today. The stream of biographical narrative coming out of her makes me sleepy, and I can't keep track of any of it. She's telling me about her second husband, Kenny, who's a guitar player for Kenny Chesney ("So confusing to have two Kennys in one band!"), her love of Pilates, and the way microdermabrasion has made all the difference. She seems to be suggesting that I would benefit from microdermabrasion. I lead her to the living room, and she sinks into Ginna's downy sofa like a very small child. Dust motes rise from the chenille, a vague cloud in a shaft of light. Her thighs are the size of my arms.

In a blink, Brandy changes channels. "Delia. I am just. So. Sorry. Iamjustsosorry about Ginna. You know how much I loved that girl. All y'all are just so smart, and she did all that stuff for poor Arabian children, I just can't get over it." She shakes her head, mystified. "Right there on Hillsboro Road. Can you stand it? Can you believe it? I go through that intersection five times a day. Just yesterday there was a minivan coming through—" She looks up to find me blinking back tears.

I try not to think about the way Ginna died. It's easier for me to imagine that she has somehow evaporated, vanished into thin air. Sometimes, I honest to God find myself thinking that's she's simply lost. Maybe she's down in Pulaski. But Brandy has triggered the vivid image of my sister, in her damn Volvo-because-it's-safer, on her way home from taking Cassie to school, an airbag blasting into her face as she met that oncoming delivery truck, and I can't stand it. I can't believe it. People don't die when the airbag works.

"It's OK," I say, mopping my eyes with a sleeve. "Always think I'm done crying, but I never am."

Brandy's face collapses in concern and embarrassment. "I'm so sorry. I just hope you know I want to do everything I can to help you with this house." I almost turn off the spigot, but seeing Brandy reminds me of high school, and high school reminds me of Ginna's high school graduation and the way she let me wear her cap and gown around the house, and I slump to the side of the chair, sloppy weeping all over again. I almost wipe my nose on the arm of the leather chair but catch myself just in time. We sit while I try to collect myself.

"I've done a lot of estate work," she offers in a semi-whisper, sliding a finger across one of her pale calligraphy eyebrows. "There's a process to it, and I want you to know—" she's looking at the bookcases stuffed with Ginna and Bennett's books. She sees the art and photographs climbing the walls. "This is going to be . . . a prrrrrrroject."

"Yeah. I'm just wanting to get a sense from you of how long this will take. I'm thinking the house will sell in a couple of weeks."

Brandy nods, then stops. "What are you asking?"

"The price?" It seems so embarrassing to talk about price, like asking somebody what size bra she wears. Two million? I don't know. "I'm still working on that." Must sound confident.

"Well, you know the market is awful right now. One of Kenny's friends is trying to sell his house, and it's taking forever. People want everything for nothing. It's crazy."

I have heard this but I am ignoring this.

"You know, what you need right this minute isn't an organizer—it's a fluffer. I don't fluff, but I have a friend who does. She's fluffed for Faith Hill and Amy Grant. You need Angela," Brandy says, squirming her tiny body off the sofa to have a look around. "Yeah," she says, peeking into the dining room with its wall of china-crammed display cabinets.

I'm relieved, actually, for Brandy to recuse herself from my case. While she blathers on, I'm studying my bootleg Gap jeans, which hit my shin at a capri length, unlike her skinny $300 denim which hits at the precise bottom of her gigantic wedge heel. It's clear that hanging out with Brandy will do nothing but make me feel awful. We part with superfakeynice promises to get together soon, and she evaporates seconds before I pass out from the exertion of dealing with her.

I return to the kitchen, where Shelly is fixing grilled cheeses. She turns to face me, eyebrows raised. "How 'bout that?"

"Brandy says we need a fluffer."

My phone vibrates.

"Did you mail your taxes?"

Susan's like this.

"Um. No."

"You have thirteen hours." She pauses. "Have you even done your taxes?"

I like to think of myself as organized, but somehow, I have become the partner in this business who's the slacker, the B team, the forgetter.

"I don't forget my taxes, Susan. Jesus!"

I absolutely forgot about my taxes. They're still in the tote bag in the mud-room, tidy forms cooked up by my accountant, done yet undone.

Susan is chuckling at my indignant tone. "When will you be able to take calls?" We divide our clients up, depending on who's got more time. Susan has three kids and a computer programmer husband. In our nine years of business together, I've met her family maybe three times. We have an abstract relation-ship, Susan and me.

"Neverrrr."

"The Jenkinses are heading out Thursday."

"Where?"

"Playa del Carmen."

"Nothing to worry about there."

"Mexican drug lords. Betty's worrying about them."

I laugh. "Wrong coast."

"Whatever. Do you want to take them?"

"Maybe the next one? I can't do much until—Susan, you can't believe the woman who just left here. This classmate, oh my God. Gwyneth Paltrow is going to clear out the house."

"How's it going?" Susan has heard all about my house-selling scheme.

"Don't know yet. A lot to do."

"Well, good luck with that. Takes time. And your mom?" Susan has heard even more about my mother.

"Four miles away. Dangerously close."

————

I'm still shaken by my unexpected breakdown with Brandy. This place is so saturated with Ginna. I'm shivery with sadness. I hadn't expected it to be so hard to be here. I'm not what you would call a sentimental person, but this is tough. Ginna is everywhere, in every scrap of paper.

She was so good at this way of life. I open a drawer for a spoon, and remember the trip to Corzine's to do her wedding registry, awed at the way she could rattle off silver patterns, one after the other, the way birdwatchers name sparrows. She was 21, and I was 14. It was the most grown-up thing I'd ever seen. Ginna had her pick of the four sets of sterling that Mother had accumulated from long-gone Ballengers. To me, a dozen place settings of Fairfax looked impossible. To Ginna, it was what you used every day.

"How's Mother?" I ask Shelly. It's a prurient interest I have.

"Fine. She's got a big conference to run this week, bunch of judges, so they're setting up the house today for a dinner on Tuesday. Tents, tables, it's a mess."

"Why aren't you over there?"

"Because they're setting up the house today," she says with a squint and a smile. "And I really need to take care of this cat. Might take all day, this cat."

We're refugees.

The girls sit across from me at California Pizza Kitchen. When I invited them to lunch, I suggested Obie's, which was the cool pizza place near Vanderbilt when I was growing up. Amelia was mystified. "Seriously?" she asked. "That's like on Elliston Place or something," near Pluto, apparently.

Amelia, now sixteen, is a pretty version of Bennett, dark haired and angular. She has these sharklike eyes, almost black. I wonder sometimes if temperament is attached to appearance. She's hard to read, Amelia, much like her father. Cassie, thirteen, is a girlier version of Ginna, a softer face, lighter hair, a bit like me, actually. Do these girls know how much they resemble their parents? People always said I was the younger twin of my sister, that we resembled each other so much. Ginna and I thought we looked wildly different: I called her Fattie, and she called me Paleface.

At the moment, they look very much like girls who are waiting to see the dentist. I don't know how to talk to them. At all. Girl things are so mysterious to me: when I pass by the Claire's shop in Chicago, with the racks of earrings and hair thingies, it all seems so tribal. Which are the right ones? What if you pick the tiny little Peace necklace instead of the little tiny Love necklace?

"I'm going to Mexico with school this summer," Amelia throws out there.

"Cool! What will you be studying?"

"It's not studying, it's service learning. We're supposed to be digging a well, but the regulations won't let us dig because we're too young, so Mr. Bartholomew is going to do the digging. He loves service learning."

"And you don't?"

She shrugs theatrically. "Grandma's paying for it. I like burritos."

Cassie says "Burrrrritos" in an exaggerated hick accent, and they dissolve into laughter. "Inside joke," she offers.

We have managed to get through our pizzas within a half hour, and I can't possibly return them to Bennett after a measly one-hour reunion. What crummy sort of aunt does that?

"Do you all want to go shopping?"

Cassie brightens. "Vintage?"

Amelia rolls her eyes. "Smelly old grandma clothes."

"Not."

"Are too."

"Shutup."

We head toward Belmont Boulevard and the vintage store. I'm with Amelia: the clothes all look like Mother's Dallas phase from 1982. I avoid picking anything for Cassie, because it all looks so hideous that I can't imagine her wearing any of it. She comes out of the dressing room in a sleeveless canary yellow polyester dress with orange top-stitching, probably the least flattering color possible for her blonde looks. She loves it, I am mystified, and I fork out $21 for the thing.

"Thanks, Aunt Delia," she says as we walk to the car far down Belmont. I covet the sidewalks in this neighborhood. Nashville is so spotty. I feel a sharp pang of homesickness for my street in Chicago and for my simple, abstract life there. These girls are tricky.

"You're a vision in that chemise," I tease.

"A nightmare, you mean," Amelia adds.

"Shut. Uppeth."

"Have you seen Grandma lately?" I ask, hoping to divert the sniping. At what point do girls stop bickering? I don't remember sniping like this with Ginna. Maybe it's because she was so much older—almost eight years older— or maybe I've just forgotten it.

Amelia says, "Uh, we saw her a while ago. A month? She's so busy."

"Yeah, but we did stay there that one night."

"Yeah, back when." Amelia sighs. "Right after."

"The country club." Cassie snickers. "Sweet."

I pull up to Bennett's condo, in an undistinguished complex of brick townhouses on the other side of Green Hills. Creek Valley Close. It's painted in an unloved way, a dim greige slathered over the brick, the trim, the door hinges. Nobody's training rambling roses on trellises at Creek Valley Close. This place is a storage facility for humans in transition from one marriage to another. "Hope Busty isn't around," Amelia says.

Bennett's girlfriend? "Do you see her much?"

Cassie rolls her eyes. "Not really. She's laying low these days. The Walrus."

"Cassie!" I say.

"She does. Looks like a walrus." They eject themselves from my car. "Bye! Thanks, Aunt Delia!"

I drive away, and relief washes over me. What are they calling me behind my back? Ratface? I do have a pointy nose.

I'm relieved that I didn't have to talk to Bennett. It's not like we were close, back when he and Ginna were together, but I can hardly stand the prospect of having to deal with him. It was like kicking a puppy, the way he treated Ginna. At least she didn't look like a walrus. She was lovely. She looked like sunshine.

Back at the house, with an agenda of loathsome activities ahead of me, I decide to drink tea instead. At the breakfast table, there's a glossy catalog for Honey-Spiral Hams. Every time I sit down, I study it. There's a picture of a sixteen-pound ham that they will deliver to your house for $99.95, to serve 28-36 people. Was Ginna a Honey-Spiral Hams customer? "Better than home-made," they promise. I try to imagine what it would be like to get four pounds of Yukon Gold mashed potatoes in the mail.

A Very Challenging
Real Estate Environment

It's 6:30 in the morning, and I can't believe I'm already in my car, summoned to Jackson Boulevard. Mother leads such a complete existence that the only way to participate in it is to catch her at the margins. I never see this time of day unless I'm in the full-out nocturnal phase of my ever-drifting schedule and I've neglected to go to sleep at all.

Cassie is right: Mother's house does indeed bear a striking resemblance to the Belle Meade Country Club. In this early morning spring light, it glows, white clapboard, rambling, set back from the road. Columns and boxwoods piled up front. It's a house that I never lived in. She moved there after she got her federal appointment ten years ago. "Cabin fever," she told me the first time I came to visit there. "Needed a clean slate." It is almost exactly like our old house on the inside: mahogany and silver, silk draperies like ball gowns, fantastically gracious living for a woman whose home was in her courtroom, not this place.

The thing about Mother is that she has been, as long as I can remember, an independent woman. My father died when I was one and Ginna was eight—he fell out of a Piper airplane, incredibly, when he was flying to Memphis with his law partner who liked to ferry them around the state on business. Daddy had apparently failed to latch the airplane door shut properly, and the way his law partner told it, they were both laughing so hard at a story he was telling that Daddy leaned against the door and slid right out.

Will Ballenger was a dog, Mother always said. Drove her crazy, she told us. She made it clear that in the scheme of things, it was probably best that he had fallen out of that little plane, because otherwise she would have eventually come after him with a kitchen knife. Through the years, after growing up with Mother and her distracted yet domineering ways, I developed a pretty good idea of who was driving whom crazy. I'm not saying I could throw myself out of an airplane to get away from my mother; I'm just saying I understand. "You're better off without him," she told us, time and again. I found that impossible to believe, judging by all the newspaper clippings of our smooth-haired father standing in front of banks of microphones, talking to the press about his legal cases. He looked noble. He didn't look like a dog. All my life I've carried the image of him floating through the air, laughing like a cartoon character who hasn't discovered he's not in his tiny airplane anymore.

I often wondered, as I grew up, why Mother never remarried. She never discussed it, never brought home a gentleman caller, and never gave the slightest indication that life was anything but work. I took that lesson to heart early, of course—school became the thing I was going to nail. Maybe I wouldn't be beautiful like Ginna, with that cloud of friends around her, but I knew how to get an A.

Wandering through the polish and order of her house, I find Mother in her breakfast room, buttering a croissant. Mother butters everything, yet her astonishing metabolism keeps any of it from landing on her hips. She's a coat hanger of a woman.

"Tired?" she says. It's more an observation than a question.

I had rubbed my cheeks hard in the driveway to give me that bright-n-perky look, but apparently not enough. "Phone call from Helsinki," I shrug.

"How's Greg?" she asks.

"Fine. Busy. He really is dreamy," I say, ripping open a croissant.

"Hope I'll get to meet him sometime."

I sigh. "It's so hard being apart."

She quizzes me about my house-selling project. "Why don't you just get a realtor and be done with it?"

Such a typical lack of comprehension of the particulars of my situation. Does she not understand how incredibly expensive a real estate agent is?

"It's a lot of money, Mother."

"Time is money." She draws this out as if she's explaining a carburetor to a customer. Her accent becomes cranky country girl when she's irritated.

"Exactly, and I have time but no money."

Mother contemplates this as she sips her Sanka. She has to order Sanka by mail at this point; she is Sanka's final customer.

I feel the need to make it sound like an easy project. To Grace Ballenger, nothing should ever seem hard. Mediocrity is a failure in her eyes. Period. I say, breezily, "It's not a big deal. It's a good time for me to do this."

"And why is that?"

"Exotic travel is our specialty, and as you know, there isn't much exotic travel going on these days."

"Well," she says, "that is the God's truth. You should call David Peek. He'd take care of this in a minute. You'd make plenty on the house, Lord knows, even if he gets the commission."

"I'm not interested in making plenty on the house—I told you, the proceeds are going to the girls. But I am going to keep the fee, because I'm doing the sale."

"The fee," Mother says, voice trailing off in a leading way.

"Yeah, well, I don't think Ginna would have left the house to me if she didn't want me to benefit from it."

"What did Virginia want?" she asks idly. "I do wonder. It seems like a bad joke, or a clerical error. Still can't imagine why she'd leave that house to you, of all people. Can't believe Bennett would just let it go like that. Never gave you any business about it?"

I shake my head no, flattened. "Maybe she just wanted me to have it."

Mother sniffs. "Delia Ballenger in a house like that." A pinched smile. "It boggles the mind."

"I don't want to be here any more than you want me here," I say.

"What do you mean?" she says, stung.

"You know what I mean. This. Your world. I'll be out of town as soon as the house sells, don't worry."

"I love it when you're here."

She's so infuriating, always saying the exact opposite of what she means. I squeeze a lemon into my tea so hard that the rind breaks.

She sharpens and stands up. "OK. Off to court. Just leave the dishes for Shelly. If she shows up. Honestly . . . And Delia, really. Have you ever sold a house before? Have you even paid a mortgage? This is not like selling a bicycle, I promise you that." She is gone without a peck on the cheek or a tally-ho.

Love you too, Mama. I set my plate in the sink. I can't let it go. I move fast toward the front door. The gravel in the driveway crunches with the sound of her Cadillac backing up. Her window slides open, and she sticks out an arm, waving limply.

"You're a horrible woman," I call out, almost yelling. I'm standing directly in front of her car, and my heart is racing.

"What?" She leans her head out the window, puzzled.

"I can totally sell that house. You're so wrong. You have no idea."

"Qualifying ratios," she says. "I know you think about that a lot."

"Why can't you just let me do my thing?"

She looks hard at me. "I have done nothing but let you do your thing. Whatever that is. Delia—" She has backed into a boxwood to the point that the end of her car is consumed in shrubbery. "Dammit." She shifts into Drive. "Delia. Don't come to town and be this way."

"What way?"

"This." She flaps a hand. "Way. Awful. Ginna was never like this."

"Ginna is *gone*, Mother," I yell in what feels like a roar. "I'm your precious remnant!" She flinches, I step aside, and she blasts past me down the driveway without another word.

Heading back toward West End Avenue, past the mansions of Mother's stultifying neighborhood, I feel the adrenaline finally wear off. How does she manage to insult me on such a daily basis? It is so amazing. And I can't believe she forced two lies in a row out of me. I haven't had a client in Helsinki for two years—I looked tired because I keep weird hours that I don't want to explain to her. And Greg isn't dreamy, in any traditional sense of the word. He lives in London where he runs high-end tours through scenic places in England. Greg is adequate, and willing, and distant enough that I don't really think about him all that often. I don't have a boyfriend these days. I have a Greg. I guess.

You would think that if a woman's daughter dies in a tragic car accident, the grieving woman would turn to the surviving daughter for comfort and succor, transformed by the bittersweet revelation that life is precious and at least you still have one daughter. I actually wonder if Mother even feels the loss. She never talks about Ginna, not in any normal way. Such a disconnect. And seeing Mother always sets me jangling. When I'm in Chicago, she melts away. But here, she's an iceberg. Maybe she's only ten percent visible, but the ninety percent lurking right there under the surface is a killer.

I hate it when she gets to me like this. I pull off Harding Road into the Kroger parking lot, turn off the engine, and the sour tears come. I rest my head on the steering wheel. Ginna's face flashes, her officially smiling smile. It's that Easter photograph of Ginna hugged up with her girls, with Mother behind them, arms around their shoulders like she's caught them all. The smocked dresses and baskets and eggs—it's a riot of pastels and seasonal love against the smooth green of Ginna's lawn.

I head into Kroger to get a miserable coffee. I pass a bucket of Easter-colored tulips, and I scoop up the whole lot of them. Surely ten dozen tulips will help. I don't even know where I'll put them—I've never bought this many flowers in my life. At the checkout counter, the clerk says, "Must be gonna have a wedding!"

"Or something," I mutter.

I need to activate. Between Brandy's gloomy prediction about the real estate market and Mother's lack of confidence in me as a realtor, I'm nervous. Maybe the fluffer will help.

Angela Moriarty arrives at my door almost as fast as Brandy did. Is the real estate situation here that bad? Don't these people have anything else to do?

"Love the tulips," she says as she unwinds herself from what appears to be a paisley bedspread. "Such a statement. People usually don't commit to their floral choices. Fierce!"

Somebody has given Angela a seminar in how to appear fascinated in everything the client says. I tell her that Brandy says the house needs "fluffing," and she nods, her large and watery blue eyes blinking slowly. "Yes. Yes. I know what you're saying. There's staging, and there's fluffing. When a client presents me with an empty house, that's when a full staging is needed. For a situation like this"—she sweeps an arm wide, and her bangles clank—"I envision something much more rich. There is salvageable inventory here. This will be a staged fluffing."

She leans toward me, clasping her hands together like she's her own best friend. Like Brandy, she's an accessorizer, and her earrings look to weigh about a pound each judging by the National Geographic-scale droop of her earlobes. "A buyer is looking for the story: how will my life be, when I'm in this house? Where is the me in this home? You need to have tableaux, vignettes of what life in this home is like. The fantasy of it—you need to sell the fantasy as they move through the rooms. The wow. The wow in each room. Delia, we are going to make this house into a home. Better than a home; we are going to make this into a haven."

I ask her how much a haven-making staged fluffing will cost, and she nods with profound empathy. "I know, Delia. I know. I understand this all sounds abstract, and complex, and so high end. A lot of people don't get the concept half as fast as you have. So I think you'll understand that this is subtle work, and important work, and it's the thing that will make the difference." She pauses. "In a very challenging real state environment."

She passes a sheet of paper to me, and nods as I see the bottom line: $9,000. "You will make every penny of that back, Delia." She nods again. "Remind me, please—your realtor is . . ."

"Me."

She stops nodding and cracks the fakest smile I have ever seen. "Great! What fun!"

Nine thousand dollars to straighten up the house? "Thank you, Angela. I'll be in touch. I gotta figure all this out."

"This home needs a new set of eyes," Angela says as she heads out the door. "It would be a honor to vignette this home for you."

I have a powerful need to get out of this unfluffed home, so I haul myself up to the garret to get my tennis shoes. Getting around this place is an odyssey; it's sixty-two steps from my room to the entry hall.

The leaded glass around the front door casts spectacular rainbows across the rug. The bright blue sky is Nashville's April at its most generous, but it's an awkward hike, walking in this neighborhood. The lack of sidewalks on Bowling Avenue means that I'm walking on the edge of the street or in the grass beside it. Cars swish past, too fast.

Angela's hypnotic voice echoes in my mind. Vignettes, tableaux. How would it go if I fluffed up some vignettes of Ginna and Bennett's life at 603 Bowling Avenue? "Here is the master suite, where you can imagine the long evenings of sullen conversation, the luxuriant passive-aggressive silences and flashes of white-hot fury." "And this master closet, such an ample space for hiding the perfume-soaked jacket that you wore on your rendezvous with that irresistible surgical nurse."

I wonder how I would survive a marriage. I worry sometimes that I'm too much a creature of habit, that I'm becoming Particular About Things. I still find myself wondering about Sam, who drifted away from me toward his destiny as a gene splicer. This Greg thing isn't really amounting to much. I don't miss him. I don't wonder what he's doing. I want to, but I don't. I wish I could pine desperately for somebody. I think I'd be good at it: not eating, thinking compulsively about him, running into his sturdy arms all the time. It would be great.

The merciful thing about Ginna's neighborhood is that the houses are spaced so far apart that nobody needs to talk to each other, at all. Splendid isolation. It's as if the guy who laid out these plots, one fat acre after another, calculated exactly how far the human eye can discern the features of a face, and that was the distance from the center of one lot to the next. I have no idea who lives next door. It's not a neighborhood, really. It feels like that desert in Arizona where they mothball old jetliners.

Ahead, a stacked stone wall has collapsed. Stones are scattered all over the ground, sorted by size. I see a figure moving behind the wall, down low. It's that guy with the alarm code who came up the driveway the other day. Ichabod Crane.

He stands, like a giraffe, with a pair of small stones in each hand. "Hello," he says blandly. He seems to be wearing the same clothes he wore the other day, which would be creepy except that I seem to be wearing the same clothes, too.

"Hi," I say. "Angus?"

He nods a little.

I look up at the house behind the wall; set back amid heavy hemlocks, it's the place that Ginna used to call the Castle. It's a stone manor, very severe and plain, with a riot of vines growing up the cylindrical tower. "What's their fantasy?" she'd say as we passed it on our walks.

"You live here?"

He nods silently as he studies the piles of rocks at his feet.

"Beautiful. My sister loved this house."

He nods again, a flash of recognition crossing his face. He has one of those faces that leans toward sad.

"Fell down?" I say, pointing to the wall.

"As they do."

There's something perfect about this exploded wall, the way it shifts from its tightly set, stony order to the tumbled rubble of the fallen part. Gravity holds it together, and gravity is what pulls it apart.

"You've moved in?" he asks. "You'll be a neighbor?"

"Temporarily. I'm selling the house. Unfortunately. Have to sell it, I mean." Why do I feel apologetic about telling him this?

"I figured," he says.

I ask him how he knew Ginna.

"Ah, well. The Bowling Avenue Neighborhood Association. Ginna"—he grunts as he lifts a heavy stone—"Ginna loved this neighborhood. Ask anybody. Glue," he says as he aligns the stone with another. "She held it all together."

I can't believe that I am moved at the thought that the Bowling Avenue Neighborhood Association has lost its leader. But he's so sad! What will they do without her?

There's something about this guy. He gets my goat. I have to ask. "The other day, in the driveway. You said Ginna had 'strong feelings' about me. Like what?"

Angus shrugs. "Nothing."

"What?" Can't believe I'm pushing this, but I hate that he knows something about me that I don't.

He reaches down and pulls his sweater over his head. "Hot" he says under all the gray wool, then folds it in a fussy, careful way. He seems to be stalling, or deciding. "Talked about you all the time. We all heard about The Sister In Chicago." He pauses.

"And . . ."

"Well. Do you really want to know?"

I nod.

He takes a breath. "Well. She thought you were insecure, never coming home. Thought you were mean to your mother. Said you thought you were smarter than everybody else. And, really, she thought you were wasting your time with that travel business, that you *were* smarter than that." His gorgeous southern accent is mesmerizing as he says these terrible things. "And one other thing: she wanted your help with so many things, but she could never ask. She felt judged by you, and that was hard for her." He is speaking as if he's giving a speech, or testifying. Like he's been rehearsing. Like he's actually thought about all this.

I nod, horrified. "Well," I say, stepping back. I can't believe I'm standing on the edge of Bowling Avenue, hearing this. Ginna was blabbing all over the neighborhood? "OK, then."

Halfway down the next street, my knees still weak from Angus's drubbing, I remember something. Dammit. I double back and find Angus setting up a piece of twine across the top of the gap in the wall. "Excuse me," I say, embarrassed. He looks as blotchy in the face as I feel in my gut, but I have to ask. "I forgot that code. The alarm code?"

He reaches into his shirt pocket, pulls out a scrap of paper, and scrawls the numbers with a stubby pencil. He steps over a pile of stones, eyes down, and hands it to me.

"You don't know me," I say loudly. "You don't know anything."

Through his embarrassment he looks defiant. "I know enough," he says. "I know plenty. You're . . ." He searches for the words. "Unkind." He lists as if he might tip over, then sits on the wall with a look of astonishment on his face.

I take off down Bowling as fast as I can without looking like I'm running.

All of a sudden, I'm dizzy, nauseated, can't walk. So clammy. I'm not making it home at this rate. I squat on the side of the road, in the scrubby grass, Angus's scrap of paper damp in my hand. If I close my eyes and hang my head low, I can stop the spinning. Ginna's sunny face glares at me, a watery ghost face, so clear and so hurt.

I drop to my knees, dazed, when a car slows, then stops, and a woman's voice says loudly, "Are you OK?" I wave her on, but she won't go. She's got a really ugly bowl haircut. I hate her and everything else in the world.

"Go. Away." The gravel bites into the palms of my hands. The car engine rises, then fades.

I'd like to think that I feel this way because I haven't eaten properly, but that's not it. I'm not OK. I'm not OK at all. I can't even sit up.

Thinking about a Doorbell

Far below me, the doorbell echoes. It's almost noon, and I still haven't exactly peeled myself out of bed. I've been working, if that's what you call staring at a smartphone for long periods without actually typing anything. The weight of what lies ahead is working on me like a sea anchor. Definitely feeling the drag of this place. That dry-mouthed, unfed feeling. I feel like I spent the night throwing up.

Flat out in the gravel. I've never done that before. Only embarrassment got me home. People kept stopping to help—by the fourth car, I told an old lady in a Camry to fuck off. What is it with these do-gooder types? She was probably a member of Mother's garden club. I hate Nashville.

Ginna's shimmery, furious face still glares at me when I close my eyes. She thought of me like that? And told people about it? They probably sat around the table, planning the block party, ragging on me. What the hell kind of neighborhood association was this, anyway?

She felt judged by you. Angus said this with such disdain. He was right, of course: I saw Ginna as bourgeois, compromised, so far down in the muck of worldly comfort that she couldn't even see that her groove was a rut.

However. It's painful to think that she didn't trust me, to hear this from a stranger. From such a weirdo. Awful, actually.

The doorbell chimes again, a musical bing bong bing bong. Ginna probably listened to a dozen doorbells before picking that one. I thud down the stairs, wondering if I'll get there before whoever it is gives up and leaves. Shelly beats me to the door—Shelly is pretty much a refugee here at this point, having told Mother that she needs to help me get the house ready to sell. I haven't asked Shelly to do any of this, and her hours are erratic, but having her in the house is a hedge against my going completely to seed.

I hear a cheerful reunion in progress as I round the landing.

"Delia, this is Henry Peek," Shelly says as she extricates herself from a hug. She holds him out for me to see, arm around his waist, like a mother displaying her boy. "Isn't he just the nicest person?"

He laughs. "Shelly. You're too kind."

Henry Peek is indeed the nicest person. Henry is unspeakably divine, just the way he was back in 1994 when he was a senior and I was a freshman. He has that fine blonde hair that is in the process of going away, and it won't matter when it does. He stands in the front hall, looking quite tall next to Shelly's small frame, a messenger bag over his shoulder, tidy in his dark gray pants, with an expression of slight embarrassment at Shelly's exclamations. Or maybe his embarrassment comes from getting an eyeful of me. I can hardly express how unfortunate it is that I have managed to come downstairs wearing my third-best yoga pants, a flannel shirt, and a pair of Ginna's handknit socks.

"Delia! Hi!" he says. He adjusts his glasses. His white shirt has thin blue stripes, one cuff rolled up, the other one falling down. The open door lets in a powerful scent of newly mown grass. He's the harbinger of spring. I am struck dumb.

"I've known Henry since he was a baby," Shelly says. Shelly was a baby nurse before she came to work for Mother. There is a generation of west Nashville babies that she rocked.

He fishes around in his wallet, comes up with a card, and hands it to me. Henry Peek, Peek & Peek Real Estate. "This is what realtors do," he says with a little smile. "I'm sorry for not calling, but your mother suggested I stop by. Insisted, actually. Like, six minutes ago."

"Ahhh, right."

Mother.

I am flattened by simultaneous irritation at my conniving mother and crushing horror at the way I look. If only I had washed my hair yesterday. There is a slight motion in my left yoga pants leg, and I realize that I have put on yoga pants that still contain underpants from yesterday. I have to get Henry Peek out of my house this instant. It's a race against time, whether underpants are going to fall out of my pants before I can get rid of Henry Peek. "You know, I'm going to sell the house myself. Thanks for coming, but we really don't need to talk."

While I look like this, I mean. I don't even do yoga.

Henry starts to speak, then stops. "Sure," he says. "I just wanted to introduce myself, in case you had any questions or anything. No big deal, of course.

Happy to help. However. You know."

"Right. Thanks. Have a good one." Stock still.

He turns in the doorway. "How are you finding it? Here?"

"Great. Suburban splendor." He smiles, but I realize that sounded sour.

Shelly looks irritated as Henry heads down the steps to his car. "No need to be so short," she says, closing the door.

I point to the ground, where my purple underpants have landed on my left foot. "Oh yes there was." I snatch them up in a tiny ball. "God. Flannel shirt and yoga pants. Look, Shelly, he was three years ahead of me in high school. He was this . . . other level of human." I study the card he handed me. There's a little line drawing of Henry's head, like a Thurber doodle. "He was . . ."

"Yeah," Shelly says and wanders back into the kitchen. I stare at the closed front door, stunned at the apparition that has just evaporated. He was so alive, so cheerful. Happy to help. Happy to help?

I run into somebody like this Henry Peek guy, and I crush so hard that I am dizzy.

After heading upstairs and dressing myself in my nicest dress just to prove that I can in fact wear clothes that don't look like I'm in a convalescent home, I begin my online investigation. I study the houses he's selling, the way he writes the listings, the photos he chooses to show. I read the *Nashville Business Journal* interview with him in which he explains how he does what he does. "There's no magic to it," he says. "People want a house. It's like looking for a mate, the hunt for a house. The truth is, a lot of the time my job is to separate fantasy from reality. Figuring out what's possible, what's best. That's what I do."

I consider constructing a small shrine with his photo from the Peek & Peek Real Estate website. His eyes tilt down at the outside, giving him a look of permanent empathy. I can't tell if they're blue or green, but his general fair coloring makes him look like he hails from the far north. Had to have been a towhead; he's practically one now. His smile isn't a toothy, car-salesman smile. It says he's glad to see me here at the Peek & Peek Real Estate website, but he doesn't want to impose. I think he used to have freckles.

He has a rudimentary Facebook presence, but he does seem to like Twitter. His Tweets are little poems about real estate.

HenryPeek Is refinancing a long road to a small house?
Perhaps a different house is the better way to go.

HenryPeek How much yard do you need? Well, how much do you like to mow?

I shudder with embarrassment to be chasing these Tweets. This is not what normal people do. It's pointless. Pathetic, actually. Maybe if I think of it as aspirational stalking. Field research into the habits of attractive men.

My email dings. It's Greg. He wants to Skype.

He's not British, so he doesn't have a great accent or anything. But Greg is a steadfast email correspondent, and he occasionally comes to the States to visit his family in Milwaukee. He'll catch the train down to Chicago and we'll spend a few days together, and it's fun enough. There's a term for what happens when we're together, but *romance* is not it. He's a little nerdy, frankly, and it may be that four thousand miles of distance allows me not to focus too much on whether we could ever live in the same city together. Greg does serve one important function: he does make me feel like I'm not a single woman in her early thirties. I'm involved. I've got a thing going on.

I ignore his email. Greg is a thin gruel at the moment.

I try in every way I can to figure out online whether Henry Peek is married, yet the mighty Internet coughs up no clues. He is so desirable that he's probably gay.

Shelly will know the answer. I track her down in the library, where she is dusting the tops of the leftovers of Bennett's Civil War history books. When he's not dismantling hip sockets, Bennett is something of a Civil War buff.

"Shelly, what do you know about the Peeks?"

"Mmmm, not so much now that Henry's mother passed a few years ago. Mrs. Peek played bridge with your mother." She slides a feather duster under a shelf.

"I mean, I don't need his help or anything, it's just."

"What? Henry? You want him to sell the house?" She turns and looks at me, scowling, then starts to laugh. "Or move in?"

"No. Gah. I'm selling this house." Shelly is merciless.

She's openly laughing now. "Here's the skinny on Henry. He's got a bad back. His father took him in, and they get on. But Henry is not what you'd call a salesman." She laughs, and nudges the cat, who is wallowing on the floor, with her foot. "Mr. Serious could probably make a better agent than Henry Peek." As she heads out the door, she adds casually, "And no. Not married."

"Ever?"

"No. Something about a girl, years ago. Can't recall exactly what. Believe he's gun shy."

Gun shy. Gun shy beats gay. My prospects are improving by the minute.

Standing in the kitchen, I study the contents of the pantry. "Shelly. I just have one question. All this junk food. The Cheetos. The Skittles? Did Ginna just give up on cooking or what?"

"Do you really want to know?"

"Well yeah."

"It's the girls'. Right after—you know, after everything happened—the girls used to sneak over here to the house, after school. They would watch TV, leave Coke cans all over the place like nobody would ever notice the mess, then go home. At first I thought they were gonna be having parties here, but that's not what it was. Goldilocks is what it was." She looks embarrassed. "I did throw out the liquor and hide the key to the gas fireplace. But I started stocking the pantry for them, leaving Cokes in the fridge. Just came over here, to be here I guess.

"It's just awful, Delia. You can see it in their eyes. Ginna was the one for those girls. Now they're on their own. Their daddy, their grandma. It's a cold night, every night."

So that's why their bedrooms look so occupied: they were occupied. I'm keeping the girls from their own house. Appalling. I need to figure out a way to get them over here. This isn't my house.

In the Driver's Seat

Beverly d'Angeleno's How to Sell Your House in Two Weeks says that the first open house will tell me a lot about how my house sale will go. Beverly says, "You will meet a lot of real estate agents who will urge you to list your house with them. Resist this impulse! They'll tell you all sorts of scary things to try to persuade you that you are making a big mistake, but you are the one in the driver's seat. This is your house to sell, and you are going to sell it."

I set the date for Sunday, April 25, and put listings all over the place—newspapers, craigslist, websites that don't look all that great, but whatever. I'm blitzing this town. It's *on*.

"603 Bowling Avenue: A Family Haven in the Perfect Location."

Spending Time with My Sister

I fluff the house, trying to imagine how Angela would fluff it. I can feel her right over my shoulder, blinking at me with those watery blue eyes. I am so uncertain of what I'm doing that about halfway through the week, I conclude that $9,000 would be a bargain to get out of the Vietnam I am experiencing. It starts out simply enough, plumping up chair cushions, but soon you start moving furniture around, buying houseplants, throwing out bales of newspapers and magazines, clearing out closets so that they look cavernous and one-third empty. I spend one afternoon reading old *People* magazines. I think a long while about poor George Clooney, Sexiest Man Alive 2006. Two-time winner. Has he given up on hoping for a trifecta? I punt on the basement. Looks like Hannibal Lecterland down there. I can't worry about what people think of the basement. I suck.

Every single thing I touch sends me into a tailspin of sorrow at the fact that my sister isn't here anymore, yet all her crap is. Why did you do this to me, Ginna? Why would you leave me this house? I don't want to think about your Spanx and why you have a pair of green pantyhose. I don't want strange men on the street telling me I'm insecure and mean. I don't know if I can stand to think about how insecure and mean I actually am. I'm reliving our entire relationship as sisters, and it is not so easy.

After Ginna died, I came down and spent a week at Mother's. It was such a shock, such a spectacular shock, but it felt like I was grieving alone. Mother was in some distant place, preoccupied with making the arrangements and ordering up engraved cards. "The family of Virginia Ballenger Schwartz is deeply grateful for your kind expression of sympathy." My memory of that time has a lot to do with the grief industry that popped up around 248 Jackson Boulevard. Dealing with the platoons of tenderhearted women and their somber husbands was a full-time job. Ginna's friends came from all parts of town; she did a lot of volunteer work, and her unexpected death left these strangers hollow-eyed, bearing nourishment and stories as they stopped by Mother's house. One grizzle-headed woman walked up to me, said "Ginna was," then collapsed in my arms. Crying is totally contagious for me, so we wept together for a while, though I never even learned her name. Another woman told me an elaborate story about Ginna's work teaching immigrants to knit. She was incredibly patient, apparently, and would sit with a beginner for as long as it took to get the hang of it. "So inspiring," this woman said. "She could show a room full of Arabic-speaking women how to knit, didn't need a word, only that smile of hers. She'd do anything for you."

There's a moment at a funeral, the big reveal, when the surviving family enters the sanctuary. As our small group came down the narrow hall by the chapel, the girls were in front of me, led by their father. Cassie stopped for a second, fumbling with her foot. Her shoe, a dark gray flat, had slipped off. She reached down and flipped it back over, frustrated. Amelia gently squeezed her arm, and they shared a look. I have never felt so irrelevant. I had a strong feeling that I shouldn't have even been in that heavy procession—so many others were closer to her, had treasured her properly.

When we were growing up, Mother used to take us to funerals of ancient relatives we didn't know. It was important for us to get used to funerals, she'd say. Her first funeral was when she was 20, after her mother died of a stroke. She said that growing up on a farm showed her the life cycle, but there were no funerals for pigs. I suppose my first funeral was my father's, but I was not even two. Ginna was eight, and by her description, our dad had a million suit friends. Her most vivid funeral memory was of the punch bowl. She spent ten minutes with the silver ladle, digging out a cherry embedded in the ice ring. She would have kept going except that Shelly took over and dug the rest of them out for her.

I did get the hang of funerals, but death is another matter. Ginna's is the first death that has hit this close to home.

I took so much for granted, when it came to Ginna. There was some indeterminate time in the future when we would get together. That's what I told myself. We'd do something, at some point.

The bustle of a funeral is good and distracting, that's for sure. Shelly and I spent days managing the condolence food, which was kept in a freezer truck that Mother's food-distributor friend sent over for us to use. We finally drove the thing over to Second Harvest to feed the hungry. What else do you do with sixteen frozen casseroles and mattress upon mattress of lasagna?

After exactly five business days away from work, Mother was a bear coming out of hibernation. Do not think for a minute that you can alter her course. She'll run you up a tree. She is certain. She returned to her normal schedule, and she subtly indicated that I should probably do the same. I returned to Chicago five pounds heavier and numbed by what had happened.

So here I am, finally spending that time with Ginna. I keep thinking about that moment on the side of the road, after Angus told me what she'd been saying about me. I barely made it home. Had to lie down in the front hall. I'd give anything to be able to talk to her. I can't stand this. Her beautiful face pops into my mind, scowling at me, all the time.

Things are looking better around the house, though I haven't faced into the fact that the girls are eventually going to have to come over and cull through everything: the antiques, the art, all of it. This is the sort of project that I absolutely can't face by myself. But who's going to help me do that? Bennett? Mother? The organizer? The fluffer? It's funny, but the person who is the best equipped, both practically and emotionally, is Shelly. I need to ask her how she thinks we should do this.

The yard is particularly confounding. Beverly says that curb appeal is more important than anything, that a buyer decides on a house before she even steps out of her car. If that's the case, then why am I sitting on the floor arranging Cassie's thirteen pairs of flip-flops in ranks? Why am I trying to find a less conspicuous location for Mr. Serious's litter box, which sends me into anxiety because what if Mr. Serious doesn't like the new location and starts pooping wherever he likes? In a house like this, it could be months before I discover that he's gone renegade.

As executor, Bennett has been managing the house and yard maintenance, limply, since Ginna died. When I emailed him that I was coming down to sell the house, and I'd be here for a while, he instantly sent me the phone number of Jimmy Butterman, the yard guy. "cannot deal with this guy. enjoy."

Bennett can't deal with a lot of people, but after an hour with Jimmy Butterman, I have new respect for Bennett. Jimmy, it turns out, adored Ginna, and after her death came to view his role at 603 Bowling Avenue as something akin to maintaining Arlington Cemetery. The grave of Elvis does not receive more attention than Ginna Schwartz's yard. And the thing is, he's never done talking. It's the Jimmy Butterman tango: the more I back up toward my car to escape, the closer he steps.

"I am a bit of a rosarian," he tells me in his twangy voice as we head toward the back yard. The back of his neck is deeply creased and baked by the sun, his short hair bristling gold in the light. How old is he? Not more than 40, but he has an old air about him. "Once Mrs. Schwartz had confidence in me, I took over the spraying. I think you'll find a notable absence of Japanese beetles." As he recites the many potions he uses to fight all the pests, it becomes clear that Ginna's spectacular rose garden is basically a Superfund site. And I wonder how much of that stuff has crept into Jimmy Butterman's system.

The to-do list is endless. I spend a fair amount of time trying to figure out what the house should smell like. *Beverly d'Angeleno's How to Sell Your House in Two Weeks* spends six pages discussing the hazards of house smells. "You can't tell what your house smells like, no matter how you try. This is a difficult subject, but it's extremely important to realize that the sense of smell is the most powerful sense, trumping sight and touch. Realtors will tell you that apple pie is what your house should smell like. I submit that this is overused to the point that buyers will be suspicious if they get a whiff of apple pie." I want the house to smell like Mother's house: eucalyptus, paste wax, and lemons. I want it to smell like two million dollars.

A Sighting

There are so many awful parts of Nashville—any part built after the arrival of the automobile, actually, which means the vast majority of the city. I don't know at what point the town elders decided that cars were more important than the humans operating them, but there had to have been a day when that deal with the devil happened. You see this phenomenon, the incredible swollen city, on any street map. Nashville is by no means unique. The old part is in the middle, as tightly woven as a rug. Horse-and-wagon distances. Soon, the dense streets disperse in a tangle of swirling cul-de-sacs and go-nowheres, city planning subverted by developers who got hold of a farm and laid down their vision of auto-crazy heaven, half acre by half acre. I can put my finger on the parts of town that aren't working, just by looking at where the roads hit each other. It doesn't take a genius to recognize that a neighborhood with 400 houses but only one entrance, emptying onto a five-lane highway, is going to have problems. On one of my long, aimless drives around town, I discovered that you can find the same set of superstores, again and again.

There are, however, parts of Nashville that aren't awful, a few blocks here and there where the energy seems good, where you can find caffeine, a book, a beer. Hipsters love a sidewalk. I'm walking in one of the adorable parts, Hillsboro Village, when I come upon Henry Peek, who stands in front of Davis Cookware and Cutlery Shoppe. He's gazing upward, transfixed, making a supplication to a kitchen god.

"Hi," I say.

He turns to look at me, surprised, twitching almost. He pushes up his glasses. I'm instantly embarrassed, like I've been caught stalking him, which I most certainly have not been. I would never *literally* stalk him. "Look," he says, pointing to the wide window of the cookware shop. I see a stack of expensive cooking pots and a dusty braid of garlic.

"You cook?" I say, unnerved, mulling my stunning fortune at seeing him.

"No, there," he says, pointing at a crack above the window trim. "Shhh, look." We stand there, with the traffic of 21st Avenue rumbling behind us. It's a roar of sound, but I still try to keep quiet so as not to disturb whatever it is that Henry is looking at.

A tiny beak pokes out of the crack, a narrow triangle. "That!" he whispers. The darting head follows, a beady eye, a body squirts out, a flutter of flapping feathers, and the bird is gone. The crack is maybe an inch wide, invisible to anyone walking by.

"Can you believe that?" he says. "Kills me. Wedged up there. First time I saw him he was dragging a piece of straw a half a foot long. Urban homesteader." He looks down at me. "Been stalking him. Finally got a good look at him. Pink headed."

He heads toward the used bookstore next door, which was actually my destination as well. Loners like me love a bookstore. It's one of the places you can be in the company of others without actually being in their company. Henry holds the door, as if he knew I was coming here. I'm hit with the comforting, dusty smell of old books, and I hope I can figure out some way to keep talking to him. My phone rings, tragically. Yesterday I told Susan I could take traveler calls again, so I cannot fail to answer. It could be any client in the world calling from anywhere in the world. Henry looks like he's about to say something, but when he sees me dig for my phone, he scowls, then wanders down an aisle and turns the corner. I can see his elbow with its rolled-up sleeve. White shirt with wide blue stripes.

It's the window washing company, announcing that they are on the way. This would be great news in any other circumstance, because I realized only this morning that the windows were filthy, and Beverly d'Angeleno lists clean windows as Number 2 in her Fastest 5 Ways to Make a House Look Better Than It Is. I have to go home immediately, but I feel like I'm abandoning Henry, which is stupid. I head toward the back of the store, where the blue-striped elbow has disappeared. He's hunkered down in the Nature section, bird books on the floor around him, his back to me. I whisper, "Gotta run. Window washers. Open house tomorrow." He doesn't even look up. I am an idiot. There's a slim girl on the floor tucked beside him, a sylph, laughing as she pulls a book off the shelf. She is the nightmare scenario for anybody crushing on a guy. She has tiny feet, a musical laugh.

All the way home, I think about that girl talking birds with Henry. Too young for him! He should be ashamed—he must be 35 years old. I can hardly stand it, the way she was laughing, the way she leaned toward him with that curtain of shiny brown hair.

I've got no business mooning after a guy like this. So pointless, as usual. He's got a rich and rewarding life here in Nashville, selling his houses and tracking down the underpaid cute girls in local retail establishments. He was so disgusted: I can't erase the image of Henry's expression shifting from open to shut as I answered that cell phone right in his face.

Parade of Home

Here are comments I heard this afternoon from the fourteen real estate agents who came through the house:

"You do know that the roof tile is asbestos. There's no asbestos statement in your offering."

"That basement has mold issues. I'm sure you're working on that."

"Whoever took out that wall by the kitchen sure didn't understand the basic laws of gravity."

"This kitchen is an absolute SCREAM."

"You'll be shoring up, of course. Won't you?"

"Where's your radon abatement system?"

It's a real estate hazing. They were so southernly awful, so smiley and mean. I bet they all went home and iChatted about me.

The nine actual potential buyers were nicer, though I couldn't get anybody to commit to anything at all. Only three even wrote down their names—like I'm going to sell them Amway. Beverly says that's normal, but it bothers me. This is a great house. What more could anybody want?

The comments about the price were even more interesting. How many ways can you say "overpriced"?

"Optimistic."

"On the rich side."

"On the high side."

"Costly for what it is."

"Aggressive."

"Ambitious."

"Pricey."

"Spendy."

"That kitchen is a HOOT."

"Trop cher," from one guy who thought I couldn't speak French.

"Oh em gee RILLY? Two MILLION dollars? Two?"

At 5:30, I sit on the back terrace, a glass of wine dulling the edge of this excruciating afternoon. I look up and see Henry Peek coming around the corner of the house, carrying the helium balloons that I had tied to my For Sale sign, as per the instructions of *Beverly d'Angeleno's How to Sell Your House in Two Weeks.*

He announces, "One basic rule: remove festive balloons after the open house, to avoid the possibility of deflated festive balloons which suggest a failed open house."

I am stunned that he is here. It's like I conjured him.

He ties the balloons to the back of a chair. "May I?" he asks. I nod, deciding that Jesus must be real because Henry Peek has just shown up in my backyard carrying balloons.

I hold up my glass. "Want some?"

"Thanks," he says. "I'm good."

He sits in the chair across from me, a slight stiffness to him as he lands. The bad back? I have been worrying about his bad back ever since Shelly told me about it as the root of all his troubles. "You're here to make fun of my undesirable Bradford pear trees? Rag on my unraked driveway? Who knew you were supposed to rake a damn driveway? Those agents are pitiless."

"You don't have to tell me—I have to work with them," he says in a resigned voice.

"Flying monkeys. Bitches."

"Sorry." He hands me a flyer depicting a low, 1960s brick house set in a flat, treeless lot. "If it makes you feel any better, at least your open house didn't involve a ranch-style house in West Meade."

"Great family home. Parklike lawn," I say. Beverly d'Angeleno taught me a list of phrases to use when writing ad copy.

"I'm selling a house that's absolutely going to be torn down and replaced with something monstrous."

"Well, it's not the greatest house in the world, just saying."

"I know, but it's such a charade, pretending that it's a house at all. Waste of time."

He seems to be genuinely bummed about this. He takes off his glasses and rubs his eyes with the heels of his hands. Quick, shiny blue eyes. Slender fingers. Faded, wicked-looking scar on the back of his left hand. No watch.

Circles under his eyes, not dark, but you can imagine he could look really trashed. His belt is worn at the edges. Blue is the perfect color for him. Almost straight nose. A forehead with a lot of brains in there. I'm taking inventory while I have the chance.

"So, are you here for a tour? I show only to serious buyers."

"I would have been here earlier except," and he points at the flyer.

This is so thrilling to me that I almost knock over my wine glass. "Come on," I say, picking up the bottle. "This lovely home is a haven, an absolute haven for a family."

I don't know why I'm doing this. Leading this exotic creature through this house makes me very, very nervous. I don't want him to sell the house. I do not, however, want him to leave.

"So you're a birder?" I ask.

He's right behind me, laughs. "Hardly. It's just that bird. I must have seen that bird a dozen times. Had to figure out what it was."

"So?"

"House finch. Most unexotic bird in the world. But so resourceful." Resourceful. Like that beautiful girl. I'm still horrified to have discovered him with Bird Girl. I bet they watch Nature Channel documentaries together, all cozied up under her hemp afghan. They probably do gruesome stuff like canoeing.

We head to the living room. Henry says, "My father sold your sister this house. Did you know that?"

"Really? Did you know her?"

He shakes his head. "No, unfortunately. I'm so sorry about . . ."

I'm not going to let him take me into a tailspin over Ginna. I'm all business. "I remember when they bought it. She was pregnant with Cassie. On bedrest. Obsessed. Nesting gone wild."

"Yeah, my dad was telling me how she would beg him to take her to see houses—all he needed was for a client to go into labor on a house tour. So he would sit down with a stack of photos, make house-tour videos for her."

"Were you working with him then?"

He looks down. "Ah, no. Not yet."

"You haven't always done real estate?"

"No." He smiles. "Lucky to be working with my father." He loves his dad. Of course he does; everybody loves his dad. Even my mother loves his dad, and she doesn't love anybody.

I tell him that I can't believe my mother launched him over here.

"She's not all bad," he says.

"She's not all good, either."

He shrugs. "A very smart lady."

I sink into Ginna's cavernous sofa. I am so wiped out. "One thing I noticed today is that people never sit down. They're spending a fortune for a house, but they stand there and look at the room like it's a furniture store. Isn't that strange?"

Henry sits across from me, on the edge of the club chair as if he's waiting for an appointment. "I never thought of that, but you're right."

"How do they know if the room is actually comfortable if they don't even sit down?"

"You have a future in real estate," he says in a mock serious tone.

"The other thing," I say, "is the way the agents all call it a 'home.' It's a house, not a home. Home is the place, when you go there, they have to take you in. House is this pile of sticks and bricks that I need to offload."

He laughs. "You're so sentimental."

"I just hate all that fake sentimental stuff. Home is a very powerful idea; they can't just use it."

"Oh, they use it all right. They'd tape puppies to the windows if it'd help move a house in this market."

"Is it really that bad?"

"We call it 'challenging.' We never say 'horrible.'"

His posture tells me that he is waiting for me to continue our tour, but I'm paralyzed at the thought of taking him through all those bedrooms upstairs. I'm about to boing out the window, so nervous to be right here next to him. Surely he can detect this.

My phone rings in my pocket, and I pull it out like a gunslinger. "Greg," I say and tap the Ignore button.

"Greg," Henry says solemnly.

Awcrap, now he thinks there's a Greg in my life. "Tour guide in England." He's looking at me steadily. "I'm a travel agent," I add. "Greg takes people to the land of thatched roofs. And stuff." Please shut up. "My entire life is located inside this phone."

"Right," he says as he stands. "Interesting work, I would think."

"Fascinating," I say in a superposh British accent. I stand up and move fast.

He isn't saying much about the house, which probably means that he doesn't like something about it. As I trot up the stairs, leading the way, I wonder if my backside looks big, which makes me trot all the faster.

He says, "So how are you finding it, being in Nashville? Have you been back much before?"

Such a question, asked in such a disarming way. I tell him that I've avoided Nashville like the plague since high school, and it's a lot harder than I thought to stay in Ginna's house, that she's everywhere, and that the past week has been especially upsetting.

"Sure you want to be staying here? It might be good to have some distance."

I explain that I don't want to stay at Mother's because she's kind of impossible, and I won't rent an apartment because I'm here so briefly, and as I'm telling him this, it occurs to me that he's probably right. "Nashville isn't exactly my cup of tea," I tell him as he pokes his head into Cassie's girlygirl lair.

"Not your cup of tea," he mutters. "Great light up here." He stops and gives me a look. "Nashville's not so bad. It's the greatest city on earth, actually."

"Shyeahright," I say. Did I just hurt his feelings about Nashville?

In Ginna's office, I open up one of her filing cabinets, stuffed with photographs. "This is what I'm dealing with."

"Yeah," he says. "That's what happens. A house fills up. And then comes the part nobody plans for, the emptying out." He picks up a snapshot. "Wow, she looks like you." I look over his shoulder, and sure enough, there's Ginna in a rocking chair with a bundle of baby, sleep deprived but joyous. He looks up at me, then back at the picture.

He passes the back stairs and asks if there's a third floor. I think I'm going to die. "Uh, yeah, that's my lair," I say, then head back toward the front stairs so that we can complete this tour before I do something horrible like tip my hand that I am made delirious by his mere presence. "Think *Gosford Park*. Bleak and barren. Maid quarters. That's my thang. Don't want too much upholstery, you know."

He laughs. "Funny," he says, then follows me down the steps.

In the front hall, I have the feeling I get when I have to leave a really great party too soon. I want to lay a hand on him, on that head of his.

"Your mother pretty much warned me about you," he says as he studies my sell sheet.

"What exactly? That I'm spiteful and hateful and not nice?"

"That you're stuck."

"Stuck? I'm not stuck. I'm just fine. Maybe she's lived a long, straight line from law school to federal judge, but that's not what life has to be. It's just impossible for her—no clue what my life is about."

"She meant about the house," he says, looking at me, amused. Overshare. Why can't I just shut up? "She's concerned that it's going to be a tough project."

"Well today went just dandy, seems to me," I say sourly. "You haven't told me what you think."

He gives me a look, an appraising look. "It's a good house. Has issues, but most houses do. It will sell. It's just a question of when, and for how much."

"So you'd like to 'help me out' with it?"

He smiles a little, and in that instant I see that there is an honesty in him. "Well, yeah. I would. It's what I do."

"I would love to have you sell the house," I say in my best imitation of Beverly d'Angeleno, "but this is my house to sell, and I'm going to sell it." Is it worth it to have Henry Peek sell the house? That's the $100,000 question.

He studies the cards of the real estate agents who came to the open house. "Bitch. Bitch. Crazy, stupid, BIGliar, drinker. Incompetent—oh, that one's actually pretty good."

"Which one?" I ask, looking over his shoulder.

"Think I'm going to tell you that?" he laughs. He takes out his card and lays it on the table. "You can't win if you don't enter."

Now I have two Henry Peek cards.

Luncheon

Monday, Monday. In my line of work, back in Chicago, a weekday is a lot like a weekend. The world doesn't divide into work time and play time. I don't take the 8:15 into the city; I move to the other side of the bed. Happy hour is pretty much whenever I remember that I have a bottle of wine in the fridge.

Working at home also means that sometimes it's hard to feel like I've worked at all. In the past week, however, having lifted heavy objects and read old *People* magazines to get ready for the open house, I feel like I've been doing yeoman's labourings. I deserve a little vacay, a little Me Time.

I check my Twitter feed, to see what Henry Peek is rhapsodizing about today.

HenryPeek Balloons at open house. Cheerful or scary?

I stare at this Tweet, this message in a bottle that obviously has been sent directly to *me*, even if he doesn't know that I'm reading his Tweets. The phone in my hand vibrates, surprising me. It's him? He's calling, too? I'm experiencing a multimedia onslaught from the man of my reveries?

It's Mother.

"Meet me at the Pineapple Room. We need to talk."

Mother is off today. I should have remembered this and holed up in the basement, sealed my phone in a lead box, cut the phone line to the house.

"What's up?" How to dodge out of this?

"I have been undergoing some therapy, and I would like to talk to you."

Mother veers between total opacity and unfiltered bluntness. Therapy? Oh, how I would like to have a transcript of a therapy session involving my mother. At what point does she question the premise of the entire process? When does she snatch the notepad and start writing her own analysis of herself?

"The Pineapple Room? Does that still exist?"

"Of course it exists. The aspic is delicious." The Pineapple Room was where Ginna and I would hide fig preserves in our pockets to avoid eating them while Mother force-fed us chicken à la king.

My idea of a matinee today vanishes as I forage in Ginna's closet for something Pineapple Roomish. As I remember, there's some rule about no pants. I dig out a suit that Ginna bought for a cousin's wedding years ago. It's a fake Chanel, black and white plaid bouclé with a line of pink in there. It's big—Ginna was a good three inches taller than me—but I look exactly like a girl. I will pass. I'm in drag.

It takes longer to head out Belle Meade Boulevard than I remember, and I can't really drive in Ginna's pumps, so I have to stop to take off my shoes. By the time I find her, Mother is already sitting by one of the wide windows overlooking the gardens, tea punch dispensed. As I approach the table, trying not to clomp down the steps, she is laughing so hard that she is wiping her eyes with a napkin.

"What in the world is that get-up?" she asks. She's wearing capri pants and a pair of dirty sneakers, straight out of the garden. Her white hair is pulled back in a little nubby ponytail, and she looks even more striking than she does when she's all packaged up.

"I thought the Pineapple Room was like the Centennial Club or something," I hiss at her.

"Honey, even the Centennial Club isn't like the Centennial Club anymore. They wear pantsuits now. Everything's gone to hell. You wouldn't even recognize the Junior League; it's like a Fortune 500 company." She wipes her eyes, still chuckling. "You look like you're going to—"

"Cousin Samantha's wedding. I know." I adjust the shoulders. "It doesn't even fit." I have to laugh. "I can't think of the last time I wore a damn suit."

"You look lovely, you really do. For *church*," she says, and she starts laughing all over again.

This is the first time that we have shared a joke in years. What is going on with her?

A woman in a shirtdress stops at our table and exclaims "Grace!"

"Betty!"

Another woman walks up. "Susan," Betty says.

"Grace."

"Saturday?"

"Can't."

"Dan."

"Right."

"Better?"

"A little."

"Well."

"Tuesday?"

"Yes."

Betty turns to me. "Delia!"

Susan chimes in. "Delia?"

Mother answers. "*Delia*." She nods. "The house. Ginna's."

"Oh."

"Right."

"So hard."

I nod.

"Well."

"Bless your heart."

"Isn't that the truth."

"Thanks," I say.

They disperse. Mother parses this for me. "Betty's having supper club Saturday night, and Susan can't come because Dan is still at home after that diabetes episode—now that was a mess, almost lost the poor man's foot—so Susan is getting antsy because she thinks Dan is not taking proper care of himself and she resents the way he expects her to do for him all the time when he won't do for himself. But it sounds like they're working on it. And we'll all discuss it at Garden Club next week." She sips her tea. "They all know what you're going through with that house, let me tell you."

"I don't get how can you do all this lady stuff and your career, too."

"Work is work, but this is life. We have been through it." She studies the menu. "Through it all," she mutters. "Every last bit of it." She lays down the menu and folds her hands on the table. She is staring straight at me. "Now."

Here we go.

"As you know, Ginna's death has been a tremendous shock. I have had loss in my life, but nothing like this. This one has flattened me."

She doesn't look or sound flattened. To hear her, you'd think she was describing what she had for breakfast. I haven't seen one bit of sorrow come out of this woman. In the past six months, she has called me any number of times, but she's never sounded heartbroken and miserable the way I think she ought to. I know she's not a crier; she's famous for making female attorneys cry then having no mercy on them. But how can she be so detached from the greatest loss a mother can face?

I nod.

"So recent events have led me to conclude that I should talk to someone. You know how I feel about psychiatry—a bunch of mumbo-jumbo unless you're full-out crazy. Why not phrenology? Why not just read the bumps on your skull? And you know what I think of 'psycho therapists.'" She says the words like she's saying *lap dancers*. And yes, I know what she thinks of therapists. When Ginna told Mother that she wanted to get Bennett to go to marriage therapy, Mother said, "Well, just buy a billboard on West End and tell the world about it."

"Anyway, as I say, I have had loss before, but it's never *affected* me this way."

"What do you mean?"

She seems to be considering something. "Well, six weeks ago, I failed to show up at court."

"You mean: sick?" Mother never misses work. She gave birth, nursed me, caught a nap, and was back at her job the next day. It is a pathological compulsion, Mother's work ethic.

"I mean: got in my car, headed toward downtown like usual, then got on I-65 and didn't stop until I got to Gulf Shores." She's studying her fingers, which she has spread on the tablecloth. "It was Ginna's birthday. March 15."

Gulf Shores is an eight-hour drive, at the southernmost tip of Alabama.

"Mother," I say, stunned. "What was the thinking on that?"

"There wasn't any, really. I just woke up consumed with thoughts of Ginna, when y'all were little and we'd go to the beach for spring break. It was always Ginna's birthday during spring break. So I went to the beach." She shrugs a tiny bit. "Chilly, the way it always is."

"How long did you stay?"

"A day. Didn't have any clothes, so I went to the outlet mall and bought things to wear. A toothbrush. You know."

"Did you call anybody?" I ask quietly, afraid that I might spook her and she'll stop talking in this extraordinary way.

"No. AWOL."

"Mother."

"I know."

We sit. She orders chicken divan, I order tomato aspic in her honor, and we sit a while longer. The collar of my suit jacket keeps rubbing my neck, and the room is too warm.

"So," she says. "I keep doing it."

"Road trips?"

She nods. "Places. You know. Ginna places."

"During the day?"

"Right."

"They must love that."

She shakes her head. "No, they do not. Last week, after the judges' conference ended, I asked for a leave of absence. It's irresponsible of me to be acting this way, but I don't seem to be able to stop."

This is a version of Mother that I have never seen.

"My therapist tells me a lot of mumbo-jumbo, a lot of grief therapy business that any fool can find on the Internet. But she did manage to say one thing. She thought that I might consider being in better touch with my other daughter, the one who's still here."

That would be me.

"I told her that my daughter and I don't get along. And that's when she said, 'Well, that's what therapy's for.'

"So here we are. We're supposed to have lunch or do something. Together. On a regular basis." It sounds a little like a court order, what she's handing down. Like one of her appeals decisions. "OK?" Her eyes shift down to her hands again, and I discover that she is nervous.

Spring break at the beach. I remember the time Ginna and I had an enormous inner tube, and we'd float out past the breakers. Once she brushed a foot against mine and yelled "SHARK!" at which point I flipped out backwards and took in about half of the Gulf of Mexico. She pulled me up, in tears for having scared me. "So sorry," she said frantically, face streaked with wet hair, her lips blue from the cold water. "I didn't mean it. So sorry."

How much tomato aspic will it take for Mother and me to get through this? I'm not sure there's enough gelatine in our family for us to process 31 years of a fundamentally terrible relationship.

The Deed

Bennett and I sit in the 27th-floor conference room of Davis Cranford Davidson, clinging to the edge of a vast table made of some probably endangered veneer. Nbongi-bongi wood. Bennett's skinny face is reflected in the table's mirrorlike finish, and his air of distraction is the same as it ever was. He always appears to be working on an operation, right there in front of you.

Bennett has a classic surgeon's personality. Anybody who spends his days cutting open people must have a special little gizmo inside that allows him to dissociate his actions from what the hell he's actually doing. On a daily basis, surgeons walk into a room, put on a mask, and slice into folks. That's just not a normal thing to do. I had a friend in Chicago show me her x-rays from her knee replacement, and I nearly passed out. World's creepiest carpentry project.

The view is spectacular, a clear vista to the north, with the Titans stadium looking like a bread basket right beside the fat, brown Cumberland River, which snakes back and forth like a scribble. All around, the rolling hills are blanketed in the bright green of spring. A river town. It's easy to forget that Nashville was born in a cave on the banks of the Cumberland. The river slips along, hidden, right through the center of the city.

Why do lawyers need to be so high in the air? Does it keep the rabble from chasing them with pitchforks? Maybe it puts them closer to God. Anything for an edge, I guess. I could sit here all day and study the grid below us, analyzing the traffic patterns the way I used to do in my urban geography classes.

The lawyer comes in, led by a paralegal loaded up with a stack of documents. Papers pass, a bit of legal theater, Bennett does some executor thing, and the house becomes mine. I came here not owning a house, and now, an hour later, I have a house. That I don't want.

We finish up, and I flip through the will. There it is, at the back, a lone sheet, as short as a thank-you note. Amid all the legal throat-clearing is a sentence: "I give, devise, and bequeath to Cordelia Jane Ballenger, if she survives me, the Property located at 603 Bowling Avenue, Nashville, Tennessee 37215, including the house and contents." Dated September 27, 2009. Ginna's girly signature amid the legalese looks like a party hat at a funeral. Her sunny face flashes in my mind.

As we descend, our ears popping as the floors fly by, Bennett says, "You ought to call the girls. They liked seeing you. They think you're 'cool.'"

That's a surprise. I couldn't tell a single thing about what the girls thought of our lunch. "I guess they like getting out?"

He turns to me. "What?"

"Nothing. I just mean, it must be hard for them, not being at the house anymore. I feel bad about that. And your whole deal . . ."

"My whole deal?"

"You know. Carla. It's got to be hard for them, Bennett. To lose their mom on top of everything else."

"Everything else?"

"Well, there's Ginna, wanting to get back together, and you're, you know. And the girls stuck in the middle of —"

The elevator doors open, and Bennett is out of there. He is hot. "You've got it all wrong."

I have never seen Bennett so agitated. He's talking to me like we've already been arguing for half an hour. I seem to have shown up late for our disagreement. "What do you mean?"

"Do you really want to know? 'Cause it's really something."

I don't know what he's talking about. People are peeking at us in the cavernous lobby, looking for the echoing voice. "What?" I whisper, nodding at the people passing us.

"OK, so here you are, dumping on me every time you see me—that smug thing you do with your eyebrows is so incredibly shitty, like you don't believe a word I say. Carla was the least of it. Carla was not the problem." He looks at his watch. "You know, I don't have time for this. But I'll call you. You want to hear the story? I've got nothing to hide anymore."

I spend the rest of the day in a fog, trying to imagine what Bennett is talking about. He was so wound up—he runs cool, not hot, so this is something to see.

And Mother. Holy Jebus, what a luncheon that was. I can't even begin to process what that's about.

I'm supposed to be doing work today, but I don't have much steam for it. Susan and I talk for a while about clients' upcoming trips, and we conclude that we are unsustainably low on work right now. In the past, we would get on the phones and drum up some business. But today, with the house consuming so much time, the mystifying thing with Bennett, lunch with Mother, and my perpetual study of photos of Henry Peek, I'm just not feeling it.

Susan is patient with me, but I can tell that she's frustrated. She needs this job as much as I do. But this life around me is so loud. I'm in the middle of this swampy territory. I am down in it. I look at the pile of papers from the lawyer, the deed a thick sheaf of legalese. *Beverly d'Angeleno's How to Sell Your House in Two Weeks* is on the table beside this mess, and I realize: I'm two weeks into this gig, and not only have I not sold this house, I own it more than ever.

Bennett shows up at my front door, suppertime, still in his scrubs. This house is like a soap opera set: doesn't anybody call?

"I almost didn't come," he says. "Not much point to this, but you might as well hear it all."

I pour wine, and I wonder if Bennett has even been back to this house since Ginna died.

"Hungry? I've got soup from Bread and Company."

"Nah, I'll eat later." He spreads his arms wide, like he's about to take off. "Here's what happened." No preamble, no warmup. Bennett is the least southern Southerner I know. How could somebody from Dothan, Alabama, not know how to shoot the shit?

"This was probably a year and a half ago. I was digging around in this closet one night, looking for a blow-up bed for Cassie's friend sleeping over, and Ginna was out at a meeting. I pulled out this clump of knitting, and usually I would just stick it back where I found it like all of Ginna's other knitting junk, but I saw that it was a sweater, with needles and stuff all in it, and I held it up and saw this sleeve like an elephant's trunk. Like, huge. Bigger than me, for sure. And that's when it hit me, like a ton of fucking bricks. Nobody in our family—nobody I can think of—would wear a sweater that big.

"I went crazy. I mean, I totally lost it. She was making this thing for somebody else. It was like finding out that up is down. It's like . . . finding out your wife is cheating on you."

At this point I'm thinking I have in fact gone deaf. Bennett is saying all this stuff, and all I can think is: Ginnacheated? Ginna cheated? Ginna? Cheated?

"I decided to check the sweater every night, to see how long it would take her to finish it, and it dawned on me that she was cranking on it as a Christmas present for somebody. Sure enough, two days before Christmas, the sweater disappeared. I was off from work, right? Trying to look like I'm Santa Claus myself, last-minute shopping and whatever. But I was watching her like a hawk, waiting to see if she snuck off someplace, if she was going to meet somebody. But she didn't. She was baking cookies and playing her Tammy Wynette Christmas album and carrying on like she'd never leave home again."

Ginna did a fierce Tammy Wynette imitation.

"So she and the girls went out caroling one night, cheerful as hell, and I realized: that's it. It was somebody in the neighborhood. See, that fall, Ginna started spending a lot of time on this neighborhood association, worrying about sidewalks, potluck suppers, lost dogs. All week long she was passing out paper bags so that everybody would put candlelight bags all the way down Bowling Avenue. Whatever.

"So off they went, the street all lit up with these candle bags, and off I went behind them so they won't see me, and they were in this big group, and there was this one guy drifting along with them, really killing it on 'Good King Wenceslas,' and she was laughing and calling him Robert Goulet, and then she did it: she reached over and . . ." he stops. "She reaches over and squeezes his arm." Bennett's fidgeting, pulling his fingers back, hard, like he wants to snap them off. "His arm that was wearing a dark gray sweater." He cracks his knuckles. "Guy was six five, six six."

"Oh, man." A tall neighbor.

"Didn't even know his name."

"Really?" Oh, man.

"Really. So there I am, hunkered down behind this magnolia tree, taking all this in, watching this cheerful little group drift away into the night. It's a nightmare. Ginna. I'm seeing my entire life evaporate before my very eyes.

"Listen. There I am, up every morning at five a.m., fixing rotator cuffs and sawing up people's knees, making a living for us, but for what? Ginna has checked out. Without a word." He stops and looks up at me. "I'm so sick of thinking about all this. But you ought to know the truth."

I can't even speak. In sixteen years, this is the most talk I have ever heard from him.

"So I wait. Christmas was nauseating. I literally threw up one night, just thinking about it. I watched her like I was expecting her to pull a gun on me or something. Like she was going to burst into flames. Like she was a psycho. Because the thing is, she never cracked, never gave the slightest hint that she was knitting sweaters and doing God knows what with some dorky guy down the street. I'll put it to you this way: she never knit a damn sweater for me."

At this point, I've got my head in my hands, trying to mash all this into my head. I can't process this. My brain is not taking this in. Dorky guy down the street. Oh, my God.

"I figured out who the guy was—funny how you run into people when you walk the neighborhood. Especially when they're color-coded in dark gray. The thing is, I couldn't figure out how to confront her. She's the one who's ruined everything, but I'm the one who has to point it out? So shitty. I think, If I don't say anything, maybe it will all just go away. But I'm watching her, knowing that she can lie to me with a straight face, and I see that it'll never go away."

"We were supposed to go over to the O'Neills' house for this New Year's Eve party they have every year, and we got in the car, and that was it. The new year could not begin with this hanging over me. So right there in the driveway, in the Volvo I got her for Christmas, new car smell and all, I told her that I kept seeing this neighbor, this guy, and it was the damnedest thing. He was wearing a sweater that looks just like the one stuck in the back of our linen closet. I said to her, 'Angus Donald. Can you believe that?'"

I flip back on the sofa, screeching. My first thought, I'm embarrassed to admit, is: *He's not even hot.* The second is: Ginna was doing it with The Doomsayer? Bennett says, "You know the guy?" and I croak, between howls of amazement, "A little," and Bennett actually cracks a sour little smile. "So you know what I'm talking about."

It takes me a good while to get my wits. Bennett sits, silent, aware that he's just delivered a neutron bomb.

"I don't get it," I say. "You never told anybody about this? Nobody? Why would you keep it a secret?"

He's shaking his head. "Wouldn't you?" I feel a sudden wash of pity. I forgot that Bennett actually contains a soul, that he might have feelings that could

be hurt. "The girls adored her. I mean, they couldn't handle it when she even **raised** her voice at them. I decided pretty fast that Ginna was not going to end **up the** villain." He drags a hand through his dark hair. "After all, it was because **of me** that she ended up attracted to that guy. I wouldn't admit this to her, but it's a fact, and I know you may find this hard to believe, but I'm not the easiest guy in the world to be married to." He is silent for a while. "But at least I was loyal."

I'm thinking: loyal?

"You're thinking, but what about Carla? How loyal was that? OK. So Ginna and I have it out, she's devastated that she's been caught, that she did it, I can't tell. She's actually kind of heartbreaking to listen to. Begging me to work on it with her, but all I can think about is the fact that she would do this. I shut it down. Nothing. She's getting nothing from me. I can put up with a lot, but cold-blooded lying like that is the limit."

"This went on for a while, weeks I guess, at which point I was so shut off from her, from everybody, that I just. I had to have somebody to talk to." He sits down. "And Carla listened."

The Walrus.

"I decided that I wasn't going to hide it from Ginna. It was awful, but if she was going cheat and lie about it, at least I was going to be honest. How about that?" He grimaces.

"I guess I should tell them, but I just can't. Now especially. There's just no point. She's gone. Their mother was this warm, loving person, and I want it to stay that way. But you need to hear this. I'm sick of being the villain. I mean—I'll put up with it if it keeps Ginna's reputation good with the girls. But listen. Ginna? Ginna was no saint."

He stands, heavily, and heads into the library. He comes out with a book and holds it up for me: *The Beleaguered City: The Vicksburg Campaign 1862–63*. "Mind if I take this?" He flips through the pages. "By the end of the siege, the Confederates were eating rats and mules."

I shake my head. "Bennett. Jesus." And he's gone.

Years ago, at Ginna's bridesmaid luncheon, our wizened cousin Mildred Ballenger dispensed advice to Ginna and me on the subject of marriage. Three things in particular were seared in our memories by this tiny troll. One: bathrobes. As "working women," she said, we would be seeing our husbands mostly at night, so we needed to have a lot of bathrobes. I had never even been on a date, being fourteen years old, so the concept of a husband, never mind a need for bathrobes, was completely mysterious to me. Two: "Physical affection." We were instructed to be sure to be physically affectionate with our husbands on a regular basis. She made it sound like doing deep-knee bends or brushing our hair a hundred strokes a night. It was only later that Ginna translated this for me. Three (and this was the most ominous-sounding proclamation): only the two people in a marriage know the truth of that relationship. Now, hearing Bennett's tale, I wish to hell I could hear Ginna's version. Because his story has completely, totally, and utterly blown my pea-pickin' mind.

House Continues Not to Sell

I hesitate to point this out, but three days later, nobody from the open house has followed up with me. It's strange how deeply this hurts my feelings. It doesn't make me want to try harder to find a buyer. It makes me want to lie on the wooden bench, way in the back of Ginna's yard, listening to the tumble of water in the little creek that runs along the back of her property.

It's a separate world back here. Ginna filled the banks of the creek with iris and lilies, and it's exactly the place to be when you don't want to be inside a sagging, poison-filled, unsellable bummer house. The floppy butterfly iris, hundreds of them along the creek, are the brightest blue. On a day like this, you can lie flat on your back, look up through the weeping willow branches, and just be.

I, however, can stand to do this for maybe one minute before I decide that ants are coming up my leg. I love nature, but I love drywall more. Out in this wonderland, I sit up and click through emails on my phone. It looks like Susan has been carrying water for the business in her competent way. How long will it take for every single one of our clients to evaporate? We're down to six trips set for the next three months. I can't think of the last time we had so little business. Something is going to need to change, but I have an inkling that it isn't going to be me.

I stop to visit Henry Peek's Twitter page, as I do twelve times a day. OK, that would mean I'm checking it every two hours, which is wrong by a factor of at least three. I don't want to go into how often I'm doing this.

HenryPeek Average time to sell a house: 90 days. Number of days before a seller typically freaks out: 3.

I'm halfway inclined to give Henry Peek the house to sell because then we'd have to be in constant contact. Imagine getting emails from Henry Peek, little voicemails, juicy Tweets. Skyping, texts. It is almost worth it. Maybe it would be worth it.

Mother. She looked so thin, sitting there, with the glare of the glass window behind her. I think she was telling me that she needs me. Could this be true? I can't believe she's ever said that, to anyone.

"Delia?" It's Shelly calling from the terrace. "I'm here."

"Hey," I yell back. Doesn't Shelly have a real job to go to? I can't believe Mother lets her spend so much time over here. I head up to the terrace, empty coffee mug in hand, guilty to have been caught in such abject sloth. I feel like a vampire, squinting in the morning glare.

"Sold the house?" she asks, joking.

"We close tomorrow."

"Really?" She's surprised.

"Does it look like I've sold the house?" I hate this house.

She scowls at me. "No need to be so short."

"Sorry." I am so embarrassed that I look down at my phone and click through emails I've already read.

She reaches into her pocket, pulls out her cell phone, sighs, and sits. "William got me this foolish thing." We sit for a while, Shelly playing solitaire, me staring at my phone, feeling like crap.

"I have no idea what to do," I say.

"Hm?" Shelly looks up.

"About the house."

"Your mother wants you to call."

"She called?"

"No, but she wants you to call."

"You can read her mind?"

"Just call her, Delia." She's got the sun right behind her head, and I can barely make out her silhouetted face, but I can tell she's put out with me.

"She could call me."

"For heaven's sake," she says hotly as she stands, shaking her head and picking up my coffee cup. "There she is, and here you are, moping around, worthless. I never seen such a pair."

"I don't owe her a thing. You have no idea what she's—"

"You think you're the only one feeling bad? I never. Most pitiful thing I ever saw." I start to say something, but she's already back in the kitchen, door shutting quietly behind her.

Shelly never raises her voice. I'm shocked.

Shock. I keep thinking about the physical sensation of shock, that rush of your pulse, the electricity in your fingers and toes, the way the pit of your stomach actually does feel like it's going to drop out. Shelly yelling at me is shocking.

And Bennett's tale of Ginna was a shocker. I've had this feeling before, most often while watching a TV show when the smoke monster comes out of the jungle and eats the commando. But in real life, complete shock comes along only once in a great while.

It's what hit me, last year, when I learned that Bennett had left Ginna. Virtual Male Companion Greg was in from London, back when he was kind of a new story. Come to think of it, it was April, like now, unseasonably warm for Chicago, and we were walking along Lake Michigan. Maybe I was wishing things were more special than they actually were, but we were having a sweet enough time. My phone rang. I had been expecting a call from the Castlemans who were in Vietnam trying to get an asthma inhaler for their son.

Ginna sounded congested, and at first I didn't fully hear what she was saying. Something about bronchitis and how her life was in ruins. I joked about how she should make Doctor Schwartz go get her some chicken soup.

"Delia. Thanks a lot. Why are you always so mean?"

"What?"

"As if."

Very confusing. "As if what?"

"Like Bennett's even here."

"Ginna, what are you talking about?"

"You haven't even heard, have you? Bennett's gone, sister. Bennett moved out a month ago. If you ever deigned to return my calls or talk to your mother, you might learn something."

That was the electricity-in-my-feet moment. That was the shock.

It all came out, and poor Greg had to sit beside me on the bench as I lay on my back, phone pressed to ear, stunned. What kind of sister is so out of touch that she doesn't even hear about major life trouble until a month later? I don't remember everything Ginna told me, but I do recall one thing, because it struck me as so strange when she said it. "What goes around comes around." She had done nothing to merit this sort of scurrilous treatment. Ginna wasn't the one who screwed a surgical nurse. Ginna wouldn't do that. True enough, as Bennett has now so eloquently explained: she screwed a gangly neighbor down the street.

I need to apologize to Shelly. When I go into the kitchen, my coffee cup sits upside down in the dish rack, clean and wet. I check the front driveway, and Shelly's car is gone. Electricity shoots up my spine.

Coming back from a trip to the grocery store, I discover an incandescent red pickup truck in the driveway. It's not a normal pickup truck: it has at least two feet of lift on it, a little ladder leading up to the driver's door, and a decal across the entire back window that mystifyingly says "LOVE YARD" in capital gothic letters. Just a huge amount of effort put into this ride, brand new and as shiny as a slot machine. A man comes around the corner of the house. He appears inflated, with a shaved head and long beard that looks wispily Hasidic, eyes sunk into his sunburned face like raisins in a bun. He's not all that tall, but he is wide, and he's scary as hell to see in my yard. Somewhere behind him a high voice in a foreign accent yells "Ethan! Where the fuck are you?"

"I'm fuckin' right here, sugar," he yells back blandly in a flat, nicotine-stained country-boy accent. The high voice appears, and I have to avert my eyes in embarrassment at the bounteous plenitude of her—a Partonian quantity of tangled gold hair with a small face somewhere in there, a spectacular amount of bosom, and a napkin of a dress. She's figured out how to be naked with clothes on.

"Well hey," he says to me, tiptoeing through the grass in lurid cowboy boots that seem impossibly small. Between her bosom and his girth, I'm afraid somebody's going to tip over. "This your house?" He's chewing on something, idly. "Sugar," he says, "jewgetcher shoes unstuck?"

She is indeed barefoot, carrying a pair of clear plastic platforms. There's a stripper in my yard.

"We like this house," Ethan says. I mishear him and think he said "We lack this house," which sounds so fancy.

"Oh. Yah." Sugar knocks the dirt and grass off her stilettos. This sets off a tremendous jangling of the bangles running all the way up her arm.

"Sugar's pregnant," he says. She doesn't look pregnant. I can practically see her uterus.

"So we need a bigger house like yesterday," she says, looking up at the roofline. "Is there an au pair suite?" The accent is Swedish or Norwegian or otherwise Scandinavian.

"Let's go," Ethan says. "Give us a tour. Sugar, where's my gum?"

She pulls out a pack of Nicorette and slips a piece into his mouth like she's feeding a baby pig. He bites her fingers in the dirtiest way I've ever seen, and I hope against hope they resist the urge to have sex in my front yard until they sign a contract for this house.

Off we go. "I'm sorry it's such a mess right now." The house is neater than it has ever been, but I want him to know that I have extremely high standards.

Ethan wanders into the den. "This could be the bar."

"Mmhmm," Sugar says. She seems uninterested in the house tour.

He peeks through the den window at the terrace. "Put a studio out back." Ethan has a lot of ideas. Upstairs, he takes one look at the guest room and sighs. "Nice colorway."

"You're in the music business?" I ask. Of course he's in the music business. Who in the merely mortal world looks like this?

Sugar laughs, incredulous. "You didn't recognize him? He's Ethan Hardy. You know: 'Tennessee Mud'? 'Your Love'll Make Me Quit My Job'?" She digs around in her suitcase of a handbag and hands me a CD. There's Ethan, heroically lit from behind like Jesus, wearing a lot of leather, with his beard trailing in the breeze. The album is titled *Happy as Shit*.

I'm kind of knocked out by this couple. I think I'm a fan. "You're looking for a place in town? I thought you country music stars liked to have 400-acre farms out in Williamson County."

Sugar cracks up at this. "Yah, you'd like that, right honey? He grew up in Hickman County. On a chicken farm."

He thinks this is funny, too. "You ever spent time on a real farm, last place in the world you want to be is anywhere near a chicken. I fuckin' hate chickens."

Sugar makes me show her the attic, for the au pair she will hire once the baby comes. "Now this is a dismal scene," she says. "Ethan"—it sounds like *eaten*—"could we implant some windows or something?"

He's looking around the room. "You living up here, aintcha?" he says, seeing a half-gnawed bagel on my bedside table, which is a large cardboard box with *Kotex* in large letters across the side. He looks at me sharply. "Why you selling this house anyway?"

I tell him about the situation, in direct violation of Beverly d'Angeleno's specific advice not to share unsavory information about the current ownership of a house. But there's something about Ethan—he seems kind, under all his ink and leathery trappings. Sugar says, "She didn't die in *here*, did she? No offense, I mean," she adds as she sees my expression.

Yeah, she pretty much did die in here. This flashing thought sinks me like a brick tied to my ankle. "Car accident," I say, suddenly regretting telling them this, wishing again that Ginna had just wandered off to Pulaski.

Ethan looks at me, struck. "My God, woman. You can't be living in here. You're gonna break your heart all over again. Your pain's kickin' off you like a halo of sorrow. I mean, I can feel it."

I shrug, feeling my lips go all rubbery and trying not to cry. Why is it that the tiniest expression of sympathy can have the most potent effect?

By the end of the tour, I can't tell whether Ethan is into this house or not. He's cagey about it. "OK," he says, climbing up into his truck. "You're negotiable on the price, I know. I mean, that's a lot of coin for a place like this. Somebody's gotta fix that kitchen."

I shrug and talk up to him so I can be heard. "Just let me know if you're interested. Are you working with an agent?"

Sugar snorts. "Ethan's got no agent for nothing. Thieves, he calls them."

"I'll be in touch," he says. "I got your digits."

I'm weirdly sad that they're leaving. "Hey Ethan—what does 'LOVE YARD' mean?"

"Love hard!" Ethan exclaims, twisting around to look at the window.

"I told you it's hard to read," Sugar says.

"That's my ethos. That's what drives the whole thing. You gotta love hard or you ain't loving at all."

Dream into Reality into Dream

My job is vanishing, I am learning disturbing and upsetting things about my family, and I have discovered four toilets that either flush too long or not at all. How can one house have eight toilets?

It is a minefield, this house. This morning, for example. I pass a table in the library that Ginna filled with photographs of family and friends. The frames are lined up so tightly that you can't even see them all. Collect the whole set. Permutations, occasions. Large fish being held up. One of the frames has fallen off the back of the table, and I drag it out. It's the famous photo of Mother being sworn in as the state's first female bankruptcy court judge in the early eighties. Mother has her hand on a Bible and is looking directly at the man swearing her in, dead serious. She's been a widow for less than a year. I'm on my knees, looking up Mother's robe, and Ginna is whacking me on the fanny with a gavel. Mother could have had wolverines gnawing at her feet, and she still would have made it through that ceremony.

I keep thinking about the girls. Ever since Shelly told me about them sneaking over to the house, I've been trying to figure out what to do. Bennett said they had fun with me. I find that hard to believe. Over the years, I've had a limping relationship with Cassie and Amelia. Birthdays in particular seemed impossible for me to remember. Ginna would send along photos of the girls every once in a while: a pair of lined-up, tidied-up specimens. I always thought Cassie looked a little like a monkey, a cute monkey. Now, I'm still spinning from that conversation—that monologue—from Bennett. What a tilted world those girls inhabit: a silently furious father, their mother there one day, gone the next. I can't stand that they have been cut off from this place. I dial Amelia.

"Any chance you and Cassie might want to come over for a sleepover to-morrow night? I know how busy you are, and I don't know exactly what we'll do, but it would be great to see you guys, and I . . ."

"Um, yeah hold on." Muffled talking that goes on a long time. "Yeah. We can."

This will be terrifying I mean fun.

Late in the day, I answer my phone, fifth call in two hours because the Bergers are visiting St. Petersburg and have decided they want to stay an extra week, and that involves visas, and Russian visas are scary to travelers because of the Cyrillic thing. And also 1,000 years of scary Russian government. But it's not Svetlana, my visa expert, on the line. It's Henry Peek.

"What are you doing?" he asks. He sounds caffeinated. "Like, right now?"

I am sitting in my tenement attic bedroom, in my second best yoga pants and a Chicago Cubs T-shirt, watching the sun set through the low half-moon window. I'm not lying in my bed, because at this hour of the day that would be slovenly. But I am technically sitting on it. And at this very second, I am trying not freak out. "Painting a fresco. You?"

"I was wondering if you're hungry. There's an opportunity. Something kind of great."

"Like, now?"

"Yeah."

"Does this involve real estate?"

"No, no no no. The opposite."

What could be the opposite of real estate?

To be clear, I haven't been out of the house past sunset since I arrived in town. It feels creepy to drive up this dark driveway with all those hollow box-woods potentially housing crafty marauders, and I hate coming back into this huge house all by myself. It's easier to watch the day fade from the safety of the indoors.

The prospect of going into the night with Henry Peek sends me into a delirium of preparation. I won't go into the wardrobe crisis resulting from this phone call. OK, here are highlights. The way I see it, Henry Peek wouldn't have asked me to dinner if he weren't at least, in some marginal way, interested in me. He knew I wouldn't have other plans, so maybe this is a last-minute filler-type deal. Still, he called. Calling a person is a deliberate act. I go out on a limb and declare this a date, whether he intends it that way or not. I can't blow this by not making a solid effort. It's got to be a dress. You can't go on a pants date when the guy is the one you have been cyberstalking without mercy for two weeks straight.

I think about Bird Girl's hair. If only my hair could be as silken as that.

I haven't been on a date in at least three years, unless you count Virtual Greg, who, as I think about it, does not count. Tonight is an Army training exercise with live ammo. This is different. I could get killed out there.

Henry is gratifyingly complimentary. At least, he says he likes my blue cotton dress, which is Ginna's, and he pats my wrap, which Ginna knitted out of an impossibly thin yarn and does look like something you ought to pat. "You just sit around like this all day long, dressed up?" he asks.

Yeah, when I'm not wearing yoga pants with underwear falling out of them.

He looks so scrubbed. As he drives, I steal a look at his profile. His chin is smooth. His coat has a dark, almost invisible checked pattern to it. Three buttons at the cuff. I focus on this sleeve because my eyes will burn out if I look directly at him.

"Where are we going, anyway?"

"I don't actually know. All I have is an address. Here." He hands me his phone. "You navigate."

It's an email with only the subject line "209 Shirley Street. 8 o'clock." The sender is kevinkevin@gmail.com, who it appears sent the email two hours ago.

I remind him that I haven't lived here for more than ten years and can barely find my way to the mall anymore.

"Aw, you know. Shirley Street. Near where the old Shoney's was downtown. Near where the Children's Museum used to be."

Navigating by long-gone landmarks. You're so Nashville if. "Such a local."

It's killing me that he's going to the trouble of being mysterious about our destination. We're headed toward downtown, that much I can tell.

"You're nice to call," I say.

"You're nice to come."

What is it about riding in a car with a guy you like? There you are, captured, trapped together, insulated against the elements, swallowed by his world. If you like the guy, you probably like the music he's playing. And if it's a warm April night, the breeze makes it feel like you're flying. Anything can happen in a car. You can tell somebody your whole life story. You can get pregnant. You can get in, crank it up, and drive south, all the way to Gulf Shores.

Music City Autohaus is what it says on the sign, but there don't appear to have been any autos in this autohaus for a long time. The derelict building at 209 Shirley Street is an empty car repair business, with a cluster of cars parked around it.

As we walk in, a small guy in a trashed chef's coat and a scruffy chin passes us, carrying a sizeable whole salmon in his arms. He smiles at me, and I guess that this must be kevinkevin. "Henry! Brought a friend?" he says in a teasing voice. His accent is so flat country that it almost sounds like a foreign language. "Can this be possible?"

"Ah. Kevin. This is Delia. Be kind, weasel."

"Henry is a lone wolf," Kevin says to me. "But you already know this." He holds up his fish. "Must roast. Back in a minute." He turns back and gives us another look.

It is a surreal room. The cement block walls are bare, and the floor bears scars of heavy machinery once bolted to the floor. In the middle of this barren space, one long table floats like a dream: the tablecloth is a glowing, deep orange, tall candles all the way down, with places set for at least thirty. The scent of something roasting is overwhelmingly delicious. There are at least twenty people here, and more arrive behind us. It's a Thursday night in Nashville. Henry has brought me to a secret supper. I love this, so much.

Henry passes me a glass of wine. "Cheers," I say as we clink our glasses. He has a highball with a lime. He's not wearing his glasses, which I take as an important sign of interest in appearing handsome, which at this point he very much is.

"This is unbelievable," I say.

"They're bulldozing this building on Saturday, for the new convention center. So Kevin wanted to bid it a farewell. He cooks. And he hates the convention center, thinks it's a greedy, unneighborly thing to do to a city." He laughs. "In general, he protests by cooking in endangered spaces. Kind of an anarchist."

"Where's the kitchen?"

"It's magic," Henry says.

We stand for a while, talking with Henry's friends who seem to be either music business or food business or Vanderbilt. A woman in a chef's coat holds up a tray: Kevin's fish has turned into tiny bites of roasted salmon.

"Where are all your real estate friends?" I ask.

"I don't have any real estate friends." He says this in a way that strikes me as very funny, and I laugh.

"Really. I'm probably the most self-hating realtor you will ever meet. We're fiends, we lie. We're damnable beasts." All said in the most charming way.

"So why do you do it?"

Henry shifts and avoids looking at me. "Lucky, actually. A good job is a good thing."

"You like selling houses."

"I may be the luckiest guy in the world." I can't tell if he's being ironic, but he doesn't appear to be joking. He takes a skewer of shrimp from a passing tray and gently gives it to me. "Always eat hors d'oeuvres."

We sit at the long orange table, side by side, in our own little world. He tells me about the people around us, but at this point I am finding it hard to do anything except be amused at everything he says. The wine comes around, and I start to pour him a glass, but he catches the neck of the bottle. "Thanks."

He doesn't drink. "No wonder you're so clear-eyed," I say.

"Shockingly clear-eyed."

I have to ask. "OK, Shelly told me that you had some trouble with your back, a while ago."

Henry smiles ruefully. "I blame it all on my back, yes." He is so close to me, right there. His eyelashes are as pale as his eyebrows. His ear curves like a shell. "But really, my back was the least of it."

Kevin appears behind us. "It is time for the pig. Come on." He leads us to the serving table, where an enormous pork roast is being carved. It is not, in any way, a Honey-Spiral Ham. It is magnificent, a monument to the porcine arts of Middle Tennessee.

After dessert is served—a sizeable strawberry trifle—Kevin stands. He is an elflike creature, mischievous, a friend of everyone in the room. "Now it's time for declarations. I want to hear it: something that you believe with all your heart." It's the most incredibly hicky drawl I've ever heard.

Henry leans over. "We sing for our supper. Everybody chips in for the food, but we also have to amuse Kevin. At least you missed Truth or Dare night."

One by one, the declarations flow, and it's interesting how unwittingly people reveal themselves. One tall woman, clearly in her cups, says, "I believe with all my heart that honesty is not the best policy." Another guy starts to recite Rudyard Kipling but is booed down. I am nervous that I'm going to have to say something. Everybody seems to be listening very closely.

It's my turn. I look down at Henry, who looks up at me, amused and expectant. "Thank you, Kevin, for this beautiful dinner. What do I believe? I believe that it's easier to sit at home in your yoga pants, with your Lean Cuisine Café Classic Fettuccine Alfredo. But it's important not to." This makes Henry smile, which is all I want.

Henry stands. "If you've traveled as much as I have, this is easy: be it ever so humble, there's *no* place like home." He looks down and gives me a look, like he's directing this at me alone. A chorus of awwws, and somebody says, "Give that boy a commission."

Traveling. I didn't know Henry was a traveler. When I ask him about it, he says, "It wasn't good, most of it. It was runaway travel."

I remind him that I'm in the travel business, and he nods. "You think I wouldn't Google you? Or that your mother wouldn't give me an inch-thick dossier?" God knows what she told him. "So—what's your favorite place in the world?" he asks.

Such a no-brainer. This question comes my way a lot, from clients looking for their next destination, from anybody who hears I'm a travel agent. I look at the vase of wildflowers on the table and say, "Furano. Japan. On Hokkaido, one of the northern islands. They have these vast lavender fields that I can't even describe. The scent of it—it's like the world's hugest bar of soap." I sip my wine. "And poppy fields. Like *The Wizard of Oz*."

"You like Japan?"

"I like the people more than the country. You're really out of town when you're in Japan. What about you?"

He shrugs. "Never been to Asia and can't say I'm too curious about it. My favorite place is actually right here in Tennessee. Maybe I'll show you sometime."

Sometime. The indefinite future. Henry imagines me somewhere in his sometime ahead.

"Why are they building a new convention center?" I ask. "Conventions are so 1980."

Henry shrugs, irritated. "I know. I mean, what do you do with 300,000 square feet of space when the NRA's not in town? Totally useless building. Never mind what the city is putting into the thing—the numbers don't really work. I tend to think smaller. The best thing for a downtown is to have eyes on the street—people living there all the time. The convention center was driven by people who don't really think about neighborliness. We realtors, on the other hand . . . we're noble visionaries." He rolls his eyes. "Can't sell a convention center over and over the way we can sell a condo."

I'm touched that Henry thinks about neighborliness. I tell him that I majored in geographical studies, and this is the sort of thing I think about all the time. He is surprised. "Exactly what is that?"

"How cities evolve. The intersection of humans and the places they live in. The character of place, place-making. My senior thesis was about the depopulation of North Dakota." I instantly regret telling him this.

"That's the loneliest thing I ever heard," he says with a slightly alarmed expression.

"It's not all bad, depopulation," I say unconvincingly, recalling the day I read about the way Dakotans would kill themselves by taking a walk on a railroad track. "It's great if you're a buffalo. We're supposed to live in places that get regular rain, you know. It's not good to settle in a place with a low water table." I can't believe I am talking about Ogallala aquifer at this particular moment.

"So why don't you do work in planning or something?" He looks so puzzled.

"I guess I'm just." *Scared* is the word that almost pops out, unexpectedly. I've never thought of myself as scared. "It's politics, mostly, and I'm not good at that. It's hard to make anything really change."

"I don't believe that," he says sharply. "You can change anything if you really want to. Or need to. I mean, you have to try." He sounds irritated at me, almost. A basket is handed to him. "Here," he says. "Artisan cornpone."

After dinner, an enterprising guy hooks up an iPod to a set of big speakers, and that's when the dancing starts. I'm not a dancing person, but when everyone else in the room is spinning around, and somebody like Henry Peek takes you by the hand, you'd be a fool not to join in. I tell him, "I only know how to shag," to which he responds, "I only know how to fake shag," and off we go.

He is a lower-lip-biting dancer, like me, but we dance until I have to take off Ginna's shoes, and Ginna's wrap, and Henry is down to his shirtsleeves, rolled up. We don't talk; we stop only to catch our breath, then start up again. The music is somebody's mash-up of everything from techno to "I Got the Music in Me," and it doesn't matter. He is absurdly charming, his hands warm in mine. Dancing makes it so easy to hold onto him, such a great excuse for the thing I want to do. Whoever invented dancing was a total genius. I try not to hold onto him too tightly, but I worry that if we stop dancing, the whole night will evaporate, and it won't be real anymore.

It's midnight by the time we get to Ginna's. The house looms, and the weight of it returns. I'd forgotten about everything tonight. "Open house on Sunday," I say in a fakey cheerful voice. My ears are still ringing from the music. I'm still mortified to have told him about my senior thesis on depopulation.

"They're calling for rain, you know. Big rain. Always check your forecast." He gets out and comes around to my car door. I can't believe he's like this. I catch him wincing as he rubs the small of his back, and I wonder if dancing has done something to him.

We walk up the front steps, the stone cool against my bare feet. "Here." I hand him Ginna's shoes so I can fish out my key. "Is your back OK?"

He nods, a tight smile. "Old war wound. Korea. You know. Fine." He takes the key from me to open the door. "You should let me sell the house for you," he says. "No fee. I don't care about that."

"That sounds exactly like something a drunk guy would say at the end of the night, except I know you're not drunk."

"Just a sucker for a damsel in distress."

"You're gallant."

"Think about it. You don't have to do everything all by yourself, Delia." He nudges the door open, and turns to me. "You remind me of me."

If we don't kiss in the next five seconds, I am going to die.

But the warning beep of the alarm goes off, and I have to drop everything and run to the control panel in the kitchen before the Voice of God starts yelling at us. By the time I punch in the magic numbers, I have the fleeting fear that he has gone home. I hurry back to the front hall, and he's still there, Henry Peek, holding Ginna's shoes in one hand and the key to my house in the other.

So Much

I don't know whether it's a good thing or a bad thing, but I have somehow managed to withstand the hurricane force of Henry Peek's offer to sell my house. I have not, however, been able to resist much of anything else about him.

I'm watching him sleep beside me in the guest bed of Ginna's house—my house. He is sunk into the covers, one poignant foot poking out from the comforter, an arm curled under his head. I love that foot. This bedroom, with all its lush drapery and upholstered comfort, feels like a hotel, with a slice of early bright sun coming in the crack of the heavy curtains.

I do know one thing: I was correct when I guessed that Henry was hoping for a date. I can't believe we did this, right out of the gate. I wasn't even nervous. By the end of the party, we had spent so long dancing together that it felt like we'd been talking all night.

It feels wild, and sneaky, this uncharted territory. I've caught my exotic creature, and now I don't want to scare him away.

I know so many facts about him, from all my trolling on the Internet. Such a Pandora's Box, the Internet. I wish I didn't know already that his middle name is McDougal. He should have told me that himself, confessing to a rogueish Scottish ancestor. He lives at 2109 Acklen Avenue in a yuppie condo near Hillsboro Village. I should be lying here wondering about his place, not knowing that it's across the street from the Methodist church and that the apartment next door is for sale for $328,000. He is selling six houses right now. He went to Duke. He has worked at Peek & Peek for eight years.

Mercifully, I don't know his favorite book. I don't know if he has a dog. I don't know how he takes his coffee, where he banks, whether he believes in God. Despite my spying, there's so much to find out.

I'm wearing his shirt because I had to get water during the night, so thirsty from all the wine. I want to touch him, but I'm embarrassed. What if he wakes up and decides this was a mistake? I sit for what feels like an hour, reliving last night even as I study the shiny haze of whiskers on his chin. So incredible, the whole thing.

But my mind catches on one moment like a splinter into my thumb: I lied to him. I can't believe I told him I'd been to the lavender fields in Hokkaido. For years, I've answered that question of my favorite place by saying the first place that pops into my mind. I've said Montepulciano when there's a bottle of wine in front of me. I've loved Brazil when I've had my feet propped up on a box from Amazon.com. It might be Hong Kong when I'm drinking tea or Bali when I'm folding my bras. My favorite place can be anyplace, because when it gets right down to it, it doesn't really matter. Only Susan, my business partner, knows the hideous, horrifying truth: I've never left the continental United States. Even my family thinks I've traveled, due to some vague statements I may have made to them describing my intimate knowledge of faraway places that may have led them to conclude that I had actually been to those places.

What if Henry had been an exchange student in Japan? What if his great-grandfather was an expatriate rice baron? So stupid.

His eyes open, like a turtle waking up.

I slide down beside him. "What's your favorite book?"

He looks so sleepy, the circles under his eyes. "Anything by Shakespeare."

"Do you have a dog?"

"No. But I like dogs."

"Shoe size?"

"Eleven." He yawns and scrunches his eyes, green in this light.

"Favorite color."

"Blue."

"I knew that. You have blue everything."

"Your eyes are blue. Your dress was blue."

"You noticed."

"Of course I noticed. I'm a noticer." He looks intently at me like he's studying a map. "You're noticeable."

He's very good at being charming. He reaches for me, and I feel a rush of relief. "You're stealing my clothes," he says into my hair.

I notice that the wicked scar on his left hand continues up his forearm. I trace it with my hand. "This hurt."

"It did." He looks at it as if it's somebody else's arm, as if it's a puzzle to figure out. "If I say it was a bar fight, will you laugh and think I'm joking?"

"You were in a bar fight?"

"Outside a bar, actually. In Copenhagen. Long time ago. Foxy, isn't it?"

His shoelaces would be foxy to me. "I can't believe you were in a bar fight."

"Me neither." He shifts onto his back, slowly, and I see a flash of pain.

"Oh my God, I broke you."

He laughs. "I'm not that fragile. Just busted, a little. I haven't danced like that," and he sits up, "ever."

"Me neither."

I see another scar across his shoulder. He's a Navy SEAL disguised as a mild-mannered real estate agent.

He yawns again. "You don't happen to have any Advil, perchance?"

The bad back. He slides to the edge of the bed, and I see the scar running up his spine, a wide purple line with dots alongside it. "Henry." I can't help but gasp.

He turns, eyes wide like he wants to scare me. "Gruesome!"

"No! I mean, I'm just so sorry."

"Glad I can't see it." He turns slightly, shy.

I slide out of the bed. "Be right back."

"Just Advil," he says. "Nothing fancy."

I take off down the stairs for Ginna's medicine cabinet, which is a marvel of pharmaceuticals thanks to Bennett's profession. I stand in front of the sink, studying myself in the wide mirror. My hair is tangled, hardly blonde at all in this light. Henry's shirt has the most subtle blue stripes. I look different. So flushed, so pink. I look wonderful. I never look wonderful.

I take off Henry's shirt, because he's going to need it even though I want to keep it, and I put on one of Ginna's many, many bathrobes. What would cousin Mildred think of this situation? I am concerned that a long, pink robe is dangerously close to a Lanz nightgown.

I head to the kitchen for a glass of water for Henry, and to my heart-stopping surprise, Shelly is at the breakfast table, fixing pimento cheese on toast. "Morning," she says.

"Shelly!"

"I'll be doing pots in a minute. Out back." Shelly has been sticking impatiens in the planters on the terrace as per Beverly d'Angeleno's advice about adding color to a patio. She has the most ambiguous expression possible. "Sposed to rain later on."

"You're giving me the weather forecast?"

She shrugs and returns to her precise nudging of pimento cheese into the corners of her toast. Only I would recognize the smile hiding in her face, and she knows this.

"I have things to tell you," Henry says as we stand by his car. He looks surprised, as if he just discovered that this could be the case. And he seems tired, slow, like he's had as restless a night's sleep as I had. I think his back is bothering him, but he hasn't mentioned it and I don't want to pry. "Do you ever have that feeling? Like there's so much to talk about?"

I nod. If he only knew. I feel like Jimmy Butterman, following him all the way out to the driveway. I may just hop in and go home with him, rattling on about rose mulch and fertilizer. I'm so dismayed that he is leaving.

He stands there, utterly charming, doesn't even realize it.

"Henry." It comes out like a croak. Just say it.

"Delia."

"I haven't ever been to the lavender fields in Japan." I run out of air halfway through this.

He looks at me, puzzled. "What?"

"What I told you. About my favorite place. I haven't been there, I haven't traveled at all. I haven't even left the continental U.S." I am so embarrassed that I've got my arms wrapped completely around myself in a pink chenille straitjacket.

He gives me a look of complete puzzlement. "Never?"

I shake my head.

"You're a travel agent who's never traveled." He smiles with a sort of amazement. "You fake it."

I nod. "I simulate it. You can be a travel expert but not have to do all that pesky traveling."

"Seriously?"

"I'm a good researcher. You can find anything on the Internet." How peculiar this sounds. "I had to tell you the truth. I'm not a sophisticated world traveler. At all."

He says, "It's easier to stay at home. Yoga pants."

"Right." This is awful.

"But you said it's better not to."

"Maybe I'm just starting to figure that out."

"Well, well," he says. I have no idea what he means by that. He leans to kiss me, but is it a hundred-percent kiss or a ninety-percent kiss?

He's in his car, key in the ignition, but I can't stand for him to leave without asking the question that has been driving me crazy. "What about Bird Girl?"

"What?"

"The girl. On the floor. The bookstore. The bird books."

The recognition grows, and he frowns. Thinking. "Susannah. Known her for ages. I meant to tell you." He's embarrassed, low voiced. "Very special person in my life. Should have told you."

The floor drops out under my feet. He looks at me closely, watching what it looks like when complete horror crosses a person's face. He is disturbingly amused.

"She's my cousin, Delia. Works at the bookstore."

I walk around to the back of the house, still in Ginna's pink robe. Such a lovely day, a perfect day, with extravagant clouds moving in. Surely none of the neighbors can see over Ginna's hedges. I hope.

Now I'm second-guessing myself about telling Henry about my profound provinciality. He seemed to laugh it off, and he said he was glad that I wanted to tell him, but I can't decide if it's worse that I admitted to lying to him or that he now knows exactly how weird I am. The only way to prove to him that I'm not weird is to be not weird. I clearly have some work to do.

I'm not even sure why it became such a compulsion, this not-traveling. Growing up, Gulf Shores was about as exotic a vacation as Mother's schedule would allow. She thought people could find plenty to see in their own backyards. I always resented this, and in high school I would carry around a People to People student exchange brochure, dreaming about my French homestay family, imagining me in my French family's French bed, living the French life the way the French live it. By the time I got to college, I was so relieved to get out of Nashville that that was enough. Chicago was an entire world, and I lost myself in a place filled with people smarter than me. The travel agent work was a little joke at first. I really did plan to be an urban planner—until I actually started making money at trip management, and Susan came on board. Travel became work, and I hunkered down. I had no money for travel, anyway, so it became a habit, not traveling. At some point, it became a professional liability never to have traveled, so I became very good at sounding like a traveler.

"The girls are coming over tonight," I tell Shelly, who is popping little plants out of their containers. "To spend the night."

"Hunh," she says. "How'd you manage that?"

"I asked them. Do you think it'll be too sad? I don't want to upset them."

Shelly looks thoughtful. "Who knows? Hard to know what will set somebody off." She glances up at me, and I realize that she's talking about me. That hurts.

"Bennett said they said I was cool."

She looks up at me, in my mousy bathrobe, and raises an eyebrow.

"I'm sorry, Shelly. About yesterday." She blinks. Not buying it. "I called her. We're having lunch. Today, I mean."

"Well, that'll be nice," she says in a way that I can't decipher. I feel like she's not even on my team. I hurry inside, embarrassed to be in this bathrobe in front of her.

My relief about Bird Girl cannot be overstated.

I think of myself as someone who is comfortable being alone. It has never bothered me. Most of our childhood was spent off in rooms by ourselves, with only Shelly checking in on us to make sure we hadn't set ourselves or the house on fire. I can count on one hand the number of times I recall Mother hanging out with me in my room. I've lived by myself for a long time now, more than three years, after leaving behind Costanza the roommate. Costanza made life very inexpensive, but the parade of her awful friends did me in, and the talking. One room to myself beat four rooms when one of them contained a Costanza.

But it's not that familiar solitude that I'm feeling as I head inside, up the broad front staircase, then around to the narrow back stairs to my attic bedroom. Empty. Feels empty. Having Henry here made the house right, a house where people come home late from parties and fool around all night long. Now that he's gone, I'm back to being a caretaker, a squatter, a vagrant. I don't like this feeling a bit.

I sit at the spindly table by the half-moon window, on which my computer sits like an oversized cat on a footstool. This room is like that—filled with misfit furniture stowed up here in limbo on its inexorable, slow journey out of the house. My papers are spread all over the floor—real estate listings, thieving realtors' business cards, *People* magazines from 2003. I pick up a spiral notebook open to a list of goals I cooked up before coming to town:

> Clean out house by April 25.
> Have contract in hand for house by May 7.
> Get more clients ASAP.
> Avoid Mother.

How marvelously straightforward. I didn't take into account the fact that Ginna's house is Ginna, and that living in it would be this powerful and overwhelming experience. It makes me miss her so much. What was she thinking, leaving this place to me?

I should talk to Angus. Can I bear to talk to the guy? He was so unhappy to talk to me, and now I know why. He's heartbroken. Did he and Ginna break it off after Bennett found them out? I still can't believe I never heard a word about this affair. Bennett should get a gold medal for valor. And Ginna. I never would have guessed that she would go rogue.

One by-product of my interlude with Henry is that I have conveniently forgotten about the parts of life that have been my recent, unpleasant preoccupation. I need to focus. I flip to a new page and start scribbling.

> 100% unsold house. Mobilize ASAP
> Mother flaking out
> Girls need someone
> Travel business = problem
> Henry
> Back to Chicago ASAP

I look at this last item and run a line through it.

I come down the stairs and head straight for the guest room, where I climb into the bed and pull up the covers. What is it that makes these sheets smell so good? Ginna probably used some organic laundry juice. Something on the bedside table catches my eye: a card, Henry's business card, with the little cartoon of his face peering quizzically at me. I pick it up and flip it over. Scrawly handwriting. "Delia. There's no place like home. Seriously."

It's lunchtime at the Picnic. Mother loves this place, which functions pretty much as a cafeteria for the sorority that is west Nashville. Hundreds of blue-and-white plates on the walls, a menu of hardcore girl food. I'm trying hard to get my aim right on dress code, and I'm in good shape today, though I'll never have access to the sort of wackadoodle print skirts that I'm seeing here. Where do these people find clothes like these?

Mother says hello to at least four women, then says to me, "I liked it better when it was inside Belle Meade Drugs. You could get your things right there after lunch." Chicken salad, Dr. Scholl's Corn Pads, ointment. "But really, the best of all was Moon Drugs." We pause to mourn Moon Drugs. Closed for decades.

I say, "The girls are coming over tonight. Do you see them much?"

"Well, you know. They're just so busy, with all that soccer and day camp and so forth."

Day camp? What sixteen-year-old girl goes to day camp? Mother is so out of it. "I don't know them," I say. In the interest of Mother's therapy, I add, "And that makes me kind of sad."

She glances up and looks irritated. "Went up to Sewanee yesterday."

Ginna went to college at Sewanee, about 90 miles southeast of Nashville. She declared, on the day Amelia was born, that all her children would go to Sewanee. She had that starry-eyed alum thing about the place. It's where she met Bennett.

"How was that?"

"She wasn't there."

"Want my frozen salad?"

Mother reaches over and picks up the cup of pale pinkness. "Love this," she says as she digs in.

"Are you actually looking for her?" I ask. "When you're on these trips?"

Mother looks at me like I'm crazy. "Yes, I'm hoping to see her floating along the quadrangle in her black robes. Of course not, Delia. I just." She adjusts the emerald ring that Will Ballenger gave her all those years ago, the one she never stopped wearing. "Wish I could get them back. Those days." She's talking into her plate. "Never came to see you, either."

It's true: she never came to see me in college, except graduation, but at that point I wouldn't have welcomed her anyway. It's fascinating that any of this is even occurring to her. What a stew of grief and remorse. Seeing Mother like this makes me feel sturdier than I have in recent days.

"You were always so difficult, Delia." Ah, there you go. There's Mother. "Always so sure of yourself, didn't need a thing from me."

I really, really don't want to get into a thing with her. What I want to say is, "It's easier to opt out than to be rejected, over and over." Instead, I say in a tidy voice, "I guess that's the hazard of raising independent girls. They end up all self-reliant."

She's so strange now. A gloomy Mother is something I've never seen. She's not back at work. She says she is gardening obsessively. She asks me what I'm doing about Ginna's roses as if they are small children who need a guardian. She is satisfied that Jimmy Butterman is on the case, but she mentions the floribundas as an area of concern this spring. She knows I have no idea what she's talking about, but she keeps talking anyway.

I suggest that we walk at Radnor Lake next week—my system cannot handle the mayonnaise load that our family therapy seems to require.

Driving home gives me a moment to wallow in the splendor that is Henry. I check his Twitter feed.

HenryPeek Storms this weekend. Are your gutters ready?

The girls show up in the late afternoon. I feel like I'm receiving dignitaries from a distant land, standing on the front porch, waiting, not sure I can speak their language. They come out of Amelia's dented Jeep talking. Cassie is dogging her big sister.

"When?"

"Forget it."

"When did he ask?"

Amelia picks up a backpack from the back seat with a doomed sigh of exasperation. "Yesterday. OK?"

"What will you wear?"

"A dress, silly."

"I'm not silly. What kind of dress?"

Cassie comes up the stairs, smug with her classified information. "Amelia has a date to the prom. Finally."

"Shut up, Cassie. Hi, Aunt Delia." They breeze past me into the house. Amelia has more style in her left foot than I have in my whole body. Her jeans are impossibly skinny, her Converse are plain white, and she wears the same hoodie that every other sixteen-year-old girl wears. But she looks so cute, all big-eyed with long dark hair pulled back in a sloppy ponytail. She should have a hundred prom dates.

I've been trying to figure out how to manage this sleepover, and I don't have a single idea. The last time I hung out with teenage girls was when I was a teenage girl. My plan: I don't have a plan. We'll just see what happens.

"We're here because we don't like being at Dad's." Amelia looks matter of fact. "I'm just going to put that right out there."

"Creek Valley Close," Cassie says. "Apartments of doom. Smells like food."

"He's going to move," Amelia says.

"Shaaaag carpet," Cassie intones. "Rentallllll."

"Mean."

"You said it first."

"Not supposed to repeat it." Amelia looks at me to see what I think of this. I try to look nonjudgmental. God, they're a stand-up act.

"Mr. Serious!" Cassie screeches as the cat waddles in to investigate the new voices. He is the most doglike cat, walks right up to Cassie and flops flat on his back. She and Amelia both drop to the floor and turn into four-year-old girls, so glad to see their estranged friend.

"Now this is a cat," Amelia declares.

"I forgot how FAT he is."

"None fatter."

"Gargatron. Gargatronnnnnn." Cassie speaks in a million different accents.

"Remember Ginormo?" Amelia says.

"Ginormooooooooo. I miss you so much."

This goes on for a while. Amelia stands and says she's going to her room. "Which room are you in?" she asks me.

"Attic," I say. "I like a hideout."

Amelia looks at me with a puzzled expression. The weird aunt from Chicago.

In the kitchen, I lay out the Chinese takeout that I've foraged. I'm relieved to see that this idea works—the girls seem content to manufacture tubes of moo shoo chicken, though they aren't talking all that much.

Cassie picks up the Ethan Hardy CD and laughs. "Nice. You like this stuff?" she asks incredulously. "'Halo of Sorrow'?" she reads. "What kind of song is that?"

"He was here looking at the house," I explain. She sets it down quickly. "He's actually kind of sweet," I add.

"For a serial killer," she says.

So far so good. It's raining outside, as predicted, and it's a real Maria von Trapp scene up in my attic room. We'll be making playclothes out of curtains any minute. Amelia has commandeered my computer and is dissecting the latest status updates from her electronic friends.

"How many Friends do you have?" I ask.

She scrolls down. "843."

"That seems like a lot."

"I hide most of them."

"Sort of like real life, isn't it?" I say, and she laughs.

"Exactly. Filler."

Cassie snorts. "Half of them are her environmental hugger wuggers." She's got Mr. Serious draped across her lap like an afghan.

"Are not."

"She started a group of Hypermiler Jeep Owners."

I am confused. "What's a hypermiler?"

"Geeks who try to get 100 miles a gallon. Never run the AC, never roll down the windows. Coasting down hills. Only Amelia's got a gas-guzzler Jeep. So it's kind of stupid."

"Oh shut it, Cassie—Dad made me get a Jeep to be safer."

"Whatever," Cassie says dismissively, colossally bored. "How can you stay up here?" she asks me. "So lonely. We never came up here."

"I have a fear of comfort," I joke, then realize that I've just said something that's very likely true.

Cassie launches into a story about play tryouts at school. It sounds like she's going to be in *Alice in Wonderland*? Or her friend Jessie is? The tale grows complicated with callbacks and the issue of a kooky drama teacher, and I drift.

I don't know what to think. I look at these girls and I see a pair of Ginnas. Cassie's hair is exactly Ginna's: a deep golden color, almost brown underneath. It was the hair I coveted my entire childhood, and Ginna knew it. She was so much better at being pretty. Amelia doesn't look like Ginna at all—she's dark haired and pale like Bennett—but her hands flap just like her mother's, and she often stands with a Ginnalike hand on her hip, a little stubborn looking. She sounds exactly like her, and her voice rises at the ends of sentences—not a question but a hopefulness, encouraging you to agree with her. It's uncanny.

Henry creeps into my thoughts every few minutes. What has he been doing all day long?

Amelia looks up from the computer. "Can a friend come over? I just heard from somebody I haven't seen since." This construction, this incomplete, dangling "since" is so painful to me. Since.

A guy? She wants to have some guy come over and shack up here so that Bennett won't know? How appalling! How similar to something I would have done, back in the day.

"Mary Donald. She's a neighbor, switched to a different school. Dropped off the planet, basically. I haven't seen her in like ages." She stands and performs a yoga maneuver that leaves her on one foot, arms twisted behind her back. "I know we're supposed to be having bonding time and all, it's just, I mean, it's fine if you don't like want . . . Mary's mom is, you know." Her tone drops on the "you know." No, I don't know, but I'm going to go ahead and guess that Mary's mom isn't around anymore. Since.

Hold on. Mary Donald. Child of Angus Donald? Spawn of The Doomsayer? I hadn't thought that there could be a mini-Angus.

"Bring her on. I'd love to meet her. Do we need to go get her?"

She untangles then retangles herself. "She's like three doors down. Comes through the hedges in the back yard. It's like a tunnel in there."

A secret hedge tunnel! I can't believe it. Ginna was squirreling around in the back yard shrubbery with Angus while Bennett was out repairing NFL knee joints?

Ah, life. I have to call to let Angus know that I'm here. If I talk fast, it'll be over fast. "Hello, Angus? This is Delia Ballenger. I was just calling because Amelia, you know Amelia my niece, is staying over, here at the house, and she would just love it if Mary could come over tonight. Not a sleepover, just to visit."

"That's fine." He sounds so old. How could he have a teenage daughter? "I'll send her over."

"Great. I'll watch for her."

I've just spoken with the mighty Oz. Why am I so afraid of him?

Mary materializes at the back door, wet and very tiny, with the look of a silent movie actress: huge eyes, short dark pageboy and a shelf of bangs. Angus's straight, long nose comes right out of the middle.

The three girls head off to the den, where they hunker down in front of the television. I head for the sunroom so I can turn out the lights and watch the rain. I love rain. It means you can opt out, and tonight, it gives me the chance to pretend I'm doing something other than think about Henry, about last night. I can remember every single moment in perfect detail.

Sometime in the middle of that epic night, both of us still wired from the evening and each other, we talked. It was so quiet in that room, such a funny conversation, like a radio interview. So dark. His voice was right there, but I could barely see him.

He asked me about Chicago. Whenever I tell people I live there, they always say "oh, Chicago" in a dreamy way, then they tell me the last time they went to Chicago as if to validate their credentials as a lover of Chicago. Everybody loves Chicago. Henry doesn't. He was funny: he went into this aria about how no place that flat could be good for anybody's soul, the evils of a grid, how it looks like a big city but it's still in the Midwest which cancels out everything. "Nashville people love Chicago because it's easy. It's New York for the timid."

I went into a stirring defense. I said something fairly disparaging about Nashville, pointing out how no city with "ville" in the name is a real city, and he found this funny. He thought I was wrong. "Fightin' words! You have your idea of what it's like here. You're basing everything on your life twenty years ago. You gotta move on! The Peking Garden Restaurant is no longer here, I'm telling you. I just want to show you."

"So show me."

"We civic boosters can't have this negativity. Hurts our feelings," he said in the tone of an aggrieved bureaucrat.

"Such a booster."

"Rootless child, you poor rootless child. You don't even know what you're missing, cutting off your roots the way you do. Life is so much richer, so very much more meaningful, if you plant yourself in a place that will nourish you."

He was very theatrical, declaring this. "Well that was poetic," I said. "Nashville. I can't get over all the churches. More than ever. 'What church do you attend?' This woman at the grocery store asked me. Just like that! Recruiting in the checkout line. I guess I looked unwashed."

"Church," he said. "Church is comforting to people."

Surprising. "To you?"

"No," he said quickly. "Not to me." That was a relief. I couldn't deal with a churchy Henry. "Look. What's your apartment like in Chicago? What's your life like? Who are your people?"

I described my apartment, trying to make it sound more glamorous than it is. I described my wildly convenient work-at-home set-up, leaving out the part about not always getting out of bed. I told him about my book group, though I didn't mention the fact that we haven't met in eight months. I definitely did not mention the time that a bowl of popcorn kernels in my sink sprouted when I neglected to do my dishes for a while. And I told him how Chicago was an asylum for me, an escape from my domineering, ignoring mother.

"An asylum or an *asylum*?" he asked. "Seriously. What could be so bad that you would rather live in a place without a Station Inn? They don't even have Krystal."

"You're the one who left town for—how many years?"

"A tale for another day. But I will say one thing: however hard I was running away, now that I'm back, it would take a crowbar to pry me loose."

It was right then that I felt sleep wash over me, even though I wanted to keep talking. He slid his hand into mine, and my last thought was, *We're holding hands.*

Watching the sheets of rain flash outside, I wonder what he's doing tonight. I don't know what it is about Henry. He says he has so much to tell me. He should be here right now. There's no time to waste. So why do I hesitate to make the next move? It's so old fashioned of me, but I can't pick up the phone. Even the most independent woman in the world knows better than to do that. There's modern, and there's slutty.

Curiosity takes hold of me. Online, Ethan Hardy isn't an obese biker with a stripper girlfriend and a giant pickup truck. He's an international (if you count Canada) country phenomenon. His website is elaborate, with videos of him performing his number-one-smash hit "Drink Up, Boys (It's Closing Time Somewhere)" in front of huge festival crowds. His message boards are insane with love for the guy. He's huge. For $49.95 you can be a Hardy Lover, and for $99.95 you become An Anointed One with a meet-and-greet Party Hardy at the CMA Music Festival. I read all about Hardy Aid, his charity effort in Africa. There's a picture of him in Ethiopia, holding a tiny baby in his enormous, burly arms, an inked "LOVE" trailing up one forearm, "HARD" up the other. With his arms curled around the baby, "HARD LOVE" is how it reads.

He was so sweet to Sugar, so crazy for her. What a pair. Ethan Hardy has that rare skill, the ability to connect with people. I mean, here I am on the verge of punching in my credit card to be An Anointed One to this redneck from Hickman County.

At about ten o'clock, the doorbell rings. Henry? Henry would just show up in a driving rain to see me. Wouldn't he?

The figure peering in the narrow window beside the door is too tall to be Henry.

The door almost opens itself, the wind is so fierce. "I came to get Mary," Angus says. The rain blows sideways, directly into the house.

"Come in," I say automatically.

He leans his umbrella against the wall, and it immediately flies off the porch into the boxwoods. "Monsoon weather," he says with a small smile and steps into the front hall. "This is rain."

Angus is the sort of tall that is surprising every time you encounter it. He's up there, with a view available to him that most of us never see. He can probably see into the top of the undusted light fixture above me. He takes off his bright yellow rain slicker, and there it is: Ginna's sweater, dark gray, a fine piece of knitting. For pity's sake.

Now, there have been a few times in life when I have been truly flummoxed. When I got caught with a fake ID at Rotier's. When my prom date ditched me. (I know I've mentioned this before, but I'm still working through that one.) But this sweater, this garment of infidelity, this scarlet letter done up in Shetland wool—I know exactly what it is, but I can't say anything about it. What I want to say: "I can't believe you're wearing that gloomy souvenir! Could there be a sweater more loaded with awfulness? Do you not understand that the destruction of an entire family is embedded in its every stitch! Remove that thing, this minute!" What I actually say: "Amazing rain. Quite a rain," and I find myself gesturing toward the murky living room, as if I'm going to chat with him while waiting for his adorable daughter to emerge from the den. He looks down at the puddle of water at his feet, slides off his sodden loafers, and shrugs with apology. They're the biggest feet I've ever seen, narrow and long. Snow skis.

We sit, Angus sinking into Ginna's downy cloud of a sofa, where they probably canoodled when everybody else was out at the middle school play. He lobs out a "Mary was glad to hear from Amelia," to which I reply, "Amelia says she's at a new school. That must be interesting." He nods, and we digest that. He looks less like a homewrecker than a damp college professor. I can't help but steal glances at that sweater. Does he actually wear it every day?

"I should probably tell you something," he says. He looks nervous, which makes me nervous. What? "I think your gutters are overflowing."

House advice. He's giving me house advice. "Yeah, I don't really have gutters in Chicago, so . . ."

He nods. "The source of much unhappiness, an uncleaned gutter."

Spoken like a true homeowner.

"Any takers?" He's looking around the room, like a buyer.

"Not yet. The market's pretty bad, but I'm hopeful. Have to be, I guess."

The legs of Angus's pants are soaked. He looks like he waded through a pond to get there. "The other day," he says quietly. "What I said. I came because I wanted to apologize."

Did I just hear that correctly? This slow-rolling home maintenance chat is screeching into a ditch of apology? I've been stewing about our roadside chat and his shockingly accurate summary of Ginna's feelings about me, particularly his comment that Ginna needed me but wouldn't ask for my help. That one accusation kills me. "Well, you didn't say anything that wasn't true."

"Things were not going well. That day."

"Your wall looks great now."

He shakes his head. "I don't know if you know this, but my wife died four years ago. Breast cancer."

"I'm so sorry."

"So it's Mary and me." He tries to say it in a sturdy way, but I hear the incompleteness of that situation. Angus seems to be deep in thought, pulling out the words. "There are days that just seem. Insurmountable. Difficult. Not myself, half the time. You'd think by now I'd have a handle on things. Feels like it happened yesterday."

A fresh wound. I see it. Maybe he misses his wife, but he's talking about Ginna. Clearly talking about her. He looks up at me, his patrician face troubled. "You miss your sister."

He misses my sister. We both miss my sister. I nod, and find myself suddenly and perilously close to tears. "So much. I hate this so much. Didn't know 'til I got here. It's like it just happened."

Angus is watching me closely. I can't really hide my feelings, and neither can he. The tears rise in my eyes, as they do so often these days, then leak down my cheeks. He passes a hand across his face, grinds the heel of his palm against his eye.

Mary appears, with Cassie and Amelia trailing her. Mrs. Angus must have been a small, dark-haired person with limpid-pool eyes. It must kill Angus to have this echo of his wife with him all the time. "Here they are," he says, unfolding himself from the sofa. The girls are scheming up a plan for the next day, and the evening ends with Angus stepping back into his shoes and bundling his daughter in his enormous yellow slicker, which covers her like a tent in the rain.

Increasing House Clutter

I wake up early to the drumming of rain on the roof, not far above my head. This attic room was a true attic back in the day, so there's only a thin layer of house between the elements and me.

In Chicago, I rarely check the forecast, because no matter what happens, my daily life grinds on, whether the sidewalk has snow on it, or rain, or blistering heat. But this rain, which seems awfully rainy, makes me curious, so I head downstairs to the kitchen TV.

People in Nashville love to worry about weather. Mother can wax operatic in her description of the Tornado of '98. The Ice Storm of '94 is one of her finest horror stories, with the limbs of hackberries cracking like rifle fire and the frenzied dumping of antifreeze into toilets. Mother claims that weather in Nashville is much worse than it used to be. My suspicion is that watching enough StormTrackerInstaVueDoppler2000 would make anybody think this.

The weather radar shows a long, thick line of dark red blobbiness west of Nashville, and the weather person seems to be excited. I wonder about the gutters, now that both Henry and Angus have indicated that I'm headed for trouble. Cleaning out second-story gutters on a house like this seems like something that requires trained professionals who are used to monkeying up ladders.

As I brush my teeth in the cramped attic bathroom, I see my circle of pills on the shelf above the sink. I've taken them for years now, more to cut down on cramps than to prevent a baby. It's not like dodging pregnancies is a chronic challenge, but it does give me comfort to think that I'm not going to end up pregnant after hooking up with some random guy in an abandoned car-repair building. I think about Sugar and her enormous, doting husband, and I wonder what it would be like not to take this pill, to let my hormones operate, to have a fat, blue-eyed baby. I stop, shocked, at this crazy piece of thinking. I stare at myself in the mirror: I'm imagining a baby-sized Henry, like a medieval painting of the Madonna with Jesus standing on her lap, adult-faced and scaled like a doll. A Henry baby. I have never wanted a baby in my life. I take a pill, fast, feeling shivery and nervous and embarrassed.

We head to the Pancake Pantry. The line is shorter than usual because of the rain, but Cassie would have put us through the full wait no matter what. I'm glad to get out of the house, glad to be going somewhere with these girls. I haven't been to the Pancake Pantry in decades. It seems to be in a new building, but the vibe is still the same: businessmen stoking up for the day ahead, scruffy music industry types in fleece jackets, Vanderbilt students who look too young to be in college, and one table with a baby, who blithely drops pancakes onto the ground while his mother digs around in her mini Conestoga wagon for a crucial baby supply that seems to be missing.

We contemplate pancakes. The girls debate bacon. Cassie is pro, her big sister very much opposed. How does a sixteen year old know so much about the evils of modern-day meat processing? And how can a twelve year old argue the merits of pig so persuasively?

My phone rings.

"Hey," Henry says. "Good morning."

Shudder of delight. He sounds so magnificently awake. "Hello." So embarrassed.

"What are you up to?"

"Eating. With the girls. Pancake Pantry." Henry lives less than three blocks away. If there is a God, Henry will invite himself for pancakes.

"That's funny—I live right down the street." Who knew? "Would it be rude if I joined you?"

I look at the girls and quickly realize I should see him later, after they go home. "Maybe later? I shall die if I don't see you," I say in a fake desperate voice that isn't actually fake when you get right down to it. Amelia trades a look of surprise with Cassie, thinking I don't see it.

"Who was that?" Cassie asks. I'm learning that she is as blunt as Bennett, but considerably more charming about it.

"Cassie," Amelia scolds.

"I won't actually die," I say. "It's somebody I went to high school with. Henry. Henry Peek." That sounds neutral enough.

"Not your boyfriend?" Cassie asks.

"A friend."

Amelia looks shrewd and says in a singsongy voice, "A friend who is a boy."

"He is cute," I say. "But life is complicated."

"You like him," Cassie says. She is ruthless.

"I do."

"Well, I think he's very cute."

"You know him?"

"No, but I think I'm looking at him," and Cassie points behind me to the guy who is making a big show of trying to sneak up on me. He's bundled up in a rain jacket, streaming water, such a welcome sight.

We pull a chair for Henry, and he sits, wiping his glasses with the tail of his shirt. He tells the girls that he had to meet them, having heard so much about them from me. "She says you are evil, wretched girls and she was dreading spending two seconds with you."

Amelia says, "Well, we mostly heard that she was an evil wretched aunt."

Cassie says, "Actually, we didn't know much of what she's like. Aunt Delia spends all her time working. In Chicago."

He looks at me, but I can't hold his gaze. Too much, to see him right here.

He appears to have had three cups of coffee. Did he run all the way here? "Ready for your open house? It's supposed to do this all weekend." He points at the window, where a woman passes with an umbrella hunkered low against the downpour. "House hunters hate to get wet."

"What?" Cassie asks.

I shrug. "I'm supposed to be having an open house tomorrow, but it looks like it's going to be rained out."

It floats right across her face, a cloud. She looks at Amelia, and Amelia looks down at her orange juice.

"What's up?" I ask.

Amelia has such an open face. At the moment, it looks aggrieved. "Nothing."

"Nothing," Cassie says.

We all sit, with Nothing taking up a lot of room at the table.

Pancakes arrive, thank heavens, the blessed Bears in the Snow that Cassie explains she has ordered since she was two.

"These ones are kind of wrong," she says. "The bear heads are so small."

We're outside, on the sidewalk, when Cassie loses it. She was quiet through the rest of breakfast, and I knew she was feeling something, so when I look over at her and see the tears streaming down her face, I feel the same thing. I don't want to sell the house, either. I don't want to be doing this. I shouldn't have to be selling the house, and they shouldn't have to be visitors in their own home, and Ginna should be here. Amelia wraps her arms around her sister, as I suspect she has done on many occasions, and we all cry together in a huddle, without a word. Henry, poor Henry, stands alongside us, head down, holding his umbrella over us as if that will keep us dry.

Amelia lets Cassie sit in the front seat on the way home, which is important because the front-seat sitter runs the radio, and Amelia wants to be kind. I'd forgotten about music when you're a teenager and the world is so new, how it sorts so many things, how voracious the appetite is for it, how it provides such easy and obvious markers. Cassie runs through the stations, setting my radio buttons as she goes. "Lightning 100 is the only station worth listening to," she says.

"WRVU," Amelia says.

Cassie nods and fiddles with the buttons. Even I remember WRVU, the Vanderbilt campus station. Such an oddball mix of DJs, you could get show tunes or reggae, depending on the hour. Cassie arrives at 91.1 and the long, high wail of hard-bit bluegrass. "Wait—Punch Brothers," Amelia says. This is somehow important to them both, and there is much discussion of the mandolin player's extreme cuteness, so we make our way home to the sound of this heartbroken mandolin. Schoolgirls listening to bluegrass. I give up trying to understand.

I'm still upset. I hate that the subject of the house sale came up, and I'm sorry that Henry got caught up in it. It's not that I haven't been worrying about it—the very idea of having the girls over to spend the night worried me. It's crushing, that's all, to see Cassie that way: so sturdy one minute, so melted the next.

The continuing rain makes me want to check the radar again—I'm becoming such a Nashvillian. The TV in the den is humongous. Bennett apparently had a midlife crisis involving electronics, so watching TV is an exercise that involves three remote controls and a subwoofer that makes my teeth ache. I finally locate Channel 4, the go-to station of my youth, which is Channel 232 on this insane apparatus. In high definition, five feet across, something impossible is happening: a building is floating down I-24.

Amelia comes into the room and exclaims "WOW. Is that here?" Cassie sits on the floor, dragging Mr. Serious into her lap as usual and says, "That is so epic." I immediately reach for my phone to call Henry.

"Are you near a TV?" I ask.

"What? Are the girls OK?"

"They're fine—go check WSM."

It seems that a portable classroom has floated off a flatbed truck and set sail down the interstate. Cars are strewn like toys all over the highway, flooded to the roofs. A burly guy in a tank top clambers to the top of his big rig like he's rock climbing. As we watch, the drifting building catches a corner on a truck, and as the current continues to push, the building stops, then in a matter of seconds buckles, collapses, and pretty much vanishes into a tangle of wreckage.

"That's crazy," Henry says. "That's not normal." The footage plays and replays, as if the TV producer can't believe what he's seeing, either. "Mill Creek? It runs near there. But not that near."

"When did all this happen? I didn't think it had rained enough to flood."

"Yeah. It's low over there." We listen to the reporter reviewing road closings and power outages. The rain falls in an abject, flat-out way.

"Delia. Can't believe how stupid I was to bring up the house thing. Wasn't thinking. So stupid." Henry sounds crestfallen.

"I know. It had to come up at some point. The For Sale sign's in the front yard, I mean. But we hadn't gotten to it."

"Still. So sorry."

"Anyway. Just wanted to share the floating building."

He laughs a little. "Would you call when you're free?"

"I would."

I go upstairs to find Cassie, who tends to nest in her room like a hamster. She's lying on her bed with Mr. Serious wedged up against her head, and she has a solemn stillness about her.

"This is your house now, isn't it?" she asks.

Such an awful question.

"Well, your mom left it to me in her will. But, you know, I live in Chicago, and I can't afford a house like this. So I have to sell it." I told Bennett a while back that I wouldn't get into the issue of giving the proceeds to them. Too hard for a teenager to know that she's about to inherit a pile of money.

"Why don't you sell it to Dad? He said he's going to look for a house.

Then we could still live here."

How can I tell her that her dad doesn't want to live here, that it's more complicated than she knows, that her dad specifically told me that under no circumstance would he move back into this house. "Well, he's probably wanting a different kind of house."

"Like how? Like tacky like Carla?"

"I haven't met Carla. What's she like?"

"Carla is a big fat redneck"—she has slipped into her cornpone accent—"with a nasty little dog and she smokes."

What a characterization. "But other than that she's great," I say.

She nods. "Right. She's like the opposite of Mom. Mom couldn't stand her."

"Your mom met her?"

"Sort of. Once. When Dad was dropping us back at home, and Carla was in the car too, and Mom saw her sitting there and then she called him to say it was wrong of him to have Carla around us. I don't know." She sighs and runs a hand across Mr. Serious's enormous belly. "She reads like romances and stuff."

I can remember Ginna hitting the roof over Carla. "She's just so . . . not it," she said to me after Bennett moved out. "Maybe I'm not it, either, but she's absolutely not it." But I'm also remembering Bennett's story about the Angus Donald Knitting Project, and how tangled the whole situation must have been. Bennett's furious at Ginna, Ginna is furious and guilty, neither of them are good talkers, so the marriage spirals down in a swirl of silent misery. There's Cassie, caught in the middle and watching the whirlpool head down the drain.

"Can we stay another night? Amelia wants to stay, too." Cassie says this into Mr. Serious's belly.

Unexpected. "If it's OK with your dad. You want me to call?"

A muffled "yes."

I guess I shouldn't feel proud about it, but I do feel a small triumph over the fact that the girls want to stay. They didn't hate it.

I text Bennett, because he doesn't answer his phone. He calls back almost instantly. So annoying, Dr. Passive Aggressive.

I tell him that the girls and I have had a great time, and they'd like to stay another night.

"Fine," he says. "Just as well. I'm between procedures right now. I've got a bad compound fracture. Guy swept away by the water. Out on the Harpeth. Like a blender. Things are crazy."

I go lie down in the guest room, so lush, where it is very easy to transport myself back to a recent night—two nights ago? It seems so long ago that Henry was here.

Henry. I dial. "I need some real estate advice. If you're in a metropolitan area where there is widespread flooding, is that a good time to have an open house?"

"Just let me sell your damn house, Delia. I have answers to that and many other questions. I am a trained professional. I do this, like, every day. I am highly regarded for my integrity and ability to return a phone call. I can't believe I'm bragging like this."

"I can't afford you. And." Hate to say it but have to say it. "It's awkward for us to be in a business relationship."

"I told you, I would do it for free."

"Even worse! A pity listing!"

"Not exactly. Though I admit I do have an ulterior motive."

"Which is . . ."

"Impressing you."

"You'd give up a commission to impress me?" He laughs. "I hate to tell you, but I'm a cheap date. Dinner impresses me. Bad dancing impresses me."

"My offer stands."

Lying here, in this triple-puff downy bed, I don't have a single thing to say to Henry. All I want is to know that he's there, at the other end of the line.

"Oh!" I say. "The girls are staying again tonight."

"That's great. They like you."

"Or they like not being at home, more likely. Their dad has this girlfriend that they keep describing as a walrus. I still don't know how to talk to them. They like the weirdest music."

"That was an old-lady thing to say."

Which sends us off into a discussion of music, not unlike many phone conversations I had in high school with a boy, when talking about music was how you talked about each other. It's one of those conversations that goes on so long that your ear gets hot, and you have to switch the receiver to the other ear.

———

There's a small room at the top of the main stairs, Ginna's office. I think it used to be a landing, but Ginna built a wall and installed French doors so that she would have her own little space. Why do women do this? They move into these extravagant houses, with all the space in the world, then they carve out a squirrelly nest with no room for anything, and they spend ninety percent of their time crammed into their dim lair with a computer printer stuck under their feet. At least Ginna allowed herself a view, a wide window that looks out on the back yard into the trees.

I sit at her desk, which looks probably the same as it did on the day she died. I ought to sort through all these papers, but I seem to be unable to deal with even my own papers these days.

The green of the trees is gorgeous, livid against the stormy sky. There's no texture to this sky, no clouds, only a million buckets of battleship gray paint. It's a sky that looks like it will always be there, a flat backdrop, and I can't tell whether it's two o'clock or six o'clock. I look down to see if Ginna's roses are blooming yet, but it's not the garden that surprises me. The little creek that runs behind the house has grown up. It's a big creek now, busy, crawling across Ginna's secret garden to the point that the benches are surrounded by muddy brown water. The water, which looks to have a decent current to it, is less than ten feet from the rose garden. When did this happen? Who turned on the muddy brown water spigot?

It doesn't take a licensed realtor to know that this is not something that a potential house buyer wants to see. I need to cancel the open house tomorrow. This is a relief, because now the girls won't have to witness my pathetic attempts to fluff the house. More important, they won't be reminded that their house is for sale, right out from under them.

The girls and I are watching *Sleepless in Seattle*, which Amelia gets and Cassie thinks is sort of geriatric. They think of Tom Hanks the way I think of Douglas Fairbanks, Jr. We are hunkered down with blankets and popcorn in the dark, a homemade movie theater. Amelia's cell phone glows under her blanket as she keeps a steady stream of texts rolling. Who's in there with her?

We change channels occasionally to see the weather radar. The diagonal line of red blobby looks to be exactly where it was six hours ago. Weather Lady seems to think it's not going to move for another eighteen hours, and she seems to think that the Gulf of Mexico is basically being piped into Middle Tennessee.

My phone rings. Mother. I sneak out to the kitchen to talk. "Delia. The rain. Have you seen the rain?"

"I have." Where does she think I've been for the past day?

"This is something. I just don't know." She sounds rattled, which is one of several New Mother characteristics that I cannot get used to.

"Mother, is everything OK?"

"Well, Shelly can't get home, because I-40 is flooded—"

"Flooded?"

"Out past Bellevue. So she's just sort of stuck. So she's staying over tonight." Shelly lives way out west of town near the Harpeth River, where she keeps chickens and goats. When we were growing up, Shelly would take us out there to see them. I always liked the goats, the way they thought nothing of standing on the roof of the shed, waiting for Shelly to return.

"The interstate is flooded?"

"Shelly's brother says it's like a parking lot. Backed up for miles. People sleeping in their cars. No hotel rooms left."

This rain is really something. "Hope her house is OK. Are you OK?"

"I suppose. Delia. Have you ever wondered about Ginna, why she was so distant to me?" These blunt questions of the heart are so unnerving, another aspect of New Mother. I'd love to have a talk with her therapist, to find out what exactly they're up to. Somebody has cracked open the lead casing of Mother's soul.

I never thought of Ginna as distant. I was the avoider, not Ginna. She was the one who lived here, who would go to Mother's fundraising events and kooky costume parties, who paraded the granddaughters at the requested moments. Ginna didn't seem distant at all, to me.

"She did have little kids, Mother. That's pretty distracting, you know. And dealing with Bennett was no piece of cake."

"Bennett," she says. "I always forget about Bennett. He's a cold fish, isn't he?"

We're the cold fish. We're the distant ones. Ginna was the warm fish.

Mother sighs. "I do wonder what would have happened if she'd waited. To marry him."

"Yeah." I have wondered the same thing. Ginna and Bennett married in a fever, less than a year out of college, in the gothic gloomy splendor of Sewanee's mothership All Saints Chapel, during a weekend that felt as much like an extended fraternity party as a wedding. Bennett was all about order, and checking things off his list. A doctor needed a wife, he seemed to think, and the beautiful Ginna was as good as he could hope to find. Ginna was happy to be married, pleased to have a baby at what seemed to me a shocking age. The baby Amelia turned up barely a year after the wedding, and Ginna quickly, irrevocably disappeared into a world I didn't understand at all. The first time she handed her baby to me, I felt like I was holding a piece of rare porcelain. To a fifteen year old, a baby is not all that different from a collectible. Put it on a plate stand. That thing might break.

"You know, Mother, Ginna was the one who was always trying to pull us together. You and I are the ones who resisted."

"I never resisted," Mother says, indignant. "We had a standing lunch at the club, every Sunday." Man, the things Ginna put up with, the frozen tomato consumed in the name of family harmony.

I give up. "So Shelly's staying over?"

"She is."

"Say hi to her."

"I will. And Delia—have you sold the house yet?"

"Not yet, but soon. There's tons of interest. I can just feel it."

"Is that Henry Peek helping you?"

"No, Mother. Henry Peek is not helping." No way am I going to tip my hand about the situation with Henry. If Mother knew we'd been having a slumber party over here, she would broadcast that juicy tidbit all over town. And she'd take credit for the whole thing.

"Oh!" She sounds surprised.

"What? Did you think he was going to?"

"No, it's just. He's awfully smart. He did call you, didn't he?"

"Yes, Mother. Showed up on my doorstep last week, thanks to you. Such a schemer, putting him up to it."

"If you had a bit of sense, you'd let him do it." She pauses. "Wouldn't cost you a dime."

What? "What are you talking about?"

"Oh, all right. I'll tell you. I wasn't going to. But. The commission. Really, Delia, it was supposed to be a secret." She actually chuckles. "I told him I'd cover the commission if he could get you to agree to let him list your house for free."

I've been standing at the breakfast room window, simultaneously watching the rain outside and my reflection in the glass of the window. I lean in closely to see myself, jaw dropped. I manage to squeeze out, "You never told me this."

"No sense dragging out this house sale. Absolutely no reason to drive yourself crazy. But I figured you wouldn't like it, so no, I didn't tell you."

I feel the flush creep up my neck. She did this? She did the thing again that she does. Unbelievable. "You're damn right I wouldn't like it! This is my business, not yours. You can't just swoop in and pay off a guy to sell my house for me. That's not your choice to make. I don't want your help!"

"Well, you turned him down anyway, so what's the difference?"

I hang up the phone before I can hear her try to make it sound like this was an OK thing for her to do. "Dammit dammit dammit," I say into the kitchen sink.

I turn around, and Amelia is standing in the doorway. Under all that shiny, dark hair is one of the more world-weary expressions that I've ever seen. "Grandma," she sighs. "Piece of work." And we both burst out laughing. Thank God she's here, because if she weren't, I would be crying by this point, thinking about Henry Peek, wheeling and dealing behind my back.

Overflowing

I wake up in the middle of the night, but the fact is, I haven't slept well at all. It's so dark that I can't see. There's a drumming of rain above me, shifting, rising and falling as if someone is spraying a garden hose over the roof.

What a sucker I am, what a fool. I can hear his charming voice, that night at the secret supper. "We're fiends. We lie." He told me himself, and still I fell for it.

Buying off Henry. I can't believe it. He wouldn't take the commission, would he? Surely he can recognize the craven machinations of my scheming mother. Can't he?

Did she not learn anything the last time she tried this, when she prepaid my rent without telling me? I've spent most of my life trying to escape this woman and her misguided ideas about money, about meddling, yet she continues to monkey around in my life. There she is, a woman who has spent her entire career in legal courts, where evidence rules the day, when precedent determines what happens next. Yet she has this compulsion to go renegade when it comes to me—there are no rules, apparently.

She has a complicated view of money. When my dad died, back when I was a toddler, my mother became a rich woman. She was also stingy, having grown up on a farm south of Nashville, where she learned how to make milk last longer by watering it down. She thinks money corrupts young people, that it can be just the thing that sucks the starch out of a person, so she used to give us measly allowances and make us get summer jobs. She also believes that a Cadillac is a lot more fun than a Toyota. She once told me that the secret to happiness is services.

She cannot understand that I don't want her help. She has failed consistently, over a period of decades, to do the little things that any normal mother does, but she whips out her checkbook in these grand gestures that totally undermine me. It's so stunningly inadequate.

I head down to the kitchen to find whatever I can that involves chocolate. The girls have laid waste to the Mint Milanos. I head for the failsafe option of Ginna's freezer. She hoarded Girl Scout Thin Mints the way survivalists stock up on freeze-dried beef.

My plan is to eat the whole box.

The TV in the den is still flickering, so I go in to see what's happening with the rain. I'm feeding myself Thin Mints, one by one, then two by two, my disbelief about Henry giving way to something more pitiful, that feeling of having dropped something fragile on the floor. The reporter on slicker duty is standing in the dark on an I-40 overpass, explaining how backed up the traffic is because of the flood, the rain flashing in the glare of the camera, the occasional raindrop blurring the lens. The line of red taillights extends behind him to infinity.

Henry is so sincere. He wouldn't take it. I think. My insecurity about Henry is now complete. I have no idea what to make of this.

I head toward the back stairs, finally sleepy, when a crashing sound in the basement makes me jump so badly that I trip over Ginna's pink bathrobe and slide into the wall. What the hell was that? This is why I live in a one-room apartment—I can see all four corners at all times. I consider the possibility of hiding in the attic until daybreak.

But that sound was not a wild animal loose in my house. It wasn't a home invasion. I tell myself it was just something doing something. Gravity. Or something. I open the basement door, and I reach in to turn on the light. Jebus, what a basement. The wooden stairs haven't been painted since 1942, and the bare bulbs cast a harsh, shadowy light. I can't believe my courage at opening this door.

I also can't believe what I'm seeing at the bottom of the stairs. A batch of clear plastic bins are floating, bobbing a little because of some recent disturbance, in about a foot of water.

I don't know how long I sit at the top of the stairs, watching this Poseidon Adventure in my own house, but it's a good long while. My stomach aches from all the chocolate, and my feet are cold. The bins seem to be rising, slowly, and at one dramatic point they slip over the bottom stair and float into place one step higher. They're coming to get me. It's a slow-motion horror story.

I can't help but watch this watery drama unfold. Ginna's basement runs under the entire house. This is a tremendous amount of water. How high will it go? The silence of the basement is broken by a splashing sound, and I see a crack in the old stone foundation spouting water like one of those fountains where a little frog spits at you.

Somewhere in a fog of sleepiness, I have the sickening thought that Henry is a gigolo. I imagine him in his velvet smoking jacket, wandering the suburbs of west Nashville, smooth-talking a helmet-haired matron in her Lilly Pulitzer capri pants. No ranch house is safe from his intentions. She touches his ascot; the deal is done.

There's a loud knock at the front door, insistent. I stand, so stiff from my basement vigil that I have to stretch for a minute. Somewhere under the thick clouds, the sun has risen, and the dim day has begun. I look out the breakfast room window and find that Ginna's yard is covered in deep puddles of water, saturated. The ground has absorbed all it can and has given up.

The improbable duo of Mother and Shelly stands at the door. Each has a small suitcase in her hand. Shelly is wearing a plastic rain bonnet of the sort that was popular in the 1960s. Mother looks pale and old, no lipstick.

"Hi," Mother says.

I'm still furious at her. "Hi."

"We're flooded out."

"Come on in," I say.

It sounds pretty bad out at Mother's. Richland Creek has overrun its banks, wild, and unfortunately, Mother's house backs up to it. "It happened just like that," she says. "Right in through the den, the kitchen. A river, right there. The furniture . . . I don't know. I just don't know. Still rising when we left. We were up all night." She is definitely rattled, talking about the flood as if it's a puzzle she can't solve.

Shelly doesn't even know what the deal is at her place. Her brother, who lives next door, isn't answering his cell phone. She is very worried. "The goats'll figure out what to do," she says. "They're goats. But the chickens don't have a lot of sense."

"Stay here," I say. This seems obvious. You can't kick out your own mother, even if you mostly want to. Home is the place where, when my mom comes over, I have to take her in. And Shelly. I wish Shelly would stay here forever.

"I'll try to find us a hotel for tonight," Mother says.

"Don't worry about it. Plenty of room. You may have to bail water at some point." I try to keep it perky for Shelly, but I am sodden with anger at my mother.

Amelia comes into the room, wearing those little shorts that girls wear these days, and a pair of tall rubber rain boots. "Grandma! Shelly!" She gives each a hug. "Mary's coming over. We're going to go play in the creek." Cassie trails in after her, in pink Crocs and those same tiny shorts. For the first time in my life, I think, *Those girls need to cover up.*

Shelly looks skeptical, too. "Y'all stay out of the water, OK? They're saying it's full of all kinds of nasty."

I haven't even gotten dressed yet, so I go up to the attic, and on the way, I decide to call Henry right this minute. I'm not sure what to say to him, but I need to say it fast before I lose my nerve. He answers with a cheerful "Hey," and I launch.

"Henry."

"Delia." Playful.

"I." Don't know what to say.

"Hm?"

"Look. I." I feel a strand of resolve pulling me forward. "I don't usually use a lot of profanity, but I fucking can't believe my mother would try to talk you into a back-room deal. Involving ME. I can't believe it. She told me all about it." I am shaking. It hurts my feelings so much. "She's."

"Delia."

"It's like doing a deal with the devil! Don't you know? I can't believe . . ." My resolve is slipping fast, my upset billowing over the top. "Look, the basement is leaking like the Titanic. I have stuff to do. I can't believe you wouldn't even mention this to me," I squeeze out with one last semi-gaspy breath. "Goodbye. Henry."

I hang up and glare at the phone, then of course I dissolve into sloppy tears, mopping my eyes with a sock. The crying goes on and on, waves of it, the sucking, sour crying that's like throwing up when you've already thrown up everything there is to throw up.

Hysterics combined with lack of sleep leaves me trembly and queasy, and I flop on my miserable canoe of a bed, boo freaking hoo.

I wake up, face down on my bed, drooling like a baby, a tremendous crick in my neck. My scratchy eyes have run out of tears. Somebody is calling me, far downstairs. "Delia! Come down!" I slide into whatever clothes are on the floor by the bed and hold my head at a crick-minimizing tilt that makes me feel like I was assembled wrong.

"Our hero," Shelly says cheerfully as I come around the landing on the stairs. She has her arm around Henry, who stands in the front hall with a Black & Decker 12-gallon Shop Vac and an apparatus that looks like a science fair project.

"I was just going to leave these. But she wanted you to come down." He looks terrible, absolutely terrible. His quick eyes have a crashed look to them. He points at the gizmo. "It's a sump pump."

I nod. I can't even say words. It's so upsetting to see him, so generous of him to come, so crushing that Mother has come between us. He brought me a sump pump because he knew that I would have no idea that I even needed a sump pump.

He turns to go, wordless as well, and I sit on the stairs, watching him through the leaded-glass side window as he makes his way in the rain. He wears tall rubber boots. His hood slides off his head as he opens the car door. He turns and runs back up the steps, head down against the rain. "Shelly," I say. "He's back at the door."

She opens it, and Henry stands there, dripping wet, glasses blurry with rain. I am swamped, myself, by my confusion at seeing him so soon. I can't find any words. He says apologetically, "You need a hose. For the pump. You hook it up to a garden hose and run it out a window."

"OK," I say. "A hose." He's trying to leave, but he wants to stay. He is here because he wants to help, and he knows I need help. "OK. We got it," I say, in as dismissive a tone as I can muster. He nods, hesitant, then turns and leaves. His hood flies off his head again in the wind.

Shelly shuts the door and turns to me, mystified at this Kabuki play. "No need to be so short," she says.

Mother comes in from the kitchen as Shelly and I contemplate the equipment sitting on Ginna's prized Heriz rug. I'm thinking about help, about what it means to show up like that, immediately after being yelled at.

"I made some more coffee," Mother says, then stops. "Sump pump! That's a fancy one." Mother's farm upbringing pops up at the strangest times.

"Where'd this come from?"

"Henry," Shelly says. Mother steals a look at me, and maybe I glare back at her.

"Mother, you take Ginna's room, OK? And Shelly, guest room?" I stand, the crick in my neck making me list to the left. Mother wanders off, shaking her head.

"That basement is filling up," Shelly says. "I never seen anything like this rain." She looks closely at the sump pump. "Wish Henry stayed. He could rig this up." She looks up at me. "Give him a call?"

"We can figure it out," I say, but Shelly looks at me with a puzzled expression, as if I am crazy not to have her beloved Henry on the scene. If she only knew the story.

"He's not all that," I hiss. "He's a schemer."

"What is with you, Delia?"

"Not everybody is what they appear," I say. "Not everybody is so noble and good."

"You're rigging up this thing?" The pump looks completely mysterious. "OK. I'll call."

At the top of the staircase, I stop in Ginna's office to use the phone. The morning's vista into the backyard below is a stunner: a chocolate brown mirror, water up to the edge of the terrace, as if the big creek of yesterday melted into the back yard. Is it going to come in the house? It doesn't even matter—it's already in the house. Ginna's rose garden has vanished. Only the tops of the roses show now, an outline of what was there before. We have set sail in this colonial revival ship of fools.

Ginna's phone cord is so twisted that I have to hunker down low to use the receiver. Had she never heard of a cordless phone? Did she not know that technology could solve this?

"Hi," I say. It's just a river of embarrassment flowing through me today, that churning combination of terror and self-loathing.

"Hey."

Just say it. "Shelly thinks—you could help. With the pump. If you have time, I mean."

"Be right there."

"Thanks."

I sigh and recall Shelly's face staring at me. No need to be so short.

I rest my chin on the desk, flattened by the effort just expended, and study

Ginna's girly handwriting on the list of phone numbers taped to the side of the phone. "MESSAGES *98" it says at the bottom. Aha—the code I've been meaning to ask the girls about.

I take a listen to who's been leaving voicemails on Ginna's phone in the past six months. Cable TV offers, mortgage refinancing, pollsters, nobody who would know that the occupant is never, ever going to return the call. Then, a voice. "Ginna. See you there at 9:30. Just checking in. Hope you're better this morning."

Angus. A message from Angus, in that unmistakable accent. I sit up, stung. I listen to it again and again. The timestamp is October 22. I think hard. When did Ginna die? Right in there. It was the 22nd. Definitely the 22nd. This message was left on the morning she died? Where were they going? Hope you're better? What was wrong in the first place?

Mother has been wandering around the house, commenting about things. She seems to be thinking of Ginna's house as some kind of museum. I find her in Ginna's room, unpacking her bag. "Positively eerie, isn't it? Like she's not even gone. You can feel her in the very draperies," she says. She's put on her face and looks less like a castaway now. Even in a disaster, Mother travels with her cosmetics.

"Tell me about it," I say. "I've felt like I've had a roommate, the hand of Ginna on everything."

"Do you believe in fate?" Another Grace Ballenger whiplash question of the week.

"You mean, are things destined to happen?"

"Destiny, fate, predestination, whatever. I think about this all the time."

"Like how?"

"Like Ginna's will. This business with the house."

"Do I think it was fate that she would leave me this house? I don't know, Mother—most of the time, coincidence will explain just about anything. It's a big world, you know. Things are bound to bump up against each other eventually."

Mother shakes her head and sits on the edge of the ottoman, a shoe dangling from a finger. "I mean the timing. It is so strange, that she would change her will only a month before her accident. Don't you find that uncanny? It's like she knew something was up."

"It is. It's very strange." I think about it all the time, but I have no insight about it. "Henry's coming over. To help with the pump. Shelly wanted him to come."

"A good head on his shoulders, that one."

"Don't want to talk about it. Or him." Your co-conspirator, I think. You nutty old spider.

"Just trying to help," she says in a voice with no fight in it.

"I don't need any," I say, feeling the age-old irritation.

"I know you don't. From me, anyway."

My pulse races. "I really don't. You know? I haul myself down here, ditching pretty much everything to get this thing done, and the minute I get here, you're monkeying around with it. I don't need anybody's help. And dragging Henry Peek into it—for shame, Mother! This is my house to sell, and I'm going to sell it." Such a flash, this fury, out of nowhere.

"I just can't imagine why you'd want to stay here, that's all," she says calmly. Did she even hear what I just said? "I'm about to come out of my skin, seeing all this." She lines up her shoes, nudging the heel of one with her toe. Those nylons. Hold on: she took the time to dig out her nylons in the middle of a house flood evacuation?

"She makes a good roommate," I say sourly.

"Such an angel," she says, looking at a photograph of Ginna and baby Amelia. She eases down on the loveseat in the corner of Ginna's bedroom and puts her feet on the fat ottoman. "Delia, do you remember when you were nine and got stuck in the tree house, and you sat up there for four hours because you didn't want anybody to help you down? Or that time you applied to the University of Chicago without telling me because you didn't want any of my friends to write letters for you?" She laughs a little. "Or that surprise eighteenth birthday party, and you walked in, then turned around and left in a huff?"

I remember them all, of course. The birthday party had some kind of Caribbean theme, and she hired this Rastafarian band who got everybody high out behind her garage. Everybody at the party loved it. I spent the evening at the Krispy Kreme on West End, reading a biography of Robert Moses, pissed at my mother for hijacking my big day.

She is lying back now, therapist style, eyes closed. "Life is a ferocious thing, at your heels every day. It's nigh impossible to get through it without people around you. I just hope you let somebody into your life, Delia."

"I have a lot of people in my life," I say.

"I'm sure you do."

Ginna's bed lures me with its smooth pillows, and I stretch out in its delicious softness.

Mother sighs. "Well, I just want you to know that I do actually get it." Get what? That my life has been an exercise in trying to live without the long arm of Grace Ballenger sliding in the window? "I get that you're a little stubborn, and a little prideful, and it's pointless for me to try to help you, because you don't want it. Ginna never seemed to mind my help. I guess Charlotte has gotten me to see that I need to stop. I need to listen. And I need to figure out what you're actually needing help with, not just the things I think you need help with."

At this point I'm stretched out on Ginna's bed, listening to my mother's sonorous accent, and I'm thinking: my mother sounds exactly like Eudora Welty, and I love Eudora Welty. I don't know what to make of her offering. But it sounds like this Charlotte therapist person has done something extraordinary: she has managed to get my mother to say the words "I need to listen," and that is something I thought I would never hear. She needs to listen, so what is it that I need to tell her?

Ginna's room is such a cocoon. We actually doze off amid the striped draperies and the soft rug, the never-ending rain tapping on the windows.

Shelly must think I have narcolepsy, because she is forever waking me up. "Delia," she whispers, trying not to awaken Mother. "Henry's in the basement. He didn't want to bother you."

Henry's in the basement. I am so crazy about him, the big fat liar.

Not only is he in the basement, he is wearing waders so that he can slosh around in my underground basement lake. He still looks trashed, but the high-waisted overall waders make him look like a big baby. The flood is waist high, a murky brew of dirty water and things floating on top of it. So many soccer balls and Barbie dolls and clear plastic bins. A crutch drifts by.

"Waders?" I ask, sitting down on the top stair.

"Dad. Fly fishing. So much gear. You'd think he'd caught all the trout in Tennessee." He is corralling the bins toward the steps. "Let's get these out of the way. What is with this yarn?"

"Ginna had a habit. Wait"—I remember his back—"I'll get them." I stack the bins in the back hall. Some of them are leaky, cracked at the bottom, so I take them to the sunroom with its brick floor. There's water all over the house, from people coming and going.

"You actually have a sump pump down here, it's just not working. Looks like it's from the Civil War," he says, shining a flashlight into the dim water. "This is the sort of basement that gives house buyers the freakouts. They can't handle an old basement that has actual dirt visible at any point." He shines the light to a far corner, where raw earth is carved out above the foundation. "People can't believe that a house is actually connected to the earth."

"I think the events of the past day pretty much make that clear to me," I say.

"Pass me that hose, willya?" he asks. He's all business, setting up the sump pump. "This is going to take a while. But you want to get it moving as soon as you can. Once it gets lower, we can bail into that utility sink to move it along." He looks up. "Fun, huh?"

Henry. Look at the guy. I'm dying.

"Run outside by this window, and pull the hose out as far away from the house as you can, downhill. Obviously. You know, toward your storm sewer?"

I look at him, incredulous—as if I have a clue where the storm sewer could possibly be—and he laughs. "Never mind. They're all flooded anyway. On the way over, the manhole covers looked like fountains, water squirting up out of them. Unbelievable. These are strange days, Delia, strange days."

His words hang in the air as I head outside into the rain. I don't even hunt for a raincoat. The ground is spongy and cool under my bare feet. It feels good, actually, the wettest wet it will ever be. I stoop by the basement window and watch Henry as he herds the floating junk out of the corners. I sit down on the edge of the window well to get a better view, my feet in the water that has caught there. It's a gutter that feeds this flood, I discover, right there by the window well. All the water off the roof is funneling straight into the basement. I'm there a good long while, feeling the water creep through my shirt, stream down my neck. I watch Henry work until he looks up, stops, and sees me sitting there. He smiles, up to his waist in muddy water, a smudge across his cheek, and he wades toward me. When he arrives at my window, he reaches up and presses his wet hand against the windowpane. I reach down and match my palm to his, the glass cool under my hand. A drop of rain hangs on the tip of my nose.

I come in the kitchen door, streaming water, and Shelly lets out a hoot. "Forget something?"

"I was communing with nature," I say. "Baptism." I wrap myself in one of the towels the girls used to dry off after their backyard adventures. Drying off with a wet towel is a good way to get even wetter than you were, so I run to Ginna's bathroom for a dry one. Godawful clammy. Mother is still zonked out on the loveseat, and this makes me somehow glad. She has the most peaceful look on her face.

I end up in one of Ginna's terrycloth robes, a blue one with tropical white chenille flowers all over it. So many godawful robes. I head for the attic to get some more clothes, and as I come around the corner for the back stairs, I just about bash into Henry.

"It's not what you think. The thing with your mother."

Henry seems to have caught a case of Grace Ballenger Bluntness Virus. I squint at him, trying to catch up with the debate that he seems to have already begun in his head.

"The thing. What thing?"

"The commission thing."

My hair is wet, and I look awful with wet hair. "Hold on. I gotta get dressed," I say as I head up the stairs. He stands for a second then comes behind me. "Henry."

"I need to talk to you." He's on my trail, and he's not stopping, following me all the way up to my attic dungeon.

"There are people everywhere," I hiss. He shrugs. He is more persistent than I thought.

I sit in a wrought-iron breakfast chair with metal grape leaves that poke into my back, and Henry ends up in the taupe leather Barcalounger that I can't believe Ginna ever let into the house. He looks ready to settle in for an afternoon of NCAA football.

"This is the worst-looking place I ever saw. You are such a hermit."

"I told you not to come up here."

He's looking around at this gloomy space, shaking his head in wonderment at the squalor that I inhabit, collecting his thoughts. He is here to Tell Me Something On His Mind. "Look, your mom came to my dad a few weeks ago. Told him that she had never been so depressed in her life. They're old friends, you know. He helped her find a therapist.

"When she found out you were coming to town, she was so excited. She felt like it was some kind of sign. And she thought you were crazy to sell the house yourself."

"Believe me, I heard about that."

"Well, she thought it would be a burden for you. So that's when Dad told her to call me. She did offer me a commission on the house. It's true."

"Can't believe you wouldn't tell me that."

"Hold on—I'll explain. Your mom. She was doing it from what seemed to me a real intention to help. She knew you wouldn't let her cover the commission. She knows how to make an argument, I'll tell you that. Brilliant."

"Intentions—it's always intentions with her. And she knew I would fall for it because you're so dashingly handsome." Henry rubs his face in embarrassment, and I can't frankly believe I just said it. But it's true. He was the bait. Surely he must know this. "I can't believe you're defending her. You have no idea."

"Maybe I don't know everything," he says.

"Trust me, you don't."

"Seriously. What is it? Why are you so hard on her?"

"It's not one thing. It's a lifetime of things. The basic situation was that she wasn't there. She was unavailable to us. It just hurt my feelings, Ginna's too, so much. So maddening because she could fake it well enough that we couldn't even put our finger on it. It sounds petty to complain about her. It just wasn't interesting to her, raising girls. It just wasn't her thing."

"Well, I know what I saw a few weeks ago. She's a very sad person."

"Who's ready to give you a big fat payday."

That was low. He gives me a look that lets me know just how crappy that is. "I turned her down, OK? Look. It kills me that you think this was . . . I would hope that somehow you could tell that I was sincere." We sit on that for a moment, the obvious and spectacular sincerity of a guy who has just spent an hour wallowing around in my flooded basement, who found me a damn sump pump in a city where every single house has a flooded basement, who came back to help me.

"There was something about you, the first time I saw you." He looks down, the slightest amusement crossing his face. "You were so pissed off, that time I came by. It was so comical, like you would snap in two if you made a single move." Purple underpants. "I actually decided right then not to take her commission. I wanted your listing for the pure comedy value of it. So stubborn. And that house tour. Wish I'd videotaped it. Like Jackie Kennedy giving a tour of the White House. 'And this lamp was made by Benjamin Franklin.' Why were you so jumpy?" He looks at me, his face open. "I don't expect you to believe all this, but there it is. Believe it or not, I'm not in this for the money." He pulls on the tail of his shirt. He's in sock feet. I can't stop looking at him. "I don't blame you for thinking the worst of me."

And with that, the Barcalounger does the thing that doomed it to exile in the attic: it flips backwards, sending Henry heels up, upside down almost, Henry yelling "crap!" I hurry over to give him a hand, which he takes, and he pulls me to him, just like in the movies, or high school actually, with me hoping that my mom downstairs doesn't catch us up here in the attic together.

We get to a pretty serious third base in the flipped-over Barcalounger when I remember that my mom actually is downstairs, and I actually don't want her getting in my business.

"Come on," I whisper. I am treacherously close to not caring. He is so great at making out, totally game. It's like we just invented making out. "We're gonna get busted any minute now."

Henry slides onto the floor, buttoning his shirt, looking around the room, shaking his head. "Delia, you have got to come down from here."

"Maybe I will when I have a reason to."

"What do I have to do to persuade you?"

"You're being pretty persuasive right now. Just saying." I snug up Ginna's chenille robe and give the belt a yank. "I don't wear these, in real life. I just want you to know that. It's important that you know this. Now turn around. No peeking. We've got to clean up our act."

Is this a short cut? Am I giving Henry a mulligan when he doesn't merit one? Does the realtor tell the truth? Does my mother? Does any of this matter, right this minute?

I keep forgetting about the girls—they've spent the morning over at Mary's, and I guess that's a good thing. Cassie comes bounding into the kitchen like a rabbit. She seems to have stopped worrying about whether she's wet or dry, like she's having a day at the beach. She's breathless. "Aunt Delia! You have got to come see this. This is incredible." She stops when she sees Henry sitting at the breakfast table with me. We have been talking with Shelly and trying to act like we're deeply concerned about the flood in the basement. Shelly's trying to act like it wasn't odd for her to discover Henry coming down the attic steps in his socks.

Cassie looks at me, quizzically, then at him. "You can come, too. You need rain boots."

She is skipping, almost, as she leads us down the driveway. There's a break in the weather, and a hint of sun glows deep within the clouds. "Mary's dad is so hilarious," she says.

Angus?

"So great. So great. Such a crack-up." She slides into his southern accent. "Casseh, ah do bleeve ah'll build us an ahrk."

She leads us down the driveway to Angus's house, the Norman castle that was Ginna's favorite. Henry says, "The Donalds'. House never goes on the market."

"He's completely inscrutable," I tell him. "I cannot for the life of me imagine anyone ever describing Angus Donald as a crack-up."

"Come on!" Cassie yells.

As we come around the corner of the garage, squishing in the spongy grass, we see what has so amused Cassie: there's a black pick-up truck caught high in a tree, flipped upside down, with a violent, churning whirlpool of rushing water just below it.

"Whoa," Henry says.

"See?" Cassie says.

Amelia and Mary stand with Angus watching this spectacle as if it were a TV show. This is the same creek that runs behind Ginna's house, but another, bigger creek converges in this back yard as well. It's at least ten feet deep where there normally is nothing. It is mesmerizing, the force of the water. It looks totally dangerous.

"It just showed up," Angus says, studying the truck. "Floated down the creek, caught the whirlpool, and up it went. Never seen the like of it." He extends his hand to Henry. "Angus Donald."

"Henry Peek."

"I know your father."

Henry nods. Everybody knows his father.

"How's that basement doing?" Angus asks me. The slightest amusement.

"A little damp. Maybe a gutter issue?"

He actually cracks a smile. "If it makes you feel any better, I've got water, too. Not a gutter in the world can deal with a water table like this. Coming up through the cracks in the floor. Just too much."

Cassie scoops up an armful of glossy, leathery leaves from beneath the magnolia next to the house and tosses them into the whirlpool. They float slowly at first, then spin crazily as the water pulls them into the center of the watery tornado. They vanish. "Isn't that incredible?" she yells with glee.

As she runs back to get more leaves, I notice that Angus has taken on the posture of somebody with a crushing migraine: he's pressing the heels of his hands into his eyes, hard. He stays like this at least a minute, and I worry that he's crying, but when he finally lets himself out, he's blinking like he's come out of a cave.

"Are you OK?" I ask.

His eyes narrow, and he squints. "I'm sorry," he says. "I just had a vision." He does seem like he's in a trance.

"A vision? Like . . ."

He shrugs. "I couldn't say, actually. Just a thought."

This seems odd, but he is done talking about it.

Henry says he needs to check on his dad's house. Angus waves a hand at the girls, who continue to watch the TV show that is this backyard flood. "I've told them they cannot be back here unless I'm here with them," he says. "I'm here until they leave."

"Thank you, Angus," I say.

The voicemail. I need to ask Angus about it. I can't get up the nerve, so we leave him with his surreal scene.

On the way home, Henry says, "Seems like a good guy."

"Nice sweater, right?"

"What?"

"My sister. Knitted that sweater for him."

"Really?" He gives me a knowing look. "Like, knitted it for him?"

I nod. "I mean yes. Like hand . . . knitted. A love token. You can't believe the stuff I've heard in the past two weeks." I tell him the whole story as we make our way home.

"I guess you never know what people are up to," Henry says.

"Never would have guessed she would do it. She was such a goody goody."

"He must be superhot in the hay," he says.

"I literally cannot imagine it," I say, but unfortunately, I get a flashing glimpse of Angus laying a big one on Ginna, and I let out a howl of dismay. Henry shakes his head and heads straight for a deep puddle beside the road. He walks with a bit of lope in his stride, as if he might break out into a trot at any moment. "This is so great," he says, sloshing through a foot of water. His rain boots squirsh. "Isn't this great?"

I can't express how great it really is, so I nod. "So great," I say.

———

There's a shiny white minivan in the driveway as we return to the house. As we come up the drive, the doors slide open and three children tumble out, along with a mommish-looking woman who looks like she is about to kill them all.

"Hi," she says breathlessly. She has a diaper in one hand and the classifieds in the other. "Am I too late?"

"For what?" I ask.

"The open house."

I look at Henry, who raises an eyebrow back at me. I thought I cancelled all the open house ads. He cracks his humble and magnificent smile, extends his hand, and says, "Of course not. I'm Henry Peek, of Peek & Peek Real Estate. This is Delia Ballenger, the current owner." He looks at the children, a sticky, feral pack wielding Pixie Stix and Twizzlers, none older than maybe seven, and says, "You must be relocating to Nashville."

Surprised, she says, "How'd you know?"

He smiles. "Because only someone in urgent need of a house would be out crawling open houses on a day like this. With kiddos. Your husband's coming to Vanderbilt?"

"He's down there right now," she says, surprised.

"Congratulations!"

"Yeah, well, our agent bagged on us because of the flood, but I cannot go back to Palo Alto without some idea of what the deal is here. We have a flight later on."

"Or not," he says. "The airport closed this morning. Which means," he glances at me, "that maybe you'll have a little extra time to see the house."

No way. I am mentally telegraphing him. I'm blinking Morse code. Forget it. There's five feet of water in the basement. Refugees camped out in every bedroom. The back yard is a swamp. This is madness.

"Let me ask you this," he says, so relaxed that he appears to have nothing else in the world to do. "How good is your imagination? Because this house is a great house that at the moment happens to be trashed. This is the sort of house that can handle whatever life brings to it, that's for sure."

"I'm sorry to just show up so late, but you know."

"Well, no time like the present. My only advice is that you have to be able to envision this house on a sunny day, because this ain't one of those days," he says.

It really is unbelievable, watching Henry Peek take this woman and her mob through this house. It's not a soft sell; it's a no-sell. He tells her every single problem, from the asbestos shingles on the roof to the sagging beam in the back hall. He announces that the kitchen cabinets are at least fifty years old. He introduces them to my mother, who sits in the sunroom reading, surrounded by dozens and dozens of balls of wet yarn that Shelly has laid out to dry. He leads the whole crowd up to my attic tenement nookie palace, with the flipped-over Barcalounger and the warehouse of abandoned furniture. As if that weren't enough, he concludes this tour at the basement door, where I glare at him with a white-hot panic. "Theresa, this is something that you will rarely see. I guarantee you that on this day, 80 percent of all houses in Nashville have this issue. But nobody will admit it to you except us." Before I can wedge myself between Theresa and that door, Henry has opened it and led the two oldest kids down the stairs. "Cool!" the boy exclaims. "It's like a tidal pool in the basement!"

"Theresa," he says with mock solemnity, "every one thousand years, you're going to have this problem with this house. Full disclosure."

By the time the kids are packed back into the minivan, Henry and Theresa are swapping phone numbers and emails. He is devastating. That other agent will never hear from Theresa again, after a performance like this. The thing is, Henry is absolutely artless. He doesn't sell her anything; he shows her my House of Horrors, such as it is, and she loves it. Or him. Or both.

Henry has to go check on his dad's house, which apparently has the damps, too. I don't want him to leave, so I lean against his car door to keep him out. I point out to him that he technically does not have my house as his listing, and he smiles in a sly way.

"What else was there to do? She just about killed herself to get to your house. It's like traveling with squirrels, those kids. She obviously wants to buy a house. You would have sent her away, right? Just chalk it up as an experiment."

"You do have killer charm, you know."

He looks mortally embarrassed, actually flushes and looks at me in a puzzled way. "The odds that this woman will buy this house are low. She's from California. People from California don't buy old houses. They have this morbid fear of termites. But her kids are going to University School. Any doctor whose kids are going to University School needs to be on Bowling Avenue.

That's just a fact." He stops and looks at me, as if he's just remembered something more urgent than analyzing this home tour. "Thanks for letting me come over."

"I didn't let you come over. You just came over. With your gizmos."

"You called me back."

"Shelly made me."

"I love Shelly."

"Me too."

We stand there by his car for a while, talked out, exchanging a long and life-changing gaze filled with deep and profound meaning. Or something. I mostly like to look at him. His face is so angular, strangely similar to the drawing on his card. His eyebrows have the slightest curve to them, punctuation to his quick eyes. I take his hand and study the scar running up his wrist. "You have to go now," I tell him, running my thumb over the hurt part. "Before my charm wears off."

Back in the house, the girls are celebrating the news that their school has cancelled classes, and Mother has taken it upon herself to tell them it's fine to stay the night. I have no idea where Bennett is, but I need to call him at some point.

Shelly is in the kitchen, trying to figure out some food for us. She's standing at the counter with a huge foil-wrapped object.

"What is that thing?" I ask. Mr. Serious slides against my leg, then flops at my feet. He likes to be where the action is.

"From the freezer. Here," she says, pulling off a holiday card with a soft-focus photo of a Christmas dinner table. "'Wishing you a meaningful holiday season and a happy 2009, from your friends at OrthoBioMed Distribution Co., LLC. A Division of Kramer Pharmaceuticals Inc.'" It's an orthopedic gift ham.

"I don't know, Shelly—a sixteen-month-old ham? How long can a ham sit in a freezer?"

"Maybe we thaw it out and see."

"How long will that take? A month?" It all seems worrisome to me. I've never had to do food service like this, and I'm not in the habit of freezing enormous hunks of meat, ever.

I hear voices in the front hall. Bennett has come to take the girls home, not having heard their message that they're staying another night.

Amelia is explaining how they want to stay, and he protests that he hasn't seen them in two days. "It's fun," she says. "Grandma's here. Shelly's here." He looks besieged by his two girls. He doesn't have a chance.

"It's fine with me," I add. "Come sit for a minute." What is with me? Since when do I pull up a chair for the likes of Bennett? Maybe it's because he looks so exhausted—he doesn't have five o'clock shadow, it's more like a scraggly beard, and his scrubs make him look like he's escaped from a pajama party.

Bennett looks warily at me. "OK. Pit stop. Hold on," he says, and heads down the hall.

I'm just settling into Ginna's lush sofa when I hear a tremendous crash in the kitchen, a dense thud, and a "fuck!" I head for the noise, surprised to hear "fuck" at such an uncontained volume. There's a scramble at my feet, and I nearly wipe out on Mr. Serious who is hauling it out of the breakfast room. The scene in the kitchen: Bennett is on one foot, holding the other in his hands as if it were a precious object. The frozen ham is on the floor. "Goddamn it that fucking cat!" He's panting with pain.

We help Bennett to the library and stretch him out on the leather sofa. Mother emerges from her lair. "Well, hello Bennett," she says coolly. I'm guessing that they haven't seen each other since the funeral. Mother still thinks Bennett is a homewrecker. I feel sorry for Bennett these days, preserving the legend of Ginna at his own expense. At what point do I tell her about Ginna's slutty knitting habit?

"Do you think?" Mother asks, studying the mound of ice on his foot.

"Yeah. Metatarsals. Fourth and fifth. Hate that cat."

"It's your right foot, too." Mother does not seem too concerned.

"Yeah." He looks extraordinarily grumpy. "Hurts like a bitch."

"Well," she says, drifting out of the library, "I'm sure it does."

His phone buzzes in his coat pocket.

"Yeah. At the house. Just broke my foot." Pause. "A ham." Long pause. "How bad?" A very long pause. "OK. I'll figure out something. You just do what you need to do." Pause. "No, yeah, it's really broken." He hangs up and sighs heavily. "My apartment is trashed. Haven't been home since yesterday, but sounds like the whole back side of the complex is flooded."

"So stay," I say automatically. "You can't even drive."

He shakes his head. "No way."

I shrug. "You're welcome here."

"Oh, right. Bunking up with Judge Ballenger. She'd love that." He rubs his beady eyes with the heels of his hands. "I am so fucking tired. Three surgeons out right now. It's a zoo down there." He throws an arm, dark hairs on pale skin, across his face. "I can't work with my foot like this."

Amelia comes in. "Dad," she says ruefully, studying his foot. "Are you staying here?"

He looks around the library, with his collection of Civil War books lining the walls. "Been meaning to catch up on my reading," he says dryly. He could not possibly look less happy about it.

So endeth the day. I'm in the attic, my head spinning, trying to settle down. I can't believe Bennett actually decided to stay. He said he couldn't deal with trying to find a hotel room, and he made no mention of staying at the Walrus's. He said that he really couldn't stand for hours at work with his foot the way it felt right now, so he didn't have much choice.

What must it be like for him to be back in the house he left behind? It's haunting me, all the time, and I never even lived here. I can only imagine how strange it must seem to him.

My phone buzzes. It's Susan, calling from Portland.

"Delia! I saw the news! What on earth is going on down there?"

Mother is in Ginna's room. Shelly is in the guest room. Amelia and Cassie are in their rooms, and Bennett is on the sofa bed in the library. "Boarding house. We still have one sofa available, if you're in town. Shared facilities, full breakfast. Indoor swimming pool."

DAY 20: MAY 3

Relief Work

Out my low, half-moon bedroom window, the day has exploded in a bright blue sky. It's cruelly beautiful, as if the weekend flood had been some kind of supercomplicated practical joke. First thing, I check Henry's Twitter feed.

HenryPeek Hope everybody's OK out there. I think this is the part where we all pitch in? #nashvilleflood

From anybody else, this would be so sappy. But it's Henry. He's not like that. He's so optimistic. I love that so much.

The girls are still in high spirits. It doesn't seem to bother them to be back in this house. Maybe it's the snow-day feel of it all. Shelly sent them to the grocery store with a list, having figured out that a house full of people can't subsist on Lean Cuisines and leftovers from Bread and Company. I'm struck with how Shelly is affected by her knees. She's the same age as Mother, and she's hobbling around. This must mean that Mother is getting old too, and I can't deal with that, either.

"Where's Mother?" I ask Shelly.

"Out back."

"Swimming?"

"Go see," she says with a shrug in her voice.

The sun is warm on the back terrace, as if it's making up for lost time. Sure enough, Mother is in Ginna's rose garden, wearing Henry's waders, with a wide straw hat topping it all off. Up to her knees in water, she is pulling debris out of the roses, which remain flooded under two feet of water. Sticks, branches, pieces of lumber, a flip flop. "Look at all this," she says. "I just don't know. Do not know. I do not know where all this came from. Look at that," she says, pointing to a five-gallon bucket beside me. "That's twenty inches of rain we had in two days."

I sit on the wall of the terrace and watch as Mother fools around with the garden. "How's it going?" I ask. What's on her mind? Is she planning any Ginna Schwartz Heritage Tour outings?

"Well," she says. "I am about to come out of my skin, not working. Haven't gone this long away from work since, since never."

That is the understatement of the century.

She is absorbed in dragging things out of the wrecked roses. "The girls are something, aren't they? So mature. Amelia says they're going to have the prom Saturday no matter what. She was telling me about this boy who asked her. Such an intelligent girl." She pulls a dead rose bush out by its base and sloshes over to throw it up on the terrace. "This one's tired. I remember your prom, that time when that boy was so . . . that boy was so awful, I called his mother."

I can't believe she remembers that, or that she would go to my defense. "You did?"

"I most certainly did. I told her it was a reprehensible thing to do—you don't abandon a date at a prom—and she probably wasn't going to hear about it from her son, so I wanted her to know that her upstanding young man was anything but."

"Well, why didn't you tell me about it?"

"Thought you'd be embarrassed. Wouldn't want me meddling."

True.

"You were a prickly one, Delia." She holds up her hands in Ginna's rose gloves. "Had to be careful around you." She pulls a long vine from the water, reeling it in like a rope. "Where did this thing come from? Looks like kudzu." It trails all over the garden, and Mother wades along, looking for its roots.

She stops and looks up at me, her face in shadow from that enormous hat. "Amelia says she needs a dress for Saturday. Maybe we could take her out to find one. Assuming of course there's a dress in town that doesn't have wet hems." She pushes her hair off her forehead. "Do you think she'd want to do that?"

Such kindness in her voice. She's asking my advice. I bend down, pretending to pick up a trowel, so she won't see my tears. "Yeah," I say. "I think she'd love that."

The situation with Bennett is very mysterious. Overnight, he seems to have lost the will to live. He's hunkered down in the library with three stacks of Civil War books on the floor beside his foldout bed, foot up on a pillow. Shelly has brought him chicken noodle soup and saltines. She says he won't get out of bed.

"Hey Bennett, what's up?" I ask.

He looks up, over the top of *Railroads in the Civil War*. "Not much."

"How's your foot?"

"Broken."

"Do you need anything?"

He sighs. "No." He looks down, then up again. "Actually, ice."

"OK." I turn to leave.

"Carla broke up with me. Last night, late."

I turn back. "Oh."

"Surgical supply rep."

"Sorry."

He shakes his head. "He has a bass boat." He chews on this for a moment, and I feel for a guy who loses out to somebody with good fishing equipment. "I know you don't care, and I know what the girls think of her, but she's not a bad person." He adjusts his pillow. "I can't do this by myself, you know."

"The girls seem good."

Bennett looks at his hands, stretching those steady, steady fingers. Is he making sure they're still good? "Amelia . . . struggles. She's lost weight, since. I don't think it's a real problem—you know—but she sleeps a lot, keeps to herself. Her grades are not great right now. The girls were seeing a therapist for a while, but there's no way to undo the basic fact of it all."

"I can't believe she's gone."

"Yeah. That."

The sad twinge bites me. I hate that she's gone, and it's so heartening to hear Bennett feels the same way. "If I could have ten minutes with her, there's so much—"

"Right." Bennett has a flatness to him. "The thing for me is how wrong it all feels, how derailed it is. Don't know where I screwed up." He wrestles his pillow higher. "I try to figure out the exact moment that Ginna said, 'OK, this is it, this is the moment that I can do this, that I am going to drop the vase and let it shatter.' Because there had to be a moment like that, and I can't stand that I didn't even recognize it, even as it happened. I probably wasn't even here. Or worse, that it happened right in front of me."

"I don't know, Bennett. I wish I did." Man, do I not know anything about marital dynamics. I imagine it was a glacial slide of missed moments, things not said, chances to be together that slipped by. Their marriage slid right past me, that's for sure. I had no idea.

"She ended it with the guy right after I found out about it." He bites his lip. "Said she wanted to stay married. I was totally deaf at that point. Didn't want to hear any of it. Wouldn't give me the divorce because she thought I was suffering from Physician's Lust Syndrome, she called it, that I'd get over it." He looks up at me. "Thing is, she was right. If she hadn't had that accident, we'd probably be back together by now."

"Bennett, that's hard. Who knows?"

I remember him at the funeral, sitting right next to me. Of all the shocked and miserable people sitting in those pews, Bennett seemed paralyzed by grief. He got through it—he brought the girls, did the things he was supposed to do, but I was struck by his absolute stillness through it all. Mother saw it as his typical cold fish response to everything, but I saw a guy who was stunned, as if he'd been hit over the head with a board. He spent most of the service staring at the leaflet, "In Celebration of and Thanksgiving for the Life of Virginia Ballenger Schwartz." I couldn't believe it, either. It looked like a typo, the wrong name.

"The girls are having fun," he says. "Here. With you. Camp Delia."

"They're amazing." It's true. I watch them together, these gangly girls, so strange and unfamiliar, and I see Ginna and me. Not in any particular way, but in the orbit they keep around each other, the mutual gravitational pull even as they tease each other without pity.

The echo that comes from them is so strong. We were young and left to figure it out on our own. At least, that's how it felt at the time. I think about Mother busting my prom date, how much that pleased me just now to hear that she might have been watching out for me, and I almost laugh.

Bennett lets a sour little smile slip out, and I know he's done talking. "Ice?" he asks.

How did I manage to miss a call from Henry? I stare at my phone in amazement. Not possible—I carry this thing around like it's the nuclear codes. Eight years of travel advice have made me a cell phone junky. "Good morning, Delia." His voice is so warm, captured forever in my voicemail. "I have a red alert from Kevin. The Cumberland hasn't crested yet, and they're worried about the water treatment plant flooding. Call me if you want to help. It involves hushpuppies."

The news coverage of the flood is wall to wall. We may have a flooded basement, and pick-up trucks may be landing in our trees, but now that the rain has stopped, we can see the city in its breathtaking ruin. The Cumberland has run rampant, crawling up Lower Broadway, flooding the new Symphony Center, the Country Music Hall of Fame, all the downtown district. The Titans stadium is a pond for football now. The most upsetting sight to me is the view from the TV helicopters, where the curving rows of roofs in suburban subdivisions float in broad sheets of shining brown water. Thousands of houses have been swamped, entire neighborhoods. Each one of those roofs is another family with a suddenly flooded life.

Shelly is transfixed in front of the huge screen, hoping that a helicopter will go far enough out past Bellevue that she can see how her house has fared. She still hasn't heard from her brother, and her claim that she's not worried sounds awfully thin.

"Why don't we go out there?" I ask. "I bet we could get through."

Shelly shakes her head. "They just flew over the Ashland City highway. Can't get through there, can't get to my house. We'll just wait it out."

I have this fear that Henry's going to regret everything, that he's going to decide that it's a bad idea to be hanging out with the attic-dweller from Chicago. He seems glad to see me, but he can't possibly be as happy as I am to see him. Khaki shorts and a faded Duke T-shirt. A Timex watch, old looking. Hair still damp in the back. I always take inventory when I have the chance.

Mother comes around the corner of the house, still in Henry's waders. She looks vaguely like an EPA worker, or a beekeeper. "Well hello," she says, brightening at the sight of us.

"Your Honor! In the waders!" Henry looks both embarrassed and amused. "What brings you here?"

"Flood stuff. We're going to make lunch for the guys sandbagging the water plant."

Mother is calculating something, and you can see it in her face, the moment that she figures out that this is basically a date disguised as humanitarian aid. I try to look nonchalant.

"Have fun," she says. "Save the city."

Henry's chef friend Kevin has decided to feed the inmates who are sandbagging the Omohundro Water Treatment Plant. He has activated his secret supper squadron to help out, and Henry has been assigned hushpuppies.

"The inmates volunteered," Henry says. "The mayor asked for help, and they stepped up."

"Wow."

"I know."

"So the water treatment plant might flood?"

"One of them already has—this is the last one. If it goes, there's no water in Nashville. Like, none. Stop drinking water!" He smiles. "Ironic enough for you?"

We make it to the Sysco on Charlotte Avenue, a food wholesaler where things tend to come in colossal quantities. It's busy—the businesses unaffected by the flood seem to want to do whatever they can to help the rest of the city. We load up on the ingredients Kevin has texted Henry to bring: 100 pounds of cornmeal, jugs of peanut oil, cases of eggs, jalapenos, onions, buttermilk.

"How many inmates are we feeding?" I ask.

"I don't know. Hundreds? Kevin's insane. He's bought piles of catfish."

I am trying to envision how this will work. "Wouldn't a peanut butter sandwich do the trick? How do you fry catfish and hushpuppies for hundreds of people at a water plant?"

"Ahh, that's the genius part," Henry says. "Wait til you see." He studies a shelf of five-gallon buckets. "What is Chocolate Lite 'n' Fluffie?"

"Better than Banana Lite 'n' Fluffie."

I tell Henry about the arrival of Bennett last night, and the rogue cat and the falling ham, and the morning's despair after the Walrus dumped him.

"Poor guy. How long do you think he's going to be laid up? You could end up with a long-term boarder," he says.

"All of them, actually. I never imagined that I'd end up in this situation. They're all flooded out."

"It's like some group therapy family rehab clinic. What are the odds of that?"

So funny. He's so right. He hasn't heard the whole story of what's going on in the house on Bowling Avenue, but I'm guessing we are going to have a long day of hushpuppies ahead of us. I plan on finding out the Story of Henry while I'm at it.

The Omohundro Water Treatment Plant is located on the banks of the Cumberland in a bleak industrial area, the land of granite and wire and tremendous piles of sand. Henry keeps singing "Omohundro" to the tune of "Oklahoma." We can't get very close to the plant, but even at a distance, it's such a surprise. It looks like a textile mill in New England: brick, many windowed, sturdy. Noble and old. It warms my heart to see our water plant behind a barbed-wire fence with a gatehouse. Protect our water! It deserves it.

There's a lot of activity going in and out. Dump trucks are carting sand. The prison buses roll in, exactly as scary as prison buses should look. The inmates' faces are ciphers, absolutely unreadable as I glimpse them through the barred windows. Those are our customers today. I'm nervous to be anywhere near so many prisoners. I've never been near prisoners before.

It becomes obvious where we are going to be frying up all this catfish and hushpuppies. Parked outside the fence is a vehicle surrounded by people working at folding tables.

"Oh, man." I get it now.

Kevin may cook high-style secret suppers in abandoned buildings, but his daily gig happens in a food truck he converted from a recreational vehicle with "Leisure Life" in swirly letters on the side. He added "Restaurant" underneath in stick-on mailbox letters that make anything look demented. "We Br ng The Crispy 2 You" it says across the bottom.

"Kevin's specialty is fried things," Henry says. "Believes everyone should have something fried every day." I am laughing. "Mobile Fry Daddy."

Kevin is running around, small and manic, demonstrating his breading technique, fussing at people in his flat country accent. He's the ultimate conflation of high and low: a trained chef who sounds like a character on *Hee Haw*. There are maybe a dozen of us there, ready to do this thing. The flood has triggered a citywide rush to help. All over town, thousands of volunteers are ripping out wet drywall, buying diapers, collecting supplies. Squads of church volunteers mobilize in their matching T-shirts. Kevin had to turn away potential hushpuppy volunteers. "You gotta make these in batches," he explains as we unload our supplies. "Double it, but don't triple it."

"How many batches are you talking about?"

"I dunno, fifty? A hundred? Til we run out. Y'all just crank this deal, OK?" He seems unconcerned and scurries off to talk to the prison guards. I look at Henry in amazement.

We're in this group of animated people, all increasingly breading ourselves in cornmeal and buttermilk, nobody any good at this, scooping flour, but it feels like Henry and I are here alone. We have this little table, in a gravel parking lot, in the shade of a hackberry tree. Just us. He has on a long apron. His hair is all rumply. I can't help but study him.

"We should be filling sandbags," he says.

"I know."

"Ridiculous."

"Yeah. But catfish is so tasty. Couldn't hurt."

"Exactly," Henry says. "At least we're here, not watching this on TV. You can't just let somebody else do it."

We have a long day ahead of us, it seems. "OK," I say. "Not long ago, you said you had a tale for another day. Well, this is the day. Here we are."

Henry looks like he doesn't know whether to get into it or not. "Ah, it's such a beautiful day." He's chopping jalapenos, with rubber gloves making his hands look like cartoon hands. "OK. Do you want the long version or the short version?"

"Start with the short."

"Left home, came back."

I shake my head.

"Left home, traveled, came back a changed man."

"Henry."

"Religious crisis, opted out in an unproductive and self-destructive way, got in trouble, came back."

I point at his faded T-shirt, which I now see reads "Duke Religion." Quite a shirt. "Not the basketball team?"

He smiles. "No, the literal kind of religion."

Religion? He said before that he wasn't churchy. "What flavor? What were you aiming for?"

"I don't know. Maybe an Episcopal priest, maybe a professor. I guess," he says with a laugh.

That's a shock. "You? A man of the cloth? You look good in black."

"I loved the smell of candle smoke. I'm not kidding."

"I'm not religious." I lob that out there just to make sure he knows this straight off.

"Me neither." He smiles, but it's not a happy smile. "But I was, all through college. It seemed like a puzzle I could work on my whole life." He puts down his knife and pulls off his gloves. "Hold on." He comes around the table and holds me so close, and kisses me so certainly, that I kind of forget about the hushpuppies. "This is not a good story," he says, "so I wanted to make sure I got to kiss you today. Because you might not want to later."

How bad could a story be? I suspect he just felt like kissing. Right in front of his friends. I don't think this is something that he is in the habit of doing.

He returns to his chopping, but he's not doing a very efficient job. Preoccupied.

"You don't have to tell me."

He shakes his head. "I sort of need to." He dumps a pile of minced jalapenos into a bowl. "I'm sorry, but jalapenos are not a traditional hushpuppy ingredient.

"So there I was, at Duke, reading all this stuff, interested in the early church. You know, back when it was very young, before Constantine converted. Monasticism, solitude. Contemplation. Christianity is fundamentally about the individual, not the group, you know?"

"I'm no theologian."

"Crap! I can't believe we're getting into this."

"I'm in."

"Well, it's interesting the way Christianity has been distorted to be this religion of community, but it has."

"Henry! Blasphemy."

He shrugs. "It's true. It's very useful for an emperor to have everyone stoked up on the same god. For a priest to have a large group of people hanging on his every word. And when groups of wigged-out Christians get going, well."

"Not every Christian is a maniac," I say.

"True, but once you start reading about centuries of hardcore intolerance, large scale—the institutional kind—it left me asking why I was associating myself with any of it."

He knows he is being puzzling and gives me an apologetic look.

"Doubt. It was a soup of doubt. Too many things sounded wrong. I know it seems strange, but the whole thing felt tragic to me. A loss, a death. I wanted it so badly, my faith, but it evaporated. Organized religion is such a mess. The real estate component of Christianity alone is so comical—the amount of time and money churches spend on their buildings. On stuff. You know? So it just vanished. The closer I looked, the more I read, the less I could find. The net result of all this was that I checked out. Drank. A lot. I did graduate, in a fog, basically, on momentum. I went to Europe, because I thought I could figure out my problem there. I knew I couldn't do it in Nashville. Anywhere, really.

"I hunkered down in Copenhagen, mostly because I figured if it was good enough for Kierkegaard, it was good enough for me. Thought it might help me get his vibe. Beautiful, too. I told my parents that I was going to study philosophy, which sounded plausible. I couldn't bear to tell them that I was so off the rails.

"It turns out that Copenhagen is a great place to spin out. Spent most of my time feeling ripped off, like I'd wasted my time investing in all this religion when all it's done is to separate people, cause wars and suffering, give men a way to abuse power. Didn't see the value of it at all."

"A full-out religious crisis? That's so tender."

He shakes his head. "No," he says emphatically. "It is not tender. It's the opposite of tender." This is the angriest I have seen him. "Just the stupidity of it. So wrong. So careless. That's it—I just didn't pay attention. Careless. I couldn't care less. About anything but myself and my poor sad pathetic little destiny."

I'm stirring a vat of batter with a giant spoon. I can't tell where he is headed, at all.

"There's a strange kind of art in Danish churches, really haunting. Medieval chalk paintings, up in the ceilings, primitive, colorful against a white ground. I became obsessed with them. They fit my mood. I set a compulsive little goal of seeing as many of these paintings as I could, all over the country. I'd go to churches, and almost always, there'd be some small, old woman sitting in a pew, in the middle of the day. These women, I'd seek them out, and I'd ask them why they were there. 'Comfort,' they'd say. 'Peace.' They'd tell me they were heartbroken, or grieving, or angry, or confused. Praying for something they'd lost or never had. Waiting. It was sweet or depressing depending on the person, but I always left thinking that they were wasting their time, sitting there with those strange drawings over their heads. Didn't they understand that no answer was going to come from above? Didn't they see that praying was just thinking?"

At this point I have filled three buckets with hushpuppy batter, and I can't believe I am hearing this story from Henry. He is mesmerizing, and I have no idea where he's going with this.

"You were asking me about my scars. One is from the bar fight. The rest are from an accident."

"I can't believe you were ever in a fight. I just don't believe it."

"It wasn't heroic, I promise you."

The back scar was from an accident? I thought he'd always had a bad back, from what Shelly had said. I'd assumed it was some chronic thing.

"Along the way, I met a girl in Copenhagen on a fellowship, for a wind power project. From Dublin. Very idealistic. Pretty, too, I have to say. Almost as pretty as you."

I look up to give him a glare of incredulity.

"I wasn't in a mood to be with anybody much, but she was persistent in her way, so we ended up spending time together."

"Not because she was hot, of course."

"Of course." Henry picks up a bucket. "You know, I think I'm going to go make some hushpuppies now," he says, and he walks away, just like that.

It's as if he doesn't want to tell any more of the story. He walks slowly, with his heavy bucket of batter, yelling a greeting to Kevin up in the truck. "Got some slop for ya, son."

"Bring it on."

So Henry makes hushpuppies, for such a long time that I wonder if he is personally going to fry every single hushpuppy today. It occurs to me that he may have decided that hanging out over a deep fryer filled with boiling peanut oil is somehow preferable to talking about whatever it is that he isn't telling me.

A question I have, all day long, is whether the sandbagging is supposed to work. I remember a book I loved growing up, *Alexander and the Magic Mouse*, about a thirty-day flood and a kindly alligator who saves the day. Their sand-bagging worked. What if, in our case, there's more river than sandbags? What if the plant fails, and we do run out of water, in this ridiculously watery city?

Another question is: accident? What kind of accident? The word runs through my mind so often that it starts to sound like nonsense. Axy din. Acts o' dint. Acks! A dent! And the foxy Irish wind power girl? I keep imagining them—her name is Fiona, no doubt about it—holding hands, wearing match-ing fisherman sweaters, looking out at an ocean filled with spinning turbines, sighing at the environmental sexiness of it all. I am so jealous that I can barely catch the hushpuppies that rain out of Kevin's trailer window like crispy, brown hail.

Lunch goes well, I think, though we aren't allowed anywhere near the in-mates. It's the guards who tell us that the catfish and hushpuppies are a success. They seem excited by the day, the strangeness of it.

The way Henry talks about religion is so careful, so reasoned. He has thought about this so much. Yet to have left it all behind seems like such a drastic break. It would be so hard, I would think, this leavetaking. I can hardly imagine what it would be like, but I believe it could send him into a ditch.

Henry doesn't say another word about any of it all day, and he manages to slide out of conversation with everybody. He does tell me that he believes he has perfected his hushpuppy technique and would go head to head with Kevin, anytime, on fry skills.

We finally leave in the late afternoon. The river is still rising, but the officials tell us that shifts of inmates will keep working through the night. The morning will tell whether the Omohundro Water Treatment Plant will stay dry.

Henry is quiet on the way home. "I feel like I have myself been deep fried," he says, and I have to agree. We are trashed, both of us. I will have hushpuppy nightmares tonight. "Do you mind if we go by my place to clean up?" he asks.

"Thought you'd never ask."

I have been so curious about Henry's apartment. It's very new, this small building, sleek and airy, so different from Ginna's upholstered, faux colonial suburban splendor. It's probably low-carbon-footprint environmentally perfect. Probably has a solar dishwasher. Fiona probably helped him pick it out. So not Nashville, this place. "If I'd known you were coming, I'd've baked a cake," he says, unlocking the door.

There's a lot of mossy green and gray. An avalanche of magazines and newspapers by his sofa. His laptop on the table. A wall of books. There's no womanly touch anywhere in this place, I am relieved to discover. No cute lamps. No potted palm behind the sofa. No set of six attractive botanical prints over the mantel. No photos of ringlet-headed young women in Irish fisherman sweaters.

I don't know what happened earlier today, but Henry's mood is unlike any I've seen from him. His fundamental cheerfulness is missing, and he's lost in thought. "Are you OK?"

He glances over at me. "I guess it got to me, seeing all the inmates go by. Hadn't really counted on that."

I don't buy this. It's something else. "Henry."

"I gotta clean up," he says, and he's off to the shower.

"Save water," I say to his back.

I feel like I'm intruding to be in his apartment without any warning. I'm seeing his life exactly as he leads it, not as he wants me to see it. It's not messy, really, but his shoes and socks are on the floor, an open bag of Trader Joe's Pita Chips on the sofa, stacks of papers. It's certainly less a wreck than my attic, but I think that on a different day, he would have invited me over with a lot of ceremony, and it would have been fun.

One of the bookshelves holds a batch of family photos, the largest a picture of Henry in a front yard, next to a woman who is surely his mother, with the same wide set of the eyes and fair coloring. It looks recent; Henry doesn't look all that different now. She is smiling, he is not, but he leans toward her as if he's mooching her warmth on what looks like a very cold day. He wears a knit hat that stands up funny.

My hair is full of peanut oil, I have cornmeal under my nails, and I need a steam cleaning. I hope the prisoners liked those hushpuppies.

What was the accident? What could be so horrible? I have to know. I go into his bedroom to find him. He's standing in the steamy bathroom at his sink, in his boxers, not shy as I come in. That scar on his back startles me. It just doesn't look all that old. It looks like something isn't quite healed under there. "What happened?" I ask.

He takes my hand and leads me to his bed, where we sit on the very edge. His shiny hair is slicked straight back, very wet, and he smells soapy. His skin is pink from the hot water, the hairs on his knees shiny and blond. I hold his hand like it's going to slip away.

"You know the drill," he says, "with recovery." He lays out the word in quotation marks, and he glances up to see my reaction. "You have to tell your story over and over, the whole thing, because you have to remind yourself that you could go so low."

"You didn't drink at the secret supper. I figured something was up."

"Right. Funsucker."

"No," I say, remembering that night. "There's never been a party like that, for me anyway."

He smiles a little. "I just didn't want to tell you. All this. I'm so tired of it. I want to be beyond it, but I don't guess I ever will. That's the point, I guess. I can't be with you and not tell you."

This is so upsetting. Recovery could mean anything. I have a strong feeling that I don't want to hear this. He seems determined to tell me anyway.

"This girl, Clare, ended up being a lot of trouble, because she liked to drink even more than I did. I would put her squarely in the category of bad influence. I take responsibility for my actions, but I wonder, often, what would have happened had we never met. She ran with this crowd of expatriate types, you know, trustafarians. Not all that different from me. Smoking just bales of pot. Pot was not my thing. I have simple tastes," he says sourly. "Drinking works great. It was on one of those bingey weekends that the wheels came off."

He looks up at me from time to time, checking to see that I'm getting all this. I'm focusing on his kneecaps mostly, because his face upsets me. It's a crying face, even though he's not crying.

"I decided to take her to see this one church, out west of Copenhagen, the one I absolutely had to see. They're very trippy, these chalk paintings. I was driving, because I was in better shape than she was, but neither of us should have been anywhere near a car. And I was doing OK until we got to the coast—this wild piece of road. The thing was, her car's steering was on the right, being Irish, and I wasn't used to that, shifting with my left hand and everything. At this one curve, I turned right, when I should have turned left. And we launched, right off the road, down a gully." He looks up and sees me watching him steadily. "There are not many gullies in Denmark, but I managed to find one."

He flattens out my hand and stretches out my fingers, one by one, like little puppets. "You know how they say that drunk people don't die in car accidents? Well, that's just not true."

I shake my head, disturbed. He nods. Not this. The accident is this.

"I've relived this story so many times, but . . ." He sighs. "Yeah. Her name was Clare Murray, and she was beautiful, and it was a nightmare. We rolled and rolled, and out she flew, sort of. Car rolled right over her."

He lies back on the bed, stretching his back, his bony feet dangling off the edge. Those poignant feet. The flat of his belly rises as he takes a deep breath. He's talking to the ceiling.

"The Danish government really hates it when people drive drunk and kill people." So quiet. "So. I broke my back, my leg, and my collarbone. Took out my spleen. After about ten weeks in the hospital, I was told that I would have a trial, and probably go to prison. And I did."

"What did your family think?"

"My parents came over, right away. I will never forget the look on my mother's face when she saw me. I had two black eyes and a broken nose."

He's silent for a long while. His nose does have a slight bump to it. I watch the rise and fall of his chest, trying to imagine what he went through, and I see for the first time a pair of small scars under his ribcage.

"I talked her into going. Totally didn't want to go, but I sold her on it. Thought I was so charming. My powers of persuasion."

"Oh, Henry."

"You know those prisoners today? Those crappy buses? Those jumpsuits? So crude, so brutal. Nothing like that in a Danish prison."

He actually was upset about the inmates. I see now.

"How long were you there?"

"Almost a year. Danish prisons are like what would happen if Ikea designed a jail. At least the one I was in. It's a whole different model of justice. There isn't even much of a fence, just this surveillance system. Intense. They explain exactly how they're watching you, and what will happen if you cross a line. Psychological prison. Totally works.

"It was the most surreal experience of my life, this place. You cook your own food, there are inmates' kids running around, it's like an apartment building. Men and women in the same place. You can date."

"You dated in prison?"

He turns on his side and props himself up on an elbow. "Trust me, I was unfit for human consumption. Really. It was one of those be-careful-what-you-wish-for things. I achieved my monastic lifestyle, in the most ironic way possible. Piles of time to think. Drifts of it, deserts of time to contemplate the mysterious and juicy nature of God. But what I mostly thought about was how I'd screwed up, how far from home I was."

He stands and goes to his closet, where he pulls out a lovely shirt, blue and white stripes. Blue. He should always wear blue. "Before I left for home, I managed to get out to see one of those Danish churches again." He laughs a cheerless laugh, as if he can't believe himself. "There's another thing about these churches. They hang these ship models from the rafters, right there in the sanctuary—these elaborate models of sailing ships. It was some kind of tradition. Sea captains. I have recurring dreams about those ships, floating above me, weightless, perfect."

He finishes buttoning his shirt, buttons the collar, rolls up the sleeves. He finds a pair of khaki shorts in his dresser and steps into them. "There's more to the story, but you've been patient to listen this long." He stands, so clean, arms out, presenting himself. "It's not something I talk about."

"This was eight years ago?"

"Almost nine," he says. "Delia. You are so beautiful. I've waited so long for you to come along. I'm so tired of being a monk, and I think you're tired of being a nun."

"A nun? You think I'm a nun?" This actually hurts my feelings.

"I do." He looks very serious.

"I can't tell if you're joking."

He shrugs. "You tell me."

I stand up, wanting to be as clean as Henry is. I go to his closet and pull out one of his beautiful shirts. I go to his dresser and find some shorts. In the bathroom, I turn on the shower, and I take off all my hushpuppy clothes, right there in front of him. It's funny, but I don't feel the least bit shy. He, on the other hand, blushes a full-out crimson.

"A nun," I say as I drop my clothes in the trash can.

I stay in the shower forever. I wash my hair three times, using Henry's orangey shampoo, washing away the day. I have heard sad stories before, and I've been confessed to, but not this way. He knows this is a game changer, that I will see him differently now.

We don't even speak on the way back to my house, but I feel his clothes against my skin. My feet are bare because I threw away my ruined shoes. I feel as light as a breeze, and as heavy as lead.

When we arrive at my house, he comes around to my side of the car. He looks at me, up and down, wearing his clothes. "There's a thing that happens in my line of work, a phenomenon. Somebody comes in looking for a house. He starts out on this exhausting search. Eventually he gets frustrated because the one he wants isn't there. But there comes a time when he's looked and looked, and he's seen a lot, and it happens: he walks in the front door, one that's just come on the market, and he knows, just like that, that this is the house. Doesn't take a second."

"Two seconds."

He smiles the tiniest bit. "I'm just saying. Sometimes things are obvious." He is so close, right there, but we don't touch. "I've been to enough open houses, that's all."

I walk up the steps, barefoot, and I feel Henry watching as I reach the door. At the top, I turn to wave goodbye, and he says, "I don't think you came to Nashville to sell a house. I think you wanted to come home."

I can't believe he just said that. He's told me his story, and now he's doubling down. He's all in. What in the world am I supposed to make of him?

What to Keep and What to Discard

The basement is nasty. After a day of the shsh-shsh pump steadily ejecting the basement floodwaters, spoonful by agonizing spoonful, I take an early morning tour of the subterranean vault beneath the house. I don't see how it will ever dry out. It's going to mold, and mildew, and eventually the dank ooze will creep up the stairs and kill us all. We're going to have to fill it with cement; bulldoze the house; flee waving our arms in the air, screeching in horror.

A fan is a good weapon, apparently. Yesterday, while I was out at the water treatment plant, Bennett showed a mild interest in this basement project—maybe he was hallucinating that he was a Confederate corps of engineers officer. From his foldout-bed command post, he activated his daughters to go track down some fans. When you put five fans in a basement, crank them all to high, and point them into every corner, the wind tunnel effect will crank a beehive hairdo in about fifteen seconds.

I don't know. The house is so full now. Everywhere I go, there's a human hunkered down doing something. Bennett does not seem to have moved since I left yesterday to make hushpuppies. The library now looks like a dorm room. I can't read his frame of mind at all, though it does feel like he is in no hurry to leave. He says he doesn't even want to get his foot examined. "I am a doctor, you know." So strange.

In the laundry room, Shelly has decided to dismantle the washing machine to fix a leak, and it's not clear that she quite knows how to put it back together. She sits on a stool, muttering "hosepipe" and "wing nut." Amelia is on the floor, doing whatever Shelly tells her to do, an apprentice repair technician. Shelly launches into a lecture about the dangers of lending tools.

Cassie calls me into the den. "Aunt Delia! Your prisoners are on TV." I see the inmates working, lifting the heavy sandbags, an endless task, one after another. A dump truck pulls up behind an inmate being interviewed, and deposits another small mountain of sand. "Feels good to help," he says. The river is right there, sloshing around on the other side of the sandbags, so close. The moment comes—yes!—when they show an inmate holding a plate of our catfish and hushpuppies. "That's my puppy!"

Cassie applauds ironically. "Beautiful, Aunt Delia. You should be so proud." I can't believe the chaos in the den. The girls had Mary over last night to spend the night, and evidently they have embarked on a project involving a bedsheet and every craft material in the craft closet that Ginna so lovingly filled over a period of ten years. "We're doing a flood mural," Cassie says. "Dad says this is historic, so we need to make a memorial about it."

After tracking down some coffee, I discover Mother in Ginna's bedroom, knitting on the unfinished blanket that Ginna had left by her bed.

"I didn't know you could knit," I say.

"Of course I can," she retorts, adjusting the wide blanket across her knees. "You think I'm just a home economics failure, don't you?" I think about Shelly and how she was the one who taught us to knit, to polish silver, to make a bed with hospital corners. "Well I was raised on a farm, you know. Not every minute of my life has been spent in a law library." She's fast, it turns out. "Wax a floor." Chugs along. "Pickle okra."

"I get it." It's so strange to see her doing something so domestic, so old-ladyish. I don't think of her as anything but a blinding force of legal brilliance, this brain walking around in low-heeled pumps.

"How was your flood relief work?" She says this with a wink in her voice.

"Humbling."

"How so?"

"It didn't feel like I was helping. On the news this morning they showed the inmates filling sandbags, working like Trojans. There I was, stirring batter and hanging out with Henry's yuppie friends."

Mother shrugs. "So go fill some sandbags." She yanks a length of yarn from the ball. "Actually, I think we might need to go out to Shelly's. She finally heard from her brother last night, and it's sounding like a real mess. The goats have gone missing." She knits. "Of course."

"Henry is an interesting person," I lob out. I wonder what she knows about Henry's convict history. I try to imagine him in that stylish Danish prison. I keep seeing Marimekko sheets on the bunk beds. So stunning. Henry's story has seared its way into my mind, the contrast between his past and the guy I see now. The dissonance of it all makes it hard for me to think straight about him. I can't snap all the pieces together.

"Hmmm?" Mother is lost in thought about either the goat situation or the dropped stitch she is fishing back onto a needle.

"Henry. He was telling me about what happened in Copenhagen, back when."

"Such an accident. Such. An. Accident. Bless his heart. Bless. His. Heart." She's off in a zone. "A handsome pair you are," she says almost to herself.

"Mother," I chide. She glances up.

"You are," she shrugs.

It was so hypnotic, Henry's story. He mesmerized me. "I feel so sorry for him," I say. "That poor girl. I mean, I can't even imagine."

"What girl?" Mother looks up.

"The girl in the car."

"What girl?"

Does she not know about the girl? "Henry's accident."

"Was there a girl?"

How strange. Mother looks up, confused. Did Henry just tell me something that nobody here knows? Is that why he was so affected all day? He said he didn't talk about this, but never? He was telling me something huge. I feel suddenly protective of him. "I don't know," I say. "It was hard to follow the whole thing. It was sad, that's all, to imagine him so hurt."

"David and Eleanor were over there for weeks. Like they'd dropped off the face of the earth. Just undone by it all, that precious child. They thought he wasn't going to walk again. Took more than a year for him to get home." Mother thinks he was on the mend for a year. She doesn't know he was in jail. My head spins. Henry hasn't told anyone about what really happened.

Henry.

My first thought this morning was a slightly panicky realization that I don't know Henry at all, that I'm in too deep, too fast. If you had bet me a thousand dollars that Henry had been in prison, I would have taken that bet, easily. I mean: no way. What has he been doing for the past eight years? I don't even know what he's doing this morning. Surely he hasn't actually been a monk, as he says. I can't believe he wasn't out and about with someone. And calling me a nun. Do I seem that cut off from reality? At least I have a glamorous career. On the phone. Talking to people taking glamorous trips. To places I've never been.

Speaking of blowing off work, I need to call Susan. But I dread hearing what she'll tell me. I have a feeling that things might not be going all that well, and she's being kind by not bothering me. How long do I want her to be kind? At what point do I need to knuckle down and focus on work?

"Of course I can knit," Mother mutters to no one in particular.

We all have our trials.

The sunroom is a warehouse of yarn at this point, and in a fit of order I begin to put away the skeins that have dried. I wipe out one of the bins and pull out a stack of damp papers stuck in the bottom and spread them out on the glass-topped table to dry. They look to be old medical bills, insurance stuff. It's going to be a long day, dampness everywhere, with a field trip to Shelly's in the offing, as I put my head down on the table and stare at the papers at close range.

Blue Cross Blue Shield Blue Moon Blue Christmas. Am I blue? I'm suddenly very sleepy. Wet paper dries so warbly, doesn't it? I'm staring at the page directly under my nose, my eyes crossing.

Boneopsy. Binopsy. Bone biopsy.

I sit up, electrified.

Flipping through the papers, I discover a paper trail, a story of Ginna going to get a bone biopsy, an MRI, X-rays of the pelvis, and some blood tests. In September last year. Insurance was put through on it all, and it looks like the grand total out-of-pocket expense to Ginna was $94 for $8,409 worth of medical tests.

I didn't know a thing about this. I feel like I just stuck my finger in a socket.

Bennett has a quilt pulled up to his chin. Has the loss of Carla been so profound that he can't get out of bed? I kind of want to meet her now, to see who could break his sunken heart this way. I hope the girls don't know why he's behaving like this. Maybe they're used to his ways, but I can't imagine how any kid could think that lying morosely in a foldout sofa bed for two days is normal, even if you do have a broken foot.

"Bennett. I just found these papers. Ginna's. Health insurance stuff, some clinic bills. Do you know anything about this?" I hand them to him, then wedge myself on the edge of the foldout sofa bed as far from him as possible, because there's no place else to sit. The library at this point is covered in open books draped across the back of the chairs, in the chairs, on the floor. He seems to be reliving the Civil War, volume by volume, with his Ace-bandaged foot propped up like a war wound. He fishes out his reading glasses from under the covers and takes a look at the first paper. He stares at it, head at a tilt, then shifts his head in the opposite direction, as if a different perspective will make it say something else. He flips to the other pages, examines them the same careful way. As usual, he doesn't say a word, and when he finishes, he lays down the papers.

"No. I don't know what this is about." Then, as he takes off his reading glasses, I see something I've never seen before: tears welling up in his dark and beady eyes, a rush of red across his face.

In a flash, I get it. He's not grieving the loss of Carla, in this gloomy foldout bed bunker. He's been missing Ginna.

He doesn't acknowledge his tears, but they fall freely down his cheeks, as sorrowful a sight as I've seen. "Oh, Bennett," I say, affected to see him like this.

He wipes his face with his sleeve. "Never forgave her," he says. "Never let her off the hook. I didn't care if she dangled forever." He lifts the pages limply, as if they're contaminated. "She was going through this? I don't even know this doctor. She's going to Murfreesboro for a bone biopsy? She wouldn't even come to Vanderbilt? She didn't even want me to know."

"Or me." So contagious, this sadness. My throat is tight. "What was it?"

He frowns. "Bone biopsy is not routine. Could be she was having bone pain from an infection. Or they could be looking for a spread from another site."

"Spread?"

"Metastasis. Cancer spread. Maybe there was something somewhere else." He frowns again. "Or," he says, reading from a page, "how about mesenchymal chondrosarcoma?" He looks up with a resigned expression. "There you go. That's what it was."

Sarcoma. I know what that means.

"Mesenchyme is connective tissue. It's a cancer of the cartilage, a bone cancer basically."

My heart lurches. Cartilage? How can your cartilage have cancer? That's like cancer of the fingernails. Sounds all wrong.

"That's a real diagnosis?"

"What it says here. Usually aggressive." He wipes a hand across his face as if to erase it. "Where did you find these?"

"In the bottom of a yarn bin. Floated up from the basement in the flood. Like a message in a bottle."

He shakes his head, so disgusted. Here we are, dissimilar in almost every way, but we are now yoked by the fact that we both failed Ginna, failed her to the point that she wouldn't turn to us with what had to be a crushing piece of news. Ginna, why wouldn't you tell us this? You'd do this alone?

"We suck, Bennett. We totally suck."

"Didn't want anybody to know. Jesus. Surely somebody knew?"

Mother comes wandering into the living room, then sees us in Bennett's dorm room. "Delia, do you have any scissors?" She is like an untethered moo cow these days. We have got to get this woman back to work. I am now actually missing my bossy, driven mother.

I look at Bennett, who shrugs. *Ask her*, he's saying.

"Hello, Bennett," she dispenses dryly. She may be distracted, but she keeps track of her distaste for Bennett the homewrecker. It doesn't help that he nods back at her with as sullen an expression as she has given him.

"Mother. We just found something sort of upsetting. Here, have a seat," I say, scraping *Battlefield Dentistry* and *Nine Thousand Confederate Souls* off an ottoman. "Before the accident, did Ginna ever mention any health issues to you?"

Mother is wearing one of Ginna's cardigans. At this point, we are all wearing Ginna's clothes because we don't have enough of our own. Bennett is working his way through her collection of Boulevard Bolt 10K T-shirts. I thought I was going to be here for two weeks, so I'm wallowing in her long cotton skirts. "No, well. Let's see. Health issues. Health. Issues. No, nothing. She did have that bum knee, from all the running. But nothing in particular, nothing I recall. Why?"

I hand her the papers. "These. From the basement. Bennett thinks she had some kind of cancer before she died."

"Cancer!" She almost yells this. "Ginna, with cancer? I can't imagine . . ." There is something tender about her mystified expression. She's trying to imagine, and she can't. She looks very young, a girl who's just gotten the news about the tooth fairy too early.

"Right."

Mother is doing the calculation. "So. You all didn't hear anything about this."

We shake our heads.

"She was getting tests and never told us?" She passes a hand over her hair, instinctively checking for smoothness. "For heaven's sake—was she going to have chemotherapy on the sly? Why on earth would she not say anything?"

"I don't know, Mother. It's too strange."

Bennett says he's going to call the doctor in Murfreesboro, but he's not sure how much he'll be able to get from him. I want to go lie down and wallow in this latest version of Ginna's life story, the story that keeps changing the longer I'm here. At this rate, we're going to find her stash of voodoo priestess gear in the guest room trunk.

Shelly comes into the library. "William just called. Says the highway is finally open." She stops when she sees the three of us sitting in numb disbelief, the guilty trio. Nobody says a word.

Mother stands, trying, I think, to put on a good show for Shelly. "Well then, shall we get to it? Delia, how are you with a crowbar? Shelly's got some things that need tending to."

Shelly sighs. "Got to clear it out before it molds."

I smile at Shelly. "I'm better with a sledgehammer," I say. "Do you need more helpers?"

"Misery shared is misery halved," she says with a little smile. "William said it could have been a lot worse. But he says that about everything. Wonder what he'll say when he's laid up in his coffin: 'Coulda been worse.'"

Bennett looks at Shelly, embarrassed. "I'm sorry not to be able to come," he says.

"I know," she says. "Appreciate the thought."

Bennett stands on the front porch, leaning on a crutch, dispensing parting advice. "Masks. Gloves. Do not inhale."

"It's going to be a short day, Dad, if we don't inhale," Amelia says. She leans up to kiss him. So alike, their dark eyes and hair.

The girls want to come help too, so the five of us pile into Mother's tank-like Cadillac. Mother has a crazy way of driving, with her basic philosophy being to accelerate until it's time to brake. The drive out west of town is a tour through a dystopic science fiction movie, plus free carsickness. As we wallow in the car's spongelike suspension, Harding Road is revealed to be a ruin, with slabs of pavement in the middle of fields, the long, stacked stone walls scattered like pebbles. The saplings planted alongside the railroad tracks look blasted by some fierce wind. There's junk up in the trees, six feet off the ground.

When I suggest that we drive by Mother's house to see how her cleanup is going—she lined up a crew to clear it out—she is wholly uninterested. "Not going to worry about that now." She has been like this since she and Shelly showed up at my house. There's a fortune of old furniture in that house, things handed down from my father's family in Virginia going back to the 1700s. She has always tended to these ancestral objects as if they were fragile relatives. I can't believe she isn't over there, tamping down warped veneers and rubbing everything with paste wax.

"Don't you need to see about your things?"

She shrugs. "It's just a house, Delia. They're working on it. Need to focus." She looks at me in the rear view mirror—I'm right behind her—and she widens her eyes and looks to her right as if to say, *Focus on Shelly*.

Like we didn't with Ginna, she means.

It doesn't take long to leave Nashville behind. I forgot how fast you can move from crowded city to pristine, rolling hills. The green of this place continues to astonish me, the gentle lift of the hills, covered in the moss of a thousand trees, velvet soft to the touch, surely.

"William said there was a lot of water," Shelly says. "But he said it's all gone now, so all we have to do is clean it up. Insurance will cover it all."

"You had flood insurance?" I say. "The news was saying that nobody had flood insurance."

Shelly looks back at me. "Maybe nobody did, but I did."

The highway crosses several bridges, each with a mountain of junk caught against it—pallets, fishing boats, entire trees with roots intact. The farther we drive into the country, the quieter we become. At one point we have to slide past a washout where the asphalt has been eaten away by a current. The violence of the landscape makes me think that a huge water monster has swept through, then evaporated. The day could not be more sunny, but it feels like lions and tigers and bears oh my.

The dirt driveway to Shelly's house, and her brother's beside it, runs straight across the edge of a field, a bright green stretch of soybeans, then dips down, unfortunately, toward the tree-lined creek that runs behind their houses. As we approach, we see cars parked all over the place. "Oh my," Shelly says. "What's all this?"

The thing that William failed to tell his sister is that her church congregation would turn up to help, all wearing pale blue T-shirts that read "Glory Baptist Church. Bringing A Flood Of Love." There must be twenty people milling around our car, all armed with pickaxes, buckets, brooms, and armfuls of towels and rags. They could not be more cheerful as they welcome Shelly back to her house. It's a beautiful sight to see, the reunion of all these people with Shelly. She receives all this attention with good humor until the crowd parts, and she gets a close look at her house for the first time since the flood.

"Oh, Lord," she says, then dissolves in tears, like she's melting. "Oh, my. I told myself I wasn't going to cry about this." Mother fishes a tissue out of her pocket and hands it to her.

It's a disaster. It's the thing you want never to happen to your house. The high water mark is obvious, about a foot below the gutters, with the wood siding below it covered in streaky brown mud. The windows on the left side of the house are all blown in, with branches and debris caught in the window jambs. The windows on the right side are a tangle of blasted curtains blown out the broken windows. The path of the current is obvious: straight through the house. The most unnerving thing is that the entire building seems to have shifted on its foundation. It looks like cubism.

Leaning on her cane, Shelly wanders over to a pile of shattered clay pots caught in a privet hedge. "My impatiens," she says. "Just put them out." She reaches over and pulls out a tangle of bells and string. "My wind chimes."

Amelia is wiping her eyes. Cassie leans against me, upset, too. A tall, stout woman from the church comes over and consumes Shelly with her broad arms. "We got this," she says. "Piece of cake, honey."

Shelly wipes her nose and cracks a rueful smile. Her brother, small like Shelly, and wiry, finds his way through the crowd. If they hug each other any tighter, somebody's going to snap in two.

"William, if you tell me this coulda been worse, I'm gonna kill you."

He looks up at the water line. "Coulda got into the ceiling," he says wryly. "Could been a lot worse."

I turn to ask Mother if she brought the old towels, but she's gone back to her car, sitting at the steering wheel with a handkerchief over her face. I sit down in the passenger seat and shut my door, watching the silent movie of this scene in front of us. Mother is more upset than I have ever seen her. Little gasping cries, quiet sobs. I thought I was going to get through this in a sturdy way, but Mother crying is more than I can stand. I lean over and pull her close to me, such an awkward angle to hug her, but I can't bear this, and I feel her relax against me, her head on my shoulder, mine on hers, and we cry together, sad upon sad. The whole damn day has caught us and won't let go. I see Ginna sitting alone in a doctor's office, with that brown Coach bag on her knees, waiting for a doctor to drop a bomb on her. I see Shelly pointing at a window and shaking her head. The soft scent of Mother's perfume, that rosy scent she always wears, surrounds us in a pale cloud, and I feel her warm hand on my wrist. "Delia," she says.

Over her shoulder, I watch a burly older man pull a bucket from the back of his pick-up truck, and I cry all over again to see his wide smile as he jokes with another man. "Mom," I say. "We're still here."

She presses the handkerchief against her eyes, wipes her nose, then lifts away this weepy, damp shroud. Thin rivulets of tears follow the creases by her eyes, but I can see that she is very much herself, in there. "We are that," she says. "Such as we are."

She watches the silent movie, too. Shelly sits down on the steps while her friends swarm into the house. "She's lived here forty years," she says. "She and Danny built this house right next door to William and Sarah because they knew it would be safe out here. Danny put that house together himself, every stick of it. And now she can't even find her goddamn goats."

"They'll have this rebuilt in a snap," I say despite the fact that I don't actually believe this.

Mother turns in her seat to me, miserable. "That's not what's really going on here. Shelly is wishing for that, but William wants her to move into town. She says this is the final straw. Needs to get her knees done, but the doctor says they'll never be much good. William wants her to use the flood insurance money for an apartment. Can you imagine Shelly living in an apartment?" She says *apartment* as if she's saying *rendering plant*.

No, actually, I can't. Shelly has lived close to the land as long as I've known her, with her garden, her chickens, the goats. Now I understand why Shelly has put up with her bad knees. As long as she could get around, this life was possible.

"Can't you just help her out? Get a helper for her?" I ask.

Mother frowns, then shakes her head. "Delia, do you hear what you just said? You want me to fix Shelly's problem with a big check. Can you believe it? You just suggested the very thing that you hate about me!" She's actually amused by this, and I have to smile. "I know you don't believe that I know this, but money can't fix everything, Delia. It doesn't rebuild bad cartilage. In fact, it doesn't fix much of anything. Just pays for things." She wipes her nose. "You've taught me that, at this point." She seems steadier now. "Shall we? The goal, according to William, is to inventory everything that was ruined, for insurance purposes."

And that means listing every single thing down to the half-empty box of Kleenex swollen into a misshapen blob, the can of allspice that dates from 1962, the crushed box of Q-Tips. Cassie and Amelia are the listmakers, and the rest of us work inside, bringing out all the belongings for Shelly to declare up or down. I feel so awkward, going through Shelly's things. I know she feels even worse, but it has to be done, and the sooner we finish, the better.

I can't get over how complete the devastation is. Six grown men use every ounce of their strength to get the waterlogged mattresses out of the house. "Like a dead elephant," William says. "Nothing has ever weighed this much." The dishes in the cupboard are so full of water that the cabinets are sagging off the wall. I open a kitchen drawer, and it's a tiny pond with a sunken treasure of spoons and forks at the bottom.

At lunchtime, a big box of peanut butter sandwiches and potato chips appears. We work until late afternoon, and it feels very special to be a part of Glory Baptist Church's flood of love. These people are so contagious. Shelly is the project today, we all know. Shelly is what we're going to fix, on a day when a lot of other things can't be repaired.

At the end, it's as if Shelly's whole life has been spread out in her front yard for everyone to see, sorted into two piles: the salvageable (small) and the ruined (a small mountain).

We are all exhausted on the way home. William asked Shelly to stay at their cousins' house, but she declined, saying she was settled in at our house. I had a moment of hospitality pride that my innkeeping skills won her over, at least for the night.

We come up the front steps, and there's a box sitting on the porch. Honey-Spiral Ham Company, it says on the side. It's the size of a doghouse.

"What on earth is this?" Shelly asks.

"Dinner," Mother says. "I thought we should at least have some kind of supper." I look at the label, and sure enough, I now know what it's like to have four pounds of mashed potatoes arrive by overnight delivery from the Honey-Spiral Ham Company. "Knew this would be a long day. There was a catalog in the kitchen."

"Everybody likes ham," I say.

"Except Dad," Cassie says as she goes upstairs. "Flying ham."

"I heard that," Bennett says from the library.

"It's a turkey," Mother calls out dryly. "Not a ham."

Mother and I unwrap all the dry ice, all the containers of the dinner while Shelly rests upstairs. It's all in the box, from the dressing to the gravy to the cranberry relish. The potatoes come in a heavy plastic bag, like a giant packet of ketchup. I guess this counts as mother-daughter cooking? She's very good with the box cutter. She slides the enormous turkey, already a golden brown, into the oven to warm. It's *like* cooking.

We settle in at the long mahogany table in the dining room: Bennett and his two girls, Shelly, my mother and me. Amelia has fished out the silver and china.

"It's Thanksgiving," Cassie says. "Only faster."

"Magic," Amelia says.

"Caramel cake. Mom's cake."

"I know," Amelia says. "The best."

It's true: there is a hole at the table, the obvious lack of the caramel-cake baker. Bennett looks very low, as if he feels personally responsible for her absence. For him, this dinner is rhyming badly with many other, better Thanksgivings. Mother pats Amelia's hand—since when has she been a hand-patter?—and Amelia lets a small smile out. To my surprise, I find myself saying "Shouldn't we have a blessing?" and Shelly—who has had one of the longer days of her life—nods and asks us to bow our heads. "Lord, we thank you for this food, and this roof, this ark. And we thank you for this flood that has brought us together and reminded us of the power of nature. And the power of family. We remember Ginna and know she is with you, and we hope she can see us here, tonight, together in her home. We praise you and thank you, Lord. Amen."

That just about does me in, all of us. The power of nature and the power of family. I think of all the places I could be tonight, and this is it. There's no place else I could possibly be.

We all mop our damp eyes, unembarrassed. Amelia passes the green beans to Cassie, who is unaware that her father is studying her as if he has never seen her before. He sighs heavily and adjusts his knife into perfect alignment with the spoon beside it. And he starts talking.

He lays out a chronicle of his day spent in the basement with the wet-vac, doing his limping best to help get rid of the last of the floodwater down there. He seems to have some EPA-level understanding of the insidious nature of mold, and he could not stand the thought of what could be spawning down there while he sat in the library, doing nothing. "The silent killer," he says knowingly. I'm trying to remember how many mold-related deaths I've heard about on the news. He tells us how he managed to end up stuck, wedged under the ancient boiler, on the prowl for spores, and we can't stop laughing, and neither can he.

The potatoes are delicious.

Sunburn

I wake up early these days. Mr. Serious has taken it upon himself to sleep at the top of my bed, right by my head, an obese and furry nightcap, and he's an early riser. The house, too, tends to wake me up. All the people downstairs make the place creak. It's not noisy, exactly—the house is too big for that. But there's always the feeling that someone is closing a door, running a shower, having a conversation. In Chicago, my strange hours sometimes make for nocturnal, raccoonlike behavior. In Chicago, there's never the smell of cinnamon rolls and coffee to tantalize me out of my bed.

Shelly thanked God last night for the flood. It figures. She teases her brother about saying that things could have been worse, but the fact is, she is the one with the chronically half-full cup. I remember all those years with her so vividly now. She has found a lot of joy and a lot of hope in the way she holds friends and family so close.

How strange it is. If there hadn't been a flood, this house of damp family would never have happened. I would be here, upstairs in my hermit attic, counting the minutes until I could return to my hermit loft in Chicago. Bennett would be over at Creek Valley Close Condominiums, distractedly managing his girls and pouring his frosty heart out to the bass-boat-seeking Carla. Mother would be careering off to Cookeville visiting Ginna's childhood Girl Scout camp, and Shelly would still be telling herself that her knees aren't that bad. Henry would be stewing over trying to sell that ranch house in West Meade and still looking for a girl like me. The girls—actually, the girls would still be sneaking into the house, trying to find someone who's not here anymore. At least there are people in the rooms now.

Mother. I can't recall the last time I saw Mother crying. She was steady even through Ginna's funeral, which annoyed me so much.

It's Wednesday, I realize as I stare at the ceiling. It feels like a month since the flood. It's been four days. Four watery days. Four weeks ago, I was helping the Patricks buy ferry tickets on a Friday in the Czech Republic for a ferry that only sells tickets on Tuesday afternoons. It was one of those moderately challenging problems, but I nailed it. Aftermarket ferry tickets. So on it, so sharp!

Now I'm blurry, not an edge to be found. I've got a houseful of relatives I thought I knew so well. There's a guy, right there, who wants to be with me. The certainties I carried around like little notebooks are all missing. What I know has dissolved into what I would like to know. Very little is obvious to me, except for the lone fact that I feel like I have a lot to do here. I have lost my focus, but I have never felt so loose, open, available.

My back aches from yesterday's Shellyfest. I think of Henry. What was his day like?

HenryPeek Full disclosure on a house = best way to go, even if it hurts. They learn you're honest, at least. #tipoftheday

I think of supper last night, of the Thanksgivings that Ginna hosted. She had this crazy way of wrapping bacon around her turkey. It was so incredibly bad for you, and so good. Why didn't I come down more often? I had so many solitary Thanksgivings in Chicago. Museums were the way I would pass holidays like that, wandering the galleries at the Art Institute with the herds of families who were walking off their big dinners. I thought I was so sophisticated—I was *looking* at the paintings, unlike these drowsy people drifting by. Ginna would have been absolutely mystified to see me doing something like that. It would never have occurred to her to spend a holiday by herself.

My first job of the day: I need to talk to Angus. Yesterday I was wiping the mud off Shelly's answering machine, and I remembered that voicemail he left for Ginna.

Mary is back, on the floor of the den, gluing spirals of brown feather boa to the sheet on the floor. They seem to be working up the Cumberland as a showgirl flood. There's glitter all over the place. I wonder when school is going to reopen. The girls' school had four feet of water in the mechanical room, so it will be a while.

"Mary, is your dad home?" I don't even know what Angus does for a living, but it certainly seems like he's always around. I think of him as some kind of country squire, out mending his walls and puffing on a meerschaum pipe.

"Um yeah, I think so."

"I'll be back—just have a question for him." I study the firmament of gray clouds they have created from spray-painted cotton balls. "Amelia, dress shopping today?"

Amelia swings her dark hair as she turns to me. "Yeah. That would be great. Grandma was talking about it. I don't know what to get."

"We'll find something fabulous. Hey Mary—what is it that your dad does? You know—work?"

She looks up, her dark eyes enormous under her bangs. "He's a lawyer, sort of. Something with stocks and law. He works at home. Reads a lot."

He's a spy. He's got to be a spy. Who hangs around the house on a Wednesday morning? I remember that lugubrious expression on his face the first time I saw him coming up the driveway.

I feel jumpy, walking down the street. To get to the bottom of all this, I'm going to have to let Angus know that I know everything. What does he think I know already? He knows that Bennett knows, but beyond that? That night of the flood, when he came to pick up Mary, he let on absolutely nothing about being friends with Ginna. No more chat about the neighborhood association. Too close, I guess, even to say her name. I have the wrinkled papers from the yarn bin with me, and I hope he will explain all this.

Angus's stern stone house looks like Errol Flynn will come swinging off the turret, but as I approach the front door, I see little signs of life: a patch of pansies squeezing out their last blooms before the heat gets them, a row of white peonies bent over in heavy bloom. Mary's rain boots are tipped over beside an urn with a little evergreen tree in it.

I doubt my knock even penetrates the heavy wooden door. I peer through the small window, but it's pretty dark in there. Angus's long face suddenly appears, right in front of me, and I jump. Ichabod! Right there! There's a medieval clanking sound, and the door swings open.

"Hello Delia," he says. Dark gray sweater: check. It's eighty degrees outside, and he's wearing Ginna's souvenir Shetland wool.

Gah. So nervous. "Hey. Angus." He looks at me expectantly. "Would you mind if I came in?" I hold up the papers, curled into a tight tube. "I just had something I was wondering about."

He steps aside. "Please."

No suits of armor, no dank tapestries. It's surprisingly soft and pretty, a place anybody would feel happy in. How could Angus have such a welcoming house? I'd imagined that he spent his time in a lone chair in front of a vast fireplace, *Citizen Kane* style.

He leads me to a library off the entrance hall, we sit, then he stands quickly. "Coffee. What about some coffee?"

He's not a natural host. He's making an effort here.

"I would love some. Thank you."

He looks rueful. "Would you mind? If you could come with me. I don't often make coffee, and I could use your expertise." Such a lush accent, somewhere between old money Yale and old money Vanderbilt.

"Oh, tea's fine. Or water. Water's great."

"No, no. I ought to know how to use this contraption."

"I can try."

"Augusta was a coffee fanatic. Prissy about it. And Hilda, our housekeeper, will be off for a while—her house was ruined. She holds the keys to the kingdom around here."

The kitchen is down the long hallway—such a big house for just the two of them. He walks under a light fixture and I almost yell "duck!" but I remember that he probably knows he has one inch of clearance.

"Such a home you have," I say, meaning it.

"My grandparents built it after they came back from their honeymoon in France. Living some fantasy, as you can see. I suppose they imagined themselves some kind of French nobility, which they most certainly were not. Nashville, Tennessee." He almost chuckles. There's somebody in there.

The coffee maker is a mess, the Maserati kind that I can't figure out. But we dump beans and fill reservoirs and push a button. "It'll be either coffee or we'll discover a new element," Angus says.

"A person needs to be fully caffeinated to operate this thing," I say. Hey— we're cracking jokes! This is going swell.

There's something comforting about waiting for coffee to make. It takes the edge off my nerves, and I sit on a stool. This kitchen is about a hundred times nicer than Ginna's. "Do you cook?" I ask.

He rolls his eyes. "My wife did. Constantly. I've lost thirty pounds since." I nod. "Cream was one of the four food groups." He starts to say something, then stops. "I ought to live in a smaller place, I suppose."

"I wouldn't want to leave either. If I could afford it."

He glances up at me. Is he thinking about Ginna's house? "Well, it's loaded with memories. It's the easiest thing, to stay in a place that you know well."

Ginna used to sigh a lot when we'd pass this house on our walks in the neighborhood. Once she and Angus got together, she had to have been in this very room. It gives me a chill to think of her here, on the sly, nervous and excited. Ah, Ginna. What were you thinking?

Angus is watching me, waiting for me while I zone off into talking to my dead sister. I need to get down to business. I can feel his anxiety about why I'm here. He's as jumpy as I am. I pour a mug of coffee and head back down the hall to the library.

"Angus. I have some questions, and I could use your help."

He looks down at his shoes. I look at his shoes, too. We are talking to his carefully polished loafers.

"My sister."

"Ginna."

"Right." Where to begin? "Angus," I say to his shoes. "We found some papers."

"What kind of papers?"

"Medical bills, some insurance stuff."

"Really."

"We think Ginna was sick. When she had her accident."

Angus is not moving. I think he's hoping that I will forget that he's here.

"Just found them. We had no idea. This is really, really upsetting to us."

He studies his thumbnail as if he just discovered it exists. He traces the edge of it with a finger, looks at his fingerprint, then lets it drop to his lap. He sighs. "Well, what do you want to know? Why does any of this matter? There's only one fact relevant here: she is gone, and we're all miserable."

"That's two facts."

"I don't care to go into details." Angus shifts in his chair. He does indeed look miserable, but he also has a stubborn set to his eyes.

"Look. I know about that sweater," I say. He glances down at it, then back at me, his face open, searching almost. "I know everything. Bennett told me about you and Ginna. What was going on. There's no reason to pretend about anything."

"I'm not pretending," he says quietly.

"What happened, Angus?"

I look at him in that sweater, which honestly is a fine piece of knitting. He's listing to the right a little as he sits in the wingback chair. Maddening. He shakes his head slowly. "It's just. It's just a shame, that's all."

Infuriating. "A shame? Like you broke a shoelace? Like somebody forgot to water the asparagus fern? It's a good deal worse than a shame, Angus. Over at my place, we're all suffering aftershocks from an earthquake that hit us six months ago. We're sleeping in the streets because we're thinking the roof might cave in. I assure you, it's not just a shame down at our house. We are good and freaked out over what happened, and the news seems to just keep coming." I am so pissed. "Furthermore, after a few weeks of being down here, I'm concluding that the one person who has any clue about the last days of Ginna's life is you."

"It's not my place. To say anything."

"What do you mean?"

"Her wishes. I'm just honoring her wishes."

"For what?"

"For privacy."

"Her wishes or yours?"

He sighs. I've never seen such a combination of sorrow and defiance. "Perhaps it's best if you go now."

He's doing this? He's not going to tell me anything? He's like Tar Baby—the less he says, the more I want to poke him with a stick. "There was a voice-mail from you on Ginna's phone."

He looks at me sharply, hearing the accusation in my voice. "What did it say?"

"Something about meeting her at a clinic, and hoping she felt better that morning."

He leans back in the tall chair, head propped against the wing. Then, swiftly, he stands as if lifted by a breeze and heads toward the front door. "I'd like you to go now," he says in a low voice. "This is not something I am prepared to discuss."

He stands with the doorknob in his hand, the door wide open to the bright day outside. I am trembling at this point, so upset that he won't talk. "Angus," I say, standing on the front porch, "I don't know what you think you're protecting, but Ginna isn't here anymore. There's nobody to protect but yourself. And there's nothing good going to come from that."

He's kicking me out, silently. He would probably wait there all day from the look of him. I give him my most irate glare and stomp down the driveway. I am halfway home before I remember that I left the insurance papers in Angus's library. Maybe those wrinkled, sorry pages will make him see how little we have to work with.

I don't know. I want to punch the guy. So infuriating. He knows. He knows all sorts of stuff, and he's sitting there all buttoned up, like he's preserving the sanctity of his beloved Saint Ginna. For crap's sake. Makes me crazy. It's like he's going to torment us with this. Can't stand it.

I get back to the house, hot as fire about this Angus thing, and I find Amelia and Mother sitting on the front steps, waiting for me.

"Shopping time!" Mother says cheerfully. I wonder, suddenly, if she is on some kind of antidepressants. Isn't everybody? Why am I not?

"Hi," I say, trying to fake an equivalent amount of cheer.

Amelia stands. "You guys are so nice to do this."

"Can't wait," I say. "This is going to be great." I have got to calm down. My head is still spinning with frustration at The Doomsayer.

"I don't want anything dumb," she says. "Some girls have these ... dresses. I just want a dress that's normal."

Good job, Ginna. You raised a good girl. I feel a huge responsibility to make this all work out perfectly for Amelia.

We launch the Cadillac—truly, it's a river barge on wheels. I regret not taking a Dramamine, what with Mother's accelerator/brake technique and Angus's $400-a-pound coffee sloshing around in my gut. "So who are you going with?" Mother asks.

"Carter Phelps. He's a senior. He's just a friend."

That's what we all say.

"He wasn't going to go, he said, but then he said he wanted to. He knew I wasn't going with anybody because Melanie told him. So."

"Where to?" I ask.

Mother suggests Faber's, a dress shop that's been around for decades, and when she mentions it, Amelia brightens immediately. "Oh! They have the coolest stuff. Like Grace Kelly. Have you seen *Rear Window*?" Aha, so our Peace Corps volunteer has another side. Carter Phelps has no inkling of what will be heading his way on Saturday night.

This is one of those times when I miss Ginna so much that my head hurts. The empty chair. She ought to be doing this motherly rite of passage. This is what you dream about—a teenage daughter who will actually let you shop with her. Mother and I sit in the dressing area, and the saleswoman is a tiny, sharp-eyed lady dressed entirely in black with a tape measure dangling around her neck. Scary and perfect at the same time. It's probably extravagant to be shopping here for a sixteen year old's dress, but what gorgeous dresses they are. Amelia beelines straight for one in particular, a short tank dress, and when she comes out of the dressing room, the emerald green silk looks fantastic with her dark hair and pale skin. She knows this is the one, just like that, taking a turn for us and smiling. She reaches under her arm to find the price tag, and Mother says, "No peeking! This is our treat," but Amelia has already seen it, and her eyes widen.

"Oh, Grandma, I couldn't possibly."

"No worries," she says. Mother is as taken as I am by Amelia, so striking to see in something other than her jeans and Converse.

"Seriously. This is awesome. But I could never do something like this. After yesterday." At Shelly's, she means. "I mean." She looks like she's been caught stealing a candy bar.

"It's OK," I say. "We can find something else. There are a million dresses."

"I saw one in Mom's closet," she says. "I think if we shortened it, it would work. It's green, sort of like this."

Oh, man. There's no way I'm going to let Amelia wear her mother's old dress to her prom. "Tell you what—we'll go poke around at the mall." Amelia looks doubtful. "It's so good of you to be thinking of Shelly—"

"It's not just Shelly. It's the whole city. There are a bunch of teachers at school who've lost everything. What if we put the dress money into a donation or something? I mean, I appreciate your bringing me out like this."

I glance at Mother, who has an unreadable expression. "I think that's a lovely idea, Amelia."

When we get home, Cassie greets us at the door, curious about The Dress, and immediately lets into Amelia. "You didn't get a dress? What are you waiting for? The prom is in three days, girl!"

Amelia explains how she just couldn't stand to buy a dress like that, and Cassie says, "Oh. Well. You should go rent one at the vintage shop. They have like party dresses from the fifties and sixties. Like forty bucks. Hey—you should get all your friends to do it. And then you could all donate the leftover money, and it would be like noble and awesome and everything." By the end of this she is talking in her singsongy hippie voice.

I am amazed that there is a girl in the world who would forego her prom dress for flood relief. And another one who would scheme up a rented-prom-dress charitable effort. But then, these girls surprise me on a daily basis. They're like little line drawings coming to life.

"Here, Aunt Delia," she says, picking up a small card on the front table. "I think this is for you." She rolls her eyes. The doodle of Henry's face.

"Oh. Thanks," I say, attempting to take it in a nonchalant, distracted, uninterested way. Trying not to grab it.

"Came by," it says in Henry's scrawl. "I have an offer for you."

Just for the record, I went almost two hours there without thinking about Henry. It's just about impossible for me to resist wondering what he's doing. Right this moment, for example. This business card is a colossal relief. I want to frame it. When he left the other day, we didn't make a plan to see each other again, which left me in that endless eddy of call/don't call. Guileless/coy. Dignity/no shame. I'm way too old for this.

What is his offer? I can think of at least three different meanings for that. I go looking for a quiet place to make my phone call.

This house. I feel like we should be offering lunch buffets and shuffleboard. At what point do people start asking for shore excursions to the rum factory? To my shock, I find that Bennett is sitting on the Fiesta Deck in the back, outside the house, not in his sofa bed, with a pair of surprisingly cool sunglasses on, reading the *American Journal of Orthopedics*. "There's a stack of these here I never even read," he says.

"Fun! Did the war end?" He shakes his head, so misunderstood.

"I have got to get back to work."

"I bet."

Amelia comes out from the kitchen and puts a plate of leftover yeast rolls on the wrought iron table. "We were dress shopping."

"I heard," he says. "Find anything?" Is he going to talk hemlines with Amelia?

"Yes and no. Working on it." She glances at me and smiles. "I love yeast rolls." She stands and stretches into one of her pretzel yoga poses. "You should try yoga, Aunt Delia. You would like it. It's good for people at computers all the time."

"Trying to drum up business for your dad? You don't want to see me do yoga."

She laughs and bends down into a long stretch. "I'm just saying," she says, then rises in an impossibly graceful swoop and disappears into the house, munching on a roll.

I wonder what Ginna told them about me all these years, how she explained the aunt who never came to town. *Girls, your poor, employed aunt sits at a computer for weeks at a time, never leaving her depressing little room. She even got carpal tunnel syndrome once. Never be like her, children, whatever you do.*

Bennett shifts in his chair and stares at his propped-up foot. "I hate this."

I wonder what of many things he could be referring to: his foot, his flooded-out apartment, being in this house, me, Mother, Ginna dying on us, that particular issue of the *American Journal of Orthopedics*? "What?"

"The girls. I hate that they don't talk to me."

"Well, do you talk to them?"

"I try." I have never seen them carrying on with any real warmth. "They don't even try."

"Want to know what I think?"

He looks up at me, frustration in his eyes. "That's what I'm asking you." He acts as if he's trying to communicate in a language he doesn't speak.

"I think you have a lot of work to do. And you have to decide if you can do it."

"Ginna was the one. It feels . . . impossible."

"It is impossible, basically. We're not her. We don't have that thing."

"You're better at it than I am," he says. I think: Mr. Serious is better at it than he is. My hairbrush is better at it than he is.

I decide to go for it. "They hate Carla. That didn't help."

He shrugs. "That's over."

"Well. But you got to understand. That was a big deal."

"This house is like being in the worst dream I ever had. Here we are, back, but there's a glass wall between me and everything I had. I can see it, get this close to it, but I can't have it anymore. Can't touch it. And it's all I want."

"I keep thinking it will get easier."

"It won't."

"I'll help," I say. "The girls. We're tight. They think I'm funny. I need that kind of approval."

He scowls, deep furrows between his dark brows. "You're in Chicago."

"I'll be here." I can't believe I'm saying this. "To visit."

He looks at me skeptically. "Really?"

Henry's beautiful face flashes in my mind. "Well, yeah."

"I'll believe it when I see it." The scorn of one who recognizes a fellow introvert.

"Thanks a lot."

"I'm going on past history."

"Maybe we should all just let go of past history, don't you think? Maybe that's the job right now."

I wish Ginna were here right this minute, seeing Bennett and me on her terrace, the two least capable human beings in the world. She would be laughing her ass off at our ineptitude.

The only place I can get any privacy is up in my attic. I dial my phone, Henry's card a winning lottery ticket in my hand, the prize being an excuse to call him.

"I just have one question," I say, diving right in to avoid that awkward hey-how-are-you thing that is so embarrassing. "Who did this little drawing of you?"

"Hi. Delia," he says. "Could you hold on?" He sounds like he's in an echoing room with other people.

"Where are you?"

"A meeting. Call you back?"

"Yeah sure."

"My mother," he says.

"What?"

"My mother. Did the drawing. Talk to you soon."

I sit, slack, on the edge of my bed. I could wait, right here, for the next six hours, no problem, sustained by the fifteen seconds of Henry's live, actual, human voice. I don't know if it's possible to describe the chronic buzz of Henry that hums in my mind. It spikes into conscious thought every so often, but it's never not there, the thin line of Henry running alongside all my other thoughts.

His mother did the drawing. Shelly said his mother died a few years ago. He hasn't talked about her.

I think about his car wreck, his wet hair, and his long body stretched out on his bed. It was such a dazzling sight that I had a hard time absorbing the story of his miserably derailed life. You can't lie there with no clothes on and tell me about how you went to jail. He told it in such a hypnotic way. How could my mother not know this story? She was friends with his parents. I don't get it. At all.

I've been thinking about this prison thing constantly. How far off the rails did he go? Was he a total derelict, or just a semi-derelict? The girl in the car died. I felt a crash myself just hearing about it, this eight-year-old tragedy. Sickening. I wonder if he's ruined by it. Is that what he means by calling himself a monk? Is he somehow broken?

While I wait, I investigate the Kotex carton that has served as my bedside table. I pull off the tape on top, and sure enough, it's a case of pillowy pads, so antique that they don't even have adhesive on them. I think you're supposed to tie them on with jungle vines. What was Ginna up to? Starting a museum of sanitary history? Saving them for a feminist art project? I can't stand this house, all of a sudden.

My phone buzzes. "Where are you?" I ask.

"A meeting. Hey—I need to see you." He needs to see me. I flop back on my bed in delight. "Somebody's interested in the house." I sit up again, dismayed.

"Who?"

"Can you get out? Let's go eat. I'll come get you."

His embrace, there in the driveway, is a drink of water. I try not to overdo, but I have craved his touch so much, and I hold on until I can feel the warmth of him soak into me. Henry surely must know the effect he has on me. So thirsty for him. He won't let go, either, I'm relieved to discover.

"Where are we going?" I ask.

"Where do you want to go?"

"Anywhere."

He is heading down West End, toward downtown, but I don't sense that he has a destination. He looks tired in the eyes, his hair rumpled.

"I think about you. All the time," I say. So much for coy.

He looks embarrassed. "Me too. I mean, worried actually. What you think. About everything." He is so transparent. He glances over at me. "I've wanted to talk to you so much. What have you been doing?"

I smile. "Henry. I don't know what to say." I have piles of family drama to tell, but I feel like we have an endless amount of time to talk about these things. What is urgent, right this minute, is the sensation of being beside him in his car, riding someplace, watching his hand on the steering wheel, the knots of his knuckles, the shadows of veins under his skin. "You're all sunburned." His arms are red, his cheeks and nose a hot pink against his white shirt. His high color makes his eyes an even more vivid blue.

"Running around," he says. "Kevin. We have fed every hungry person in Davidson County. Nobody's hungry anymore."

"Who knows what happened in Denmark?"

He glances over at me, puzzled at the change in subject. He doesn't say anything for a second, then exhales heavily. "Nobody, really." He bites his lip, thinking. "The accident, yes. But the prison part, no. Other than my fellow convicts, a bunch of mental health care providers. And rooms full of superdepressed mental patients, oh and people I know only by their first names, I've told three people—civilians, I mean. Two were my parents. The third is you."

"No way."

"It's a true fact."

"Mother didn't know."

"Right. Did you tell her?" He's curious, not anxious.

"No. Almost did, then realized she had no idea." I'm so amazed. "You would tell me this, after not telling anybody."

He nods slowly. We're at a stoplight. He's looking right at me. "It's kind of a big deal. To tell you." I can't hold his gaze.

He pulls to the side of the road, in front of a cozy-looking restaurant, Tin Angel. He turns off the engine and shifts in his seat so I can see his extravagantly sunburned face. He rolls down the windows to catch a breeze. I exhale and realize I've been holding my breath.

"Really wanted to tell you, that first night even. Never wanted to talk to anybody so much in my entire life. I could tell, right from the first, that you would get this."

I'm overwhelmed. This feels like I've just been diagnosed with a disease. Henry is the doctor delivering the news, so calm about it. It may be an old story to him, but it sure as hell isn't old to me. I can't imagine how a human being could haul this experience around all by himself. It's the loneliest thing I ever heard.

"What about your friends? Didn't they wonder what you were doing in Denmark?"

"You know how it is after college, everybody moving all over the place, so into themselves. You can vague out if you try."

"Vague your way out of prison?"

"I was motivated, believe me. I was 'recuperating.' I was 'traveling.' One friend, Danny, a roommate from college, came through Copenhagen, but I was 'out of town.' Like three-card monte. Just keep moving. People knew I had an accident, just not the whole story."

"That's a lot to keep to yourself."

"Yeah. No burden on you, right?" He smiles a little, takes my hand.

"How can you joke about this?" I ask. "How could you not tell anybody?"

"I don't expect you to keep it to yourself. I wouldn't ask that of you."

I can't digest this. "I thought you're supposed to go make amends with people. In . . . recovery." I'm embarrassed to say the word.

"I did go to Dublin, after I got out. Her father saw me, her mother wouldn't. A nightmare, the whole trip. He had these hollow eyes, deep down in there, like looking into a cave. She had eyes like that, Clare did. Only sparkly, not flattened like his. It was like I'd killed him, too."

I can hardly imagine how that meeting had to have gone. How did he not rot from the inside, dissolve into a puddle of guilt and regret?

"You should tell people stuff. It's not healthy to keep all that inside."

"Uh, yeah," he says, as if I've suggested that vegetables are good for you. "Maybe I was waiting to tell the right person. Maybe it had to be someone I wanted to know." He says these sweet things in such an unembarrassed way. "If you tell this stuff in therapy enough times, in enough meetings, you're sick of the sound of your own stupid story. It's not that I haven't told it—it's that I just wanted a life where I didn't have to tell it. Where it didn't happen."

"Can't believe a therapist wouldn't make you deal with this."

"I dealt with it, in my way."

"I don't think keeping this a secret for eight years is exactly dealing with it."

"You don't actually know that, do you?" There's an edge in his voice, and he sounds tired again. His eyes follow a woman on the sidewalk beside our car, led by her loose-jointed Labrador retriever on a slack leash. Henry drifts into a trance almost, then notices me and perks up. He reaches for the car key, turns the ignition, and starts the engine.

"Tuckered out," he says as we turn right at a light.

Misery shared is misery halved, Shelly says. Which means, for Henry, that his misery is whole, undiluted all these years.

I have to ask. "So. No confessions to old girlfriends?"

Now I've embarrassed him, and myself, too. "Yeah, a string of them. Right. Nobody who," he pauses. "Nobody who stole my heart," he says lightly. "What about you? Where are all the old boyfriends who wrote poems about you?"

"Henry," I say, incredulous. "When you called me a nun, that bugged the crap out of me. Maybe because it was true."

He smiles a little. "The convent lifestyle."

I seem to be stuck on the words "stole his heart." I stole his heart? He thinks this? I thought he had stolen mine. "Please stop driving this car," I say.

We are at his apartment. I slide my hands around his neck. I don't know what is wrong with me: I want to possess him, lay claim to him. His sunburned neck is hot against my fingers as he leans to kiss me. He's surrendering, collapsing against me. He smells so clean, his warm shirt. I want to do this all day, here in Henry's car.

He stops. "Come on," he says, opening his car door. As we approach his front steps, he says, "Hey guess what—the water treatment plant. It's safe. They just announced it." Solemn.

He knew this would make me happy. He might as well have handed me a bunch of tulips.

I go into his bathroom to find lotion, anything to soothe his hot skin. His medicine cabinet is as tidy as the rest of him, minty floss and seven bars of soap stacked up. An industrial-size bottle of Advil, Tylenol, and there in the corner, the pale person's remedy—a luminescent bottle of green aloe gel.

"Delia?" Henry calls from the kitchen.

As I take down the aloe, I see some small bottles behind it. "Hold on," I yell back, and I shut the bathroom door quickly. What are they? So nosy.

I lean in, not wanting to touch them. "Virginia B. Schwartz," says one. All three, I discover, carry this name. Ginna's. Oxycodone. Percocet. Dilaudid. A smorgasbord of narcotics.

What in the world?

How did he get these? Why did Ginna have these, so many of them? I slide a bottle of rubbing alcohol in front of the prescriptions, my hand shaking, and I sit on the edge of the tub, knocked out, numb.

"Delia?" Henry's voice is right outside the bathroom door.

"Hey," I say. "Just a sec." I lean over, flush the toilet, and feel vaguely like dying. I turn on the water in the sink and watch it run for as long as a person could plausibly be washing her hands, then I stand and study my stunned face in the mirror.

He sits on the edge of his bed, and I reach down to unbutton his shirt. I paint his nose, his cheeks, his ears with the cool aloe, smoothing his forehead with the heel of my hand. I slide a hand behind his neck, as lightly as I can, and he kisses the inside of my arm. He is so fair where the sun hasn't touched him, and so red, so hot where it has.

He can keep a secret for eight years. He has my sister's pills in his bathroom. I don't know this person at all.

He watches me solemnly, then undresses me just as I've undressed him. "You are so pale," he says, and kisses my stomach. "Ghostly person."

I tip him back on the bed and take his arm by the elbow, holding it up to examine the long scar down his forearm. "Henry." I try hard not to cry as he kisses me. I'm dizzy, actually, wobbly.

I wake up, confused, with the weight of Henry's arm across me, his leg over mine. The late afternoon light makes his room glow. I can feel his exhaustion in the way he sleeps. Worn out. How long can we stay in this bed, under these covers? Fooling around in the middle of the day is not even on the long list of things I'm in the habit of doing.

I'm here. He's here, sleeping, his cheek against my shoulder. I don't want to lose this feeling, this person. But what am I to do? Ginna's painkillers are in Henry's medicine cabinet. It makes no sense. Or, rather, it makes sense only if medicine bottles have little feet and can wander into somebody else's house. Or it makes sense only if Henry has been up to something, and that's what is so upsetting. Pills aren't a cup of sugar, or a shovel. Nobody borrows pills. Not three bottles of them.

He can't be sneaky. He's not supposed to be like that. But he kept the secret of his prison time for eight years. That's sneaky. That's awful.

I have so many stories to tell him, but I don't want to hear about those pills, can't bear it. "Basically," I say into his arm, "I cry all the time. We all do. I was crying into a throw pillow this morning, wondering why Ginna invested in so many goddamn throw pillows. It's like she upholstered the upholstery. How cushy does a house need to be? I had no idea it would be like this. We're all there, in that house. It's the craziest thing. Ginna's right in there with us." Something occurs to me. "You didn't ever meet her, did you?"

"No," he says. "My dad did, though. She sounds so great."

"She was." I sit up and look closely at his hot-red nose. "Your sunburn is epic." OK, so he couldn't have taken the bottles at some distant moment. It had to be recent. He's been in my house exactly twice. I imagine him rooting through Ginna's bathroom, a bleary-eyed, pain-demented fiend in the night.

"How could you not tell anybody about going to prison? Seems impossible."

He runs his hand across my hip, so distracting. "Sort of like not telling people that you've never traveled?" he says.

"That's different."

"Is it?"

"I was embarrassed."

"Exactly. Imagine embarrassed times a thousand. A million. It's not hard to keep a secret that ruined your life."

"It's not ruined."

"It was ruined," he says. "Maybe a life can be unruined, or deruined. That's all I want," he says, and he catches my face in his hands, devours me with a kiss, then gives my lip a gentle bite. "All I want."

A pain-free life. I don't know what to make of this. I can't bear to ask him about those pills, cannot make the words come out of my mouth.

I tell him about going to Shelly's but can't do it justice. I describe prom dress shopping with Mother and Amelia, but I can't convey the expression on Amelia's face when she figures out what she wants to do about her emerald green dress. And I try to explain the peaks-and-valleys experience that is Bennett, the way I keep laughing at him at the same time I'm crying with him. I tell Henry about the appalling discovery that Ginna was sick when she died. It's such a failure, the fact that she wouldn't tell us. I am so embarrassed that this is the state of things in our family, but he doesn't seem horrified at all.

He tells me about his days with chef Kevin, picking piles of beautiful lettuce from somebody's garden, fixing beans and rice, vats of gumbo. Kevin's mobile kitchen has taken them to four different places around town, each place more wiped out than the next. He is so moved by the way people are responding to the disaster. He says he's working from dawn to dark. It seems a little compulsive. When I compliment him on what he's doing, he rejects it. "Kierkegaard said that one can do works of love in a self-loving way. One test is: who feels better at the end of the day? The person you fed or yourself?" A self-hating do-gooder. Henry is the most confounding person.

"I was telling my dad about you," he says, reaching for his glasses on the bedside table. He looks so different with his glasses on, like a grownup. He is big eyed and young without them.

"What were you telling him?"

"That I met a girl. And when he asked me who it was, I told him it was you." He laughs, and his eyes squint up like he's trying to read print that's too small. "He already knew, it turns out. Then. He starts laughing, and I say 'What?' and he says, 'Well, I just met a girl, too. And you won't believe it, but—'"

"No." He's not saying this.

"Yeah. Your mom. And my dad." Henry finds this bit of news very funny. "Known each other for thirty years. 'Just met.'"

"I don't believe it. Not possible." I can't even begin to imagine this. Mother? And David Peek? She did say he had been helping her get a therapist, which seemed like the strangest thing I ever heard. But I never would have guessed this. In all these years, the lifetime since my father died, Mother had these relationships that I only glimpsed, that she rarely referred to, that seemed never to turn into anything. And she absolutely never talked about remarrying. She was an ironclad battleship, plowing through life under her own steam.

"She called him up last week and just invited him to dinner at the country club. He likes her. Says she's sweet to him."

"Sweet? Must be some other Grace Ballenger."

"She's over there drying out his garage right now," he says. "He said she feels like she's back in college, back at Vanderbilt."

"I'm not double dating with my mom."

"You should see Dad. Trying to play it cool. This is the first time since Mom died that I've seen him show an interest in anybody. You can't believe the parade of ladies, dropping off soup and books and *New Yorker* magazines folded back to an article they just thought he might be interested in reading."

Can't believe it. "I wish you could have seen her at Shelly's. It's like the Arctic ice pack melting. She cried, Henry. It's like she's become some slightly different person."

Henry has a look on his face.

"What?" I ask.

"Funny. That's all."

"Don't you have work to do?" I ask. We seem to be stuck in bed.

"Don't you?"

"Tell me about this offer. Who is it?"

He looks skeptical. "Well, it's one of those good news/bad news things."

"The mom from California?"

"No. She's coming back in a few weeks, though. It's somebody else, a health care guy. His wife, actually. She's running the show."

"Great!"

"Yeah, well. She loves the location, loves the neighborhood." He sits up. "It's just that she doesn't exactly love the house."

"You mean."

"Yeah. Wants to build a Mediterranean villa."

"A teardown."

"Right." He could not look less happy. "They'll even pay your asking price." He takes my hand and plays with my fingers, puts my hand over his heart. "Which is wild. In this market."

I feel like someone just stole my bicycle. He knew I wouldn't like this. But he doesn't know exactly how heartbreaking it is for me to imagine Ginna's house gone, a pile of rubble, replaced by some crappy, overwrought nightmare house. It's not an option. I surprise myself with how instantly and vehemently I decide that they'll never get this house, at any price. "Out of my cold, dead hand will they pry this key," I say.

Henry smiles. "Kind of thought you would say that. But you do know that it might be months before you get another offer. The flood has trashed the market. Nothing's going to sell until everything dries out. Every house under contract has to be reinspected. A massive real estate do-over. It's a mess." He lies back on his pillows, holding my hand. "You probably ought to consider it. You'd be done. You could go." He says this last part so quietly that I think he's hoping I don't hear him.

I'd be done. I could go. I could check this off my list. I could be back in Chicago. I put my pillow on Henry's chest and rest my head on him. I hope he understands that this is my answer. But I can't stop thinking, as my head rises and falls with his breath, about his medicine cabinet. I'm going to pretend that I didn't open that little door.

Weaving Demonstration

Jimmy Butterman is beside himself, standing on the terrace like a sea captain at the rail, surveying the ruin of the backyard. The water has receded, but it looks like somebody poured a dump truck of hot chocolate four days ago and never rinsed it off. Everything is flattened to the right, like a steamroller has come through.

"Lord. Al. Mighty," he says, "I knew it. I just knew this was going to happen. Look at this. Just look at it. I'd a been here sooner but I just got my own house cleaned out." He tells me about his neighborhood, which I saw on the news this morning, a sprawling, huge subdivision by the river, now a surreal landscape with mountains of dead carpet and drywall lining the narrow streets. The houses have all been turned inside out to dry. "That Army Corps of Engineers is gonna catch all kinds of hell once it all comes out—I heard there wasn't anybody minding the store Sunday morning, when they should of been releasing water. Released it all at once, which is why that Opryland Hotel flooded." He looks out, shaking his head. "Piranhas loose in the Opry Mills mall, you hear that? Flooded waist high. Escaped from the Aquarium restaurant. They're freshwater, you know."

We contemplate the flesh-eating outlet-mall fish. He heads down the steps to study the wreckage, and I follow. I don't know how to tell him that I don't think it's worth it to restore a garden that's just going to end up in somebody else's hands.

"How long did you work for Ginna?" I ask. He's on his knees, seeing how the roots on the roses have fared.

"Well now, I'd say since they moved in. Eleven years? I do your mom's house, of course, and the Averitts down the street, and the Donalds, but this here"—he gestures over the ruined roses—"was special." He runs a hand across his forehead. "She was. Special." He pulls the brim of his ball cap low. "Can't believe she's gone."

"Yeah."

He clears his throat, trying to shake a rattle. "Insulation, nasty stuff. Anyway, your sister helped us out, my wife and me."

"Ginna?"

"She did. She didn't ever want anybody to know it, but I'll tell you now. Andrea and me were having trouble, you know, getting pregnant. Nobody in the world wanted a baby more than Andrea, I'll tell you what. Thought it was going to kill her not having a baby, so anyway, one day we were back here, Ms. Schwartz and me, doing rose stuff, and for some reason I end up talking about it, and how Andrea wanted to do the in vitro thing but it was just too much and all, and I look over, and she's all choked up, trying to act like she wasn't, and that got me all choked up thinking about her thinking about Andrea that way, and anyway, it was one of those awkward-type moments but she laughed and just wiped off her eyes and said that things just work out sometimes, right? Well anyway, she went off to some meeting and she left me my check the way she always did—taped to the back door in an envelope—but inside she put another check and this note that said that she thought Andrea and me were real lucky people, and we needed to give it a shot." He looks up at me. "So that's how we got Jennifer." He laughs. "I told Andrea we couldn't name her Virginia because it would be awkward, so we went with Jennifer. Jenny." He pulls out his wallet and shows me a red-haired girl in a white tutu. "She's eight." He looks at her for a minute, then folds her up again.

"That's wonderful," I say. Jenny. His accent turns it into *Ginny*.

He looks at me with a straight gaze and nods slowly. "It is that. Andrea sees the hand of God in things. I don't know." He looks around. "Who's been out here? Somebody's been cleaning up."

"My mom. She was out here in waders, yanking vines."

"Judge Ballenger? Doesn't strike me as a waders type of person."

"Yeah. I don't know. Things are strange around here, Jimmy. It gets stranger by the minute."

"I hear that. We're living in Andrea's cousin's garage. It could have been so much worse, I tell you what. Some people got it bad," he says, and shakes his head. This from a guy whose house flooded to the rafters and is living in a garage. "Mulch," he says. "That'll be a start."

"Thanks," I say. "Thanks so much, Jimmy." There is absolutely no way that

I will tell Jimmy Butterman not to work on Ginna's garden. He's welcome to it for as long as he likes.

So Mother is probably skunking around this morning with dashing local real estate legend David Peek. She's certainly not in the house. I still can't get over that. She's getting out of her head. It's kind of great, actually. Right on, Mom.

Shelly's gone out to her own house with her brother. There seems to be some reckoning going on with her. She is calm this morning, steady.

The girls are off helping make sandwiches for people at Mobile Loaves and Fishes. Cassie and Amelia are the most unjaded volunteers. I can't get over their earnestness, their engagement with the world. When I was their age, all I thought about was how similar I was to Jane Eyre, how poor, obscure, plain and little I was, and why couldn't I be an actual orphan so I could get some sympathy for my lonely life? I used to think about porridge a lot. I just don't think that Amelia and Cassie are worrying about porridge, or why there's no Mr. Rochester falling off his horse in their general direction.

Bennett turns up in the kitchen, in the surgical scrubs he was wearing when he landed the ham on his foot four days ago. He is wearing a walking boot, and he's on the move.

"So what did he say?" Bennett asks. He's in the superprickly mode that until recently I assumed was his only mode.

"Who?"

"Him."

"Him who?"

"You know who. He came by yesterday afternoon. Said you'd left some papers at his house and he was bringing them back."

Angus. Oh crap. I didn't tell Bennett I was going to talk to Angus about Ginna yesterday. It just felt too awkward to get into all that. Did I need to tell Bennett that Ginna's final voicemail was from the guy who cuckolded him?

"You talked to him?" I can't believe I missed this. It's probably the first time that these two ever spoke.

"Barely." He shrugs, belligerent. "I opened the door, and at first he didn't even know who I was. Incredible. Asshole. Sweater-wearing idiot."

Oh, man. What a clash of the bereaved. I hadn't thought about the possibility that Angus might show up here while Bennett was around. The fact is, these guys would actually have a lot to talk about. If they didn't despise each other with a ferocious loathing.

He's giving me a major stinkeye. "So why were you asking him about those medical bills?"

"I don't know, just figured that maybe he would have some idea." It comes out thin and high. It's just too awful to tell Bennett that his wife was getting phone calls from Angus. I keep thinking about Bennett in his sofa bed, so undone.

"They were still seeing each other? Did she tell you that?" So jealous. She's not even here anymore.

"We never talked—remember? I didn't even know she was sick, Bennett. And Angus wouldn't say anything."

"Wouldn't say?"

"Totally stonewalled me. Said he was respecting her wish for privacy."

"Privacy? Which means . . . they had to be together, or else he wouldn't have known that she had any privacy to protect."

"I don't know, Bennett. He wasn't talking. At all. I wanted to punch the guy, I'm telling you."

He's headed for the door. "Sounds like a great idea to me," he says, sarcastic jolly, as if I've just suggested we go have a beer.

"Bennett!" I trot after him—for a guy with a bum foot, he's making pretty good time down the front steps. "I don't think it's a good idea for you to talk to him."

"Why not? You guys keeping secrets from me?"

"No, it's not that—it's just that."

"What?"

"What's the point? I mean, maybe he'll talk when he feels like it. I don't think he's going to want to tell you—"

"What? My wife's boyfriend doesn't like me?"

"I don't think that's what was going on."

"Well how the hell do you know?" We're crunching along the shoulder of Bowling Avenue, almost yelling over the noise of the passing cars. I give up trying to talk and just try to keep up with him. This is not good.

Maybe I can redirect him. "I thought you were going to talk to that doctor in Murfreesboro."

"I did. Fucking HIPAA. Privacy laws. She signed a thing saying that they couldn't release her information to anyone. Anyone. Court order to get them to release anything. Incredible."

At the massive wooden door, I say, "Let's go home, Bennett."

"Let's don't," he says and beats on the door.

Angus opens the door but looks like he wants to shut it. I hang back, not wanting to get whacked with a stray punch.

"Hey," Bennett says.

"Hello," Angus says.

They stand there like two cats waiting for the other to do something. Bennett shifts on his good foot. "How could you not know who I am? How the fuck could you not know that?"

Angus looks at Bennett's broken foot. "Of course I know who you are." He chews his cheek. "It was a context problem. You're shorter than I remembered. Confusing."

"Delia here seems to think that you know what was going on with Ginna." Nothing.

"Does this give you some great buzz, knowing something that we don't?" He shakes his head almost imperceptibly.

Bennett is twitching, he's so mad. "Well here's something to put in your box of juicy nuggets: Ginna was sick, and we didn't know it." Singsongy, mocking. "We just want to know. Need to know. What happened."

Angus steels himself and stands at his full height. "Look. I've got nothing to say to you. Ginna told you what she wanted you to know. Or not. What she told me is between her and me." He begins to close the door.

"You can't just—"

"Sorry," he says, and the door shuts.

"Fuck," Bennett says as he turns to me. He looks like he's going to burst out of his scrubs. He stumps his way down the driveway. "Who does he think he is? So smug. What an asshole. Jesus."

"I think I can get him to talk," I say. "It may just take some time." I remember sitting with Angus in his library, and I could see how upset he was, how stuck. He brought those insurance papers back to my house. I think he was going to tell me something.

"Well good luck with that. It's like talking to Lurch." He stops and turns to me. "Was she seeing him again? I just need to know." He percolates with frustration. He wants to know something, anything.

I take a deep breath. "They were in contact, Bennett. There was this voice-mail I found. From the day of the accident. He was going to meet her at some clinic."

He deflates, instantly. "You knew this."

I nod.

"But you didn't tell me."

"It just seemed sort of depressing."

"Yeah well. Yeah. Thanks a lot for helping, Delia. You've always been so sweet to me that way."

"I'm really sorry, Bennett." I feel crummy about this. We walk in silence for a bit, mulling my perfidy.

He stumps along, calculating something. "She called me, about a month before she died. Said she wanted to meet me about something. But I blew her off—even the sound of her voice would set me off. So I guess she turned to him." He rubs his face with his hands. "Such an idiot."

"He's not that bad, Bennett."

"Not him—me."

So now Bennett's furious at Angus and at me. He's right, of course: I should have told him. But I just couldn't. I feel oddly protective of Bennett, all of a sudden. He's not the villain in any of this, yet he's catching crap from my mother, from Angus.

Bennett does manage to squeeze out a thank-you once we get back to the house, for letting the girls and him stay at the house. I think this is his way of apologizing for yelling at me. He says that he wants to move into another unit at his apartment complex over the weekend, and he hopes that he can get in on Sunday. He leaves for the hospital. So much on his mind. His head tilts a little to the side with the weight of it all.

I flop on the big sofa in the living room. I keep thinking about that tear-down woman. Who is she? Who would want to tear down this house without even coming inside? I have half a mind to call her up and let her have it—how dare she assume this house isn't worth saving. The nerve!

But how simple it would be, to do this deal. I would be done. The girls would have their money, I would have mine, and it would be over. We could throw all this furniture into storage for six hundred years until the girls discovered they needed a Kazak rug and a ten-foot dining table.

Chicago. What would I be doing right this minute, back in Chicago? It's warm, probably, the great thaw in progress. People practically sleep in the parks, warming themselves like lizards on any piece of granite they can find. I'd go over to the lake, probably, take a book. I'd ponder, as I do from time to time, whether I should get a little dog like the one passing by. Enormous ears on that tiny dog. Who's walking whom? But I would end up thinking, as ever, that a dog is a lot of trouble. It would limit my flexibility. To sit in my apartment and stare at my computer all day. I'd have to take care of that dog. Every day.

I pull out my phone. "Henry. What are you doing?"

"Talking mold with a mold guy."

"When will you be done?"

"An hour?"

"Come see the river with me."

"OK. If we can get through. It's all blocked off down there." He pauses. "You OK?"

How could he tell?

"Just want to see you."

My last thought as I drift off is about Jimmy Butterman, and Andrea, and Ginna sitting down at her kitchen table to write them a check for their baby. She would have given them an actual baby if she could have. Ginna. Jenny.

I awake to the sound of Mother whispering "Delia." Ginna's sofa is like sleeping in a cloud, a downy pillow. The scent of Mother's rose perfume slips by. I open my eyes, and she's sitting beside me, on the tufted ottoman.

I am so sleepy. "Hi."

From this low angle, I get the full effect of Grace Ballenger's natural poise. You could float a phone book on the top of her head. I wonder whether this regal bearing is the result of her years as a judge, or whether good posture put her on this career path in the first place.

"Delia." She is wearing, I see, a golf shirt with a little emblem that reads Pebble Beach Golf Links, several sizes too large for her skinny frame.

"Mother," I say. "Golf?"

She looks embarrassed and pleased. "David needed some help. With his house. Messy. Had to change." She likes wearing his shirt. I have to smile. She looks off to the window. "Delia, what are we going to do?"

I'm trying to wake up, but it's just so deliciously comfortable to be in this sofa. "About what?"

"The girls."

I yawn one of those crazy air-sucking yawns like I've been trapped in a box. "I don't know. I think we're doing it."

"Bennett is a mess."

"He just went to work," I say, feeling a flash of sympathy for the guy.

"I mean big picture. That bosomy girlfriend." Mother has always been skeptical of too much figure, the same way she considers any heel higher than two inches a sign of inner decay. Do not even bring up the subject of pierced ears.

"She's out of the equation. Broke up with him a few days ago."

"Really? She broke up with him? Interesting. Serves him right."

"Dang, Ma."

"It's just so morally reprehensible, the whole thing. How could he have treated Ginna like that?"

She still thinks Bennett was the cheater. I halfway want to tell Mother that he wasn't the villain, that it was the saintly Ginna who cracked the window. But it's Bennett's bomb to drop, not mine. I want to tell her that I kind of like the guy now. Bennett is a walking O. Henry story, realizing so very late that he should have said yes when he said no, that being too slow to forgive can mean you never get to forgive at all, that the train can leave the station without you on it.

"He's complicated," I say. "He says he can't do it alone."

Mother leans in to me. "That's what I'm talking about. It's abundantly obvious that he can't. Somebody's going to need to step up for those girls."

And Mother thinks we can?

"Mother, what kind of mood-enhancing medications are you taking? Never seen you like this."

"I'd say the same of you," she says right back. "I hardly recognize you these days. It's like," she scowls, "it's like you're actually here. You're never actually here." She's correct. "Remember those 21-hour visits to Nashville? One foot out of the car, hello then goodbye? You seem . . . not yourself."

"I know. I'm not." I can't believe I just said that.

She has the most extraordinary expression of surprise on her face, then recognition. "They're unusual," she says. "Aren't they? Like a tonic, a balm."

"The girls?"

"The Peeks."

A balm. Mother goes biblical sometimes.

Most days, the Victory Memorial Bridge soars high over the Cumberland River, connecting the courthouse to the Titans stadium. Today, the bridge feels low, like its pilings have sunk into the mud of the riverbed.

Henry leans on the railing with me, hypnotized as I am by the slow water and the hot sun. "The water is so close now. I've never seen anything like this before," he says. Buildings have lost their foundations, roads vanish beneath the brown water. Suddenly, the city is an unfinished drawing.

I tell him his tennis hat makes him look like Bing Crosby. "Bing Crosby never got a sunburn," he retorts. "One of the paler crooners."

"I like it. Here," I say, fishing in my pocket. "A picture." I hand my phone to him. "Your arms are longer." We turn our backs on the river, the skyline of the city and the ruin of the flood behind us. He pulls me close to him, and we smile. He takes three pictures, and I check, wanting to be sure his whole entire complete face is there. We're peering into a well, squinting into the afternoon sun, and I have to say, we look great.

"Look at that," he says. "We're floating over the water."

We are not the only disaster tourists downtown. "I feel like we ought to be pumping out somebody's basement," I say.

"This'll go on for a while," he says. "You'll have your chance, once your house clears out. So much to do. Never saw anything like this before."

"My mom is wearing your dad's shirts."

"Ballenger women. Thievin' bitches."

We're standing there, doing nothing, and all of a sudden I have a vivid image of Angus and Bennett in their Mexican standoff, Angus towering over Bennett in the shadow of that doorway. There's no fix for them, no solace to be found. Maybe they should have just started punching each other and gotten it out of their system. Angus looked consumed by this thing with Ginna, like some wasting disease is getting the best of him.

I say, "How do you get somebody to talk about something they don't want to talk about?"

He glances over at me quickly. "Like what?"

"Suppose somebody has some thing, some experience. If he would just tell it, just get it out of his system."

Henry leans way over the railing and looks at a tree trunk drifting toward a bridge footing. "What are you talking about?"

Do I want to get into it all? Maybe Henry could help me figure this out. Or maybe not.

"Ah, never mind. Come on," I say, heading back toward the courthouse. "I want to stick my big toe in, just so I can tell my grandchildren I swam the

Cumberland in the Flood of 2010."

Henry is quiet all the way down to 2nd Avenue. The streets near the river are all blocked off where the wandering river has crept up Lower Broadway. ServPro Disaster Remediation Service trucks have descended on Nashville in force, labeled with their home cities so that we can see that help is coming from Terre Haute and Binghamton and Cleveland. The bigger the building, the bigger the trucks, with hoses coming out of basements, air tubes blowing in dry air, and water squishing out, bucketful by bucketful. Much of this water appears to be heading right back into the building next door to it. At a street corner, where the river has run out of steam, I squat down, flatten my hand, and feel the cool water, as shallow here in the street as the edge of a pond. Henry is not interested in swimming with me. "Any more of that and you'll need a tetanus shot," he says. He reaches down to help me up, and I put my wet hand into his.

Henry still has my phone, and as we walk, he studies the pictures of us. He's frowning, then clicks the buttons and holds up the phone. "Look at that," he says quickly. "How your hair does. You're so pretty in there."

"Unlike out here."

He scowls. "When are you going to give yourself a break? You have got to learn how to take a compliment."

There is something so safe about idle walking with someone. It's the least lonely thing possible. "Did you ever come downtown, growing up?" he asks.

"To Mother's office sometimes. Downtown wasn't anything like it is now. So dried up back then. Remember the concerts at Municipal Auditorium?"

"I went to see Poison once because Tommy Hubert made me. And Rick James. After he got creepy. Municipal Auditorium is all about the languishing career."

"And wrestling."

"It must have been hard, not having a dad," he says.

"I had a dad, if by dad you mean a workaholic who was never there—it was a mother I was missing. Shelly was closest I ever got to a mother."

Henry takes me by the elbow and stops me, a gentle tug. "Sorry. But I still don't get why you're so hard on her. Imagine what it was like."

Our walk has slowed to the point that we are drifting along aimlessly. "I guess I can't," I say. "I can't imagine how she could have been so—so uninterested. We were very interesting. We were adorable."

"I don't think it was that simple."

"I don't know what it was. Awful. But it's the sort of thing that I just put out of my mind, once I left town. It's only when I got back here that all this came flooding out. Do you think sometimes you can live with something so long that it doesn't even seem real anymore?"

"Yeah," he says. "And the opposite, too: you can make unreal things real, inside your spinning little mind." He turns and waits for the light to change, even though there is no traffic in either direction.

We are standing in front of Fort Nashborough, which has managed to avoid the flood, though the water is unnervingly close. It's a reproduction of a stockaded log fort, scaled to fit 1790 humans. It smells like creosote and wetness. Come to think of it, everything in Nashville smells like it's not drying out very well. This moldy city. "Do you know about this place?" he says.

"First settlement? And weaving. Or something. Why is there always so much with the weaving at places like this?"

"I need to tell you something," he interrupts, in a suddenly somber tone. In this bright light, his eyes are pale blue, washed out.

"Jesus, Henry, what else do you have in your bag? You don't have to tell me every little thing, you know."

"Actually, I do. Since the other day . . . If I don't tell you, how do I get out of bed in the morning?" He pauses. "Don't you have shocking things that you're just not saying? Surely the judge's daughter can't be that virtuous," he teases.

He catches me off guard. What does he know? What to tell, what to let go? I think about this all the time these days. Even a trip to the grocery store can send me into a sinking spell, going past a house where I, say, spent New Year's Eve in a less-than-productive way.

"Do tell," I say. He pulls me down to sit beside him on a bench by the entrance, and he holds my phone between his hands like it's a baby bird.

He is reluctant, stymied, stuck. "It's what happened after I got back to Nashville. After Denmark." I've been dying to hear the second part of his story, but it's like looking under a sticky bandage. "I hate telling you."

"So don't. Or do. It's OK. I can handle it," I say. Not really.

He shakes his head. "Pretty bad." He takes off his glasses and rubs his eyes. He gives me a here-we-go look. "I got back here—this was probably eight years ago—just after all that. So full of myself, so sure I was on the far side of a bad time. When I tell you there's no place like home, you've got to understand:

when you've been away, the way I was, home becomes this monumental thing, this goal.

"So I got back, and Mom and Dad put me up, and there I was, twenty-four years old, back in my room with my Clapton posters and my bed that's too short. Dad wanted me to go into business with him, to teach me real estate. So generous. He'd never had a partner, never felt the need to have a big office full of people working for him. Honestly, I think part of his success was this mystique that he wouldn't do what other agents in town did." He stops. "Do you want to hear this?"

"You want to tell me, so."

"Anyway. I have to say, my back never was the same. It could have been so much worse—I was about a half inch from never walking again. But I rarely took anything for it, because, really, I felt like this was the price for surviving that crash. That I had to carry that with me."

Henry has this way of talking. You can see it in his eyes, the constant search for the way to say something. He has the slightest, leftover southern accent that comes out only with certain words, in the vowels. I could listen to him all day. Seriously, listening to him talk is an activity for me. I keep imagining him up in a pulpit, laying out a sermon. He would be great at sermonizing.

"So I study up for the real estate test, I'm waking up every morning, but the adrenaline I had at first wore off."

I was wondering about that. To go from the mystery of God to the mystery of the Tennessee Real Estate Board had to be a severe letdown. "My back got worse, and I finally decided to see the doctor, and he said he was amazed that I hadn't come to see him sooner. Lined me up with some stuff that gave me relief that I had only dreamed about. So." He is stuck.

"And?"

"I got totally hooked. It wasn't a slippery slope—it was a straight line from pain to no pain." So bitter. "They say it's not addiction if it's relieving a symptom; it's a dependency. Whatever—I just got to the point that I absolutely could not function without them. Or function with them. It was two problems: the back. And the soul-sucking depression."

He looks at me with the flattest expression. This is it. This is the real part.

"After I got back, it got so bad. Delayed reaction, I guess. What happened, with the accident. Clare Murray's face, right there next to me in the car. You want to talk about haunted. Charmed her into that car. Begged her to go with me. Used to be so good at that."

He still is.

"And then. Here. Life had turned into something so plain, so different from my exotic semi-scholarly ambitions. And the painkillers flatten things to the point that you don't much care that you're miserable. Deadens you. Such a perfect word for it. I don't think you would have recognized me if you'd seen me then. I know you wouldn't have liked me. Bed. Bed was it." His voice is so quiet that I can barely hear him. "The moment I dowse the candle, pull the eiderdown over my head."

He looks at me, and I can't hide my stricken expression at whatever this sad quote is. He doesn't show any surprise. He doesn't try to cheer me up. He wants me to feel this. "My mom. Saved me. And Dad. She and the doctors got me to the hospital, which let me tell you is the sort of place that makes a Danish prison look like fun. It's about four blocks from my apartment, felt like going to the end of the world. Nothing like hanging out with people more incoherent than you are. That alone was pretty motivating." He's trying hard to find the right words. "You know that drawing on my business card? She was always doodling like that, and every day she would bring me a note about her day and a cartoon she cut out of *The New Yorker*. Instead of writing 'Dear Henry,' she'd draw my face, and sign it with her face. I have a whole drawerful of them." He takes a deep breath, like he's about to go underwater again.

I feel like shit. I feel nervous for him, jittery as I imagine him sitting in some harshly lit room with crazy people all listening or not listening to what he was saying. Little cups of pills. Sleeping badly. Coming home, finally, only to end up in a place like that. I hate that he had to do this. I hate that I wasn't there. I hate that he has to tell me this. I reach out to touch his face, to feel the curve of his warm cheek in the palm of my hand. He leans against it, heavy.

"The thing I think about, a lot, is the fact that I came back to Nashville. It would have been easier in some ways to go someplace else, back to Durham, New York, whatever. But I didn't. Sometimes I wonder what would have happened. If I hadn't come back here. She wouldn't have known. My condition. She couldn't have done anything." He is talking to my hand, which he has been holding very carefully. "Without her, I don't, honestly, think I would be here at all." He tilts his head back and looks up at a lone, tiny puff of a cloud. A cotton ball. "God and Zoloft," he says. "And Nashville and Mom. My dad took me on." A small smile crosses his face. "Nashville is where I got a life back. This is it. This is home."

He takes off his hat and puts it on my head. His hair shines, so rumpled.

There's a little red line across his forehead from the hat. "It took a while before I was off everything. Plenty of bleak in there. My proudest achievement was the day I called Mom to tell her I had sold my first house. Feels like a long time ago. And also not."

He hasn't mentioned Ginna's pill bottles. How can he tell me this story and not tell me that? Is he off the wagon? He seems sleepy today, not as sharp as usual—is he on them right now? "Do you take anything now?" I'm horrified to ask. My voice has shrunk to a little squeak. "I mean, is your serotonin reuptaken?"

"Nothing psychotropic, if that's what you mean."

"But what about . . . " He looks quizzically at me. I can't ask him about Ginna's pills. It would ruin everything. Instead, I say, "Vitamins?"

"I eat a lot of spinach," he says.

The word *spinach* hangs in the air a good long while as we watch a log drift down the river. I can't bear to go any further on this.

He asks, "How long have we known each other?" Is he changing the subject on purpose?

"Depends on how you figure it: either three weeks or fifteen years, right?"

He looks slyly at me. "I looked you up. You're in my senior yearbook. Cordelia Jane Ballenger, freshman."

"Not fair."

"The loyal daughter. So young. Such strangely fluffy hair."

The Perm. Henry has seen The Perm, part of my fruitless quest to look like my thick-haired big sister. Mother just about killed me. At least he cares enough to be digging up my super-unflattering photos.

"I have exactly one memory of you in high school," I say. "It was in the parking lot, and you were standing by your Dodge Dart Swinger"—

"World's greatest car."

"With that girl, what's her name? Janet something. I was so envious of her. She had hair. And she had your attention, I mean totally. Mr. Class President. Mr. Dreamy."

Henry remembers this girl. "Yeah. Janet. She was something. Don't worry," he says, "she lives in Sydney, Australia, married to a banker, four kids."

"That's almost far enough away."

"You were in the Pep Club, Student Council, and the French Club." He's merciless.

"Résumé padding. All I wanted in high school was to prove that I was the smartest person in the room."

"How'd that go?"

"Well, it goes great when you design your life so that you're the only person in the room."

"Listen," he says, his tone higher. "About ten times a day I want to ask what your plans are, what you're going to do."

"I don't seem to be having much luck selling the house."

"That house is not the thing. It's going to sell, somehow, to somebody. Trust me, I know nothing in this world but I know real estate." He's frustrated. "I also know a lot about delayed reactions. Seems to me like your whole family is just now figuring out what it means for your sister to be gone. That's what seems like the real project for you."

"Delayed reactions," I say. We sit for a while, thinking on that.

He says quietly, "One day you're going to answer the phone and tell me you're back in Chicago, that you've up and gone home. I know you're thinking all the time—I just wish you'd tell me. So hard to read. Why are you such a cipher?"

"Don't mean to be." I lay my head on his shoulder. "Things seem to matter a lot." Say it. I'll just say it. I turn to face him. "I can be blunt, you know. How about this: I think about you too much. I keep you in my head, right behind my left ear, all day long. Do you know the quantity of time I have spent looking at that *Nashville Business Journal* picture of you? I have never in my life had a feeling like this, and I'm thirty-one years old." He is embarrassed, and I have to look away and talk to a recycling bin across the path. "You tell me all these terrible stories, Henry, and they just make me want you all the more. You shouldn't have to carry that around all by yourself. You're telling me all these things, and it makes me so nervous for you to be so open with me. Maybe I'm not the right one to tell. Maybe you'll figure out that I'm not the one. I'm just scared, Henry." I'm reading Dear Diary out loud in an auditorium, the scariest thing I've ever done, and my heart is racing.

"I'm not scared," he says softly. "I told you before, sometimes things are obvious. OK, I was scared that first night. When I called you to go to Kevin's thing. That was scary. What if you'd said no? But there you were, when you opened the door. Nothing was hard, after that. Do you know? I mean, look at you. In that hat." He kisses me, such a gentle, confident thing, even though I'm pretty sure this is a hat-based pity kiss.

There have been no visitors to Fort Nashborough in the time we have been sitting here. A mousy-haired woman in an itchy-looking pioneer dress and a long apron passes us and sets a sign outside one of the small cabins. "Weaving Demonstration 4 pm." She goes inside, busy as hell, scurrying around as she prepares for her audience of nobody. She settles in, and we listen to the steady thwack-thwack of her loom for a good long while. Henry slides down the bench on his back and uses my legs for a pillow. He closes his eyes, arms crossed on his chest, and he says, almost as a sigh, "Stay, Delia. Just stay."

He drifts off to sleep, right here at Fort Nashborough, his head resting on me, which gives me the excellent opportunity to study his sunburned face for as long as I like. I slide my hand inside his shirt to feel his heart beating. He keeps falling asleep on top of me. I worry about his back against this hard wooden bench. I worry about those three little bottles, unconfessed on a day when he seemed to want to confess all sorts of things. Why couldn't I ask him about that?

The Teardown

We're sitting around the breakfast table, watching flood news on the little TV.

"Water," Cassie says. "We need water."

"A nice, long, refreshing bath," Mother says. "In my fifty-gallon bathtub."

"A real shower," Cassie says. "Where you leave it on the whole time fifteen minutes full blast until you run out of hot water."

"The dishwasher," I say.

"Ice," Amelia says.

The city is still running on half its normal water supply. If the Omohundro plant had failed, we would have no water at all, so we're supposed to continue water restrictions until the plant that did flood is back in service, which will take weeks. It's become a game, trying to figure out new ways to conserve water. This seems to suit Amelia the environmentalist. Cassie calls her a water Nazi.

"We could just stop drinking water, dry up, and die," Cassie says. "How about that?" Our little libertarian.

Amelia gives her a complete eye roll.

I somehow feel responsible for the lack of water in the house. "Such spotty accommodations," I say.

"Yeah, some hotel," Cassie says. "Dad says we're leaving on Sunday." She's building a tower out of English muffins. I ought to say something motherlike along the lines of "Don't play with your food," but I'm not her mother, and I'm liking her Le Corbusier hut. "Aunt Delia, have you sold the house yet?" She says this in a matter-of-fact way.

"No. I don't think it will sell for a while."

"Is Henry helping you?" Mother says this to her coffee mug. "Never knew how that all shook out. After all that."

It's funny how little I begrudge Mother her most recent subterfuge—now, anyway. If her scheming ways meant that Henry Peek ended up on my doorstep, how mad can I be? "He's helping. I mean, actually, we don't have a contract which I guess we should. But he did bring me an offer the other day."

"What offer?" Cassie pipes in. I forget that the girls have ears.

"Yeah, well, it was a lousy offer. No way."

"Who was it?" Cassie is alert.

"Oh, this woman. And her husband."

Cassie's shiny face is right next to me, so intent.

"Why was it lousy?"

I'm not going to tell her that somebody wants to bulldoze this house. "Not good people."

Cassie says, "Well what does that matter? If they have enough money, I mean."

Surprised, I say, "Well it matters to me." Mother looks at me, eyebrows raised. "I don't want some jerk family in here. They can't be awful."

"If it can't be us, then I don't care," Cassie says, balancing a muffin atop her little building. "I just can't believe you're kicking us out on Sunday."

OK, that hurts. "I'm not kicking you out. Your dad is just . . ."

"Is kicking us out," Cassie says in a low voice. I've been imagining how the girls must feel about the house, but I hadn't heard it expressed. She looks up at me, a wash of disgust and hurt across her face. How strange all this must seem to her, sitting in her own kitchen, with her weirdo aunt and imperious grandmother.

"Cassie," Mother says, clearing her throat as she speaks. "Your dad wants to get things back to normal."

"Whatever that is," she says. "We don't have normal. We have un-normal." She shrugs. "I still don't get why dad won't buy it. Or whatever."

Mother says, "It's tricky, you know. Your dad has a lot on his mind. Sometimes a place has a lot of memories in it. And it may be that he just can't be here."

"Well he's been staying here now," Cassie says. "He seems OK about it."

I see a flash of the seriously not-OK Bennett sunk into the covers of the sofa bed at four in the afternoon. "Well," I say. "I think Grandma's probably right." Man, do I hate this feeling of leaving Cassie high and dry.

I turn to Mother. "How's your house?"

She looks up from her newspaper, and the expression on her face is absolutely extraordinary. She looks as light as schoolgirl. "A mess," she says. "A godawful, expensive mess." She smiles.

"When do you expect it to be done?"

She shakes her head. "Delia, it's just not something on my mind right now." I hardly know what to make of this woman.

"I'm quitting work." She bends to pick up a napkin from the floor.

I drop my spoon. It's a sentence I would have bet serious money that my mother would never, ever say. She's a federal judge. She's worked forty years to arrive at this most difficult peak of achievement, the judicial gravy train, the life appointment. She left us at home with Shelly while she worked herself silly. There was no boundary between work and home. Actually, it was all work. It's the thing that stole her from us—that billowing ambition, that grinding drive.

Amelia is as dumbfounded as I am. "Grandma, really? You love your work."

She nods. "I do."

Amelia is perplexed. "I mean, why?"

She stirs her coffee, with an impossibly placid expression. "Things are . . . changing . . . for me." The sentence drifts from her, as if the sentence itself might change before it is complete. I can't stop staring at her. "Delia," she says, "you know what I'm talking about."

I realize suddenly that David Peek is somehow a part of this decision. This is one of those rare moments in life when my mother and I have the same feelings about the same thing. Things are changing. Things aren't the same. I think about a course I took in college, where we were supposed to design a city grid for the most efficient flow of traffic. I imagine my mother's route, the straight line up the gut, thirty stoplights in a row. And mine, with sixty-three left and right turns, all side streets, dodging traffic. But here we are, at the crossroads together.

I look at Mother, who understands the surprise of her announcement, and I say, "Why? When? Does anybody know this?"

"No, nobody except David. Such clarity he has." I think about Henry. Is that genetic? How come the Ballengers seem so low on the clarity? "My father's on my mind these days. He understood a lot about nature, about the rotation of crops. Being a farmer gives you clarity, that's for sure. Cash crops, cover crops, green manures. Keep the soil fertile, keep pests down. He was big on root depth, thought you should vary how far down the roots go. He had the loveliest soil, magnificent soil. He was the first to plant hairy vetch in Tennessee. With his winter rye." She nods, certain about my grandfather's skill as a farmer. I never knew him. He died when I was four.

"Time for some hairy vetch?" I say.

"Things are pretty hardpanned. May be too late."

"You don't know that."

"I am worried." She sighs.

"What do you mean?"

"Well, I'm not positive, and I could be wrong, but I'm starting to suspect, at this very late date, that it could be possible that it may not be all about me."

She's cracking a joke. Amelia is watching us closely. "You can't quit," she says. "You're a judge. That's what you do."

"We'll see. I find you all a good deal more interesting than a courtroom full of suck-up lawyers."

We're in my car, Amelia and me, on a last-minute quest for prom shoes that will be superior to the perfectly good ones that she was planning to wear until she decided this morning that they would not work at all. I recognize her pre-prom countdown freakout.

"You do know, Amelia, people won't even be thinking about your shoes because they'll be so obsessed with their own. They automatically believe that your shoes are better than theirs. Always."

"I know. It's just."

She is such an unmaterialistic girl that I am not about to talk her out of a pair of party shoes.

We pass a truck loaded with flood-ruined carpet. I wish I had a carpet business right about now.

"Grandma won't really quit her job, will she?" Amelia asks.

"Isn't that something?" I stop. How much can I say to a sixteen year old? "You might call it a transition."

She doesn't say anything.

"We miss your mom. So much," I say.

"What does that have to do with her quitting work?"

"Well. It makes you think, losing a daughter—or a sister, for me. And it was such a shock, so fast. I think Grandma missed a lot, working. She's very sad these days. I've never seen her like this."

"But work is her life. That's all she does."

"She's wondering what she's missed. Grieving for all that. I think she's in the middle of what you call a midlife crisis, coming on the late side."

"And yours is coming on the early side?" How did she know this? She smiles a little at my shocked expression.

Shoe Heaven is one of those places with 10,000 pairs of shoes, where you can try them on yourself all day long. I find this sort of store hair-raising, but Amelia is primed to try on all 10,000 pairs if necessary.

I sit down at the end of a long aisle of boots, 80 percent off. "Lots of options, Amelia." I begin the arduous task of trying on a pair of thigh-high pirate boots, and we laugh. I look ridiculous. Amelia is suddenly not laughing anymore.

"Mary Donald told me there was something going on with Mom and her dad."

"Like what?" I feel the electric zing of shock in my feet.

"Like Mom used to be over there, at their house, a lot. Before Dad moved out."

Observant Mary. Big eyes. Of course she would notice. "One time Mary said she came home and they were sitting in the kitchen, and they were like laughing superhard at something, and then they stopped when she came in. So she started noticing that her dad was doing all this stuff, neighborhood stuff, and it seemed like Mom was around a lot. And then, one day." She stops. She's studying my pirate boots. "Doesn't matter." She shakes her head. "Those are a bit tall for you. No offense."

"What?"

"So one day her dad came in, and he looked all happy, and he told her that winter was his favorite season, and he put down a grocery bag which she thinks he didn't mean to leave out, because she looked in it after he went upstairs and it had an empty bottle of wine and two glasses in it." Amelia lays this out in a flat way, like she's recounting the synopsis of a bad TV show. "Lipstick. On one."

"Wow," I say.

"Yeah," she says. "I couldn't believe it. I told Mary she was crazy, but she had all these things she'd noticed. Like a scarf. That she found. She gave it to me—it was Mom's. Definitely." She has an impatient look in her face, wanting to get this story out as fast as she can.

"I'm so sorry."

"Yeah." She wanders off, and I can only imagine what it felt like when

Mary handed that scarf to her.

I ditch my boots and catch up to her. She says, irritated, "But then Mary said that it all stopped, and she didn't come over anymore, and her dad was even more bummed out than he was before." She squats down in front of a batch of shoeboxes. "The thing I don't get, and I really don't get it, is why Mom and Dad were so lame about it. I mean, they were married. They were parents. It's like they didn't even try." She shakes her head. I'm struck by how calmly she is dissecting this. "Dad sucks, I mean, I get it. But she did that? Sneaking around?" She pulls a shoebox from the stack. "Is that all there is? You get married, then everybody starts cheating?"

"Never been married," I say. "So it's hard for me to say. But God I hope not."

"Did you know about this? Did Dad? Because I really don't get it."

I'm so tired of secrets. Amelia is looking closely at me, expectant. What was it like to be sixteen? How much did I understand back then? This girl, this young life in motion, is so tender, so uncured, so curious. She can still absorb things; she's got no crust. She can handle anything I tell her. She wants to know. "Yeah," I say. "I just found out about it, when I came to town. Your dad told me. I had no idea. I couldn't believe it."

Amelia has a deflated look to her. "Why didn't Dad tell me this?"

Such a good question. "You know, he said he didn't want you to feel differently about your mother."

"Yeah, well, he's right about that." Amelia is so mystified. "I mean, my mom. So sneaky. She was so . . . not like that." She shakes her head, and I am unnerved at having to see this girl sort through the family garbage like this. "And the thing is, Mary was actually sort of OK about it. She thought her dad was so happy. Said he hadn't been like that since before her mom died." She slides her foot into a perfect shoe. "And she said Mom looked happy, too."

"Those are good," I say, looking down.

She shakes her head. "*Happy* is not the word I'd use to describe Mom. At the end. When Dad left, it was—well, you know how it was."

No, I mostly don't.

"They acted like we were six year olds. 'We still love you so much,' blah blah. We didn't doubt that. We just hated the whole thing. Cassie kept falling asleep in those family therapy sessions. Hanging out with Dad, without Mom, was like drinking a flat Coke. The worst. Checking his BlackBerry all the time. And then Carla turns up—oh my God, I can't even tell you how wrong that was. Asking us to help plan his birthday party. Like we were pals. She had these plasticky fingernails. No wonder Mom was so depressed.

"Mom was so mean to us, to Cassie especially. So critical. She was always after Cassie about her clothes and school stuff. It was like she all of a sudden decided to be this hardass. It was like she wasn't even herself. That summer—last summer—was so bad. I spent as much time as I could at Melanie's. Her mom was like 'oh, my other daughter.'"

We are both talking to her newfound party shoes. "It sounds so sad," I say. "I'm so sorry I wasn't here to know all this."

Amelia glances up at me. "You were working."

The excuse. What Ginna must have been telling them all this time. "Not really, Amelia. It's not like I was on submarine duty. Or saving orphans in Namibia. I was just there, up there, doing the same stupid stuff I'd been doing ever since college. While you all were going through this." She probably doesn't understand what a failure this is. People come and go. Someday she'll wonder how I could have opted out, floated on the margins for so long.

"Aunt Delia." A cloud crosses her face. "Cassie and me. Dad. We don't. Dad's just. He's." She shakes her head, flummoxed. "We know he loves us. We just."

"He does love you."

"I know."

"He's just not very good at it," I say quietly. Like Mother. How do I tell her that Bennett will never be much help? How do I tell her that I know exactly how she feels? Just say it. "I know exactly how you feel. I know what you're missing. I think you just have to take what people can give you. Do you know how long it's taken me to see this? Until about three days ago. Do you know how long I wished my mom would be momlike? She's the least momlike mom in the world." Amelia smiles. "Would it have killed her to take me shopping for a freakin' prom dress?"

"She's not a great shopper," Amelia says. "I mean, you know."

"Yeah. Well." I sigh. "I think the hardest thing for me is the fact that I've basically lived my life just like she has. Head down. It's so lame. I can hardly stand it."

"Grandma's not going to quit her job, is she? No way."

"I wouldn't dare guess. She's surprising me on a daily basis."

"I like these," she says, looking at her high heels. "He's pretty tall, so."

"You're more coordinated than me."

On the way home, we listen to the radio, with Amelia microadjusting the stations as the songs come and go. It matters so much.

"You know," I say, "I think I'll be here a while."

Amelia gives me a quick glance, an assessing look. "Your friend? He's nice. Isn't he?"

"Yeah."

"Mom used to say that you worked too much."

"It's fun to hang out with you guys."

"It's going to suck when you sell the house."

It is indeed going to suck when I sell the house. My passengers are going to be disembarking soon. Shelly is out at her cousins' now, and Bennett and the girls will be off to their new apartment by the end of the weekend. Bennett's over there now. He couldn't stand another minute in this house, he said. Mother will be getting her house back before long. Which leaves the prospect of me, back in the house alone again, as I was when I first got here three weeks ago, itching to sell the place. If Henry Peek does his job, it won't be too long before I'll be on my way as well, back to Chicago, back to my room in the sky with the mingy balcony and the four easily viewed corners. I can go stare at Lake Michigan again. I can keep not having a dog. It can be like this never even happened.

I see that Henry has forwarded to me an email from an agent who claims to have an Atlanta couple that needs to move to Nashville, soon. Henry writes, "Remember the three immutable forces in real estate: death, divorce, and Atlanta. These are the things that keep me in business."

I write back: "No thank you. I hate Atlantans."

He replies: "What about rich Atlantans who pay cash?"

"Better."

He writes that he is incredibly busy and will be in touch when the dust settles. He signs it "All best." All best? What about "Love"? "Your devoted companion"? Why does it sound vaguely like a business letter?

In my visit with my computer, which has happened all too rarely in recent days, I find that Susan has been cranking a lot of emails to me. She asks if I can dig up the name of that breakfast place in Playa del Carmen, the one with the wine bottles embedded in the cement ceiling. Susan is losing her edge. Come on, girl. You know this stuff. I dial her.

"La Cueva del Chango," I say.

"I knew that."

"I know you did."

"The Jenkinses are wearing me out. I feel like I'm there with them."

"How much longer?"

"They come home tomorrow. It's fine. So. How's it going?" I hear her dogs woofing in the background. Susan's world is a series of sounds to me—children, the TV, the clicking of her keyboard. I haven't thought about work in the past three days, in the past three weeks if I'm being honest. I feel so guilty, all of a sudden.

"It's kind of crazy, here. I didn't expect all this . . . stuff."

The great thing about Susan is that she is not a judgmental person. She never gives me a hard time, about anything. I think it comes from her years on the phone with people, working with clients whose demands are either reasonable or not, in situations that either work out or don't. I have learned a lot from her about not taking things personally, so when she says, "Delia, I have a bone to pick," I feel a jolt shoot up my spine. She never picks bones with me.

"What?"

"We need to have a talk. I mean, I know you have a full plate. But I've been sending you all this stuff, and you're totally not responding." She sounds short of breath. "It just feels. I don't know. It's not. It's like a one-legged ladder, all this."

I'm upset too, just like that. I'm horrified to hear her slightly strangled-sounding voice. "Well," I say. Then I realize, nervously, I can't say what I was about to say. I don't have it in me to say the thing that I ought to be saying. I can't say I'll jump right back in. I don't know how I can do that at the moment.

"Are you OK?" she asks quietly. "We can figure anything out, right?"

I can tell Susan anything. Pretty much. But it feels like such a betrayal to tell her, after all these years, that this job, this abstract job helping people I don't even know or see, who go on trips I've never taken, with a business partner two thousand miles away—it feels like a job for some other person, not a job for me. I can't not be in the world. I can't sit it out, anymore. I've got to try.

I don't think that Susan, in asking about the name of that breakfast place in Mexico, had any idea that she was going to end up on the phone for two hours with me telling her about Amelia's prom dress and the pick-up truck in the tree and Angus's sweater and Bennett's foot, and Henry's hushpuppies and

Mother's waders. But that's what she gets, and by the end, I think she has some idea of what's going on down here. For the moment, we leave it as it is.

The combination of nerves and relief that washes over me feels like a mud bath. I told her. It was awful, but it was good.

Angus has been on my mind this afternoon. Long, spindly Angus. Clammed-up Angus, shut-down Angus. It's Mary's view of her dad, actually, that has me thinking.

He was happy, she says. Ginna was happy. That's what stays with me. Amid the streaming details of everyday life, the chronic grind of a difficult husband, Ginna found a chance to share a bottle of wine with the widower down the street. What miracle of suburban air traffic control had to occur for Ginna to find the time and the place for something like that?

I have got to crack The Silent One. He needs to let go of whatever he's scraped into his box of woe. For us, but mostly for him. I see this now.

On the way to his house, I plan my strategy. At no point will I say anything sarcastic, challenging, or mean. I'm going to keep my cool, and I reserve the right to throw Bennett under the bus if I need to, but I'm going to stay at Angus's house until I have the story from him about my sister and her last days.

Coming up the drive, I feel like I'm selling something door to door. Something unpopular, like cream of wheat.

Angus regards me as if I might whack him on the nose with a newspaper. "I hate to bother you," I say. Crap! I didn't work out my opening gambit. "But Bennett said you came over to bring back those papers. So I came over to come get them. If you don't mind."

He gives me a long look, decides something, and says, "Come in. Please." He is compulsively, southernly polite. The insulating power of good manners.

We're back in the library, this lovely temple of thinking. I'm feeling a strong déjà vu, yet he seems different today, less frozen in the joints. Maybe he got out a can of WD-40 since his run-in with Bennett. Anger can be so delightfully lubricating.

He clears his throat. "Do you remember the day you arrived here?"

Of course I do. I still have the ringing Voice of God in my ears. I almost got back in my car and drove back to Chicago.

He looks out the tall, narrow window. "I came to the house that day because I was afraid that I had somehow fouled up the alarm."

"What do you mean?"

"Well, I had been in the house until just a few minutes before you arrived." Wow. "I had a habit of coming to the house." I look up at him. He nods at my astonishment. "To be there."

I am as still as he is. We look at each other, knowing.

"I know it sounds peculiar," he says in a low voice.

"So," I say.

He nods in a tiny way. "It's not so easy. This."

"The back hedges?"

He nods. "The girls would turn up sometimes, or the housekeeper, and I'd have to get out fast—it would have been so bad for them to find me there."

I can only imagine.

"Excuse me," he says, as he stands and leaves the room. He returns with a file folder. "Here," he says.

Medical bills. Envelopes from Blue Cross. A pile of stuff I have never seen before. The tab reads "VBS." "Paid," it says in the corner of each bill, in precise, small handwriting.

"I was intercepting them, after everything happened. She didn't want anybody to know."

"Did she ask you to do this?"

"She died in a car accident, Delia! Of course not! I just figured that the bills would start showing up, and she didn't want anybody to know, so . . ."

"So you broke into her house?"

"I had a key," he says defensively. "She'd given me one, back when. The housekeeper would stack the mail up in the kitchen. I took the bills home, paid them, and that was that. I don't know why he didn't come get it, but it just piled up until one day when it all vanished." He pauses. "I kept coming to the house, worrying that I'd missed a bill—for months I would come to check, and I finally concluded that I'd caught them all." He looks up at me, abashed. "At that point, it was so calming. To be in the house. It's as if I could feel her there, right there in the rooms with me."

He wants there to be a ghost for him to meet. He's looking for the specter in the Lanz nightgown. He probably never even got to see Ginna in her flannelly glory.

"I was helping her. Giving her some peace. Until the flood." He shakes his head, incredulous at how close he came to keeping the secret. "Stashing away papers in her yarn bins. Just goes to show that you can think you've thought of everything."

What a sneaky, compulsive thing to do. I can't believe it. I'm about to bust a gasket, but I don't want to shut him down. "Angus. All we want is to know her frame of mind, those last weeks."

He stands, agitated. "Come on," he says, already in the front hall. "I need to see something." We head down the driveway at a pace that will put us in Kentucky in an hour. I'm almost trotting to keep up with his long stride. We head up Golf Club Lane. A flatbed trailer carrying a huge backhoe trundles past us. It stops up the street and begins a lane-blocking parking maneuver.

"They're tearing down the Sullivans' house," he says sourly. "Eighth tear-down on Golf Club."

I think of the offer on my coffee table from the doctor's wife who wants to tear down my house. "Was it a bad house?"

He snorts. "Bad as in falling apart? Or bad as in doesn't have a four-car garage? Won't be long now before Golf Club looks like any street in Brent-wood." He says *Brentwood* like he's saying *polyester pantsuit.* "Ginger Sullivan loved that house."

"But she's not here anymore, I guess?" Angus is so sentimental!

"Thank goodness. I'd hate for her to see this. People have lost all sense of proportion." This from a guy inhabiting a 6,000-square-foot castle with one daughter.

We stop in front of the Sullivans' house, because it is impossible not to watch. The backhoe crawls off the trailer, treads caked in dry mud. The house is already on its last legs, its warm, old brick stripped away, in a tremendous pile waiting for some other destiny. The windows are gone, too. The remaining skeleton is oddly shocking to see, like a skinned rabbit. I can't believe it upsets me to see this, but it does. "If we'd put the historic overlay in place, this wouldn't have happened. But Ginna just stopped pushing for it, so. And then. There goes the neighborhood," Angus says dryly, and turns to walk.

"You were asking about Ginna," he reminds me, as if I could forget why we're together. "I'll tell you, but I won't tell him. He doesn't deserve to know a bit of this." Angus's fury about Bennett is like those fires you hear about smoldering away inside piles of sawdust at a lumberyard. "The funeral, the way he just sat there. The way she would talk about him, how it was like being married to a marble statue." He is so disgusted. "She got nothing from him, nothing that was going to sustain her. Took no interest in her, in those girls. A perfect imitation of a marriage. She was turning cartwheels trying to get his attention." We wait for a car to pass, then we cross the street. "I'll tell you what.

I'm not sorry. Not a bit. That bastard." He is so different today, off the chain. "What is it you want to know?"

Everything. I want to know everything. He's this oracle, this time traveler who can put me back there with my sister, at least closer than I can get myself. I need to hear this, so desperately. "Whatever you can tell me. Look, Angus, I'll just say this: I feel so terrible about what happened with my sister. For not knowing what she was going through. That she wouldn't tell me about this. I feel terrible for her daughters, my mom, for you. I feel terrible that I don't even know what I should feel terrible about. But it's awful, I'm telling you. Hold up," I say. There's a rock in my shoe, and I'm winded anyway. Angus stops as if someone's yanked on his rope, and he waits.

Squatting to retie my shoe, I say, "Since I've been here, I have come to see just how bad our family is, how we suck. We've all had buckets over our heads, looking down at our feet when we should have been paying attention." Off we go walking again. "I have a friend who's carried something around for years, and it's just about eaten him alive. It's not good, Angus. It's not the way to go. Misery shared is misery halved, you know."

We finally hit sidewalk alongside the soul-sucking subdivision that somebody plunked down on the old Richland Country Club site, and Angus is moving even faster. We arrive at Elmington Park, only a city block in size, always busy with a baseball team on one side and a medieval foam-bat-whacking group at the other. Today, a guy in a tie-dye T-shirt is giving his border collie a whale of a workout with a Frisbee. Angus sits on a bench, and I collapse beside him.

"Your sister called me, for the first time in more than eight months, upset. Desperate almost. This was in September. From an imaging clinic in Murfreesboro, about to go in for an MRI, and she wanted me to come with her. Said she couldn't do it alone—it's a strange thing, an MRI, claustrophobic.

"Keep in mind that the last time I had spoken to her was on New Year's Day, when she told me she never wanted to see me again, that she and he"—he says it with utter disdain—"were going to work things out. Showed up at my back door in the middle of the afternoon, such a strange time of day. It was like seeing an owl in daylight, unnatural. Told me that her husband had ... figured out everything." He says this with embarrassment. "I stayed away. That's what she wanted. But it almost killed me. Three doors away, might as well have been the moon. I stopped even driving down that end of the street.

"When she called, in September, I didn't even know he had moved out.

Months earlier. If I'd only known, I would've . . ." and he shakes his head. The layers of regret that Angus lives under must be so suffocating.

"I knew so little about what she was up to," I say.

An older woman pushing a stroller passes in front of us. A baby foot dangles out, a biscuit foot. "So when I heard her voice again, right there, asking me to do this, I thought I was dreaming. Didn't even seem possible." He sighs. "I made it to Murfreesboro in thirty minutes. I would have flapped my arms and flown if that would have been faster.

"When I got there, she had the look of a frightened deer. Somebody had already planted some notion of what they were looking for. Said her hip had been bothering her. I think it bothered her a lot."

I'm so furious at him. "Why didn't you tell us this?"

He sees my expectant, angry face and blinks. His eyes, so near, look like they used to be blue. "I'm telling you now." He shifts. "It was the little girl. Cassie. In my back yard, standing by that whirlpool. A dead ringer for her mother, isn't she? I don't know if you could tell how dangerous that water was, but anything that could throw a truck upside down is treacherous stuff. I was terrified that somebody would slip and fall. As I watched the girls, I thought about Ginna, and how she would want me to watch out for them. And it was then that I realized—I felt it very powerfully—that she would hate for me not to tell you everything."

He may be the saddest person I've ever known.

"I don't know if you know what it's like to be alone," he says.

I snort. "Remember who you're talking to."

"I'm not talking about living by yourself. I mean completely at sea. After Augusta died, I convinced myself that what I was doing, what my life had become, was enough. That I could just limp along, sweet little Mary and me." He looks across the park, at nothing. "Then I met your sister. She was . . ."

"Yeah," I say.

"She was tremendous. A galaxy. A world for me to inhabit."

My anger ebbs, just like that, as I recognize what he's talking about, that feeling. "True love," I say, louder than I intended.

He looks up, startled, and nods. "Imagine finding it, then losing it. Then finding it again, and losing it again."

I don't want to imagine that. Angus's grief scares me, such a vacuum, a black cavern. Henry's sleeping face flashes in my mind—lifeless?—and I'm horrified.

We sit for a good long while. He seems in no hurry to talk.

"I just don't get it," I say. "Why wouldn't she tell us about this? That just doesn't sound like Ginna. She was never the sort to keep stuff to herself."

"Well, what would you have done? You look around: husband has checked out with a nurse. Mother has never been on the scene. Sister's a hermit living in another city." Ouch. "What are your options? We talked about it a lot. I told her she needed to tell you all. She was still trying to decide what to do, when the accident happened. It was only a few weeks since she'd learned the news. But you know, I honestly don't think she was going to go ahead with the treatments."

"Seriously?"

"No." Dejected is the best way to describe his tone. "With Augusta, we had time together, and it was the most precious time you can imagine. Heightened reality. Everyday life but cast in this richest glow. Gorgeous days, those days, even at the end.

"But Ginna's frame of mind was not good. She wanted to get back together with him, but it just seemed impossible. He resisted every attempt she made. Wouldn't go to counseling. Wouldn't talk about anything but what time he should pick up the girls. She called him, wanted to tell him about the diagnosis, but he wouldn't even talk to her. I hated him so much for that.

"Maybe she would have told you all, after the shock wore off. But the accident came before she had the chance."

The border collie is so quick, so hellbent on catching that Frisbee. Angus is watching the dog, too. "I never saw her, that day. The last day."

"What do you mean?"

"Well, I was going to meet her at a doctor's appointment that day—remember the voicemail? She didn't want to go alone. But she never showed up."

He looks terrible, fiddling with the buckle of his wristwatch. A wave of pity hits me.

"I waited and waited at the clinic. I called her but got no answer. Nothing. I went to her house, but her car was gone. It was as if she had vanished. Couldn't find her. I retraced her route to the clinic. I thought, This had to be the way she went. She'd go this way. I knew her so well. But for some reason, she'd gone down Woodmont, up to Hillsboro. Maybe she had an errand. I don't know.

"He was the one they called. He was the one in her wallet, not me. He was the one holding her hand at the hospital."

It's right about this moment that I get it, that I see what Ginna saw in Angus. He loved her. It's so simple, so obvious. Her world was his world. I imagine my warm-hearted, loving sister with Angus, and for the first time, it makes sense.

He's tired of carrying this around, I can tell. He's not wearing Ginna's sweater. I do notice that.

Elmington Park isn't much of a park. You're not going to find a Frank Gehry pavilion in Elmington Park. The playground is apparently designed to make it impossible for mothers to keep track of their toddlers. The playing field has a drainage ditch running through the middle of it, and the whole park is shaped like a bowl. After the flood, the mud is considerable. Still, it's a good place to people-watch. Angus and I sit on our bench, his legs stretched out like telephone poles. It's such an odd thing, to be sitting here with this recluse, but a feeling of calm is washing over me. We watch a pair of teenagers lobbing tennis balls to each other on one of the dilapidated courts over in the corner of the park. "When I was young," he says, "I played a lot of tennis. Everybody wanted me to play basketball, as you might imagine, but for me, tennis was the only sport that made any sense. I loved it, good at it. But one day, when I was in college, I blew out my rotator cuff, just that whole shoulder, and I quit the team, never played again."

Why is he telling me this?

"I still think about tennis a lot. But I don't play."

"Well, you could, couldn't you? I mean, that was a long time ago."

"It's just that some things get ruined. That was what tennis was for me. And that's what Ginna was. I will never not think about her, never stop wondering how I could have done things differently, what could have kept her here."

"There's nothing you could have done, Angus." He is so very sad. "It was an accident."

"You're so dogged, Delia. You really want every crumb, don't you? Well how about this: did you take a look at the police report? After the accident?"

"No."

"Well I did, and it said that she was basically in the wrong lane, making a turn across three lanes of traffic."

I look at him, puzzled.

"Maybe I knew she was taking a lot of pain medicine. And maybe I should have been the one to take her to the doctor."

The three bottles.

"I should have insisted. I absolutely should have taken her. She was so woozy. Maybe if I'd been driving, we would have crossed that intersection five minutes later, and that delivery truck would still be on its way. Maybe she'd be sitting quietly in the seat next to me, wondering about what her day was going to be, what the doctor was going to say. Maybe she'd be thinking how nice it was to be with Angus Donald again. Maybe she'd be here right now."

I don't know how long we sit there, watching this border collie, but the light shifts, and the heat of the day relents. Finally, the border collie catches a Frisbee, sits, then rolls onto his back, exhausted, limp.

Angus, whose gentle nature has emerged in the course of our talk, looks steadily at me. "She was intimidated by you. You were the one person she wished would be in her life." His tone is so quiet now, so wholly different from his earlier belligerence. "She felt . . . alone. In the swirl of all those friends she seemed to collect, she was missing you, missing your mother."

"Such a mess. Angus, I've had it so wrong."

"I don't know that your mother provided much in the way of tenderness for you two."

Tenderness. The way he says it is so utterly tender.

I am finding it possible to sit with Angus without the electric jitters running up my spine. "Angus, what was the deal with the house? Why did she leave it to me?"

"We spent a fair amount of time together in that last month. It wasn't the same anymore—she was so unsettled, nervous. But she knew I would do anything for her, so she talked to me, often. She was so much smarter than she gave herself credit for. A few days after the MRI, she showed up at my door, such a shock. She asked me if I would help her change her will. I told her it was precipitous to be doing something like this, and we should just see where the treatment took us, but she was very clear headed."

"That's so fatalistic," I say. "It just doesn't sound like her."

Angus shrugs. "She was not optimistic about this. She thought that stress had to have been a factor."

"Still, I can't believe she would just give up."

"Well, we'll never actually know what she would have done, will we?" We sit for a while on that one.

He says, "The will. I thought she would want to do something about Bennett as her beneficiary, seeing as how they were separated and he wanted that divorce. But it was you. She wanted to change the will to leave the house to you. She said she hadn't left anything to you, and she wanted to do something that would help you."

Gracious, generous Ginna.

"So I helped her do that."

What. If. What. If. As we trudge down the sidewalkless street, the what-if march brings me home. Angus seems literally to have lightened his load. He walks less like a worn-down camel now, more like a loping greyhound. I feel the burden of what he's given me—the thought of Ginna in so much pain leaves me dragging home.

And to think that those pill bottles are causing more trouble over at Henry Peek's place. I can't face into that situation, can't square the facts with whatever story Henry would tell me about them. I can't make the call. He hasn't called, either. He ought to own this. But he doesn't want to.

We pass the Sullivans' house, and I can't even stop to look. The house is gone now, a pile of rubble in a cloud of dust so thick that the smell of old plaster reaches us on the street. The backhoe is taking a slow bite of the wreckage, pulling on a board that won't come loose.

Angus is behind me, so he yells over my shoulder, "Mary was saying how much fun she's having. Sounds like a carnival over there."

"Zoo, maybe. Everyday life will return at some point, right?"

"Don't even know what that is anymore," Angus says. His warm hand on my shoulder startles me, and I turn. "You have a tremendous opportunity, Delia. It's the most ridiculous thing," he says. "There you all are, packed into that house, and you can't even see how rare that is, how precious."

Get with Your People

There's a house I pass on the way to the grocery store, a Williamsburg cottage but bloated, like many other houses along Estes Road. Frank Harrell, Prom Date Loser, lives there. I Googled him before I came to town. Sells insurance, has three pasty daughters. His wife's name is Tammy. Runs a boutique filled with bed linens and expensive candles and crap, and she posts a lot of Facebook photos of herself having girls' night out with other fat-cheeked raccoon-mascara galpals. Tammy obviously has no understanding of Internet privacy. I've been passing it for weeks now, this house, and every time I see it, I wonder what he would think if he knew I were here. I wonder what his wife would say if I told her what had happened.

My bowling ball. I forget about it for long stretches of time, then I discover it in my tote bag, on the seat of my car, right there beside me. It's always there, the weary load, so tiresomely, boringly sad and old that all you want in the world is to leave it behind.

I have a friend in Chicago, Debra Farmer, who had a fear of stairs, a full-out phobia that made life hard in a place like Chicago. She engineered things so that she lived on the first floor of a row house in Lincoln Park, worked in a grocery store because it was a ground-floor sort of career, wouldn't even take the El. Stairs made her crazy. After years of being paralyzed by it, she was invited to a party by a neighbor, this nice guy who lived in the apartment upstairs. And she had to say no. It was then that she decided to face into her fear and get over it. She found someone who was a phobia fixer, and they spent days doing strange things, like standing in front of a staircase for ten minutes, a half hour, an hour, just being there with those terrifying steps. After a few days of this slow, slow business, Debra took a step, like a moon landing, and found herself on her way upstairs.

That house on Estes. There it is, for the twentieth time. I see now that it's just a house, with some guy in it, with a wife and some pasty kids. I think I could run into Frank Harrell at the Harris-Teeter, and I wouldn't hate him. Much.

In Chicago, grocery stores always depress me. I avoid them whenever possible. Whole aisles stacked with things I never need: pet food, baby wipes, bags of charcoal briquettes, beets. Whoever eats a beet? What do you do with a whole snapper? The long aisle filled with cleaning supplies is there for somebody with a compulsion, or a stupefying variety of dirty surfaces.

These days, I find myself going down aisles I never visited before, and I kind of like it. We need all sorts of stuff at the house. Amelia asked me to get her some Tampax, which just about killed me. Growing up, I would have died rather than ask somebody to do that for me, never mind say the word *Tampax* out loud. Mother asked for Sister Schubert cinnamon rolls. Bennett needs razors. Shelly said to get more food for Mr. Serious, reminding me that Ginna was adamant about the brand. The back of the ViaNature bag is covered in pie charts and an essay: "Our regional ingredients are approved 'fit for human consumption' by the Government of Canada and arrive at our door fresh each day." No wonder Mr. Serious is so fat: he's preservative free and bursting with forty-bucks-a-bag goodness.

I've been coming to the grocery store so often these days that it feels normal to go home with six bags of stuff. We have a household. The checkout line is keeping me up to date on movie stars' children and Six Ways to Be Sexier Now, which is three more than I really need. I hand the cashier a coupon for two-for-one cream cheese, and I feel pretty clever.

My phone rings.

"Hey." A gristly accent with a rushing sound in the background, somebody in a car? "This Delia?" I can barely hear.

"Yes."

"Ethan. Ethan Hardy. Sold that house yet?" He dissolves into a roar of laughter. "AS IF! As if anybody can get a damn thing done around this town! Sugar!" he yells. "Tell 'em I'm comin'. Goddamn promoter. I know—I know." He seems to have forgotten that I'm on the line—he's in a conversation with Sugar. "I told 'em I ain't doin' no finale. You get up there, somebody else picked the goddamn key, and it's always 'Will the Goddamn Circle Be Unbroken?' and I look like a damn fool. If the finale ain't 'Tennessee Mud,' I ain't doing it." Long silence. "Now." He's back. "Sorry. Flood benefit."

"You're doing a flood benefit?"

"Oh hell yeah, isn't everybody? Six of 'em, actually. Give 'em an inch, before you know it, they talk you into five more, whatever. Six nights at Bridgestone Arena, god*dam*mit I need a smoke. People are hurting, I tell you what. I never seen such a mess. Hey—you out of that house yet?"

"What?"

"Honey, I been thinking about you up in that attic."

Ethan Hardy has been thinking about me?

"Listen, it ain't a bit of my business, but a pretty girl like you needs to move on with it. Your sister ain't comin' back. I lost two brothers in Afghanistan, and I tell you what: it hurts like a bitch, won't never stop. You need to get with your people. We're all half dead anyway, right? Just get on with your livin'. Hey—you ought to come to a concert. Sugar"—he's yelling again—"the house? That girl? Get her some passes. OK. Well." And he hangs up.

I call back, but it goes to his voicemail. The house is still here, I tell him. Nobody's bought it.

It's hard to say what moment of life here at 603 Bowling Avenue has been the most memorable, but I don't think there's much to rival the tender sight of Amelia Schwartz waiting for her prom date. She perches in her bedroom on the very edge of her bed, the green silk of her bargain vintage party dress billowing around her, Tibetan prayer flags festooned across the ceiling. She has managed, with the help of Mary and a hair iron, to make her hair perfectly smooth, a curtain of dark silk. Her straight eyebrows give her a solemn look. She's reading a book, *The Heart Is a Lonely Hunter*.

"That's cheerful," I say, sitting down across from her. "Deaf mutes, suicide, injustice."

"Yeah. Southern lit class. So de*pressing*." She looks down at the back cover, at the sunken-eyed photograph of Carson McCullers. "Unlike real life, of course," she says slyly. "Which is such a picnic."

"What is the deal with real life, anyway?" I ask. "It's so relentless." Hold on, now—she's going to a party. Steer it out of the ditch. "Where are you going to dinner? You look so pretty."

"A bunch of us are going to Belle Meade. Can't stand that place, but whatever. Such a Grandma hangout. Somebody's mom practically organized the whole thing. Carter is kind of like that. These are good," she says as she looks at her new party shoes. I caught her practicing in them earlier today.

"Perfect," I say. Her father can repair her ankle after she wipes out in them.

"Shelly told me about the guy who ditched you at prom," she says.

"She did?"

She laughs a little. "That's just awful. He just . . . left? Didn't you hate the guy?"

I sigh theatrically. "I carry it with me to this day." She laughs. "Whatever you do, do not let Carter Phelps out of your sight. He goes to the bathroom? You wait outside. Or go in. Just go in there with him."

Amelia laughing is the most beautiful thing, such an echo of her mother.

Mother has come upstairs, to my attic room, to say goodnight. It's very late, and we've packed an exhausted Amelia off to bed. The lighting up here is remarkably bad, just a study lamp with a 60-watt bulb and two little lamps shaped like palm trees. She heads for the ejecting Barcalounger, but I steer her toward the chair with the back-gouging metal grape leaves. She sits, as usual, with such fine posture that her back doesn't even touch the grape leaves.

"What a happy night for Amelia."

"Yeah. She seemed so good. And Carter Phelps didn't ditch her. Strong work."

Mother is wearing Ginna's worst bathrobe, an orange-striped, zippered caftan that makes her look like a beach cabana.

"Mom. I want to tell you something."

She shifts in her chair. "Like what?"

"It was something that happened a long time ago. Back in high school. I never told you. But I need to tell you. Now, I mean." My mouth is so dry. I didn't expect that I would feel like a teenager all over again, telling this to her. I'm so nervous. Mother is staring straight at me, unnervingly alert. "Well. When I was a senior, do you remember the prom?"

"Of course."

"Well. There was more to that whole thing. He. A few days later, he was. He said he was sorry—and now I'm guessing it was because you had told his mother about it."

"She wasn't much, that Linda Harrell."

"I can't believe you called her. Anyway, he said he felt bad about what happened. I was so stupid, and so wanting a boyfriend. Told him it was OK. And then." I feel the words slowing, sticking to the floor. "And then, we started going out, not in any high-quality way. They weren't dates, I guess. But it was something. And then I found out I was pregnant."

"Delia."

"So I went down, you know. And I took care of it."

Mother has a ghostly look to her, in the shadows of this attic. She is sitting absolutely still, as if she's hearing testimony of a witness who can't speak very loudly. "You didn't want me to know."

"No."

"Who else did you tell?"

"Shelly."

She leans forward, elbows on knees, and holds her face in her hands.

"And the boy?"

"No way."

"You did this all by yourself."

I nod.

"Delia." Her eyes are sunk so deep in shadow that I can't see them. The sap has run out of her, her beautiful posture now a slump. "You'd do that all by yourself instead of coming to me."

It's funny: I've had this conversation with my mother a hundred times, a thousand times in my head. I've imagined her reaction, every possible reaction, and I would conclude, again and again, that I didn't want to give this to her. I didn't want her to know how she had hurt my feelings, for so long. There wasn't a scenario where I saw this conversation going well. I thought she'd argue her case with me about the sacrifices she made for her career, or find some fault in what I had done, or—most likely—say some careless thing that would break my heart all over again. I imagined her shock, and her typically cool reaction. It would be talking, Mother's response. She would do the thing she does so magnificently, which is to parse a situation and decide, make her call, judge. I thought she would operate in a consistent way with the sort of person she is. I never would have guessed that she would simply stand up, sit beside me on the bed, and wrap her arms around me, as tightly as possible, without a word.

She feels so skinny, a bag of bones, thin. This is so sad to me that I am lost in tears. I feel her ragged breath against my shoulder, and I know she's crying, too.

"I'm so sorry, Delia," she says, muffled.

"Me too."

She sits up, a weak mother I've never seen before. "I need to tell you something, too," she says, a note of surprise in her quiet voice. She gives her face a swipe with the sleeve of her caftan, and she waits for the words to come. We sit. She is silent.

"What?" I say.

She shakes her head, then touches her throat as if to remind it to work, but nothing comes out of her slightly opened mouth.

She's sick. She's quitting work because she's sick. I understand now: she's too thin. "Mom," I say gently. "I can handle it."

She shakes her head as her face crumples again, and she catches it in her hands. "I know you can," she says. "I just don't know if I can."

"It's OK, Mom. There are good doctors."

Her head snaps up. "What?"

"What *is* it, Mom?"

"It's not that," she says, surprised. "I'm not mortally ill, if that's what you mean. It's"—and she stops again. "It's your father." She steadies herself by pushing her hands against the mattress beneath us. "It's about your father."

This is weird.

"You know what happened. With the airplane. But that's only part of the story. There's more." She swallows, clears her throat. "Your father was the love of my life. I adored him, from the very minute I laid eyes on him."

That's news. I've never heard her say that. Stories of my father were usually accompanied by a disparaging comment and a sour edge. We were better off without him, she would tell us.

She sees my astonished expression and says, "I know."

"You never . . ."

"It was a mess, really, to love someone who never quite loved you back."

"You really loved him?"

She has such a strange, guilty look as she nods. "Will Ballenger was *it*. Most charming creature I had ever seen. Ever. So smart. And when we started dating in Washington, it was . . . He had this way of making you feel like you were the only person in the room."

I don't get this, at all. "I thought you sort of just put up with each other. You said he was awful."

"He was wonderful. That was the thing. You know how you can talk yourself into something? How you can engineer a reality that you want, even if it's not actually right, or true, or good? That's what happened with your father and me. We both had a powerful need. I had to have him. And he had a need for a certain kind of life. A wife." She says this last part slowly.

"His political ambitions?" I ask. Mother said he had always planned to run for office at some point. As a girl, I imagined him as president, bitter that I would never get to grow up in the White House like Caroline Kennedy did.

She nods, then shakes her head. "I didn't understand anything. Until right before the plane accident. Married ten years, did not have a clue. I look back, try to see what I missed. But there wasn't anything."

I touch her arm. "What are you talking about?"

"He was involved with somebody. At work. And no, it wasn't a cute little paralegal. That would have been easy." She puts her hand over mine, lets a sliver of a smile out. "Put your eyeballs back your head. It was a partner."

"Like . . ."

She gives me a look of deep knowing. "There were no female law partners in Nashville at that time."

"Mama!"

"I know!"

"No way!"

She shrugs. "I'd been down in Atlanta for a conference, decided to come home early. I drove back, had to be midnight when I got home. Shelly was in her bathrobe—she was staying over with you two—and told me Will was in the library, in a meeting with Ben Hill. In the middle of the night? She was acting so odd, like I'd caught her doing something wrong. I wandered back there, but they were nowhere to be found, so I looked around and saw a light out in the pool house, one dim little bulb. It was all too peculiar. I stood at that back door for the longest time, calculating, waiting. Hoping that Will Ballenger and Ben Hill were somehow not in that pool house.

"Well, of course, they were. Eventually, Ben headed out around the side of the house, and Will walked right toward me, barefooted, as handsome as the head on a coin. When he saw me, oh my Lord, Delia, I honestly thought he was going to have a stroke. It was all there, right there on his face.

"So humiliated I was, so furious. As if I could talk him out of this? So ridiculous." She stops and shakes her head, lost in her story. "He was devastated, so ruined. Begging me to give him another chance. We were up all night, talking in circles, nothing resolved. And then he left for work. The next thing I hear is he had fallen out of the plane. He and Ben Hill had apparently taken off that morning, told everybody they had a meeting in Memphis."

She shakes her head, minutely. "I have no idea what happened. Ben Hill never said a word, other than expressing his grief over the accident. Not. A. Word. Told me Will was such a nice guy. Said he would miss him at the office. To this day I see him around town—I used to play bridge with his wife." There's a distance in her voice, wonderment. "The latch was faulty. But who knows?"

The veneer is still there, the Grace Ballenger paste wax gloss, but at least now I've had a glimpse of the heart underneath. I believe that she was furious and humiliated enough to retreat into a compulsive silence for thirty years. I see it. It's not pity I feel, but something like it.

She touches my arm and I jump. "I was going to tell you," she says. I actually believe her.

"Why didn't you tell me before?"

She rolls her eyes. "It was ages before you were even old enough to tell. And by the time you were, it didn't matter. He broke my heart, really crushed it. And that was that. At least, that was what I told myself." She shakes her head. "For a long time, I had this thought that if you didn't say it, it wasn't real. Very southern, foolish. You can imagine what Charlotte the psychotherapist thought of that. If you kept a feeling inside, maybe that was the safest place for it. That's what I thought. I actually believed that."

Answered Questions

I wake up in the middle of the night, stunned. I dreamed the answer. I get it. Angus.

I think about Mother, asleep now downstairs, and the way I could feel her skinny bones as she held me in her arms and we cried our hearts out. I think about the way it feels, this moment, here in the dark, knowing that she knows about me, and I know about her.

I don't really understand how I told her in such a simple way. It certainly hadn't been the plan. All day long, watching Amelia get ready for her prom, I had been planning to tell Mother my story. It was time. I wanted to tell her. I had a whole speech worked out, this thing about how being here had been this astonishing journey, how I had been revisiting these memories, how I could see now in a way I couldn't back then. I was going to tell her about the way I'd carried this experience, this crappy, lonely misfire, for so long and how I resented the fact that I couldn't tell her. How I resented pretty much everything about my childhood.

But I was also going to tell her that this trip to Nashville was not anything like what I'd anticipated. It's a rare thing in life to feel the earth shift under your very feet, to know as it happens that some profound alteration is under way. I was going to tell her that maybe she was a terrible mother, back in the day, but maybe I wasn't such a great daughter, either.

Last night, all that fell away. I see now, suddenly and clearly, that I will be telling her these things soon enough. I look forward to this—look forward to seeing my mom? If that isn't a seismic alteration, I don't know what is.

I can't stop thinking about my father. I can't believe it. I can't believe Mother would keep that to herself, all these years.

———

I think about Angus, coming in the back door of this house, wandering the rooms, looking for Ginna. He loved her in a way that Bennett never could. How wrong was that, really? I've never been a cheater, and it stunned me to learn that Ginna had done that. But what happened? What sent her over the edge? What let her cliff-dive away from her careful, measured life?

I don't want to be in this narrow daybed anymore. I have barked my left shin on the wooden frame of this ill-designed thing four times now. I wish Henry were beside me. The longer I don't hear from him, the more wound up I get. Why hasn't he called? He hasn't called me since our visit to Fort Nashborough. Two whole entire complete days. It feels like a month. It feels like he's dead. He keeps Tweeting about Hands on Nashville, about the beautiful things he's discovering about Nashvillians under pressure, how he now knows the count on a pallet of FEMA diapers (3,000). He's still cooking with Kevin and the Leisure Life food caravan, and he's not calling me. This is driving me out of my mind, but I can't pick up the phone.

He said he eats a lot of spinach. He had such a weird expression on his face when he said it, like he couldn't believe the word was coming out of his mouth.

At least I've figured out why I can't bear to do it: if I call, it might not work out. If I pull on the wrong stone, the whole wall might collapse.

As soon as the light comes, I head out to Angus's. Tucked under my front doormat is an envelope with "D. Ballenger" written in loopy letters. Inside are two lanyards with laminated passes: "Anointed One. Extreme Access. Ethan Hardy's House Party for Nashville. Bridgestone Arena. May 11-16, 2010." For a guy who can't seem to complete a phone conversation, Ethan Hardy makes things happen. I slide the lanyards over my head and feel the awesome power of laminated access. I need to get on with my livin', Ethan told me. I need to get with my people.

It's sprinkling this morning, for the first time since the flood. It feels scary, rain, in a way that I've never worried about it before. What if it doesn't stop, again? I can't believe that a drizzle is making me nervous.

There was something so unsatisfying about what Angus told me, about why Ginna would leave the house to me. It didn't make sense. I've been chewing on this for months now, ever since that incredible phone call from Bennett that the house was mine. Ginna was the least interested person in the world when it came to legal stuff—she barely renewed her car tags. It wouldn't have occurred to her to change her will. That's just not how her mind worked. She wouldn't have left the house to me, just to give me something. She probably didn't even know where her will was.

I find Angus out in his yard, staring up at his roof, with all the sprinklers in his lawn shooting jets of water up into the rain. His yellow slicker makes him look like a crab fisherman. I have a sudden craving for a fish stick. "Can't figure out that damn system," he says, pointing at the low, misty clouds. "Thinking of putting in a moat," he says. "Has your basement dried out?"

"Angus."

He peers at me under my umbrella as if I'm some kind of peculiar animal let loose from a menagerie.

"It's not my house, is it?" I say.

Angus doesn't move. "What are you talking about?"

"The house. That codicil is not a real codicil."

"I have no idea what you're talking about."

"You changed Ginna's will. You didn't want Bennett to end up living three doors down from you for the rest of your life. You didn't want him to live in the house he didn't deserve to be in. You saw what was ahead for Ginna, and you fixed it. It was you."

He says nothing. All I want is a clue, a sign, an acknowledgment that I'm right. I know I'm right; I just want to see it in his face. "I don't get how you did it. I mean, I saw the codicil with my own eyes. It looks real. It has Ginna's signature on it. It has witnesses. It was stapled right in there, right in that document. How did you *do* it?"

There is the slightest flicker of something across his face, but it might be one of his rabbity tics.

"I mean, the witnesses. They said it was genuine, that they'd seen her sign it. Bennett said."

He shifts minutely from one foot to the other.

"But why me? Why would you engineer this so that I would end up with the house? You were so incredibly sour that day, when I first showed up."

He smiles as if I've finally said something in English. "Sour? I was just surprised, mostly, to see you in the flesh."

"Angus, you told me I shouldn't go in the house."

"Well," he shrugs. "Wasn't I right? At any rate, I was surprised. Didn't remember you from the funeral. Different from the photos. You have a very young look about you. Ginna always said you were so mature for your age, so I guess I was looking for someone older." He folds his arms across his chest, settling in for a chat. "It's strange. Ginna and I spent most of our time talking. That was her charm, once you fished it out of her. She told me story upon story about the two of you, your childhood, your mother. And Shelly. I thought you sounded like an interesting person. And she always said that you and I were so much alike." A strange feeling creeps up the back of my neck. He looks like a contented crocodile.

"How did you do it, Angus?"

"I don't know what you mean, Delia. The house is yours. The papers say so, right?"

In the drizzle, on the way home, I think about the dilemma Angus has put on me. He didn't admit that he'd monkeyed around with Ginna's will, but he didn't really deny it, either. Now I know why Ginna left me the house: she didn't. But here's Angus looking at me with that long, bony face of his, as blank as a wall. I have to give the guy credit. Pretty spectacular, the whole thing.

It's not his house to give away. It's certainly not mine. But do I want to undo this? Not so much. Bennett doesn't want this haunted house. I surprise myself at how fast I conclude this.

I honestly don't know where Bennett spent the night last night, but his exit yesterday included the phrase "get the hell out of here before I blow my brains out." At any rate, he's back now, coming out of the house with a box of what is likely Civil War history. The girls are with him, lugging bags of clothes in the rain, piling things into Amelia's Jeep. It looks an end-of-year dorm exit, the big loadout.

Cassie looks glum. "Aunt Delia. Mr. Serious? When you sell the house? You're taking him, right?"

I have given zero thought to the issue of Mr. Serious's future, but I realize even as she is talking that I am about to become the owner of a large, crotchety cat who occasionally poops in the wrong place. "Of course, Cassie. We're besties. Laughs at all my jokes."

No smile. She is not going to play today. She knows she's leaving this house, and this time it's for real. "What about Mom's stuff? What happens to that?" She says this in a low voice so that Bennett won't hear.

"We'll go through it, and save whatever you want to keep."

She looks at me, horrified. "And get rid of the rest?"

"You can keep everything, if you want. There are storage places that keep stuff as long as you like. When you get older, it will be like an incredible Christmas to get all these things. You'll see—when you're old like me, things like breakfast room chairs are deeply thrilling." I don't even want to think about what fifteen years of storage fees will cost. Probably cheaper to buy a house to dump it all in.

She crams a bag into the trunk of Bennett's car and opens the car door. "Oh—my pictures!" she says, and runs back to the house.

Bennett swings into the driver's seat. "Ginna was right about you," he says to his steering wheel. I wait expectantly, but he doesn't seem to have anything else to say.

"Like . . . what?" I nudge.

"You're just afraid." He shrugs and looks up at me, his caterpillar brows so dark against his pale skin. "You shouldn't be afraid." He studies a hangnail on his very clean thumb. How many thousands of times has he scrubbed those fingers?

"Afraid of what?"

"Everything."

"I could say the same of you," I say hotly.

"Exactly," he says. "I shouldn't be afraid. But I am."

This strikes me as crushingly ironic, like we've been hide-and-seeking in the woods and backed into each other. "Bennett, you are such a weirdo."

"Takes one to know one."

"I'm not going anywhere," I tell him.

"Really." He is gratifyingly pleased.

"Really. I'm feeling kind of brave, actually. You said you couldn't do this alone. Well. Neither can I. The girls need taking care of, and we're going to do it. Mother, me, you." I sound so confident. "I figure that three of us equals at least a half-Ginna, and that's better than nothing."

"Judge Ballenger," he says with scorn. "Despises me. And I despise her."

"You should tell her about Ginna." He shakes his head. "Seriously. You shouldn't be the villain in all this."

He squints and sighs noncommittally. "Not worth it."

"I don't get it."

"Forget it." He runs a hand across the top of his black hair, arguing in his head, then looks straight up at me. "OK. The morning of our wedding, your mother"—he leans toward me to whisper—"who has got to be the biggest pain in the ass I have ever met—sat Ginna down. Told her she didn't have to get married. Said we were rushing it. Basically told Ginna I wasn't good enough for her. Just said it, right out loud. Ginna was so upset we almost eloped."

"Crazy old mom," I say. I remember that wedding photograph in Ginna's bedroom, the happy couple.

"Has it occurred to you that telling your mom about Ginna, maybe it would confirm what I don't want to confirm? That maybe I wasn't enough? That maybe your mother was right."

This sounds so much like my kind of pointless thinking that my head feels light. "Oh, Bennett. That needs to go."

"Nope. Not giving her the satisfaction." He looks behind me. Cassie is back, lugging a corkboard covered in certificates of accomplishment, field day ribbons, and faces of young girls mugging for the camera.

I lean down to his window. "Hey—I have a question. You know Ginna's will?"

He nods.

"Did she keep it here at the house?"

He looks puzzled. "Yeah. Upstairs. File cabinet."

"That's what I thought. Just wondering. Also."

"Yeah?"

"This house. I keep worrying about it. The will. What if she hadn't changed her will? You'd still own this house. This is your house, really."

He looks at me, incredulous. "You're kidding, right?" I shake my head. "I'd rather live in a mud hut."

"It just feels—"

"Like the worst week of my life. Give the girls their money, do whatever you want. But do not ever make me come back into this house. OK?" He shifts his car into reverse, and I step back as they pull out.

Amelia sticks her head out the window of her Jeep. "Bye, Aunt Delia!"

"I hope it never sells," Cassie says. "I hope you're stuck here." As dry as the Sahara, she is.

"Hope you're stuck here, too," Bennett says. I give him a quizzical look, and he gives me one back.

Then they're gone, down Bowling Avenue.

I tip over on the sofa and collapse. Poor Bennett. Nothing like obsessive thinking to keep a guy down. When Mother does get wind of Ginna's affair, I'm betting her reaction will not be at all what Bennett is expecting. Until last night, I would have said otherwise.

Mother is gone, too, after several days of absolutely no comment on what her housing plans might be—at one point I wondered if she had unilaterally decided to stay forever. She was so unmoored, drifting around the house. This morning she came into the kitchen, bright in the eyes, and announced that she was going to move into the guest house in her backyard until repairs are done, so she is off with David Peek getting it ready. She was so alert this morning, so alive. When she left, she gave me a hug, looked at me very directly, and said, "I can't thank you enough. For everything." I think this might have been the first time she thanked me for anything, ever. Maybe it was the first time I'd done anything worth being thanked for.

For the first time in a week, I am alone in the house.

I look at the contract on the coffee table, the offer from the doctor's wife who wants to tear down the house. Henry's handwriting slants to the right, spiky, where he's filled in the blanks. This is it. This could be the solution to my real estate project. I imagine what it would be like, signing this document, right there on that line. Sticking the pages into Ginna's Clinton-era fax machine, dialing the number, and off it would go. Done.

Leaving would be so easy. I see myself scribbling a note for Shelly on the kitchen counter. I would somehow scrape Mr. Serious into his travel crate. I'd turn out the lamps, all fourteen of them, and throw my computer, backup drives, and tote bags into my car. Set the alarm and lock the door. At the end of the driveway, I'd yank the For Sale sign and hide it under a boxwood. Gone.

How to sell your house in two weeks. Or four. That's how to do it. Mission accomplished.

Except.

I can't stand it anymore. I pull my phone from my pocket and dial. So brave. So terrified.

"Henry."

"Delia."

"Why didn't you call me?"

"I'll be right over." He hangs up, like he's on a walkie talkie.

Was he waiting for me to call? I was waiting for him to call me. This could have gone on forever.

I'm shivery with nerves, now that I know he's on the way. I wish I hadn't called him. There have been only a few times in my life when I have wanted something to the point of irrationality: acceptance to the University of Chicago. A car for my sixteenth birthday. Henry. He's lying and stealing and avoiding the truth. It's so wrong, what he's doing. He can't do this.

I don't usually second-guess myself, but the more I think about Henry, the more I see that it's all my fault. If I hadn't made him dance all night, he wouldn't have gone into Ginna's medicine cabinet. If he'd just stayed home that night, none of this would have happened. If I'd only stayed in my yoga pants and eaten that Lean Cuisine, everything would be just fine.

I sit on the front steps, clammy and nervous, wondering what Henry will be wearing today. So pathetic. Here I am, about to give him hell about not being straight with me, but all I can do is think about that one shirt with the pale blue stripes. Henry wears these beautiful shirts, so plain but so luxurious. He told me that once he got out of jail, all he wanted was to wear shirts that fit right and weren't made out of polyester. It was his indulgence, he said. But today, he comes out of his car wearing a beat-to-hell T-shirt from Bobbie's Dairy Dip. "Tasty Treats" it says above a smiling soft-serve cone. It's the color of chocolate ice cream. His nose is peeling in a worrisome way. I fight the urge to peel off a loose layer. His eyes are hidden behind his sunglasses.

"Got to go down to Murfreesboro Road. Come on." He's distracted by something, and when I look into his SUV, I see why. It's crammed with sleeping bags and air mattresses, dozens of them. He's got one wedged between the front seats. The car smells like warm plastic.

"Slumlord," he says. "These Egyptian immigrants have been fighting with their landlord all week. Took almost a week to get anybody in there to start ripping out carpet and drywall. The kids have been sleeping on wet carpet for days. Ridiculous. You speak Arabic, right?" he jokes.

"Who are these people?"

"Brought here by a church charity. They're all legal. Imagine being here for one month, no English, with your family, trying to get a job at the chicken plant in Shelbyville, then your apartment floods." He shakes his head. "Friends of mine have been working on this all week. Busy." He glances over at me. "I've been missing you." He says this in a matter-of-fact way, as if I'm the guy in the next cubicle who has been out on vacation.

Missing him. There's no way Henry could understand the way I think about him: he's a balloon, a Thanksgiving Day parade balloon, outsized, so unwieldy up there. He drifts along, above my every thought, hard to steer, impractical. I can't make my speech, my indignant declaration that I know about his pill thievery. I can't say anything much in the face of this morning's errand. "Missed you, too," I say. I can play it cool, too.

Murfreesboro Road is less than six miles from Bowling Avenue, but it might as well be a thousand. It has changed so much since I grew up here. Henry explains it all to me. If you're new to Nashville—here by the hair of your teeth, with no English, no money, and no job—Murfreesboro Road is one part of town that has a place for you to stay. You can find an apartment for $500 a month, and you pick your complex based on your ethnicity. Everybody drives 20-year-old cars, and the shop signs are in Spanish, Kurdish, Arabic.

Henry is quiet, but as we turn onto a side street, he says, "There's hush-puppy help, and there's this. This is the sort of situation that my mom would call a pickle." He shakes his head, disgusted. "This whole deal is a huge fucking pickle."

I grew up in this city, but I have never been inside an apartment complex on Murfreesboro Road—nothing even vaguely like the Granada Apartment Houses. Mill Creek, the source of so much trouble with this flood, runs right alongside these charmless, boxlike buildings. The water line on the buildings is about five feet high, and you can see what it left in its wake: the towering crapheaps of ruined everything, universal all over town these days. The difference between other neighborhoods and this, of course, is that there's no money anywhere here to repair what has been lost. It's simply lost.

Now that the drizzle is clearing, people sit on their concrete slab patios in mismatched chairs, milling around. Children everywhere. Displaced, everybody. Solidly Egyptian. If it weren't for the open doors and windows, it would look like some kind of lethargic block party is in progress. It certainly doesn't feel like anything much is getting done. Not what you would call an urgent vibe.

"There she is," Henry says, seeing a chunky woman with bright red hair standing by the apartment complex office talking to a group of men. "Bobbie!"

Bobbie has a clipboard, which is encouraging. "Henri," she yells in a fake

French accent. "Ze bedding!"

Bobbie, it turns out, is a grad student at Vanderbilt Divinity School who speaks Arabic, enough to suss out the basics of what's happening here. She and Henry seem to have a groove going on this sleeping-bag thing. Bobbie has the master list of who should be getting what, but mostly, she has the air of someone who is game for anything. When a small boy runs to Bobbie and puts his hands up, Bobbie puts down her clipboard and, apparently not for the first time, turns him upside down in a backward flip, sending the boy into screeches of joy.

Henry and I trail behind her and two other volunteers. "Bobbie is deeply and totally inspiring to me," he says. "You can't make up somebody like Bobbie. She's pretty much Jesus, only with jokes. Completely unsentimental, so matter of fact about stuff." He glances up at me. "And not a bit cynical. That's the thing. She sees good everywhere. She sees it right here." He squints. "Her father is a wheeler-dealer. Owns four river barge casinos and six strip clubs. Gives Bobbie a lot of material to work with."

"Such a mess this is," I say. "How do they get back up after something like this?"

"I wanted to show this to you." He touches my shoulder, but he's barely here. It doesn't feel like he wants to show anything to me. This feels strange, awkward, and I've never felt this way with him before.

At one apartment, the man of the house is agitated and wants to be sure we all come inside. He's small, very dark skinned, and wears gray dress pants, a white T-shirt and plastic sandals. I couldn't say how old he is: he could be thirty or fifty. We all sit in a row on the lone piece of furniture in the living room, a tremendously long plaid couch that lets you know after a minute that the cushions are, at their core, wet. The carpet is damp, too, and the sour smell of old wet is almost overwhelming. He tells Bobbie that they came to America six weeks ago. He explains that he won't put the sofa outside to dry because he is afraid someone will steal it. He tells a story, fast, gesturing a lot, and ends up in tears, complete frustration coming from him. Bobbie says to us, "It's the landlord story. Same story up and down the place." The man glances up to see two girls approach the sliding screen door to the patio, a teenager and a younger girl. They are talking almost simultaneously, analyzing something, and in the time it takes for them to come in, this man's expression melts to utter blandness. He swallows it. He doesn't want them to see him that way.

"Whose birthday?" Bobbie asks in English to the girls, pointing to the banner that fills one wall.

The teenager looks shy. "Me," she says. "Sixteen."

His wife, smiling and nodding in welcome, brings us a tray of small teacups. We each take one and sip on iceless Coca-Cola while Bobbie explains FEMA to him. Henry passes over a FEMA handout in Arabic. Welcome to the United States, sir. Here's a great, mystifying bureaucracy to get you started on the American Way.

The man says something to Bobbie, and she translates to me, "Have you ever come to Egypt?" He's making small talk? This man is chatting with me amid this utter ruin?

"No," I say, glancing at Henry. "I haven't traveled much." Bobbie translates this, and the man says something else.

"You should," she translates back. "It's good for you."

Henry looks at me over his teacup, amused. I nod. "Yes," I say. "I need to do that. I really ought to."

Henry seems very much in his element as he and Bobbie sort out their distribution plan. He has made three young moms laugh with his charades explanation of the blow-up beds. Maybe Henry's divinity school is right here, on Murfreesboro Road. Maybe he's already figured this out. Maybe that's what he wants to show me.

It doesn't take long to distribute a carful of sleeping bags. It has the feel of pouring cups of water into the waves on a beach. It was only the steady face of Bobbie that kept me from dissolving into tears while sitting in the living room with that family. That teacup of Coca-Cola. "It's not enough," I say.

"Well, it's not nothing," Henry replies, as we sit on the curb of the parking lot. "A little is better than nothing." I can tell his back is bothering him from the stiff way he sits. We watch the horde of kids playing in the center of the complex, kicking a soccer ball, swinging on the rusted swing set. They screech at each other, laugh, sit on the ground, dig in the dirt. Does this situation, this flooded-out disaster, seem any weirder than what they have already experienced? What would it feel like for me to go to Egypt, with no money, no Arabic, with only the people around you speaking your language, where you can't even tell if people are being straight with you? This is home. This is what they have. I have a sudden and powerful urge to find more sleeping bags, and pillows, and jobs, and somebody needs to open up a can of legal whupass on this landlord. Obviously. This is something that needs doing.

In my distraction, I've zoned out. I look down. Henry has been busy lining up prescription bottles on the curb between us.

Henry is not looking at me. His brow is furrowed. He is very, very upset. It upsets me to see him so upset, and the scene around us upsets me even more, so there we are, scowling hard together and trying not to lose it.

Those crappy bottles. I can't stand the sight of them.

He won't look up at me. "After you left, that day, I checked my cabinet. Delia. I could tell you found them. I hoped like hell you hadn't. God, I wish you'd called me on it then." He is hunched over, chin on his knees, fiddling with his shoelaces, sticking the ends into the holes on his sneakers like an old-timey telephone switchboard.

"Didn't know what to make of it. I couldn't," I say.

"And when we were on the bridge, and you said all that about somebody keeping a secret, and how he should just tell it—"

"Actually, it was Angus I was talking about."

"Well I thought you were trying to get me to talk, but I couldn't do it. Couldn't stand what would happen. So I didn't. Even though I knew you already knew. Shit," he says. "I've been so miserable, since." It radiates off him. Tears slide down his cheeks in fat, slow drops. "I told you so much. I couldn't tell you this. All I want is to be honest with you. But."

"It's OK, Henry."

"No. It's not," he says and smears his tears across his jaw with the back of his hand. He's dissolving, right in front of me.

"And something else," he says.

"What?"

He looks up at me, such shadows under his eyes. "What's the deal with Greg?"

Greg? He's wondering about *Greg*? "What about him?"

"There were like fifteen texts from him on your phone." He's embarrassed. "I saw them when we were taking pictures."

"Is that why you didn't call?"

He shrugs. "A guy wants to come all the way from England to help you with your flooded house, you tell me . . ."

It's true. Greg is in Wisconsin right now visiting his parents. When I failed to answer his texts or emails, he called Susan, who told him about the flood, and being helpful, he wanted to come down. I told him thanks but no thanks, but he kept texting me anyway.

"Greg was an on-off thing. Mostly off. It's what I had instead of an actual relationship with anybody. He's a nice guy, but he's no . . ." I shake my head. "He's not you. I was going to tell him. As soon as I knew what it was that was happening to me. To us. But honestly, he's such a non-factor that I didn't even . . ." He frowns, deeply skeptical. "I told you, Henry. I haven't felt like this about anyone in my life. Can't you tell?" I lean close to him. "Look at me." He keeps his eyes down, which hurts my feelings so much.

I look at the bottles. "Where did you find these?"

He leans back on his arms and arches his back in a gingerly stretch. "The cat. In the middle of the night, I went downstairs to get something for my back, and I came through Ginna's room, and I scared the cat, and he scared me, and he jumped off the bedside table, and it tipped over, and the bottles fell out of the drawer. Just like that, the thing I was seeking magically appeared. It would be funny except it isn't."

"Fucking cat."

"Right." He looks at his stack of Arabic FEMA papers, lays them down on the pavement. "I can't tell if these are where-to-get-diapers or aid-for-dependent-children." He is so frustrated. He turns to me. "My back was killing me that night. Sometimes a person wants to appear strong, and whole. And irresistible." He sighs and gestures limply at the bottles. "After a fair amount of self-loathing and deliberation I took them." He shakes his head. "Delicious."

My fault. All my fault.

"I went six years, until this. So disgusted after I left your house. I went to NA. I came straight from there to the Pancake Pantry. I called you. To tell you. And I would have except for what happened with Cassie. Didn't want to intrude."

Showing up at the Pancake Pantry in the rain. I was so happy to see him, so charmed that he would just turn up that way.

"And then. It got harder and harder to bring it up. I tried to, the other day. I'm sorry. Delia."

I look at him, so red in the eyes. "What did you think would happen if you told me?" I whisper.

"I thought you would go back to Chicago. That you'd pack up your attic and leave. And the whole thing would feel like it never happened." He looks up at me, bites his lip. "I figured, hell, she's lived by herself a long time. She doesn't need this."

"You thought I would leave?"

"After I told you everything that happened in Denmark. And when I got home, the hospital. It's just too much. Who wants to deal with all that? I wouldn't blame you, not a bit. Thought you would never trust me again, especially after that thing with your mom. Because I don't seem to be able to trust myself."

Trust. Honesty. It's a Boy Scout jamboree, this conversation. "Did you really have so little faith in me?" I ask.

"I don't want you dragged into this. Backslide."

I stretch out my legs and notice, as ever, how pale I am. Henry's legs are so beautiful with all their shiny hairs. They should be swimming, such legs. He likes to swim at the Vanderbilt pool. He says it's a relief to float that way. I feel a similar floating sensation creeping over me, a suspended feeling, a certainty. He will not backslide without me.

"I need to go," he says and stands. He runs his hand through his hair, pulling on it as he heads toward his car. I follow right behind him.

"I've been thinking about this for days, you know," I say loudly. "You're not the only one stewing about this."

He turns. "Stewing only begins to describe it."

"I don't really blame you. I mean, I can see why you didn't tell me. It's just—I need to know. If this is manageable." Just say it. "I need to know if you're having some dire kind of trouble."

He stops. He doesn't say anything, thinks hard. The set of his mouth is so unsmiling. This version of Henry unsettles me. "Well," he says quietly, "I need to know that, too."

I was hoping for a quick no. I'm crushed, in fact, to hear otherwise. Dammit. Couldn't he just say it was a flukey mistake and he didn't know what got into him?

"Come on," I say, leading him across the parking lot into the scrubby, flood-twisted honeysuckle that lines Mill Creek. I chuck one of the bottles into the meandering water, the least threatening body of water imaginable. "Begone," I say. He throws the other two listlessly.

"Yeah, that'll fix it," he says. I've never heard sarcasm from Henry before.

"It doesn't seem complicated. Just tell me things," I say. "And I'll tell you, too."

"Simple things are complicated, and complicated things are simple," he says. "This is what I think about, all the time. Paradox. The best day was the worst day. The day I felt the strongest was the day I was the weakest. The day

I caught you is the day I lost you."

"I'm still here, Henry. I'm not going anywhere."

"If this can return, these pills, then what else? What about the slough of despond? This miry slough is such a place as cannot be mended. You do not want to see what happens if I go there. Again."

"That's where you're wrong. I do."

He looks so distant, so sunk in his thoughts. The slough of despond? I don't have a clue as to whether he wants anything to do with me at all.

Such a glum ride home. He's got some seriously depressing blues on his CD player, some old guy singing that the sky is crying.

"Listen to this a lot?"

He sings along: "'I got a funny feelin' my baby don't love me no more.'"

I eject the CD. "This is not helping. This is not the Mississippi Delta, OK? Banjo music. That's what you need. Pan flute. Maracas." He keeps his eyes on the road, as if he'll turn to stone if he looks at me.

We arrive back at my house.

"Hey," Henry says, looking up. "That's so great."

Before they left, Cassie and Amelia hung their banner from a second-floor window of the house. "We Are Nashville," it says in block letters, with the tops of three pink and green houses surrounded by the sparkly feathered, brown Cumberland River, and a cartoony trio of cats standing on the roofs, dancing with their cat tails in the air, waving their cat cowboy hats.

"Empty house," I say. "Can you believe it?" I'm nervous all of a sudden because I don't want Henry to leave me, but he doesn't seem to be getting out of his car. "I'm going to miss this place, once it sells, which it never will, come to think of it, which means I'll end up running a boarding house here on Bowling Avenue, which wouldn't be the worst thing, I guess, once I learn how to poach an egg, which seems impossible, frankly, but—"

"Delia." He touches my arm. "What I was saying, how the day I caught you was the day I lost you. You know what I mean. I wanted everything to be so perfect. You were so easy to be with, so familiar. You make me so happy. But I just can't deal with the possibility that I can't shake this thing. It's wrong to drag you into this. I don't—"

I eject out my door, not wanting to hear whatever the end of that sentence is going to be. I come around to his side of the car and open the door. I take him by the arm, gently, and stand him up next to me. "I want you to stay here with me." I don't know how to be more straightforward than that.

He squints at my stubborn expression. "I'm going," he says.

"Not a good idea," I say. "I am discovering that not talking is a great way to not solve problems." There is no way I am going to let him suffer this alone. He was so willing to try, to leave his mossy green apartment and take me to dinner when it wasn't at all clear whether it was a good idea. He wanted to be in the world with me. He had an idea, an inkling, and he was right. The flood of tenderness that washes over me is so warm, so complete.

He looks at me skeptically. "I don't know what to say." As ever, he searches for the exact words but seems stuck. "I love being with you. I love every minute. But."

"No buts," I say, irritated. "Please. I don't know what I'll do if you go." He scowls. "You can't go, actually. I won't let you go. You help me, so much. You are making my life so." What is the word? "So living. Liveable. Possible. Beautiful. This is it. You're it."

Henry's hair is sticking straight up on top, like he's been electrified. It's so fine and blond that it does all sorts of random things. I reach up and run my hand across his warm head, smoothing his hair. "Your hair sticks up a lot."

Is love ever simple? It feels that way, right now. If there were some way that I could keep a constant hand on him, like this, I would do it.

Henry lets me lead him inside, his hand in mine, a sad hand but a warm one. It is almost as though he has given up fighting me, as though he's run out of words and wants only to sit down somewhere.

I think it was the patting of his head that did it, actually. We loners don't get a lot of patting on the head, so when it comes our way, it is impossible to resist.

Ever Closer

This day arrives so bright, so shining. We forgot to pull the curtains last night, so I slip out of bed to close them before the light wakes Henry. I sit in the chair beside him, watching his sleeping face as I love to do. It is early; I'm wide awake.

After a while, I leave him to go downstairs. Through the window of the den I look out at the brilliant greens of the backyard, wondering when our lives will settle down. What will we do? I will stay here—I feel as sturdy as a tree about this—but how will I stay? What will that be like?

Out the window, beyond the terrace, I see pink, and crimson, and white: Ginna's roses have exploded. I hurry to the kitchen door to go outside. I don't want to miss a thing. There's a small wooden stool by the kitchen door, and I bring it with me as I walk through the rain-washed grass to the center of the broad circle of her garden. So many roses, dozens upon dozens, tight buds and loose ones, and the bravest of them wide open. They have come through the flood so well, with the tender care of Jimmy Butterman. My feet are wet from the dew, and my nightgown is damp at the hem. I sit, and I breathe, and this gorgeous scent envelops me. I have to laugh at myself: it's my mother's perfume, this soft fragrance, and my sister's roses, all around me. I don't miss Ginna—she's right here, laughing at me, too, for loving the place I used to tease her about. I have come so far, and here I am.

I remember one day with Shelly, long ago, when we'd go behind Mother's garage to find the honeysuckle. She'd stick her head right into the thicket and breathe in the scent with a lot of drama. "That's it," she'd say, rapturously. "That goes right inside, all that sweetness. Those tiny particles of sweet go right into your body—you smell a flower, it becomes part of you." She'd pull off a flower, pinch the base and pull out the stamen with its drop of sugary nectar. "Heaven," she would say, tasting it.

Henry finds me sitting on my stool. I stand to hug him, then he sits down and pulls me on his knees. Warm against the cool of the morning, he makes such a sturdy chair. Never has a chair been so loving. His feet are bare, with bits of grass on his toes. He has scratchy whiskers. His ear is cool against my cheek. I take inventory whenever I have the chance.

Finally he leaves, solemnly kissing me and reminding me that today is a Monday, and some people have to work for a living.

The emptiness of the house roars around me. I can hardly bear it. Henry can't keep vanishing like this. I haven't even had a boring afternoon with him yet. We have a lot to do before he can just wander off to work.

I've got to talk to someone about all this. I've never been one for gossipy galpal lunches, mostly because I don't have a lot of gossipy galpals. But it occurs to me, as I'm dialing Susan, that she is and has been my confidante for just about everything. We talk for a long time. I tell her about the Egyptians, and the sleeping bags, and I tell her about Henry in such detail that she tells me to hush up, that I'm going to embarrass her.

I tell her about capacity, how I've been thinking about the way our hearts can expand, how there's so much room in that rubbery balloon.

As we talk, I hold the business card that Henry left for me on my bathroom sink. "Love sought is good, but given unsought, is better. Thank you D."

The house feels enormous, now that everyone has gone. And it's a wreck. It's going to take forever to wash all these sheets and towels, but it seems like a good morning thing to do.

In Ginna's room, I pull off the sheets, then sit on the edge of the bed. I open the drawer to the spindly bedside table. Amid the birthday cards, stubby pencils, and emery boards, there's a small calendar, the Episcopal calendar that the church sends out every year. Feasts, festivals, the lectionary laid out, day by day. All our childhood, this sort of calendar sat on the windowsill in the kitchen, and I'd puzzle about saints while I washed my hands. Hilda of Whidby was the saint on my birthday. Ginna's calendar is open to October 2009. Numbers are penciled in on the days, "4 am, 8 am, 11:45." Times of day. Ginna was keeping track of her meds. I run my finger across the faint pencil marks, those pale last tracings from my sister. So unsettled, Ginna's final days, so unlike the rest of her life. Nothing was turning out the way she had expected. Such an unspeakable mess for her, trying to wind up this unraveling life.

I think about Angus finally telling me what happened, letting go. I was so furious at him, that squirrely secret-keeper. But he hated keeping all that to himself, I could tell. He wanted to tell me. By the end of our walk to the park, I could feel the relief radiating off him. It's like Shelly says: misery shared is misery halved. He talked at one point about his unresolved feelings, how frustrating it was for him to be caught in this limbo where he would never see Ginna again. I told him then, and I really believe this, that there isn't really such a thing as resolved feelings.

And there is absolutely no such thing as everyday life.

I'm such an idiot.

So many sheets. There's a mountain of laundry in the upstairs hallway. In the guest room, I strip the luxuriant bed, wondering which parts should be dry cleaned and which should be washed. I never dry clean anything, never understood how you could get something clean without getting it wet. I flop on the bare mattress, remembering Henry there beside me. He was so worried last night, so tired and upset. But he stayed.

We talked about the NA meetings. He said it was like morning prayer but without the candles. He told me about it in a resigned voice, this ritual resumed after not going for more than a year. I told him I'd been reading the NA website, and I couldn't believe how many meetings there are every day around town. They have kooky names, these groups—"Over the Hill Gang" and "Late Afternooners." It's a secret world out there, so much hidden struggle. I asked him if I'm supposed to go to meetings, and he said only if I liked being bored out of my mind.

He told me he's working with his doctor to figure out some way to manage his back. "I want to figure this out—I'm highly motivated," he said, as if it were a mountaineering expedition he was planning. I don't think he understands how nearby I will be, maybe two feet away from him.

A text appears in my phone: "backpacks? if u have time today" It's Bobbie. Yesterday I told her I wanted to help however she needed it. According to Henry, there are dozens of Bobbie disciples who are doing her bidding for the immigrants of Murfreesboro Road. I start making calls, between loads of laundry. By the end of the afternoon, I've sweet-talked the manager of a Nolensville Road big box store into drop-shipping a gross of $5.97 backpacks to Bobbie's church. The manager explains to me how their ordering process works, gives me the charitable contributions contact in Minneapolis, and I conclude that backpacks are not all that different from travelers. I can move stuff the same way I move tourists. Logistics. There's a system to crack. I think I could be good at chasing stuff for people who need it, helping them get what they need. It's so obvious that I can't believe it took me this long to see it.

That teacup of iceless Coca-Cola stays with me.

I'm a little embarrassed when Henry comes home to find me lying on the floor of the den with Mr. Serious on top of me, beached, in a stare-off. "Help me," I moan.

"Oh, Delia," he says. "It's a good thing I like cats." He sits on the ottoman and stretches his back. "We've been invited to dinner. Our parents."

"Does that sound as weird to you as it does to me?"

"I can't tell what's weird anymore and what's not." He slides down to the floor and looks at me closely.

"I've been thinking about my mom all day," I say. "Not telling me. Totally outrageous. I ought to be furious at her. But I'm not."

"Our little girl is growing up."

"It changes everything. I have to go back through my entire childhood with a different filter now."

"Yeah," he says. "That's huge. Life can only be understood backwards, but it must be lived forwards."

"What do you think about anger?" I ask, studying the shaving cut on his chin. I feel so insanely protective of him. Witch hazel. He needs some witch hazel.

"What do I think about anger? I don't think about it—I just have it. Or it has me. I do think it's possible for it to burn itself out. That happens. A little ashy pile. Once you've figured out why you were so mad, I mean. If you think about it, anger is a reaction to an emotion—to pain or hurt. You don't get mad for no reason. There's always a source. Maybe the thing with your mom doesn't make you mad because it doesn't really hurt at this point. It doesn't change things, what happened with your parents' marriage. Or maybe things have already changed to the point that it isn't important." He runs a hand along Mr.

Serious's tremendous belly. "I'm pretty furious right now, actually. Can't believe I'd let you down like that."

"What?"

"Leaving you hanging. Such a fail. Do you know how many times I almost called you? Call. Don't call. Ruined either way?"

"You're always so calm about things."

"That's just temperament."

"Let it rip, Henry. I just want to see exactly what you're like when you're furious. Throw something. Cuss."

He smiles. "I'm mad at myself, most of the time. The problem is it's really hard to yell at yourself." He squints and frowns, like a cartoon character. "See that? Inside, I am a seething cauldron."

We're in the car on the way to some restaurant that Henry is happy about. "At least it's not Sperry's," he says, "but it would have been Sperry's if it hadn't flooded."

"This is not a double date."

"It is," he replies.

"Too weird. I can't deal with this."

"It's fine. I've been spending time with them. You'll see. It's actually sort of interesting."

"I like Bobbie," I say. We're stopped on West End Avenue, waiting for a light. "She seems to know everybody."

"She does know everybody. The other day she sent me out Nolensville Road, handed me a piece of paper that said 'Please give Henry Peek as many diapers as he can carry,' signed just 'Bobbie.' I ended up in a warehouse parking lot with two National Guard guys and six trailers full of diapers. They're all 'Who sent you?' and I handed them the note, and they started loading up cases of Huggies."

"I don't want to be a travel agent anymore," I say.

Henry swings a look at me, confused, then shakes his head. "Oh, man. Leave you for a minute, and look what happens."

"Bobbie."

"Yeah."

"You've got so much figured out, Henry."

"I've got nothing figured out."

We end up in Germantown, the old neighborhood right below the State Capitol, which hovers in the distance, a limestone gift box on the highest hill downtown. This early evening, with the lush light slipping sideways from the sky, makes me take Henry's hand as we pass the brick townhouses.

"Technicolor time," Henry says. "That's what my mom called this time of day."

"City House," I read as we come down the sidewalk to the entrance. The scent of whatever it is they're doing inside is incredible, even at this distance.

"Dad let me pick. I have to show you that Nashville is a civilized place."

It's civilized, all right. The likelihood of a congealed salad at City House is zero point zero. It's one of those locavore pig-crazy restaurants like the ones I used to read about in Chicago all the time but somehow never managed to visit. It's a stripped-down space, bare floors and rough brick walls, with an open kitchen where a burly guy in a chef's coat is dismantling some large roasted animal.

"This is their first night open since the flood. They've been out feeding flood workers all week," Henry explains. "It's important for us to support local restaurants. Downright noble of us, really," he jokes. He seems himself tonight, though quiet. I feel like something has shifted between us. I don't feel crazy about him. It's calmer than that. I catch him looking at me all the time, and I think he feels it, too.

I have never met Henry's dad, so when I come around the corner into the high-ceilinged dining room, his appearance is so startling that I walk right into a chair and wipe out a table full of wine glasses. So embarrassing, and the splintered glasses are a mess. But I can't get over what I'm seeing: it's Henry, grown up. Right here. He'll still wear glasses. He'll still be kind in the face and shadowy under his blue eyes. He'll be a little jowly, a little heavier. As David Peek extends his hand to me, I reach out to hug him, just like that. I want to tell him how fascinating it is, this resemblance, but he surely already knows.

Mom looks elegant, as ever, wearing nothing special but lit with some kind of amusement. I think she knows what I'm thinking—it is extraordinary, sitting between this father and son. I've always thought that children are caricatures of their parents. Big ears get bigger, a horsey laugh becomes a donkey laugh. Sitting here, with Henry's dad putting me at ease, I see where Henry gets his ridiculous charm. It's a generosity they share, and a modesty. They let everybody else be the most interesting person in the room.

"How have we never met?" Henry's dad asks. He has a version of the insurance fortune accent, so low and rumbly. It's fading with each generation—
Henry has only the faintest version of it, but it rhymes with his father's. With
Mother's Eudora Welty voice and these Peeks, I'm reminded again that I am
in Nashville, that this is the south.

"She's elusive," Henry says.

"Reclusive," I say.

"I was at work today," Mother says. "Such a relief."

This is surprising. "Work?"

"It's going to be a process, I think. It took me a long time to get into that
place, so it'll take a while to get myself out." She smiles. "I do like to work, you
know."

"She's phoning it in," Henry's dad says. "Lazybones."

"The flood came just a couple of blocks from here," Henry's dad says.
"Swamped the Farmer's Market. You could only read about half of Bicenten-
nial Mall—the most inscriptions in a park I ever saw." He shakes his head. "I
have never in my life seen a city swamped like this before. And I've never seen
people jump in so fast." There's a note of wonderment in his voice. These civic
boosters. I'm immune to Nashville pride. I mean, I thought I was until now.
"How are you finding Nashville?" he asks me.

"Well," I say, "I like it. I like it more than I thought I would." Henry is
studying his fork and biting his lower lip. "One thing: days sure do fill themselves up around here." Henry looks sly. "Seriously. It's so different from
Chicago. Whenever I tell people I live by myself, work alone, they say they
envy my freedom. The fact is, freedom takes a lot of work. Nothing more omi-
nous than a Friday night when you haven't got your ducks lined up."

"Our dizziness of freedom," Henry says. "He whose eye happens to look
down into the yawning abyss becomes dizzy." He smiles at my incredulous reaction. He quotes stuff all the time. Whenever he starts talking weird, I've
learned that it's usually Kierkegaard. He read bales of it, was obsessed by it.

"Freedom is not a problem with real estate," Henry's dad says. "There are
days when all I want is for whoever it is who's talking at me to please stop. I
just want to reach over and pinch their lips shut. Shhh! That's plenty!"

Mother sighs. "Just about killed me to move back to Nashville. Couldn't
believe I was doing it. Once I got to Washington, I swore I would never, ever
come back to this place. I'd managed to get away, but a girl will do pretty much
anything for love. Kicking and screaming. Couldn't stand Nashville, thought

it was such a backwater. Such. A. Backwater."

Mother can go baroque when she gets warmed up. I've heard the such-a-backwater story a dozen times, thought about it on more than a few occasions as I made my life in Chicago. The kicking-and-screaming part in particular. But as I sit here, I'm not kicking, I'm not screaming, and I'm mostly looking forward to whatever supper is about to come our way.

Henry catches my eye, conspiratorial. He's right: this is not a bad thing, dinner with our parents.

The menu is funny, low end and high end mashed up. "Mother, they have chicken in aspic. The hipsters love aspic."

She puts her hand over mine. "I've been thinking about your father," she says pointedly. A sudden droop, a mood shift. "I wish I had told you about him."

"Mom."

"No, really. Can't stop thinking about it. How could I not tell you?" She is mystified. Why is she bringing this up at this particular moment, with Henry and his dad right here? Does she want witnesses? Or protection?

Something in her tone gets me, and I feel a snap of anger. "Good question! Did you think I wouldn't want to know?"

"He wouldn't want you to know." She says this in a low voice.

"Who?"

"Your father."

"What? He's been dead forever, Mom. He's not here."

"Goodness," Henry's dad whispers.

"Wow," Henry says. A Peek chorus of sympathy. I think about all the hideous confessions Henry has heard in his meetings. He must have a PhD in compassion. They are watching my mom like she's pulling emeralds out of her ears, and I can't stop staring, either.

She looks at me. I can't believe how openly she is talking to us. "When someone vanishes like that, you relive those last words, pick through them. I could write out a transcript of that argument. Oh!" She shakes her head, hearing it again, right here in front of us. "And he said—I remember it like it was yesterday—'I don't ever want the girls to know this.'" She has almost run out of steam. "So. I grabbed onto that. That I could do. When there was nothing else to be done."

Henry watches her with something close to astonishment. "Yes," he says. "That's it." What is he talking about? He's so agitated. "That's the problem.

You hear something, and that's it."

His dad cocks his head, puzzled. Henry looks at him. "In Denmark. In the car, that day. We were arguing about something. It was pretty much the last thing Clare said to me. 'Henry Peek, you're not cut out for this world, are you?'" An oval platter of charcuterie has landed in the middle of our table. Henry gently picks up a small circle of salami. "Not cut out for this world. Like a voodoo curse. I thought about that for so long that I persuaded myself it was true." He places the salami on a thin triangle of pumpernickel, and looks up at me. "Until recently," he says with a tight smile. He unfolds my fingers and lays the toast in the palm of my hand. "Always eat hors d'oeuvres," he says.

"Who's Clare?" Mother asks, confused.

Henry looks up, then looks at me. I nod. Just say it. "She died in the car accident with me. Vehicular homicide. I was drunk. Went to prison, for a year, after the accident." He says this very directly.

"Oh, Henry," Mother says. She turns to Henry's dad, even more confused. "You never said a word."

"It was his story to tell, Grace."

"How could you keep a secret for so long?" She grabs his hand.

David Peek raises his eyebrows. "How could you?"

It's very late, but we can't seem to settle down. "Henry."

He puts down his book. This bed. I could stay in this bed forever, this linen-covered raft. I figured out why the sheets smell so good: Ginna kept a jug of a laundry potion called Pure Grass beside her washing machine. "I love this bed," I say.

A cloud crosses his face. "Bed," he says. "Do you know how much time I've spent in bed? Never been so miserable in my life as in bed. Not all that long ago, I slept on the sofa because I was so afraid of bed. Terrified." His voice gets so low when he talks about these things. "Quicksand. Tar pit."

"Bed is the worst place, or the best place," I say, and he nods.

"Have you ever had a pain problem?" he asks.

"Not really."

"For a long time, in Denmark, I forgot what normal felt like except in dreams. Sometimes I would wake up and realize that there was no pain in the dream. So I would crave sleep, wish for it like water in a desert. But I was twisted up with insomnia, no rest for the wicked. Paradox, once again. I remember one doctor saying to me, 'Pain is not fatal.' And I thought: 'Well, then, this is some kind of living death.' There was a time, at the hospital, where it occurred to me that my physical pain—my back—was every bit as hard to describe as my mental pain." He shakes his head. "That night with you, the first night, I was such a mess. I still can't believe I did that. Cannot believe it."

"Does it hurt right now?"

He shrugs. "Working on it. Dr. Cavanaugh is hopeful." He looks hard at me. "I want to be hopeful. It's all I want."

"Your mom is not like my mom. At all," Henry says. "I mean, at the mom factory, they must have a totally different production line for moms like yours. It doesn't even seem like the same ingredients."

"Like how?"

"Like, my mom was the least ambitious person in the world. It was all family for her, no work at all except for volunteer stuff."

"A different kind of ambition."

"She was a great mom. There's never been a mom like Mom." Henry shifts closer to me. We hang close, like sea lions flopped on each other.

"Are you like her?" I ask.

"Who knows? How can anybody tell something like that?"

"I'm beginning to see how much I'm like my mother."

"Well, duh."

"What?"

"Delia, you guys are like twins. Really."

I tell him, "I keep thinking weird things about the house. I keep thinking I should just keep it. It's a rare thing, getting a big ol' house like this. It won't happen again."

He smiles. "From 400 square feet to 5,000?"

"I know. But it feels so wrong to sell it."

He flips his pillow to the cool side. "You don't want this house. Stuff like the flood happens all the time with an old house. OK, not the flood. But it never ends, with a place like this. The plumbing alone is going to be a project worthy of the Romans. What you're wanting," he says, "is what happens inside the house."

Extreme Access

The doorbell rings. It's strange: there's a bright glow in the hallway, as if somebody's shining a stage light into the window. As always, I peek through the side window to see who's out there. Oh, man. When I open the door, I'm almost blinded by the red glow behind the silhouetted figures of Ethan Hardy and Sugar. It's a full-out tour bus, sparkling red and gleaming in the sun, with a ten-foot-wide decal of Ethan's bald head rising like a moon in front of the words "Love Hard."

"Hey," Ethan says. Sugar leans into him, her curves fitting against his like a southern-fried yin and yang.

"Hello," Sugar says. It sounds like *hollow*. She's wearing a criminal pair of Daisy Dukes and a spaghetti-strap camisole, supertight. I am weirdly glad to see the tiniest of baby bumps. She really is pregnant.

"We need us a house," Ethan says.

"Flooded out," Sugar says. "I can only live on a tour bus for so long." She sounds like a vixen from a James Bond movie. I can barely resist talking back to her in that Scandinavian accent.

I invite them in, and we sit on the terrace in the dizzying beauty of the back yard. Springtime in Nashville is ferocious, the trees competing in a lush-off. Even the hackberries are beautiful, and they're never beautiful.

"You're doing six benefit concerts this week, but you don't even have a house?"

"Could have been so much worse," Ethan says.

"Not really," Sugar says, and Ethan digs an elbow at her. "I mean, it's a nice bus and so forth, it's just hard to park it at the Harris-Teeter."

"Lost all our damn cars," Ethan says disgustedly. "Anyway, she told me she don't want to live on River Road no more, and I frankly can't blame her. Seeing as how the river come up through the second floor last week. Stanky is what it was."

I cannot stop looking at them; they're so elaborate. Ethan's wearing a vest that goes to his knees, a whole cow's worth of leather. They seem to have nothing in the world to do. "Don't you have a concert tonight? Shouldn't you be sound checking or something?"

Ethan shrugs lazily. "It'll go. We do this a lot."

He seems to want to know more about the neighborhood, the house. "You got you a historic overlay?" I must look surprised, because he says, "What? You think I wouldn't know about that stuff?"

"He's on the board of the Civic Design Center," Sugar says.

I tell him about Ginna's failed efforts to get an overlay in place, about my interest in planning, and he brightens.

"What I don't get," he says, "is how a neighborhood like this ain't got no damn sidewalks. Sugar is not going to be walking our baby in the middle of the damn street."

I think I've just identified the new president of the Bowling Avenue Neighborhood Association. I tell him, "You really need to meet this neighbor, Angus Donald. He's just like you. You guys are going to love each other."

We swap flood stories, as everybody in Nashville does these days. I tell them about the Granada Apartment Houses, and he makes a phone call right in front of me, activating somebody on his team. He tells me how his concerts will raise five million dollars for flood relief. "Can you fuckin' believe that? I can't even sing worth a damn."

I tell them about Ginna, how extraordinary she was and what joy this place gave her. I can't believe I'm showing them Ginna's baby book, but there's something about Ethan that is so irresistible, so generous.

Sugar finally gets Ethan to acknowledge that he needs to head down to the arena. "Where's the contract?" he says to me, hands spread like he wants to catch a football.

"You're really making an offer?" I don't know why I'm so surprised.

"One five."

"One seven five," I reply.

"One six and that's damn good," he says. "Cash. I don't finance nothing."

"Done." I run to grab the contract form before he changes his mind.

"Come on, Ingeborg," he says as he climbs into the bus. Sugar clambers up the steps, muttering "Don't call me that." He looks down at me from the driver's seat. "You gonna be all right," he says. "You already look better."

"Ethan!" Sugar chides.

"Well she does. Look at her. She don't got that oyster-eyes look no more."

Off they go with a roar of engine and hissing air brakes. The bus creams the Bradford pears by the entrance. Ethan drives the bus like it's a go-cart.

Only later do I wonder if Ethan decided to buy this house just to get me out of that attic. He would do something like that.

I go to Henry's to meet him for supper, and I slap down my beautiful contract on his dining table. In my most Beverly d'Angelenoesque voice, I announce, "I told you: this is my house to sell, and I'm going to sell it."

He is amazed. "Who?"

I hold up a CD of Ethan Hardy's new album, *Hell Damn Yeah*, and I hang a laminate around his neck. "We have a house party to go to. With 16,000 of our new best friends."

Closing

Hannah Pankowski comes down the stairs, carrying a bin of Ginna's family photos that she has collated into chronological acid-free folders. "Precious Artifacts," she says. "Can't believe I missed this one. This is it. We're done."

We sit on the window seat in the breakfast room, the only place left to sit. Hannah subsists on power bars and a mysterious vitamin powder she sprinkles into her water bottle. She's wiry and small but surprisingly strong, a little older than me, always coming from some yoga class with her hair in a smooth dark ponytail, rhapsodizing about her yoga teacher, Cleanth. She has a huge crush on Cleanth, who is thirty years older than she is.

"It never fails to surprise me," Hannah says, "what a house looks like when it's finally empty. So small."

"Why does it feels bigger when it's crammed full?" I say.

"It's a container," she says.

"A vessel."

"A stage."

"A loony bin," I say.

Once the Hardys signed the contract on the house, I got to work finding an organizer who wouldn't drive me insane. Hannah, it turns out, is a psychotherapist disguised as an organizer. In three weeks, she has dismantled Ginna's house in a way that felt like a magic trick, and she was such good company that the hours passed in an endless dialogue on Ginna, my family, and the Hannah Pankowski school of organizing. So many rules. Her philosophy of plastic bins? No curved corners. A nice, sharp-edged Sterilite is the only way to go. Get a huge dumpster because you'll feel liberated to throw anything away. Stop thinking of it as a house—it's a temporary storage facility. This meant she stacked Ginna's beautiful furniture on top of itself and piled treasured objects in what seemed to me a most disrespectful way. Sentimentality, in general, is her worst enemy. She has radar for the dangerous stuff—the sentimental time bombs that can shut down a cleanout effort. She spread out Ginna's four file drawers of photographs in a tremendous pile on the living room floor, and we did family flash cards at a dizzying speed until everything was sorted by date. "Date is the only way to go," she said. "Your descendants will think of everything by date. These photos make a narrative. You don't violate the narrative."

"Until this trip I never even imagined having descendants," I say.

She glances up. "Someday they'll all sit down with your stuff and do the same thing we're doing. It's called picking up the pieces. Be sure you take care with the magazine collection." She makes a face at me as we think of the nest of *Playboy* magazines I found on a high shelf in the back of Bennett's closet.

Hannah was willing to let me blab as long as I was actively putting stuff in a box. When I lost myself in the fascinating story of my sophomore year in college, she handed me a stack of china plates and pointed toward the bubble wrap. No idle chat. "Do you think we can let this go?" was code for "Let this go." Gentle and merciless. I realized about halfway through this process that Hannah's primary talent is inertia management. I would like to have Hannah nearby for every single moment of my life.

It was reverse archaeology, digging down through the layers of artifacts, with the goal of arriving at perfect emptiness, at nothing. The girls have a complete house's worth of furniture stowed over on Charlotte Avenue, much has been given to Goodwill, bales of yarn have gone to Mrs. Smith's second grade knitting class, and the house is empty.

It's done.

She offers me her water bottle, and I take a swig. It tastes green, awful, like pureed grass clippings. "Big day, right?"

She's keyed in on it, the fact that I'm feeling wobbly. "Big," I say, so grateful to her, so relieved that we've finally arrived at this moment. I'm frozen to this bench seat. I don't want to move. I know that when I stand up, it will mark the end of something straightforward and the beginning of something much less obvious.

"I have learned one thing," I say. "I sure as hell believe in ghosts now." Hannah smiles. "I mean, Ginna is sitting right here next to me. She's got those yellow flip flops on, and she's telling me to brush my hair, the way she always did."

"It's powerful to be with somebody's things like this," she says.

"It's her house. I hate to let it go." Hannah nods, then stands and stretches her arms behind her. She goes to the pantry for one last check, then sits back down beside me.

"I can't stop thinking about the flood," I say. "I'm just so sorry."

"What?" Hannah says, puzzled.

"Shelly's house was not like this. We got off so easy. I wish you could have been there that day, out at her house. I'll never forget it. It had this epic quality, everybody so focused on her. It was a disaster, and it wasn't. It was love, you know? Pure, complete love. The most beautiful thing."

"I know. I was down at the food bank, clearing out stuff. The stories keep coming. I don't think we'll hear the end of this for a long time."

We sit for at least five minutes, even the kinetic Hannah stilled by her thoughts.

"When do you go back?" she asks.

"Tomorrow morning," I say. Chicago looms. I dread it, so much.

Ethan and Sugar came over to close on the house this morning. I thought about dragging Angus in for some legal expertise, but decided he would probably sneak a page in there deeding the house to himself. Henry stayed home, protesting that he could be of help to me, that he was a Gold Award Realtor last year and had the lapel pin to prove it. I don't know why I felt such a need to do this myself, without his help, but I did. I printed out Beverly d'Angeleno's online closing forms. Bev wouldn't let me down. I'm kind of proud of myself. I actually did this.

Closing a house sale with Ethan was like trying to make a balky teenager do his homework. We had a ten-minute philosophical discussion about the deed insurance—"Who owns anything, anyway? Some guy shows up and says the paperwork is wrong? I'm the one sitting in this house, and you're gonna have to pry me loose." He didn't care about the termite inspection—"Five feet of water in the basement? Termites are the least of my problems." I managed to get him to sign enough papers that it felt like we'd buttoned up the deal. At the end of all this, Ethan handed me a handwritten check for the entire amount, shook my hand, and said, "It's good. Trust me—cash is king around my place." Henry just about had a stroke when I showed it to him, but when I took it to the bank, the manager looked at it and laughed. "Yeah, that's Ethan."

I can't really stand to think too much about what is going to happen to Ginna's house, but at least it's going to somebody with a sense of humor. Ethan said the studio in the back yard is going to be two stories tall, and I'm glad I'm not going to be around to hear the Bowling Avenue Neighborhood Association's reaction to that. And once he starts parking that tour bus in the front yard, well. Somebody's going to call a meeting.

At Mother's house, three construction trucks clog the driveway. The only sign that anything has happened here is the three-foot-high dried slime along the bottom of her creamy clapboard. Mother's at work, but she's not the one I've come to see. I'm so sentimental that my hands jingle. On the drive over here, I thought about the day out at Shelly's house, cleaning up from the flood. I will never forget the moment when Shelly sat on her front steps, exhausted at the end of the afternoon. "Enough," she said. "I am done with this." Never has a day felt more done.

Now Shelly is sitting in the breakfast room, reading the newspaper. "Got a minute?" I ask, sitting down in one of the metal folding chairs that are doing duty until the flood-damaged ones are repaired.

She shrugs. "Time is what I seem to have a lot of. Your mother won't let me do anything until I'm done with my knees."

"You're doing them?"

She nods. "Bennett is." She laughs at my shocked expression. "Couldn't have been nicer."

"That's so great," I say. Bennett.

"I know. Sat me down and laid it all out for me. Something, isn't it? Gonna be a different kind of summer, I tell you what." She shakes her head.

"Being back here has been so different," I say. "I thought I would be back in Chicago by now. I thought that some annoyingly cheerful family would be measuring for curtains. I never guessed it would be a Nicorette-abusing country singer and his Norwegian bombshell wife." Shelly smiles. "It's good, I guess. But you know, the longer I stay, the more old things have bubbled up."

She shifts in her chair. "I know that feeling. When your house washes away, you spend time thinking."

"Well. Remember when? That time? Back in high school?" I look at her intently.

"Of course I do." She's looking right at me.

"Can't believe it ever actually happened."

She nods. "You were brave."

"Wouldn't even tell my own mother."

"You told me."

"How did you keep this to yourself? Why would you?" I have wondered this for years, but only now have I found the nerve to ask her.

Shelly looks out the window. "Delia, you know what the deal was, back then. I thought about it. Believe me, I prayed about it more than you can imagine. But she was . . . difficult. You know what I mean. I just don't think it would have gone well. Wouldn't have been much there for you. Working every day of the week, gone. And I figured that would've been the hurtfulest thing, if she didn't give you her attention. Attention is the rarest kind of generosity." She shakes her head. "I thought someday you'd tell her. Or not. It was up to you."

She doesn't ask. "I told her," I say.

"I'm glad. Bet she is, too."

"Yeah. It kind of opens up the horizon."

"You were the oddest child," she says. "Off in your own little world." She shakes her head. "Loneliest child I ever saw."

Hearing this from Shelly is like hearing God tell you what you are supposed to do with your life. I look at her, stunned at the obvious truth of what she said.

"You must think we're the weirdest people in the world."

She raises her eyebrows, says nothing.

"I'm staying, Shelly."

She kneads her knee the way you rub a cat. "Your mother said." She looks pleased. "You seem good." I nod, embarrassed at all that she knows about Henry. I wonder sometimes if she engineered the whole thing. "Joy shared is joy doubled," she says.

"How's the apartment hunt?" I ask.

A twist crosses her face. "Still looking. William has his ideas, and I have mine." She shakes her head. "Those goats knew better than to stick around. I think William told them to head off to someplace else." I would like to think that Shelly's goats are simply living down the road.

I don't know how to do this elegantly, but I do it anyway. I put the envelope on the table. "Shelly," I say. "I want you to have this. It's for your new place. I hope you can find someplace that will suit you."

She looks at the envelope. "That's OK, Delia. I'm good. We've got it. Really."

"No," I say. "It's not my money. It's just money. That I ended up with. The commission from the house. It needs to go to something good."

Shelly gives me a shrewd look, then shakes her head. "This is exactly the sort of thing your mother would do." She smiles, relishing the obvious, complete irony of all this. "Your mother's daughter, you know."

I figured she wouldn't take it, but I had to try.

Epilogue

Driving back to Chicago feels exactly the way it felt when I drove down to Nashville in April: it's the worst idea in the world. I can't really believe that my life has taken such a turn, that leaving Nashville would be a disappointment, that I would want to get back to Nashville as fast as I could.

The only thing right about it is that Henry is sitting here beside me in this little rental truck. He wanted to see what my life in Chicago was like, and I pointed out that I was about to leave that life behind. This made him happy, but right now, I feel like I'm taking him to see my secret taxidermy studio. It's so embarrassing to think about my apartment, and to imagine what he will surely glean from seeing it. I wish I had a week or two in there, so I could fluff it to look like the apartment of a normal person. He is so willing to ignore the weird things about me. I never thought I would find someone who could put up with me. It just never seemed possible.

A long road trip with someone you love is a delicious bit of sensory deprivation. It is possible to talk yourself out when there's nothing else to do except drive. He drives, I knit. It's worrisome to admit this, but I've ended up with Ginna's unfinished blanket in my lap, heavy and hot, and it's addicting. One day, deep in the house cleanout, Hannah held it up, needles dangling, and said, "A shame, isn't it?" It was one of those instant decisions: it was beautiful, and I had to finish it.

"Algae libel nerd," he says, sunk into his seat, one hand on the wheel.

"What?"

"Algae libel nerd. It's an anagram of your name. I looked it up."

I laugh.

"What? You didn't anagram me? There's also 'reliable dangle.' Or 'all-beagle diner.'"

"I like that one." I poke around on my phone for a minute. "Hyper keen. You're hyper keen."

––––––––

"What is the problem with Nashville?" I ask, teasing. "I can't live in Nashville. Hellhole. Nobody can parallel park in Nashville." I am finding it so easy to goad Henry. He is as crazy as a football fan when it comes to Nashville.

"Nashville is the Garden of Eden," he says calmly. "Nashville is what some steaming pile of garbage like New York wants to be. Central Park wishes it were Percy Warner Park. Try to find a Robert's Western Wear in Chicago. Their claim to fame is deep-dish pizza? Oprah? A president? Seriously?" He leans sideways toward me. "I'll tell you the secret of the universe, the truth I have gleaned from my entire life's experience. Are you ready?"

I nod.

"This morning, I was sitting at the Shell station by my condo, waiting for the gas to fill, thinking about nothing in particular. And the most shocking thing happened: a tiny head poked out of a crack in the trash can, by the pump—another one of those house finches. It climbed out, flew off, and then after a minute, it came back, folded its wings, and stuffed itself back inside."

We drive for a while.

"It doesn't matter. You can be snake-bit miserable in paradise, and you can have paradise in . . ." He laughs at where this construction is leading him. "In snake-bit miserable Nashville."

We stop at the Welcome Center at the Kentucky-Tennessee border. I'm waiting for Henry, looking at a brochure for Mammoth Cave. We should go to Mammoth Cave. We ought to find some of those fish with no eyes. It would be fun to have a claustrophobic freakout with Henry.

He comes up behind me and buries his face in my hair. "I really believe the poets when they say that the first time one sees the beloved object he thinks he has seen her long before."

"What are you quoting now?"

"I saw you standing there, and it reminded me. I've been waiting so long for you to show up. I can't believe you're finally here."

"Mother asked me to go to church with her on Sunday. Can you believe that?"

"You should go."

"I'm not going to church."

"Don't be so literal. It's great. All the ladies will cluck over you."

"Do you ever think about going back to divinity school?"

"Never. Made my peace with that a long time ago. I like being in the world, having a job. This one, especially, leaves me room for other things."

"Can't believe you wanted to be a priest. To leave all that behind?"

"I wanted to be something. I can't connect those dots anymore. I did figure out some translations, though. Instead of *grace*, I say *luck*. Instead of praying, it's thinking. But that doesn't mean I don't think there's a God. There's something, and that's enough. It can be a mystery—it ought to be a mystery. It's interesting how simple it is."

"I still wish you'd pray for me or something. Put in a good word."

He puts a hand on my arm. "I think about you, OK? I think about you loudly and often. If anybody up there is listening, believe me: you're covered."

Downtown Chicago is so loud. And populated. Clanking, honking, yelling. I forgot how constant the noise is, what an undercurrent it makes. We park the rental truck down in the bowels of my building and enter the lobby for the ride up to my squalid dungeon.

"Fancy," Henry says as we come through the smeary glass doors to the lobby. I've never thought of it as fancy—the fake Barcelona daybeds have never in my experience been occupied by anybody, and the matted shag rug looks like a sheepdog died right there on the floor. There's a vague smell of motor oil in the air.

"Fancy on the outside, crappy on the inside," I say. "This is one of those pre-recession condo projects that never got liftoff. It's all rentals. The management treats us tenants like hostages. Which we are."

The doorman, if that's what he is because I've never seen him anywhere except on his stool, stares at his phone. He definitely avoids eye contact with us tenants. I'm not sure he can talk at all.

"So lifelike," Henry whispers.

The elevator door opens at my floor, and I hear the poodle in 1502 being poodly, nails scratching on the floor, yipping and flinging his body against the door the way he does whenever the elevator opens. I have not missed that dog one bit. There's some smell in the air that I don't recognize, a deep, multilayered combination of cleaning products, or air fresheners, or car deodorizers. The closer we get to 1515, the worse it gets.

"Man," I say. I'm getting artificial cherry, artificial pine, artificial lavender.

"That's awful," Henry says.

It's coming from my apartment, as is a low throb of techno music. When I slide the key in the lock, the door swings open, unlocked. Henry scowls. "I'll look," he says, such a hero, but what he forgets is that there's only one room to check, and it's completely visible to us at this point, and what we're seeing is a scene from the hippie episode of *Dragnet*. My apartment is covered in swaths of Indian bedspreads, pillar candles aflame all over the place, and my neighbor Marcy is lying flat on the floor with a shocked expression on her face and a hairy guy next to her with not much expression at all.

"Delia!"

"Marcy."

"Whoa," the guy says.

"You're here!" Marcy scrambles to her feet, straightening what looks like a silk sari or bathrobe. "It's like I dreamed you."

"Wow," Stubble Face says. "You're the Delia." He turns in amazement to Marcy.

"She doesn't look . . . ecstatic," Marcy says, then smiles in a way that has no connection to reality. "You said to make yourself at home." She's right. Marcy was the neighbor I gave my key to when I left for Nashville. "So we did."

"This is unbelievable," I say. "What were you thinking?"

"I know," she says. "Isn't it great?"

"No seriously. You can't do this." The dozens of candles have eaten all the oxygen in the room, so I'm getting a coal miner's hypoxia what with all the vanilla raspberry coconut pollution in the air. I can't believe she hasn't set off the smoke alarm.

Marcy confesses that she has been using my apartment as her little home away from home, six doors down from her own apartment and her awful roommate. Between the recreational pharmaceuticals and the lack of personal responsibility for her surroundings, Marcy has laid waste to my apartment.

"We should go?" Marcy says uncertainly.

"Yeah," I say. "Probably."

"They were so . . . cuddly," Henry says. He looks sort of pasty, now that Marcy and her creature have decamped. I open the sliding door to ventilate, but even the breeze from the balcony does nothing to dissipate the cloying stink.

"At least it wasn't pot. Actually, pot would beat this mess. At least pot is one flavor." I stick my head into the clothes in my closet, and it's there. In my sofa, it's there. In my bed, it's there. If I had a qualm about leaving Chicago, Marcy's aromatherapy has relieved me of it. I couldn't stay here even if I wanted to—it's as if somebody coated the place with a bucket of scented wax.

"It would help," Henry says, "if I didn't have such a strong sense of smell. I literally can't stand this." We're standing out on the balcony to take gulping breaths.

"I should have known she'd flake out," I say. "She's kind of a nut."

"Kind of? This is a disaster," he says as we watch a woman in the apartment across the street balancing on a spindly chair, trying to change a light bulb. "You're flooded out." He smiles, I laugh. "Call FEMA."

It's hard to believe how quickly an apartment can be packed up when the decision has been made to leave behind anything upholstered or made of fabric. I feel an odd liberation that I'll be returning to Nashville with only my books, my old mahogany bedframe, and my maps. I had this idea that my life here was efficient, streamlined, but I see now the smallness of it. I'm not starting over; I'm starting, period.

"Embarrassing," I say, taping up yet another box of books.

"What?"

"This. Here. So dormlike."

"It's considerably more deluxe than your attic hidey hole," he says. "I mean, the ceiling doesn't even slant."

"You're not rescuing me, OK?" I say. "I have lived many happy, productive years right here, you know. I am very good at this."

"No, you're not," he says, laughing. "I think we can agree on that."

We spend the most time packing up my maps. The single decorating statement in this apartment is my dozens of old street maps—views of cities that quickly overtook their original plans. They cover the walls like wallpaper. I read maps the way some people read cookbooks. I couldn't say how many hours I've spent studying them, wondering about the people who made the cities, that optimistic order imposed on bumpy terrain. How easy it was for me to float above these places, admiring the order and the folly of the plans.

Henry is transfixed by an old map of Nashville that Mother gave me years ago, an 1864 plan of the city during the war. "Look at that," he says. "How the river runs right through it. Most important thing in the city."

"I guess it let us know that," I say.

There's one thing I need to do before we go.

I lead Henry out to the balcony, which is such an optimistic name for this narrow concrete slab. Insulting, really, for that developer to put this thing out here and expect anybody to be delighted by it. On this clear night, however, it serves our purposes well enough. My neighborhood spreads before us in a snarled panorama, the rooftops of buildings, tangled fire escapes. I never put any chairs out here, so we sit down on the slab, with our backs against the warm brick wall, a bottle of Tweenie Gilbert's 1953 Cockburn Port between us. "I told you it was bleak," I say.

"You didn't tell me it would be so smelly," he says. He holds up my glass to peer through the almost-opaque wine. "I'm real sorry not to be drinking this with you," he says, then turns and kisses me. He licks his lips. "Sort of Robitussin."

"Remember when you told me, that night at the secret supper, that your favorite place was in Tennessee somewhere? Where is it?"

He smiles. "I was stalling. Trying to be mysterious. But I was thinking, at that moment, that sitting at that table with you was hard to beat."

"Henry," I say. "We should go somewhere."

Acknowledgments

The people of Nashville inspired much of this story. Their courage, resiliency, and good humor after the great flood of 2010 were a deep source of inspiration to me. Thank you to Heather Connelly Lefkowitz, Judy Wright, Angela Haglund Graham, Chelle Baldwin, Pam Wilmoth, Marci Murphree, and Chris Champion.

Early readers of this story provided encouragement and advice. Many thanks to Frances Corzine, Sara-Scott Wingo, Sara Nelson, Emily Frith, Frannie Ambrose, Amanda Moody, Kent Ballow, Havens McAllister, Adrienne Martini, Joanna Brichetto, Annis Cox, Betsy Hindman, Judy Lewis, Katie Greenebaum, Joan Shayne, Ted Fischer, and Joe Park.

Great thanks to:

Mary Neal Meador for beautiful editing.

Yolanda Pupo-Thompson for tremendous insight.

Bryce McCloud of Isle of Printing for the cover design.

Michael Zibart, for twenty years of friendship and wise, patient counsel.

Kay Gardiner, for being my invisible Internet friend.

Special thanks to my father, Clifton Meador, who encouraged me to write ever since I was little.

Love and thanks to my siblings Clif Meador, Aubrey Meador, Buffy Driskill, Mary Kathleen Meador, Graham Meador, and Rebecca Meador, who are teaching me the power of reconciliation.

Daily gratitude to my sons David and Clif, who are constant and patient tutors.

Finally, thanks to my beloved husband Jon, who is the secret ingredient in all this.